HARVESTING GAME

MAXIME PAUL

HARVESTING GAME

MAXIME PAUL

This is a collection of fictional works. Names, characters, places, and incidents are either a product of the author's imagination or are used fictitiously. Any resemblance to actual persons, living or dead, businesses, companies, events, or locales, is entirely coincidental.

Harvesting Game

Inked in Gray Press

InkedinGray.com

ISBN Paperback: 978-1-952969-34-8

ISBN Ebook: 978-1-952969-35-5

Cover Design by Squidblot Arts

Trigger Warnings

The following page lists several content warnings for *Harvesting Game*. If you don't like to read content warnings before you read a book, that's fine! Please skip this page and read on.

Otherwise, know that this book contains content that could be difficult for some readers, including oppression, physical, emotional, and mental violence, and transphobia.

Please feel free to reach out to us at contact@inkedingray.com for any clarifying questions or concerns and remember to take care of your mental health.

Stage 1: System Error

Chapter 1: Booting Up

Mission #1: Don't Upset Mom

Nights drained me.

I wasn't out and about, working late, or suffering from insomnia. When my subconscious was unleashed, all the pent-up dreams that I pretended weren't battling for my heart came out to play.

Sleep was supposed to be rejuvenating, but for the last twenty years, slumber only sapped my strength. The mental and emotional quests I went on during my "rest" left me sopping with sweat. My brain never switched to low power mode. Instead, it cranked into high gear when I laid down in my sad excuse for a bed.

I tossed and tumbled until I woke nestled on the now sweat-muddled floor. I laid next to my discolored, dissolving, dirty bed with a mission dematerializing from my weary mind. My bed was just a mattress so overused that it was missing springs yet had too many at the same time. Sometimes the earthen floor of my room was just more comfortable. It was definitely warmer.

My body took a while to catch up to the drama raging in my mind. As usual, my vision was distorted. Random pixels, flickers of rapid reflections all around me. My exhausted body buzzed with purposeful paranoia mixed with dissatisfaction and distress, all radiating from the fire waning in my gut. As the visceral dream reverberations dissipated from my fingertips and toes, the feeling transformed, like I'd transitioned from one simulation to another. Reality seeped into focus like a viscous slime in all its dreadful glory, always outmatching anything I'd faced in my nerve-wracking nightmares.

It was hard to nail down my dreams precisely and completely. I didn't even know what had me so triggered, but I took the momentarily mellow morning moments to process. The ending scene was the only bit I could remember: I was running down a dark, narrow hallway dragging an indistinguishable, monstrous weight behind me. No matter how much I stretched my peripherals while struggling to sprint, I couldn't recognize what was holding me back. I fought to keep moving. Everything was wet. Not only was the boiling, sour air heavy with condensation but my surroundings were slathered with musty moisture, sloshing and splashing under foot. A ringing sound bounced from every direction. A scattered, yet safe presence surrounded me. With every forced step, I shed a bit of the colossal weight behind me, dragging me back less and less until I was running so fast I was floating from a full sprint, upward into a snow-covered screen.

The most memorable morsel was the momentary lightness at the very end. The unshackling from the world made my heart drop. That microsecond was haunting. Incomprehensible, unbelievable, and impossible. I tried to recall that feeling and a sharp pain came back, scaring me away like an internal trauma defense. The pain drowned out my somatic recollection of liftoff. With each onslaught of pain, I was reminded of every odious element I dealt with on a daily basis in the real world. Every burn, bite, slur, denigration and swipe at my humanity was seared in my soul.

That bouncy lightness though, I yearned to understand it. To feel it in my daily comings and goings. To cultivate it. Alas, every morning I sifted through the night's odyssey only to be disrupted by a complex, painful, dispiriting process of reversion back to reality. Just knowing that there was a different feeling out there, one that existed somewhere, in some form, was comforting. Despite my frightened body doing its damndest to squelch my phantom joy, I knew my dreams — and what I felt in my gut — was important. Every day was a battle of dizzying dissonance I longed to resolve. A resolution made much tougher as tiredness compounded behind my eyes.

A bit of heat radiated from the ground below. I went without covers, only my ratty pajamas to keep me warm. My old comforter was so worn out the threads had disintegrated back to the earth months ago. Overall, I slept on the best I could procure from the dump surrounding our slopeside community, but I wanted better.

I stretched my arm out to reach for my Libook. It sat hidden securely inside my therapy journal, tangled in yesterday's fourth-hand clothes, resting on my growing revolutionary reference collection. I had technology books, game guides, and even trashed technology trinkets I'd resurrected or was in the process of bringing into its fourth life. Kurobans call it *fourth-hand* because Kuroban stuff (e.g. food, clothes, books, technology, furniture, damn near anything unless it was miraculously made here) typically was in its fourth life by the time it came into our orbit.

All things are born as a collection of elemental molecules combined to create a gift from our universe, then Luxites consume those gifts as some sort of perfunctory processed good, and then they are re-claimed by the earth when Luxites move on. It's at that point when us Kurobans liberate rotting rags and tattered goods for a fourth life.

I jammed my eyes shut and gripped my secret reanimated tablet tight. Only a few more minutes before I completely forget last night's sleep sermon. I squeezed out as many wisps of the airy aspiration still left over. After a few seconds, I open my eyes and started a new note:

Liberation dream recollection #7,310:

Wet hallway, massive weight behind, and a buoyant release in the end. But I still can't figure out what I need to let go of.

I need a new strategy because I'm not getting any sleep. I'm at the end of my energy reserves. Time is running out. Maybe I don't need to be so cautious anymore. Maybe I just need to run, like in the dream.
I'll run right into Robert's office to let him know what I need. I'll let him know about the video game studio I want to create. I've kept my head down and done good work for eduGames for seventeen weeks now (an eon in a typical Luxite's work tenure expectancy). How long can they keep me in this menial role when I can do so much more? I'm not like the rest of the QA-robans. I can sell myself. Give him a bit of what he wants in a way that serves me . . . and eventually Kuroba too. Interest convergence, the Trojan Horse of intentions. I've studied Luxites in the books, online, and now in person enough to make a pitch to cement my legacy. My people will listen once they see me succeed my way.

My mornings were always disorienting like that ever since my other parent was ripped away. They were supposedly locked in Lux's terrifying labor camps in the bowels of the city.

I know I wouldn't have been able to pick them out if they landed in my lap, but their bald head and speculative stories seeded my separatist sensibilities. They were swiftly judged and sensationally stolen from our *whole* community, not just Mom and I. Our leaders were forcefully compelled to make a show of it all. And my little ass was too innocent to handle the pain.

That miserable event, missing pieces and all, reverberated throughout my life. I couldn't even remember their name, just that Mom lovingly called them Baldie. It was the last wisp of cerebral storage I could recall. It was like they'd been rubbed from my memory. And Mom always avoided Baldie's government moniker. Despite that, their lessons of liberation still shined through. That was the fire raging in my gut. The confident ember that woke me up with a purpose each and every morning.

Despite the ultra-atmospheric pressure of gloom weighing down almost our entire community, especially those in my generation and younger, I was driven. I was desperate for freedom. Freedom for me . . . and freedom for my people. If I got free then I could free my people from the system grinding us into dirt – and vice versa, I suppose. I was working on a plan to make it happen. I had some of the steps approaching emancipation figured out, but the details for getting from the dump to a developer — a video game developer that is — were in flux. As I fumbled towards that freedom to create games that would liberate Kurobans I questioned everything, analyzing for any detail to save us, to save me.

Baldie couldn't do it, but they didn't have the modern knowledge I had. They didn't have the powerful technology of Lux at their whim like I did. My Libook held all my dreams, strategy, arguments, plans, gameplay, enemy stats, maps, items, and the overall walkthrough to liberation. It was how I sorted out how to play the character, the poor pliable prodigy, I was playing in this IRL RPG. It was also where I wrote down concepts and strategies essential to how I could free myself and my people from Lux's rapacious reach.

Quawd knows I needed to figure something out. My decision date was coming up. By tomorrow at midnight I had to choose a path: pursue this career deep within the Luxite metropolitan machine or scrimp and hustle within the confines of the crumbling Kuroba. The Elders say a career in Luxite is a path of destined duty to the Kuroban cause, but not for me. I needed something to excite me, develop me, and, hopefully, save me. If I chose not to work for the Luxites — the "idle" path in the eyes of our Elders — I would be subject to shame by my own people for not choosing to be employed by my oppressors. If Luxites found out I wasn't fully cleaved from their bosom through a self-serving snitch, or if some masochistic madness drew me back to Lux, that choice'd get me sent to the same dungeon as Baldie. All because of a primary, preventable violation of the Seed Armistice. Otherwise, staying with this current job was, to me, simply upgrading my dungeon to a fancier ambiance within the well-orchestrated perception of freedom.

Staring up at the ceiling of my rinky-dink room I scanned for the game I'd spit to serenade my elusive manager when I pulled up on him. I couldn't find a single hint in the hardened mud sprinkled with odd bits of trash seemingly floating in suspended animation above. As I racked my brain for what to write, I tried to piece together the haunting feeling of my dreams again. It was like grabbing smoke. I tried to reassemble the ephemeral dream into a cogent strategy for how to beat this level enroute to liberation. That same gut, the one guiding my goals began to grumble and growl with hunger.

~ New Side Quest: Eat Something~

I didn't have dinner last night and now I was suffering the consequences of working late without bringing home any food. We didn't have options here. To be honest, Kuroban meals were almost totally imported from the Luxite city. Starvation was the norm. Pooling our pittances to purchase a little Luxite feed on paydays made our Earth Going Ceremonies a must-attend event. Other than those traditional celebrations we held every payday, we never came together, never indulged in Kuroban culture. Between paydays, we scrounged for food in the dump. I jokingly asked Quawd for a quick blessing and got up to search our pantry for anything to satiate my tempestuous tummy.

I snuck by Mom's room like a spy behind enemy lines. She couldn't hear me over her stifled, shaky sobbing, but I couldn't be too certain. I craned my neck around the corner to peek in as I passed by. It was in these early moments, when she believed she was alone, that her public character broke down.

She knelt over a makeshift shrine to her long-lost lover. She may look better to everyone else, but she held the same despair I tamed in myself. My first reflex was to scan through all the ways I could save Mom from further strife. Kuroba might cave if they spy any cracks in the powerful, grounded, Elder-armor she exudes after her tears run dry. I couldn't contain myself to honor Baldie's last wish.

On the plus side, we'd *both* been getting better at performing. To most everyone else we were functional members of society. She was more consistent than me, if I was honest: the strong, wise community Elder holding Kuroba together. The last vessel of Land Healing, the most foundational of Kuroba's ancestral arts. And I was the problem-child who turned their life around and became an effective employee, excelling at a fancy job in the big city — who was about to lock down a first for Kuroba: a Kuroban in an exclusively Luxite job. I'd be pulling in big money, almost up there with the Opp-erator Corps.

I watched Mom as she wailed, transfixed. She was trying to mute it, but our neighbors probably heard her through the thin mud walls. Every vertebra pushed through her skin as she was folded over, mourning into her bony hands. Her skin seemed to sag off her scrawny frame. But we, us two and the collective we of our people, had more immediate and grave concerns to contend with than a little unshakeable sadness.

We Kurobans were wasting away. I blamed the Seed Armistice for simplicity's sake, but we all knew in our heart of hearts that Lux had sabotaged our serenity long before that. They didn't attack us outright anymore – unless we were in their urban bubble — so at a glance our lives looked relatively luxurious. As proud Maroons, we hid our hunger behind award-winning performances.

It was hard to see Mom like this, out of character, at her most vulnerable. The urge to cry crept to the edge of my eyelids. We all needed, much less earned, a break. I hid against the misshapen door frame to her room staring at her pain as if it was a way to indulge my own when a roar echoed from my midsection. My consciousness snapped back into focus. I zipped toward the kitchen before I spooked my maternal drill sergeant and had another dilemma on my hands.

When I slipped into the kitchen, I turned on our simple one-burner solar stove in preparation to cook up whatever food we had. A busted armoire served as our pantry. It was the first place I searched for a morning snack. For safety and silence purposes, I reached out with both hands to grab the only handle left. Carefully, a nanometer at a time, I dragged the door open. I didn't want to trigger the wail of its mangled, crusty hinges. There was already enough wailing going on. Fully open, the armoire was bare. A mess of dusty webs, a cloud of dank rot, and a single battered can of bubbling beans were the only things inside. Ripples ran across my stomach as it rumbled once again. Those beans definitely came from the dump but the can looked so old it probably knew Mom's great-grands. The void in my abdomen was undeterred as I propelled my hand toward the gnarled can.

Generations without nutrient-rich food had adapted our bodies to rancid, worthless morsels. We had only a brief period where we were nourished adequately since we'd been forced onto these lands, but since the Seed Armistice, all that rejuvenation had been undone. With the beans almost in my grasp, I paused my hand's shaky approach. It was all we had left.

Mom wouldn't have anything else for the day. She'd be busy tending to a never-ending list of Elder duties without the time to forage for a meal in the vast dump. She needed it more than me, but she'd never say that. The mutated bean sludge slowly leaking on one side might be the last resort to hold Mom over until I brought something home from Lux.

I needed to seek out something else for breakfast. I used my more logical, collectivist hand to pull back my jittery, frantic hand imploring me to appease my appetite. The rapid wrestling between my carnal cravings and my sacrificial spirit crashed into the door of the ancient armoire.

Crreeeeaaak.

"You better be ready for work," my mom's muffled yell barreled in from the other room. I could hear her wiping her face and drawing up snot while screaming into the kitchen. "You know early—"

I snapped my head toward her direction with my gaze

stuck to the ground, a single brow raised, and my lips primed to pounce. My reaction was to cut her off with a diplomatic dagger of disrespect, "—Is not early enough, right?" Which only led me down a much spicier path than intended, "Because Quawd expects us to bend spacetime upon itself to create a wormhole through which we can arrive before the office was even built? That's how the saying goes, right *Mom?*" As soon as I realized what I'd done, I put my arms up to defend myself.

Mom strolled into the kitchen with a playful saunter as if she hadn't been bawling. "You think you're funny." She stopped and stood at attention in front of me. "Don't start. You and your chicken legs know how long the trek to Lux is." She smiled at me with unabashed glee as if the sister had just finished a wake and bake session, strawberry eyes and all.

"Yeah, but I'm done with all of my assignments, and even if they give me anything else, I'll be done like" — I snapped both my fingers and waved my hands as if announcing the prestige of my latest, great illusion — "I can chill and read before work, right?"

Mom didn't respond. Her fists tightened so much the veins in her hands jumped out and I thought she'd swing on me. She let loose a big sigh and threw me a silent, steel glare that knocked me across the forehead saying, "you better get your ass dressed."

A dialog box with a decision popped up, bouncing in front of my vision.

Follow Mom's strongly implied threat or my gut.

I didn't want to upset her any further and decided accordingly, not without dissent though. The digital dialog box zoomed away.

I stomped out of the kitchen to wash up, hiding my face as I twisted it up and mouthed a curse, even though Mom was still in the kitchen barking. Her authoritative voice followed me as I pouted toward the only sink in our place. A greenish-brown bubble popped on its own from within the large rust-ridden basin about a quarter-filled with stagnant sludge. I sighed and turned around.

I fixed my face until it advertised glee and obedience while I crossed the hallway to get behind her. I grabbed a dented metal mug from the kitchen. I wasn't going to wash my face in that repulsive sink water. A lack of clean water might be just another sacrifice that Kurobans dealt with, but we didn't have to. And I wasn't gonna suffer in silence. That didn't seem to be working out for Mom, contrary to what her performances for everyone else portrayed. It was counterproductive to clean one's self in filth. Not only that, it was probably the speck of truth behind some harmful Kuroban stereotypes.

I heard Mom take a deep breath, loading up for a verbal offensive, and I sped up my exit.

As I scooted my flat feet with staccato urgency, she growled at me. "Where the fuck do you think your ungrateful ass is going? And don't forget to turn off the stove again. I'm not playing, I'll be happy to re-trash your heap of distractions to keep—"

I slipped out to the front yard, before she had the opportunity to launch the complete threat.

I looked up to see an odd lime-green shooting star rocket across the sky. The tail passed right through the Drinking Gourd, a constellation Baldie used to obsess over. They said it was the most important squad of stars in the sky. Stars that'd whisper the time to us Kurobans at night, if we listened. The Drinking Gourd was still faintly visible as the sun's edge peaked above the horizon.

I stepped over the moldy doormat with only the speckled

outline of a "W" visible. Mom had laid it out to make our hut more "homey." The cool, dry, sulfur-tinged mountain air swirled with the warmth rising from below my bare feet. Under each footstep the soil shifted to a deep, dark, nutrient-rich brown then reverted back to a rocky, reddish hue once my foot lifted off. The climate contrast converged at my midsection. A rush of unctuous life down below with decaying desertification swarming above. Love and lineage leached from the earth and shot up to my gut. The earthen warmth calmed my nerves.

A ramshackle water pump served as the main event in our messy yard. I navigated piles of trinkets and treasures collected from the dump to grab the pump's squeaky, reborn faucet we were testing out. This would be the newest and youngest Elder Wafaa's first offering to Kuroba: abundant, clean water.

Tightly gripping my banged-up mug, I pumped some water from our rudimentary purification and distribution system. Clean, cold water hit my lips and I felt proud. A bit of my exhaustion washed away with each gulp. Yet another small example of what my community could achieve, despite our lack of resources and "limited" capacity to create for ourselves.

Guzzling down that cool, crisp water softened my esophagus and temporarily soothed my stomach. I imagined the water was a hearty soup and its buttery taste hung on my tongue. Meditating over the theoretical soup, I swallowed slowly, staring out as I savored my internal shower. The desolate, dusty, dirt street that served as the spine of our ravaged community was just waking up.

The area was silent except for the soft rhythmic rumble coming from further up the rugged road. Like clockwork, a sea of people slowly started milling out of the shacks surrounding the street. I was enamored, truly awestruck, witnessing Kuroba rouse. As the sun rose, more Kurobans joined the communal march down the mountain. They each had a unique soft glow. In their luscious skin I saw every shade and contrast of rich Kuroban soil from the light reds and yellows to dark browns and blacks.

My people.

Most were draped in either the shabbiest scrounged uniforms or fabulously fraudulent formal wear. Few stepped out in flawless finery. The Opps were easy to tell apart from the general Kuroban. Their essential "Kurobanness," that original bright glow, dimmed day by day as they directly served the cream of the creamy crop.

The demanding duties, precise parameters for presentation, and lightweight *lux*ury tempted the most diehard Kurobans trying to make something of themselves. The Opps still living in Kuroba peacocked their rented airs bequeathed by their twisted patrons.

I've seen their evolution happen: They start with a couple fabulous trinkets until they're fully dripped out, but underneath, powered by their briefly bestowed authority, they detach from Kuroba and our needs more each day. That may not sound bad, but their detachment nullifies the near constant sacrifice of starving Kurobans working their hands to the bone, breaking back, or in my case, suffering sleepless nights. All for the immediate exponential enrichment of Luxites. Once an Opp has violently fleeced enough wealth and power to arbitrarily prove their loyalty, they're recruited to serve in a more intimate, insidious manner, thereby fully disappearing from Kuroba.

These Opps I was watching in the early sunlight, mixed in with the rest of the commuting crowd, were still early in their journey. They hadn't yet made the permanent move to the metropole yet and were still trying on tyranny. Whether Opp or not, each and every Kuroban on their way to their assigned workplace was dead-set to impress each and every Luxite when they made it to the big city.

I stood in the yard. One after another, these model Kurobans scanned me up and down and up as they rubber-necked by, giving disgusted looks and mumbled judgements. It became a walking traffic jam of hushed *mmm-mmm-mmms* and *have respect for yourselfs*. My angular anatomy was barely covered in some crusty briefs and a holey, yellowing crop top. I snapped back to my senses after taking so many disapproving daggers and washed my face under the faucet.

The early morning storm of shame activated my defenses and I searched for my pile of found garments. We Kurobans did our resourceful best to imitate the irrational ideals of our employers. Not me though, I didn't need to perform. My work spoke for itself.

On my way over to the mess of used clothes, I stunted forward at my commuting critics with pouted lips and a stern brow. It startled my disparaging onlookers. The nearest ones scrambled backward, bowling into the procession of patriotic performers. They didn't think I'd stand up to them. I chuckled to myself as I picked through my yard closet. I had already fallen out of Lux's grace once already, so I wasn't worried about maintaining my compliant character.

Now, to choose a reclaimed outfit that would match today's vibe.

~New Side Quest: Don't Let the Haters Get Me ~

I started to skip with joy towards the front door to put on my costume when Mom popped out of the door. "No shoes?

How many times do I have to tell you? You're not bringing those dirty feet back in."

I stomped and scraped my feet on our weathered doormat before squeezing past her immovable frame blocking me from stepping on our also *dirt* floors. I made my way to the shards of mirror affixed to the wall above the cesspool sink and hurriedly put on the clothes I'd picked out.

A black and yellow striped t-shirt with a fading image of a bowtie near the collar went over my head. I pulled up a jean skort, distressed, dirtied, and dilated from being overworked and under-cleaned. The jean material had been patched so many times the patches were becoming holes again, but I thought I looked cute. I never was a sheep before and wasn't planning on being one today. My clothes had to be comfortable and functional. Fixing my fro in the mirror I was reminded of Baldie in their final moments as leader of the Glowing Earth Liberation

Defense. They were facing away from me, standing above the Kuroban crowd with their arms bound together. Their bald head glinted in the sun. Our last conversation repeated in my mind:

"Lead better than me; remember we're still free."

"Ha! Of course, I'm already better than you Baldie! I can't wait until I hear about this mission when you return." I had joked innocently all those years ago with my shackled parent as they attempted to disguise their despair.

They were already being escorted away by Luxites when I caught their final words. "Sorry Copykid, this one might be a while, but it'll be a pretty epic story hun. In the meantime, don't worry about your mother, trust that her inconsistent idea of improvement is aligned. Spend your energy taking care of yourself instead." I wasn't feeling their nickname mocking my deep admiration, but I felt the love over 20 years later. I couldn't stop smiling until Mom popped up behind me.

"You're not going to work wearing that, are you?"

"Yeah, it's professional, black tie and everything, see?" I pointed at the dull, scratched screen printing near the neck of my apiarian shirt and kept primping.

"None of that is professional. You don't even have a collar. And you're running late, the sun is almost up. Good thing I had something ready for you." She handed me a thin, billowy hand-stitched sweater, an oxford shirt with no buttons and a huge bite out of the side, and two pairs of slacks. One black, and one brown.

"What is this?" I roared back with a power punch of irritation. I wanted to ask her why my attire mattered – or what professional was code for – but I thought twice about it.

Mom's anger built up around her face and neck like a bottle of boiling soda that'd been shaken heavily. Her exaggerated exhale, her stiff form, with fists clenched and chin smashed into her neck, took me back to my childhood, when she'd spout off all of her anger at how the Luxites had and continued to terrorize us. She always blamed me instead of crying out to the city and its dictatorial directors.

Whether it was getting her some food, getting out of her face, or getting back to being sad with her, anytime I didn't do what she wanted this was how she'd react. She was prepared to pounce both verbally and physically, attempting to break me emotionally and spiritually.

I took a step back before my whole day was thrown off. This fight wasn't worth it.

I pouted as I put on as much of her outfit as I could take. Just the sweater and the black slacks. I straightened up my hair after squeezing it through the stiff sweater.

The tension evaporated from her body and flowed right into giddy glee. Mom smiled at me and came in closer with a million small pats and pokes. Her instantaneous shift sickened me. It didn't seem human. I held myself together though, taking a deep breath while biting my lip.

"I'm so proud of you," Mom said, offering her particular brand of olive branch. "You won't dress professionally or be punctual, but you actually made something of yourself."

I closed my eyes and took a deep breath as I connected exactly what trauma she was projecting onto me this time. I gave my words a more caring tone. "I'm not them, Mom."

"I know, I know, b-but . . ." She turned away from me and sniffled a little before collecting herself. When she turned back to face me she had an exaggerated grin below her hollow eyes. "I get scared when you have your little *missions* or your . . . you know . . . *outbursts*. But you made something of yourself. Even after your expulsion from the Kuroban Free School!"

"Trust me, Mom. I know how to act when I need to." I moved in to give her a hug, just like I always did.

She blocked my incoming arms and hopped backwards to

avoid my embrace. "You don't need to worry about that. That is the direction the spirit of Quawd provides. Speaking of that, you're taking your meds, right?"

I looked away from the mirror so she couldn't see my face and squirted out a faint, "uh-huh."

"Great. Now take the sweater off so I can help you put on the collared shirt and see if I can do something about your hair. You got until tomorrow at midnight to decide, you know? But you can always decide early. With all the money you'll get you'll be able to buy tailored suits and exude the epitome of professionalism every day. It's such an easy decision for you. You've got a *good* job, almost as good as an Opp-erator. You don't need to worry about dreams or hustling or scraping by like the rest of us. You should be grateful to Bodi. Your little friend saved you."

"No, I'm fine, let me—"

Dum dum dum.

I was saved by a heavy knock at the battered plastic door. I zipped away from my mom's scrutiny to answer it, slipping my therapy journal into my back pocket as I dashed over.

On the other side of the door was my best – well, *only* – friend Bodi. He was as big as the doorway. I poked my head out to see him with his sister Soma and a pristine metal lunch pail dangling in his other hand. His dusty fourth-hand suit looked as if four tweed bears were making love on his big barrel body.

Soma beamed at me as she tried to squirm out of Bodi's grasp. She bobbed about beside Bodi dressed in pristine bright orange coveralls. The first day of school look gave me uncomfortable flashbacks. The administration provided free uniforms for every new inductee. Soma was just starting her gut-wrenching journey of indoctrination.

I yelled out to them. "EKs, are you with me!"

As Soma's face lit up, Bodi recoiled backwards. My boastful

colloquialism was out of character. Nobody expected me, of all people, to be excited for work. I just wanted to get out before Mom went any deeper in her bag.

"EK, where ya a—" Soma tried to reflect my energy back, but her unbending brother smashed his mammoth hand over her mouth before she finished. He shuffled with restless regard for some odd reason.

The top of Bodi's bulky body bent forward like a broken lawn chair. "Grand risings, Elder Mama. May Quawd be with you."

"And also with you," Mom responded with a cheesy smile as she squeezed my shoulder and turned her face towards me. She loved her formal title and, in particular, her actual name, Mama. She said the Kuroban Creole name reminded her of sweeter times, *"when there was more respect."* Not the struggle she lived now. I never called her that, even when she served in her official capacity, and that probably pissed her off even more.

Bodi bowed, head to the dirt, never giving Mom eye contact. "We are here to shepherd your wayward progeny to our place of employment post-haste. We must leave promptly. For we are far behind *shed-yool* and must escort my immature sibling to the glorious christening of her mind's maiden journey into enlightenment. Are my intentions and preparation approaching your expectation for representation ma'am?" He froze, like his barrel body had fossilized at our doorstep, while Soma cut her eyes at me, looking physically unsettled with the formality her brother shifted into.

"Oh Bodi, you are such a fine child. So respectful and focused on the *right* things. I hope you rub off on this one." Mom slapped me on my shoulder and raised her eyebrows before sashaying toward Bodi. A light of happiness flashed in her eyes. She hilariously attempted to give him an exaggerated church hug. He swiftly dropped onto one knee. "Psht." She waved his excessive formalities aside. "Give me a hug, baby." A true playfulness and affection that wasn't at all the deception she served me. If she had looked at me once while she hugged him, I would've had unadulterated evidence that she was punishing me for not fulfilling *her* employment dreams.

Before she remembered the collared shirt or whatever catastrophe she was about to commit to my hair, I took assured steps outside of my abode. "Bye Mom. See you tonight."

Mom snatched my hand before I was even a full step away. Her thespian smile of conditional caring returned, but not for the reason I thought.

"Wait, I have something for you. I was serious when I said I was proud of you." She ran off and returned with a hefty, brand frickin' new coat.

"Wait! Is this a mycelial joint!" I gagged and ripped it from her hands before she could renege. Sauntering around with it draped over my shoulders like I had front row seats at a Saturday Night Luxite Cage Fight — *which only had Kuroban fighters, never Kuroban audience members.* First of all, the sheer weight of the coat was notable. It was heavy enough to weigh me down, but light enough to move with the wind. I sunk into the fabric as I let it engulf me in its earthy shades of brown and gray. And it was warm, like its built-in heaters blasted my exposed skin with love. I halted my enthusiasm mid-runway. There had to be conditions attached to this ultra-rare gift.

"Yes, I had some time to abuse a little old land healing technique or two while you were at work. I know our spore supply has been dwindling, but this only took a few of the non-ideal spores I kept from the harvests me and Bee – *ahem* – Baldie saved helping with Earth Goings in our youth. I couldn't wait until your birthday tomorrow. I hope this helps you remember that good things come to those who *work* for it . . .

and make the *right* decision." She clumsily thumbed over at Bodi. "You'll turn out better than Baldie, you're already hanging around better company. I believe it wholeheartedly." Finished off with a kissy face and a finger heart over the spot where people normally had hearts.

There it was. She couldn't help herself. But it was a pretty dope present. I'd never received anything like this from her — or anyone, to be honest. It was mind blowing if you thought about it. She had to keep all of those spores through, and much after, the Seed Slaughter, maturing, breeding, shaping, refining, and sealing them. It was a wearable treasure trove of history and cultural knowledge.

I leaned into happiness despite her coercive efforts.

Nodding with a watermelon smile on my face, I motioned for her to help me put the coat on. She came over and slipped it on as I jittered with excitement. "Oh my Quawd! Thank you so much. So sturdy, yet comfortable." I twirled round and round to give the long split tail some real velocity and lift. "You hear that swish? Oooh, I love it," I squeaked as I sauntered around our hut's great room.

I flapped the lapel backwards and forwards to demonstrate the new, clean sound of the traditional Kuroban-wear for the cooler, less erratic temperatures we used to have. It was one of the very few things made from the meager resources we actually produced, on our own, right here in Kuroba. A version of this coat wouldn't have been uncommon when we lived closer to the rainforests and rivers that used to burst from the base of our mountain. A nice waterproof coat was actually necessary with all of that moisture. That luscious biosphere had become a maze of blighted, barren mines. We've long since fled to higher altitudes and deciduous trees, essentially trapped by the ever-expanding wasteband swallowing our oceanside summit. Only Kurobans tapped into the culture, the old school, or homeschooled like me would be able to tell this coat was made from hidden burial ground mushrooms and wasn't some dingy, old fourth-hand trench.

I MELTED when I moved in front of our hut's singular, cloudy window where I caught the faint outline of my reflection.

"Great. I know it's getting pretty cold in Lux. This'll help make a *good* decision a little easier. Bye now. Have a great day at work! Your accomplishments are appreciated." I only faintly heard her as I was busy peacocking.

"May Quawd – *sh-shrrrr* – shower you with infinite blessings madam." Silly old Bodi tried to mask a massive yawn while sucking up to Mom.

She replied with that strange caring accent she'd been tapping into this morning. "At rest, my child. And tell your father to remember my amendments to the armistice that I sent over last evening."

"Ma'am," Bodi replied, snapping his vertebrae straight to salute my mom. She twirled around and went inside without acknowledgement.

I took Soma's hand and pulled the back of Bodi's shirt to drag him out of there. Before I left the yard, Soma pointed at the ground. "Your feet. Y-your shoes."

"My bad," I replied, playing cool. I dug into the unorganized pile of foraged footwear I'd recently separated from a sizable wasteband haul. Out came a mismatched pair of comfortable-looking tennis shoes with the laces tying the pair together. Gold! And they were somewhere near my size. I stuffed my feet into them and gave a sanguine nod, something I felt oddly compelled to do, before strapping them up as tight as I could. "Now I'm ready."

Soma squealed. "You always have the best style by just listening." She looked down at her penny loafers. Bodi rolled his eyes and pulled her down the road.

STAGE COMPLETE

Health Points 60%
Magic Power 10%

Mission #1: Don't Upset Mom . . . . SUCCESS
Side Quest #1: Eat Something . . . . COMPLETE FAILURE
Side Quest #2: Don't Let the Haters Get Me . . I TRIED

Experience Points Gained [260]
Coins [-20]
Items Received [MYCELIAL COAT]

Chapter 2: Connecting . . .

Mission #1: Get to Work on Time

We merged into the mass of commuters streaming through the streets. The crowd wasn't as dense as before the sun-peeking, but a number of stragglers like us were Lux-bound. The thin crowd repelled from us as we walked, bending away from me in particular as if I produced a powerful magnetic field. It really could've been anything: my outfit, my attitude, or my history. As much as I tried to dismiss this ostracization as simply people that'd prefer to be powerless letting their pain be their pilot, the repulsed looks from all of those sunken faces and drooping eyes hit harder from close range. This dissonance dug divergence deeper into my psyche.

I squeezed my eyes shut to hide in my happy place where Kurobans were free and I was the one who produced the suite of role-redefining video games that'd unlocked our revolutionary potential. We were unshackled, joyous, and frolicking. I couldn't put my finger on what our community looked like or how I made the whole video game thing happen, but I did know how it would feel. The rhythmic warmth rotating and radiating in my gut. When I shut out the outside and went inward, I could focus on this microscopic spark of utopia.

Bodi's shouting broke my concentration. "Keep up, genius, we're late. We still have to drop off your little dilettante-in-training."

I sped up and spotted Soma on the other side of Bodi staring dirtward as she walked. Her slight shoulders sagged as if the world had dragged her down. I wondered if she was feeling the same thing I was feeling, albeit a different version of dejection. But I couldn't ask with obedient Bodi on watch.

~New Side Quest: Comfort Soma ~

To continue distracting myself from the looks and whispers of onlookers, I took in the view of shanties lining our singular, earthen boulevard. Our community consisted of a wild assortment of abodes, haphazardly constructed of any and every bit of trash, all held together with our proprietary mud blend. The craggy domiciles rose up above all sorts of bits, bobs, and baggage organized into various piles in the cramped dirt yards abutting the main road. A few huts were more market-focused with more massive, specialized piles. Those eager commercial-Kurobans were already beginning to trade their scavenged spoils for whatever worthwhile trinket they could mark off their never-ending list of needs.

To get to the school building, we had to walk to the other side of the sprawling summit community. But it was on our way to our work assignment anyways.

Beyond the out-of-place concrete and metal school building was the wasteband where our commute began in earnest. Along the way, Kuroba's energy filled the area with a warm, connected, congenial vibe. Destitution and debasement be damned, folks were already up dancing and laughing and tinkering. Those that didn't work in Lux held Kuroba down during the day: the Elders, the youth, and local hustlers without sufficient academic markers to fulfill their covenant with the armistice remained to run our mountaintop bastion.

The dirt road gave way to a cement sidewalk. As soon as we hit the hard surface, the energy subsided. Everything became silent and more serious the closer we got to the school building. The pristine palace was like a fur coat in a desert. A towering spectacle oozing of opulence sitting right at the edge of our crappy community.

A long line of cross caregivers and sad students formed in front of the massive modern structure with its lofty weathervane stretching high into the sky. For many Kurobans it was the pride of our former Maroon village. A sign of our "victory" over the great Luxite invasion, the Seed Slaughter. But it was no victory. I knew the harm it caused. Deep, generational, traumatic harm which traded physical violence with an unseen abuse, constantly manipulating our minds.

I saw it, lived it, and was still fighting to trust myself. Being expelled right before I received my master's degree like Bodi and the rest of my classmates didn't make me a hater. The administration just couldn't handle the truth. This school was a docility offering, part of their insidious coup de grâce. Possibly putting us in a situation more insidious than our horrendous past.

We joined the back of the queue, snaking around the building and down the street. Invisible strings of proletarian responsibility, deeply seated and implanted long ago, were tugging at Bodi to *hurry, hurry, hurry*. I watched him start squirming, pacing, and cursing under his breath.

"Pssht!" Bodi grumbled and fumbled his words. "It's

Father's fault for forcing me to escort this shrimp. She could've gone on her own or-or with him."

I covered my mouth and averted my gaze to contain my amusement with his intense frustration. A leafy light slowly circling the spire above the towering educational edifice caught my interest. Work wasn't calling to me and neither was the pressure for punctuality. I could indulge in imagining what this new light was all about.

Before I got lost in conjecture, we spotted Bodi and Soma's father, the vain Elder Anansi. Anansi was the only Kuroban working within Kuroba who wore a custom-tailored suit and spotless dress shoes. Even fully suited his muscles bulged purposefully, like he wanted us to all know he was powerful. In the dirt road slums he was almost as incongruous as the school itself. His life was spent modeling his image after the policy-making parasites he preferred down in the valley metroplex. His clothes, his hair, even the way he spoke were more reminiscent of his leash-holders than his roots. It wasn't simply that he aesthetically matched his masters, his rhetoric and resolutions realized the same egotistical anti-Kuroban hate hallucinations. I respected but despised him accordingly.

Anansi was posted up at the top of the steps leading into the school. He was greeting, critiquing, and shooing students through an array of doorless gates built along the entryway. Affixed to the left side of each inlet was an articulate robotic arm with an assortment of prodding, pointy, and potentially pernicious attachments. The students marched through each opening and waited on the other side as the robotic arm ruthlessly rummaged through their person and possessions. The line moved at a coordinated yet chilling cadence that reminded me of sheep schlepping to slaughter. I locked eyes with Anansi and he paused to flash his pearly whites, eagerly nodding us forward. Bodi exhaled loudly and dragged us forward to meet his father.

"Grand risings, sir. I ha – *hahrrr* – ve successfully escorted Soma to school. May I please be dismissed?" Bodi looked down. He had one hand clamped over his mouth. I could feel his embarrassment trying to address his foreboding father while hiding a yawn.

"Am I boring you already? These dirty shoes on your sister don't look like success to me. Can I have a brief word with you, son?"

"No sir, they are clearly unsatisfactory," Bodi answered quickly before furiously licking the inside corner of his baggy jacket. He then jumped down to a prone position on the concrete floor and hastily wiped up the stray specks of soil spotting Soma's shoes with his moist jacket corner. I watched, embarrassed for him, as he kept his head down on the floor and turned toward his father. Anansi dug down to grip the extra material bundled up in the scruff of Bodi's neck and lifted his big body like a rag doll.

They went around the building and out of sight. Behind me I felt someone slipping my therapy journal out of my back pocket. "What's this?"

With a quick spin I snatched the pickpocket's small, but solid arm before they pilfered my secret Libook. "Ow, ow, ow." Soma winced and turned away from me, rubbing her wounded wrist.

I moved closer to her and got down on one knee. "Sorry, sorry, sorry. Reflex. I didn't mean to hurt you. This is very precious to me, that's all. You understand, don't you?" I massaged her wrist as I tempered my paranoia. I was especially jumpy on school property. The problems I had here might've occurred a couple years ago, but they were still fresh to me.

Soma coyly turned around and gave me a cheeky smirk as she asked in an energetic voice, "Is it a game guide or some special book on computer-y things?"

I stood back up, satisfied that she was better, and gave her a covert signal to turn her volume down. "Not exactly."

"Ooh, ooh, are you finally creating your game? I remember you told me about that. You're smart enough. That would be so dope!" Soma's voice elevated with her excitement. She covered her mouth.

Her energy and interest may've been dangerous in our unfavorable environment, but it made me smile nonetheless.

"Not exactly. I'll tell you after school, okay." Soma's happiness disappeared. She looked down with the same disappointment I saw on the walk over. I put my hand on her soft cheeks and bent down to look her directly in the eyes. "You ready?"

"I-I guess so. I'm just, just a little worried. We have to spend more time in class than any other Grade 1 group ever. They got rid of recess! It's even worse than when y'all were here, and you know what they did to you." She moved in closer and spoke with a quiver in her voice.

"And there are these machines that seem to scan students too. But it'll be okay, Soma. I promise. Just stay you. Find your healing and stay curious. I'm always here if you have any questions." I squeezed her warm hands and locked eyes with her.

Soma gave me a little half-smile, then looked down quickly. "Thanks. But I still don't wanna go. I want to be like *you*. You didn't need to finish . . . and look at you now!"

I stepped back and chuckled. I wished I had her optimism. "It's more complicated than you think. I'll tell you about it later, I promise. You'll do much better than I did. Trust me."

"Y-you think so?" Before I could answer Soma, Bodi appeared from around the corner. With a huff he grabbed me and strangled my arm. "Let's go. We're late."

Anansi returned as well and shoved Soma through the frightening frisk machines. She disappeared into the mass of kids funneling into the school.

I was honored she saw me in such esteem. I had similar worries when I started school, but didn't have anyone that thought anything other than "follow the rules," except for the specter of Baldie.

My own worries started leaking through my internal defenses. The overthinking machine was cranking up again as we got further from Soma. I was so lost in thought I almost tripped with each step. Especially when I stepped onto the moat of trash that surrounded Kuroba — the wasteband — almost losing health points before breakfast. I caught myself with one hand which landed on a tattered game guide. Surprisingly, it was the latest release of my favorite massively multiplayer online role-playing game series, the one that inspired my personal style of divergence: Tower Ark 2200. I picked it up and the comforting euphoric potential it provided stopped my mind from going down a destructive rabbit hole. I tucked the game guide in my slacks underneath my sweater and skipped ahead to catch up.

Noxious particles assaulted my nostrils as we got deeper into the wasteband. Bodi had wrapped his shoes in old plastic bags to keep them clean. I didn't really care since I'd probably just hose off my footwear when I arrived. We'd been walking for a while, the discarded goods of Lux stretching out in every direction. The dump was growing faster than we could retreat higher up the mountain. Waste was regularly deposited out here, which isolated our community even more from the city we served. A disgusting ecosystem of deterioration, decomposition, and cross contamination crept underneath my feet. I couldn't even worry about the sanitation of it all because I had to keep my wits about me. My footsteps or any disturbance from a Kuroban-forager at higher elevation in the wasteband could trigger an avalanche. Every crunch and crumble kept me on edge.

A blood-curdling scream exploded into my ear holes. I jumped in shock and squinted to see a forager running towards us through a foggy section of the dump. Through the murkiness of the contaminated trash prairie, I saw they had a fat sack tied around their torso, probably full of emancipated third-hand home goods. In their arms they hugged a pristine full-length mirror. In Kuroba, one of those was worth more than a fresh orange. Mirrors were perfect for personal power production.

Chasing behind the forager was a mid-sized waste autotruck from the Luxite Waste Corporation, a fresh load of trash tumbling out the hopper in the back. Debris rained in every direction as the autotruck zoomed over the treacherous trash terrain. It looked like an angry robotic hippo barreling through a pawn shop after a tornado.

Bodi and I both ran on instinct, tripping, falling, and getting slathered in gunk in the process. The autotrucks were easy to avoid since they had primitive visual algorithms, but they worked in packs. If one caught us we're all done for, backup was nearby.

Sometimes the autotrucks were followed by a Blau which would definitely catch your ass, beat you to a pulp, then sentence you to suffer in the sewers. That way they could harvest you indefinitely. All because the forager was probably scrounging for a couple necessities for home. They should know we only do that at night, when there are more of us to watch and scramble their sensors. Now it was much easier for the autotruck to get a three for one special.

I yelled, "Just drop the mirror and it'll stop. It may be coordinating with others." Those bumbling autotrucks could easily track us if we clenched a reflective beacon.

They kept running with the mirror and all their scavenged supplies.

I held tight to my fungal trench coat draped over my scrawny body and ran faster to catch up to Bodi. When I finally started to overtake his stiff, but surprisingly long strides, I pushed his beefy shoulder and nodded to him.

He yelled, "Anansi would sacrifice the mirror for the greater Kuroban good. I would know. I'm his heir – *apparently*."

Crash! The forager dropped the mirror and stopped. The autotruck screeched to a halt with all of the trash flying to the front of the empty cab. It was cinematic, like a cut scene: the forager cowering beneath shattering glass while trash showered behind. Then the autotruck with a bare hopper drove off in the opposite direction back to their pre-programmed dump site.

I nervously chuckled at the sight of this simple victory against Lux. Luxites would never do any driving or come anywhere beyond their beloved factories, much less deal with their waste themselves. Underneath the organic and inorganic trash, the earth's scars were laid bare. All laid to rest by the Lux. Out of sight, out of mind. But at least, the forager, Bodi, and I were safe.

Below the hellishly humid section of the wasteband our view cleared up. A bit of the original woodlands, now-charcoaled trunks petrified in place, shot up above meters of mindless metropolitan "stuff-exhaust." A lush forest eradicated. Razed husks stretched as far as the eye could see. Nothing had grown here in over half a century because of the tremendous toxicity asphyxiating the area. Not even primitive, immortal weeds absorbed enough nutrients to survive these poisoned plots.

I was lost in thought, reflecting on our encounter with the autotruck on top of my mounting mess of worries. Walking on autopilot, I forgot I was with Bodi until I almost ran into him. We'd been silent since he literally saved three Kuroban lives. Darting around him to avoid the collision I realized he was lost in thought himself. "You doing okay, Bods?"

He turned slightly and gave me a weak smile, but kept hiking ahead of me through the trash. "Genius, do you miss being a forager? I-I mean, I know it was hard. Look at what we just saw, b-but . . . you could wake up when you wanted, you didn't have to dress up, no need to go into Lux, and none of this other tap dancing and sh-stuff?"

I was getting further behind, struggling to keep my balance, my pace, and my wits about me while trying to listen carefully. So instead of rushing to keep up, I projected my voice. "A little, but it was harder than you think. It was a death sentence deferred, amplified by powerful, purposefully-designed precarity. All the foraging and hustling in the world ain't stopping frostbite in this funky frontier or heat exhaustion, avalanches, cuts, infections, or an autotruck like you just saw. You're literally digging through trash everyday hoping to land something valuable for you or that someone else would trade for. The post-30 ones couldn't even panhandle because the Eyes of Lux are on high alert for Kurobans violating the Seed Armistice. The ones that did attempt to beg behind enemy lines were considered quitters because it was basically guaranteed to result in death or indefinite detention. All while staving off the same starvation every Kuroban dealt with. Plus, it *really* hurt my mom."

Bodi turned all the way around and kept walking backwards as I almost ate it attempting to maintain his momentum. He looked at me and our eyes connected with his sincere response. "The whole expulsion thing was messed up. I prayed to Quawd that Lux would forgive you. I know you broke the rules – and you definitely shouldn't have – but they went too far."

Before I could respond he turned back around and sped up. I raised my voice and put more pep in my step. I was already huffing and puffing. "As they always say in Lux, – *huff* – 'some bear fruit, – *pfft* – and some are duds.' I was a lost cause. No more than a rotten mango. – *heave* – In their mind I was just another point in their lengthy, one-sided list of reasons why they don't honor the Seed Armistice they hold over *us*."

Bodi whipped around and came to a halt. "If they're in violation, they know we would all stop working for them immediately, s-surely? That would be a clear declaration of war."

I took the opportunity to catch my breath. Once I was in range to speak at a comfortable volume, I stopped. "Oh, my four-sided friend." I patted him on his broad, square shoulders as I heaved in and out. "I thought it was just your communication skills that were stuck in a box, but it's your whole mind, isn't it? But for real, I admire your faith sometimes. Shit, you had the faith to recommend me for this job."

"Of course, why not? I used to come home begging for your help anyways. It just allowed me to get help in real time when I needed it. My mom used to tell me that my faith in Quawd is faith in all of the planet, friend or foe." Bodi took an extended breath before he launched back into his hurried walk. His dented, rusty lunch pail swung wildly at his side.

I lurched on, trying to match his sudden acceleration through the increasing density of decaying waste. "I feel that. By the way, did you get any more info on your mom, on why your mom hasn't come back? She wouldn't just leave–"

"Same story. She committed to a nunnery. In a temple far overseas and on mission trips even farther," Bodie said in a soft, but certain tone. He seemed to be moving faster as the distance between us grew.

I didn't dare pry any further so I switched the mood by smiling with my voice. "Back to your question. I appreciate this job a lot. It's opened my mind in unexpected ways and makes life just that much easier despite the ridiculous requirements we're forced to reach for. You've always looked out for me. Even when we were kids."

Bodi swung his index finger behind him and wagged it. He didn't even turn his head to respond. "Nah. That's only because — you may not be able to tell this about me — I didn't have many friends. *And* you seemed like you needed some Quawdly love."

"Haha. That tracks. But weren't you a Quawd scout leader? You and the other kids used to come out here to do some play foraging to supply Earth Goings, right?" I started hopping through the heavy tangle of trash in order to keep up with Bodi. I didn't want to slow him down or be any more of a burden.

"Not exactly. Father placed me in that position, *whilst also*, not allowing me to be around the other kids. He said, 'Kings don't consort with peasants. Own your power and commune with fellow Kings.' I was sent to camps in Lux and could only forage for you because the former Elders forced my pops, who then forced me."

"For real? That makes everything you gave that much more special. You must really like me or something." I slipped on an ancient grease trap and caught my coat on a sharp spring sticking out from a hollowed-out couch frame. I was lucky to not be skewered by an errant pole or a rusty knife sticking up from the rubbish below.

Bodi kept speaking as I pulled myself up and assessed the damage. "I knew you needed it with your mom in the state she was in after what happened to your other parent. You were too young to handle all of that on your own."

Luckily, I was fine, just a near-death scrape on my right ankle. To be safe, I stopped talking so I could catch Bodi.

We finally reached the edge of the wasteband and I looked down at my shoes. Muck had conquered my reclaimed sneakers, so much so that I couldn't see the little fella on the worn logo dunking anymore. On the other hand, I managed to *mostly* make sure my mycelial coat wasn't defiled by any of the decaying discharge. After a quick inspection, it had only suffered a little rip on the back, probably from when I fell in the grease trap. The hole was underneath where the hood hung when it wasn't over my head. That minor tear didn't seem like a big deal overall.

In front of us, land scars oozed and trembled as if they wailed for healing. The devastation here was frightening when I first saw it. Now, it was just a reminder of the kind of society we were walking into. Bodi and I leapt over and around these ground ulcers and entered the second stage on the trek to Lux.

In front of us was a vast forgotten mine that looked like the result of a gigantic, prolonged, jagged gnawing at the earth, crumbs and all. We moved quickly but quietly around an enormous pile of precious aggregate ruthlessly ripped from the guts of the peak. It was once a bustling extraction site for gold. Or maybe lithium? Or was it cobalt? Bauxite probably? I couldn't remember anymore, but it didn't matter since it had long since been abandoned when Lux found new places and people to plunder.

The expansive site had seen much better days. Long forgotten machines, trucks, and tools sprinkled their rust all over the mammoth munch of earth. They even left an eye-popping mound of land loot unattended. At the time, that mound was worth millions, maybe billions. And now it was abandoned. Available for anyone with *means* to claim as their own, but they'd also need the *means* to process the raw materials into products of Lux's many despotic, detached desires. But even that wasn't worth the toil.

Luxites didn't look back. They just moved their extraction effort to the next overflowing oasis to be sucked dry. It was hard to see because I knew how urgent avoiding the trash heap, proving our continued value, was to my people — the story told and untold. It made me want to hammer home my appreciation, knowing I could've been thrown away too.

"You don't know how much you saved me, Bods. You gave me life. Real purpose. Even more than this potential career. I loved getting the game guides, every broken device and tool I asked for, and the many, many technical books. And I can't forget, the meals were great too. You know, you were the only one who made sure Mom and I had sustenance? In the whole of Kuroba! Being locked in that house dealing with her *alone*, you brought the nourishment *I* really needed." I flashed the game guide I found on the way and clenched with excitement. "I still remember the first one you gave me. It was a literal *game changer*."

We walked close to one another now that I didn't have such a chaotic, unstable surface to navigate. Bodi turned his head, a flash of menace in his eyes. "Bodi is my name. No shortchanging it, please." I quickly nodded. His face softened and he rubbed the back of his head, looking down as we walked and talked. "You still remember that? I can't remember the - *uh* - sickening slop I scarfed down for dinner last night."

My hands danced as I tried to accentuate my message to Bodi. "I will never forget it. It provided the smallest sliver of hope I needed. It was a first edition, full-color, extended cut strategy guide for the hottest game in Lux, Tower Ark 2200. In it, all of humanity including the plants, fungi, water, and animals were forced into an enormous, mega-tech tower reaching low earth orbit. All because the planet had been irreversibly compromised by corporate climate corruption."

"That excites you? You're messed up in the head, for real, you odd genius you." Bodi cut his eyes at me before shaking his head and speeding ahead once again.

"N-not exactly." I gave him his space, but made sure not to lose too much distance as I defended my truth. "It was the idea, the deeper mechanics of the tower that inspired me. It got my mind working. Especially the folks locked in the basement. Their backbreaking, unabated labor ran the whole tower, though their lives were not their own. They were wedded to the maintenance of the tower above them. Beholden to the whims of the 'owners' luxuriating in the lavish penthouse. The story was an escape at first, but as I learned more about the world, I felt an ardent affinity with the basement massive." *And I used their playbook to develop my own plans to topple the intangible tower my people toiled under.*

Bodi continued hiking with hasty purpose while shouting bluntly over his shoulder. "It's just a silly game." I had to jog to keep in earshot of his sharp words floating backward on the wind of his rapid, rigid steps.

I was desperate for him to understand me. I'd already dug so deep into my vulnerability. His obtuse response hinted at frustration stirring inside him. "Yeah, on the surface, but underneath it, all games are interactive stories. Stories at least infinitesimally inspired by reality. Each one a new narrative on an imaginative simulation of alternate worlds — or possibly mods of this one. I *needed* that. Something different. Something to forget reality and forge hope from scratch. Mom and I were stuck in a poisonous psychic space spiraling ever-closer to pulling the plug." Games, or my written substitute, the guides *about* the games, were how optimism penetrated pain – or at least masked it. It rearranged something inside me and my shift sparked Mom's recovery. "Bodi, understand this, you saved us, maybe even saved Kuroba. Every item, enemy, power, location, trial, character, and potential strategy I read about was proto-revolutionary. The painstaking detail allowed me to observe nanoscopic nuances in my everyday life. Which will hopefully lead to a similar victory for us, the real-life characters conscripted to timeless tumult. Don't you see it?"

He didn't look at me, but his whole back tightened and I thought I saw his burly hands transform into cartoonishly animated bombs, lit fuse and all. "It's still a stinking game. It's not real! You don't have magical powers or-or potions or even weapons and fanciful shit like that. What we deal with day to day is totally different. Besides, the Seed Armistice forbids seditious intent!"

I blinked and saw Bodi's regular fists again. After taking a few deep breaths, I calmed myself in order to quell his irritation. "You're right. Totally correct. I'm doing everything by the book. It's j-just, the ways the guides solve problems and detail the overthrow of unstoppable systems are-are inspirational rather than instructive. I just wanted to find a bit of peace in this world. Maybe actually play a video game or two. You know I've delved deep into technology so that I could hopefully build one myself. My knowledge to bend technology to my will is my magic. Real shit!"

"What are you talking about? Lux is real. You know, where we work and earn money. To feed our families and fulfill our armistice obligations. Remember: no aggression, no seeds, and conscription by our 30th. All of this extraneous playing and plotting will have dire consequences. You could put yourself at risk like that forager we just saw. They'll put the real Blaus on you. All of Kuroba could be attacked again! We're just getting the power grid and fresh water running thanks to Wafaa' deciphering your other parent's jumbled plans. We can barely eat much less repel a full-scale military invasion from Lux. What in Quawd are you thinking!?"

I could hear his teeth grinding as he fought to hold back additional scolding, clenching his mouth so hard I could see a vein bulge across his cheek. "Yeah, I get that, but this goes beyond work assignments and seeds and policy interpretation. It goes down to our masters' true mechanics. I'm putting together my own guide for Kuroban liberation." I pulled my therapy journal out of my pocket and waved it around. Bodi didn't turn around to see it. *Ineffective.*

A brisk breeze from the upcoming Luxite cold caused me to properly put on my mycelial coat. The climate was beginning to transition again. I put my Libook back in my waistband as we continued to walk without words. I didn't want to say anything else that may stir him up anymore.

He stopped suddenly and turned to shout directly in my face, swinging his fluffy forearms around antagonistically just like my mom. "Why are you like this!? You're playing a dangerous g-g-game . . . but this is life. Dad was right about you. My lord and savior will guide his followers to emancipation. And you aren't one of his flock?"

"You really think *this* is life?" I blurted and instantly tried to grab the words back into my mouth before they reached Bodi. "Actually, I'm sorry. Do you . . ." I sighed. He wasn't ready for the whole truth. I held my tongue despite wanting to continue my dissertation. Bodi was too heated or influenced by his dad or stuck too far up Quawd's ass to see clearly now.

~New Side Quest: Discover Anansi's True Opinion of Me~

We finally arrived at the barren train station, the Western Lux Manufacturing stop. On the platform a few shabby-suited Kurobans and some broken beggars mingled. Beyond the towering wall on the other side of the tracks massive foundries growled, heaving enormous plumes of malignant exhaust into the air. The sun should've been up by now, but it was blocked by the artificial clouds coming from these factories. The source of the shade made me shiver every time I saw them, the third stockade separating us from Lux.

We waited for a while before a train arrived. Service was irritatingly intermittent going into the city after the early commute hours. Only stragglers like us were onboard: The late ones rushing to work, the despairing old beggars ready to quit, and the frightened-looking Luxite travelers.

When a train finally came, Bodi and I sat down across from one another. The warm air inside the car was soupy with tension, humidity, and pollutants. Bodi plopped his busted lunchpail on the seat beside him. No one made eye contact with each other. The few traveling Luxites didn't react well to their new surroundings, both physical and social. I watched their eyes stare and then dart. Stare and then dart. Fear was written all over their pasty skin, painting it a deep red. I saw every Luxite chest rising rapidly. After everything I'd learned secretly surfing every inch of their insipid information super highway, I knew the fear they harbored, wary of everything we did.

Bodi and I looked at each other. I wanted to say something, but didn't want to upset him more than I already had. As much as he rubbed me the wrong way with his rigid righteousness, he *was* my savior. But please believe I saved him too.

A stop or two later, I couldn't hold it any longer. He was supposed to be my friend. That biting antagonism wasn't Bodi. I whispered to him. "Bredren, what *did* your dad say about me? I know he doesn't like me. Is he still making a fuss about you recommending me again?"

Bodi threw his head back against the vinyl train seat and used one hand like a mouth to chirp out his yawn-filled admission, a sign he used to emphasize his authenticity. "Not this ti – *iiimmmrrr* – me. He just thinks I should spend less time with you and focus on my priorities, especially with my 30th coming in a couple weeks. He thinks I'm losing focus because I've been missing prayer and inter-communal etiquette meetings after work . . . because I'm still working. He's having me up late studying software testing and the good book as a "lesson." I slept *straight through* my alarm this morning. It was amazing I woke up when I did."

As he took the bait, I moved in closer to make my case. I tried to meet his eyes by using my hand to block his visual path. "But you're staying late at work because you're struggling with your tasks. That's the problem. Not your commitment. I've been helping you as much as I can, but it's slow progress. Unless you let me just do it for you, you'll never catch up. Let me help you! It's nothing for me, and I'd love to pay you back anyway I can."

Bodi looked straight at me and threw his hands up with a disgusted look on his face. "I knoooow. But that's lying. I would not honestly be able to fulfill my work assignment if you do my work for me. Thereby being in moral non-compliance of the 3rd grand mandate of the Seed Armistice. Anyways, Dad thinks it's your fault I'm failing. No matter what I say. He's threatened that I'd lose his powerful Luxite connections if I didn't shape up. And that's my only *semi*-truthful ticket out of Kuroba. You're a genius savant at this technology stuff. You'll breeze your way out by moving up at eduGames. As you ascend, I won't be able to survive without hanging onto your coattails waiting for whatever scraps you drop." The other passengers glanced over and stayed attached to our animated conversation as Bodi smiled and showed me his hand fashioned into a c-shape, our shorthand to show he was being honest.

I moved closer to my anxious friend. I held his large hand in mine. The first thing that came to me was to softly declare one of my *subtle* revolutionary facts. "Did you know their entire society runs on and worships computerized devices? They shove technology into everything whether necessary or not. It's their answer to every question, even if it causes more harm in the short run. To the earth, technology is simply an abstraction. A miserable misdirection from the indiscriminate consumption of our shared planet to feed the insatiable imperialist drilled into us all. And that, Mr. Bodi-so-Holy, is the cloaked circulatory system to their society. To coerce the resources of this planet to serve their needs for the least *obvious* cost in the short-term, while making you enlist yourself in that long-term, comprehensive global violence.

"And did you notice our little work tasks have slowed down immensely in the last couple weeks? They've been trying to supplement our struggle with basic janitorial work these days. Look, even Blaus are bots now. When we were coming up, these pigs serving as the tip of Lux's suppression spear were actual *people*. Except for the exceptionally elite disembarkment escorts for the inexperienced excursionists taking the train like us, it's all AI bots approximating Kuroban assignments. Just like what happened to their treasured enforcers. Where will that leave us post-30th career-wise? A terrible transition is already afoot. Why not? According to the rules they play by. I've spent 'nuff time trying to understand the root of Lux. To leverage it against our inevitable eradication." My soliloquy probably wouldn't interest him, but I was trying to get his mind off the pressure his pops was putting on him. As a bonus, maybe I'd also spark the latent insurgency I'd always felt deep inside him.

Bodi stared at me with a concerned face for a couple minutes. Then his cheeks shot up as he gave me a big cheese. "That's a serious rabbit hole you've found yourself in. Be careful. You only have a few days left to make your decision. May Quawd be with you."

The train thundered furiously and the lights flickered as if we were derailing at full speed. The newbies, Luxite and Kuroban alike, screamed out in the same key as the brakes screeched. The pent-up tension inside the train released like the squeal of a tea kettle. We were entering the urban core of Lux: the monumental barrier that encapsulated the wealthiest suburbs at the edge of the mind-altering valley. Outside the windows, the tempered plastic walls of the tunnel morphed into mayhem. The blinding lights, foreboding mechanics, countless screens and sounds, and of course, unspeakable opulence hypnotized me. We zipped through the gigantic shield and everything changed.

Broccoli-colored bursts of light discharged from every Kuroban. At that moment, I felt the difference. Everybody on the train transformed. The incandescent glow from my fellow cordial Kurobans wilted. Their posture fell apart as they seemed to sink into the background. The few Luxite travelers inflated in form and personality. They maintained sinister eye contact with us as they started hurling insults and feints that implied immense violence upon us. My cells quivered and my heart sank. Everything felt cold except for a little spark swirling around in my stomach. We'd passed through the final separation filter between Lux and us. If the other sinister, semipermeable membranes didn't drive home our place, this one did. Separate until they needed us, of course, to run the whole damn machine.

STAGE COMPLETE

Health Points 50%
Magic Power 8%

Mission #1: Get to Work on Time . . . . NOT LOOKING POSSIBLE
Side Quest #1: Comfort Soma . . . . AS BEST I COULD
Side Quest #2: Discover Anansi's True Opinion of Me . . I TRIED

Experience Points Gained [285]
Coins [-20] . . . Can't Wait for Payday
Items Received [NONE]
Status Effect [Dull of Lux]

Chapter 3: Simulation Running

Mission #1: Get Work Done for the Day (Week)
**Mission #2: Make It Through the Rest of the
Day without any Mishaps**

odi and I didn't speak again. Once we stepped off the train, even *I* knew to zip my lips and keep to myself. We didn't dare pollute Luxite ears with what they called "guttural glow worm grunts." It was particularly tense on the platform. Small militaristic units of pale flesh and muscle-bound bodyguards armed with electric batons checked *our* fares and chaperoned away each transformed Luxite.

Without ever putting my eyes up to see clearly, what I could gather was that these strapped up Fare Enforcement Escorts (FEEs) offered a friendly, safe face as vain as theirs. FEEs were a starting place for rookie persecutors to be showered in all the boundless, ill-begotten affluence this flush metropolis offered . . . solely for those who lacked luminosity. I assumed that was the reason for the line of freshly minted personal propulsion pods (p3s) stretching far into the LED-coated bedlam below.

The only p3s I sort of peeped was through a puddle: a reflection of the many screens advertising on Luxite city buildings and streets. It was all souped up with a remote-controlled incline bed, a wraparound TV, a jumbled tower of gaming consoles, copious sauced meats, steaming sides, and fountains filled with a drink that glimmered the same shade as fresh, uncut breadfruit. Word was that some were set up more sexually, others more brutal, but each one embodied the driver's optimal enjoyment ecosystem. Baldie used to tell me that time became irrelevant to Luxites in the city, their AI assistant guided them wherever to maximize passenger dopamine levels.

Lux was a cacophony of screaming monitors trying to twist susceptible minds to desire, to spend, to possess. Mixed into the noise was deafening p3 traffic, errant Kuroban screams, and the deadening buzz of the Kuroban surveillance system underneath it all. That final innocuous sound followed us once we stepped off the platform.

As I walked the streets of Lux I scanned the vents, hatches, and openings to the sewers. I hoped to validate one of the great modern Kuroban fables that our caregivers recited from the time we wore gently used diapers and napkins. It was a foreboding tale that terrified us into obedience.

Pre-30 we could enter Lux freely, by law. But post-30 was different. If we entered Lux without a defined career or an assigned Luxite keeper, we were in violation of Seed Armistice section 2b: The clause concerning Kuroban work requirements. According to the fable told to Kurobans from our youngest days, "idle" Kurobans over 30 were swiftly scooped up and locked in the labyrinthian sewers. I was looking for any hint of captured Kurobans trapped behind oppressive lines. Anyone'd do, but maybe, hopefully, Baldie had escaped this far. And I'd jump to their rescue. Legend has it that in those sewers they'd serve as the city's standing labor surplus. The whole subsurface situation was supervised by Blaus programmed to squeeze out every bit of productivity from each shattered soul.

Any backbreaking task that needed to be completed in Lux — ones that couldn't be automated or formally assigned to anyone in this congested metropolis — were forced upon these subterranean slaves who served in secret. Supposedly the "economic value" underfoot amounted to many multiples of the labor aboveground. But of course, I really hoped to catch a peek at Baldie. Maybe, possibly, in some parallel dimension I might see them and recognize them immediately, or the other way around. Then once I saved them, they'd help me make my dream come true. Together we'd liberate Kuroba. I don't know how I'd free them from the dungeon they'd been trapped in for over 20 years, but trust, I'd make it happen. Even that slim chance wouldn't materialize if I didn't watch every access point to the urban underbelly.

We moved past the mess of mind-numbing LEDs affixed to every inch of concrete, metal, and dimpled asphalt that made up the spacious city. We walked alone on the skinny sidewalks scrunched up against spacious, eight to twelve lane thoroughfares. These massive rivers of broken blacktop were packed with hovering p3s. Each one shifted between stuttering bumper to bumper traffic and rocketing recklessly into the next red light. Walking was hazardous, but it was the only way for Kurobans to get around.

I heard some glass cracking in the distance. Next door to the office was a massive mansion with a flimsy footbridge in the back. The detail and density of the decorations screamed *I have too much money and don't know how to spend it all*. A cohort of Kurobans were moving items in and out of the plush pad along a narrow route elevated high above the dry concrete moat surrounding the building.

To enter the eduGames office, Kurobans had to dodge p3s

unloading Luxite coworkers via the street-side delivery port before squeezing past the lofty parking structure to the only ground-level door in the back. Between the dumpsters there was a heavily-dented door with a fried security panel that used to keep the door locked. False security was enough of a deterrent in Lux.

We walked up the service steps to get to the eduGames office on the second level. Once inside the cramped janitorial closet, we could finally breathe easy for the time being. I couldn't wait for the cleaning supplies, towels, brooms, and mops that shared space with the four of us. Self-restored computers on a couple random pieces of furniture were the best we could do without any help from our employer. We hauled it all from the wasteband; nothing was provided except for the cleaning supplies. Even the slight lemony-bleach scent of our room was better than the cold, sterile, debasement-laden Luxite air.

We were spotted at the top of the service stairs. Between us and the door to our room, the space opened up into the main office area where our Luxite "co-workers" refueled. In the distance, a couple of those co-workers were filling mugs with some steaming liquid that looked to be kale-heavy. A teetering tray of Danish delights and still-simmering strips of meat sat on a tray in front of where the shifty Luxites mingled. They were oblivious, chatting and chewing with each other in between sips without a care in the world. As they chowed down, they created a major mess. Crumbs and residue sprayed out over a multi-meter radius.

This triggered a horde of tiny carpet cleaning bots, each the size of a standard mug, to slowly roll in from different directions. These diminutive dust busters sucked up the morsels seasoning the fluffy carpet. The bots attempted to climb up the leg of the table to clean the mess left above, but didn't have the necessary hardware or software to achieve such a feat yet. After bumping into the legs a couple times, the bots relented and returned to their charging docks. As we watched the bots return, we caught the eyes of the Luxites, leftovers smeared across their pallid faces.

I froze. Their sharp light blue collared shirts, crisp khakis, girthy ties, and gleaming monk straps far outshined our threadbare rags. Even still, I felt an intense scan of my unconventional outerwear. It was a judgmental look that truly rattled my bones.

Bodi and I didn't move a muscle as they stared daggers through us. We stared right back, like deer transfixed by headlights. The Luxites said nothing but their scrutiny tore through me, made me unwelcome, undeserving, and less than. It was a pugnacious gawk with a furrowed brow that looked down from on high, striking directly at my soul. The violent, yet invisible, payload stripped away my will to live. With no sewer covers nearby, my eyes walked straight into unapproved eye contact, treading out deep in their eerie blue eyes. A slight spark in my gut started sizzling and my chest filled with rage.

My brow crumpled downward and my gut spark shot up through my mouth, urging me to say something, to speak up, to scream. I opened my mouth wide to roar out all of my frustrations onto these chauvinistic cronies.

Bodi murmured something under his breath. It snapped me back to reality. In my moment of hesitation, he grabbed my head and bent it downward in unison with his. I followed his lead and kept bowing my head as we walked backward toward the door to our room. Our butts hit before our hands scrambled to find the knob without looking. We panicked for what felt like an hour. We tried with all our might to grab the knob while still bowing over and over. We stumbled and scratched and scraped to escape while our hands twisted into each other. Our frustration further flummoxed our frenzied behavior.

We both gave up and turned toward the door. We gave up our backs, multiplying the damage, and the door easily swung wide open. We scampered inside like two knock-kneed giraffe calves evading a swarm of lions. Inside the narrow room, we bumped into each other and knocked into an officemate's monitor.

One of our two other Kuroban co-workers sat peacefully in their lawn chair next to Bodi's telephone pole-sized leg. The lawnchair-Kuroban yapped at us as we bumbled into our cramped room. "Watch out, late birds, we're in here trying to actually get work done."

Bodi squeezed through to his seat. It was a teetering three-legged kitchen chair with one broken leg. "It's not my fault. *This* one made me late and froze up in front of the Luxites."

I gasped at the singular heaping of blame and stood up for myself. I climbed over — and on — my Kuroban coworkers to get to my worn-out gaming chair in the back of the room. Crowded beside me was the fourth and final Kuroban working on assignment at eduGames. They took up the most space with their ragged recliner. "There were *many* factors that made us late, it wasn't just me. But I didn't like how those assholes were looking at us. I was gonna –"

"— *not* do a Quawd damn thing," the recliner-Kuroban said. "You need this job more than us. You have to make your decision by midnight tomorrow too. You ain't got the juice to question anyone here, especially Luxites."

The lawnchair-Kuroban cackled. "They were probably insulted by your tacky sweater or those grimy sneakers. Because I am."

I kissed my teeth. "*Pfffft* – Good luck today without my help." Without paying any mind to their idle shit-talking, I finally sat down at my wobbly desk and threw my precious coat over the back of my seat.

The recliner-Kuroban replied with a healthy heap of sarcasm, "Nooo, what are we gonna do without your *help*?" But I knew that was a serious inquiry even though they wanted to front like they were capable of going it alone.

The QA-robans Have Joined Your Party

I let their bullheadedness go and straightened up my crowded workspace while everyone else sorted out the mess I made forcing my way through. A small LCD screen with a black and rainbow dead spot in the corner stared back at me. On my desk was a keyboard with missing keys and others so worn the writing was missing. Beside the dingy keyboard was an ancient mouse with sticky buttons that made every button press both a right and left click. Everything was connected by half-stripped cords to a naked, reborn desktop underneath my feet.

My three Kuroban co-workers — the QA-robans as I called them — were the only Kurobans in this entire large multinational education technology conglomerate. Our devices were tethered to a limited internet connection I secretly spliced us into. I hacked a way for us to access an emulated version of our company-provided task list so we could load up the screens we were supposed to test on an actual device. All thanks to the dump and my rebellious ingenuity. I don't know how they did any work at all before I came.

Hanging above each of our desks were said task lists. Each a translucent digital clipboard that wirelessly received assigned tasks from our corporate keepers. I looked up to review mine before I booted up my scrappy computer.

Our duties were added by big boss Robert and his team and marked off when our superiors accepted our work, typically at the end of the next day. Typically, by Thursday like today, my list was empty. Only surprise tasks or non-standard duties vaguely baked into our official job description kept me busy this late in the week. But wasn't I lucky today —my list was full. Big boss sent me a huge list of last-minute screens and features for testing alongside a number of unpleasant cleaning chores. Just because we worked in the janitorial closet didn't make us janitors.

I put my demeaning list of duties out of my mind and poured through the extensive software testing scenarios in front of me. It was littered with ambiguous explanations, blended with personal vernacular and incomplete connections. The untrained would've struggled to ascertain what Robert and his product management underbosses were asking them to do, but not me. I had this work so down pat that I'd be done in an hour, tops. I could read between the lines and translate Luxite incompetence into intelligent requests. Completing the actual tests was even easier for me. It was almost automatic at this point.

~ New Side Quest: Enjoy
Pre-Birthday Game Guide ~

I gave the QA-robans their space. I contemplated my conscripted career decision tomorrow. My dream of making video games for liberation was still so far from my grasp. I closed my eyes to remember the levity from my dream this morning. The QA-robans were still grinding away, grasping for basic comprehension with their eyes glued on their flickering screens. They clicked their mouses and clacked their keyboards. But my frustration with having to decide the rest of my life tomorrow pried my mouth open. "Y'all seen old Robbie today?"

The recliner QA-roban slapped down a crinkled plastic water bottle filled with some yellowish water and responded with their natural snark. "Why do you ask questions you know the answer to?"

"Hey, I thought today might be an exception. He might want to spend time in the office today. To be closer to us." I tried to match their playful banter to slowly release my frustration upon the room.

"Not at all. You know he's probably out at some 'business breakfast' or whatever. Schmoozing. While his proxies are out here monitoring our comings and goings and overall productivity. I'm guessing one of them sent us this mountain of tasks. And I still have my weekly psychiatry appointment this afternoon. It looks like it's gonna be a late night again," the lawnchair QA-roban said.

"Actually, I'm done if anybody needs me to help," I spouted, eager to procrastinate and be helpful, cheesing while my comrades' jaws dropped.

Bodi shrieked and almost toppled forward out of his chair. "Already! Wow. Why are you even here? To bother us?" It sounded like a joke, but I could hear authentic frustration dripping from his voice.

"You know they won't let me leave y'all in this cramped hole by yourselves. Even *if* I'm done. What would they do with the big rent they pay for this office space? Butts in seats, remember?"

Recliner QA-roban took a drink of their grody yellow liquid. "You right."

"Plus," I said, "I still have to clean the kitchen and bathroom by the end of the day. And I want to be available to help, if y'all let me."

Bodi lifted himself up and tried to make a tight turn in his hobbled wooden kitchen chair. He crashed into the recliner QA-roban five degrees into his rotation and stopped abruptly. "You know this is probably the most mentally demanding form of employment for a Kuroban? Software testing is right under Opp-erator work if you're talking about prestige."

I huffed. "Prestige? Really? I'd never be caught dead as a high paid slave. Cleaning, cooking, and culling Kurobans for a little check. Being a personal operative for the Luxite elite isn't something *I* could ever be proud of. Now this work, this quality assurance, is easy for me and only *slightly* compromising my values. It's just point, click, follow the script, and record the results. The harm is far downstream. And if you add in some design recommendations, you're golden. And you might even be able to slip in a couple emancipatory easter eggs along the way. But I'm not doing extra work for this paltry pay. This is purely a means to my own revolutionary game development studio."

Recliner QA-roban laughed. "Hahaha! A game development studio, really? Have you even *played* a video game?"

I groaned. They had a point, but still. "No, b-but the game guides and technology research are all I need. Do you know what it takes to restore one of these desktops like I did for you?"

"No, but if you're that damn slick you might have to press Robert for an actual office space for us. We've been asking for months through official channels, but it's probably nothing for someone as incandescent as you."

"Maybe I will." Everyone laughed as I tried to process how I might make that request a reality. Our boss was always absent and communicated only through his subordinates. I had my own demands for Robert anyway.

Lawnchair QA-roban was the first one to break through the laughter. "Yeah, you make testing sound so simple, but it's not like that for the rest of us. How did you get so good at this stuff, really? We went to the same school and *you* didn't even finish."

I chuckled. The positivity of that backhanded compliment surged through me. "Oh dear, that's so cute that you actually thought education in Kuroba, provided by this very *profit-driven* Luxite company, would give you the tools to succeed on *your* terms. To be real, I learned all my computer skills because of Bodi."

Both the recliner and lawnchair QA-roban twisted their necks in our tiny space toward Bodi and gave a simultaneous "Huh?"

A bewildered Bodi shifted his head from side to side, searching for an answer while he yawned. "M *–mmmrrray–* maybe."

I brought my legs up from the ground and squatted in my rickety gaming chair. Carefully, I twisted myself so my monitor wasn't blocking my face as I addressed my coworkers from the back corner of our congested closet. "Yeah, Bodi used to give me reading materials when I was growing up and dealing with my mom's – uh – *situation*. I started out only reading about games, but I'd quickly devour everything Bodi could find. My fascination was insatiable. I was stuck inside taking care of home, Mom, and myself. Those game guides were my only solace.

"When Bodi told me he couldn't find any more game guides I thought of the next best thing. I went under the hood and deep into the world I fell in love with. From software development and cybersecurity to economics and sociology. I was trying to discover what made these games tick, why they functioned the way they did, and what that meant for the world we lived in. I was especially interested in discovering how the protagonists triumphed in the face of insurmountable odds – for obvious reasons. Bodi and I kept our arrangement until I finished high school. I didn't have much reason *not* to get my own learning materials then, with my mom recovered and the head Elder at that point. Right Bodi?"

"Y-yes, I guess I did help you become the genius you are today," Bodi said with confused confidence.

"I even found a fresh game guide this morning that I was going to dive into now if y'all are interested."

"We're supposed to be working," the lawnchair QA-roban snapped back. "That's work time theft and it's surely one of the sub-points of the Seed Armistice. The Blaus could be called for such an offense. And you know what that means . . . I might be obligated to report you myself."

"You're sounding pretty Oppy. Who says I didn't get this game guide from *you*? We would *all* be collateral damage if the Blaus get a whiff of any Kuroban impropriety. Bodi, get your friend!"

Bodi grabbed an unopened urinal cake from the shelf right above his head and tossed it near the Lawnchair. It hit the door to our closet and fell in the Lawnchair's lap. "Stop it! Both of you."

I stood down. "You mind your business and I'll read my game guide. I am still here to help if y'all are tired of struggling under an *interpretation* of arbitrary rules."

As soon as I opened my game guide, the office intercom scratched on. A loud voice hollered, "We've heard that we need to increase team cohesion, so Robert, our excellent VP of Product Development, is hosting an inclusive team lunch in ten minutes. Everyone is invited. It doesn't matter if you work in the cubicles, the offices, or even the cleaning closet. Meet in the office kitchen ASAP. We'll be going to a gourmet restaurant in Midtown. Bring your wallets and a good attitude. It's going to be a great time."

Bodi jumped up. "Welp, look at that. We're being included for once. Y'all ready?"

"I'm not going," I mumbled under my breath.

"What!? You have to. You know it's not optional," the lawnchair QA-roban exclaimed.

"Too good for it, right?" the recliner QA-roban quipped.

Trying to hide my laughter, I said, "No, I'm going to do a little reading. I don't have money like that. They didn't say it was complimentary and didn't y'all bring lunch?"

Bodi huffed. "Yes, and I'm bringing my spoiled turkey and moldy cheese on stale bread with the spiced dirt cookies too." He showed his busted lunchpail dangling in his grasp. "This is a once in a lifetime opportunity to rub elbows with Luxites and even some management. I'll eat my lunch right in front of them so I won't have to spend any money."

"Sure, if you like that sort of lunchtime office theater. It's all just a covert compliance training event. I'll stick out like a decaying thumb when I don't laugh, smile, respond, order, or sit the way they expect us to. Just tell them I'm going to get started on my cleaning tasks early. That should appease them."

"I'm not going to argue with you. It's your funeral," Bodi answered as the lawnchair and recliner QA-robans squirmed toward the exit.

I breathed a sigh of relief when they walked out the door, each with their disgusting lunches in hand. Underneath my desk I hid a beat up power cord just for these moments. I opened up my game guide and pulled out my therapy journal. My mind was already revving up. I had some work to do while they were away performing.

The QA-robans always teased me for going against the

grain and doing my own thing. Well, I guess *every* Kuroban kinda gave me shit about my solitary deviations against the commanding current of society. Growing up I didn't understand the need to follow what others did. I found joy in moments of peace, especially in the company of me, myself, and I. Most others needed to fill up the silence and solitude. Not me. I took advantage of the empty office and set up shop in the main kitchen area.

The island in the office kitchen was my court. I was assigned to clean it today, but I had all afternoon before my task was due. It would probably get messier throughout the day anyways. The island was already littered with half-filled mugs, poppy seeds, little lumps of lox, and a variety of crumbs. Random green residue and sometimes complete rings of the luminous Luxite drink stained the granite kitchen surfaces. I moved what I could to the side and laid down some pillowy paper towels. Paper towels seemed like a suitable barrier between the solidifying breakfast remains and my temporary workspace.

I meticulously placed my recently-recovered game guide and my therapy journal down in front of me. My excitement rose. Opening my therapy journal to reveal my prized possession had me giddy. The scratched, partially-cracked screen of the tablet with the color receding from the edges housed pure gold within. "My Libook," I whispered to myself.

Reading, reflecting, and recording a suitable speech for Robert in my Libook absorbed me. I would convince him the QA-robans needed a better office and *I* deserved a game dev studio. I forgot where I was after I plugged in my dead Libook. I was engrossed in decoding the game guide's contents and translating my latest learnings into my final pitch to the Robster. Harnessing Baldie's revolutionary energy, I reconfigured the game strategy into something that I could use to shift my current work assignment into my dream career. With my decision looming, I needed all the help I could get or I'd end up laboring in the gutters with the rest of the failed freedom fighters, disappointing them and myself.

I was ready. This was the first step toward my liberation plan. I'd learned as much as I could about video games, gotten a job in Lux, proving my worth during my time here, and now with this speech would convince my boss, the Luxite who signed off on my career assignment, to invest in my dreams. I'd never met dear old Robbie in person over these seventeen weeks – I'd only felt his iron grasp – but maybe I could at least leverage my work efficiency and effectiveness for a career path toward my dreams instead of continuing to traverse the unpaved Kuroban side streets.

I was diligently strategizing until my stomach shrieked. A ravenous eruption of debilitating hunger tore through me. My mental faculties rapidly redirected from work strategy to food strategy. I needed to find some grub to satiate my hunger. My mind raced, picking up and putting down never-ending plans to solve my acute hunger crisis. I didn't bring any lackluster lunch like Bodi and the others. I'd planned to bum some food off the QA-robans to pull together a meal. With them gone I frantically scanned the kitchen area with my eyes and nostrils, searching for any morsel to eat.

I caught the scent of the coffee and cream cheese crusted onto the kitchen surfaces. My hands whirred as I rapidly slotted my game guide into my waistband. In my shaky rush I moved my Libook off to the side to continue charging. Once clear, I stripped up the paper towels as fast as possible to lick up whatever luxurious blended residue remained in the kitchen. The spill and scrap amuse-bouche only made me hungrier and more jittery.

My nose flared as it searched for more. I stopped and stared at the ample refrigerator. Glistening in the LED light, it made my mouth water. The bounty was right in front of me. My nerves fought against my escalating drive to open the fridge. My hands were tethered tightly to my sides. Nothing inside was mine and taking anything would only cause trouble I couldn't easily cover up. It was obvious stealing. Even if they had an abundance, Luxites didn't play around with *their stuff.*

In Kuroba, our feebly-fueled fridges were empty, non-functional, storage sheds or just holes in the ground filled with carefully-cured carcasses. We were stuck using ancient food storage solutions until we upgraded our local energy systems. Shit, us working Kurobans had to fork heavy tithes right back to Lux in order to maintain caloric intake in Kuroba each payday. Those little family style bites we enjoyed at Earth Goings were some of the most glorious I'd ever gobbled. With that as my only reference, I could only imagine what edible riches were inside this chilly treasure chest. Perhaps there was enough excess that they wouldn't notice. My voracious curiosity got the better of me and I cracked open the fridge.

Cool air washed over my famished face and dried out my eager eyes. It was chocked full of fabulous food. Just sitting there untouched. Fresh green salad slathered in dressings and topped with an array of accouterments. Juicy-looking sandwiches stuffed with moist meats that smelled of smoke, salt, and a bit of sweetness. Sodas, snacks, and sauces spilled out of the door and every nook and cranny. While we starved, tons of food just sat slowly aging in this fridge.

There had to be folks with multiple fridges like this. Out of all the food these folks had here, they wouldn't miss the little bit I needed to tame my tummy. I grabbed anything and everything from the assortment of dishes assembled in the chilly cornucopia. I feasted with the door wide open. I seasoned and sauced my next morsel while my cheeks were chewing the previous one.

In the middle of chowing down on my fourth or fifth mouthful of a particularly splendid sandwich my mind returned.

The pressure in the air suddenly increased and I struggled to move. How could I undo my mistake? I was shaking, sweat beaded on my forehead and pooled in my pits. Cleaning! That was it. Cleaning was my assignment, of course. This would be my back-to-back attack. First, I was done with my QA work and now I'd be done with my janitorial tasks early. Hopefully I'd land a critical hit.

~ New Side Quest: Hide What I Ate From the Fridge ~

I cleaned the kitchen area at a hurried pace. Scrubbing all of the counters, sweeping the floor, washing the dishes, and even reorganizing the contents in the fridge so it appeared undisturbed. I admired my work. It *appeared* the same volume as when I first opened the fridge – at first glance.

That's when two Luxites entered the office holding goblets that gleamed the color of fresh mint.

I scrambled to start washing the dishes in the sink and didn't look back. My head stayed stuck on the sink as I heard them approach. After my perilous standoff that morning, bolstered by a hefty helping of residual guilt, I was able to fight my nosey urge to look in their direction. I focused on my task. As stools scraped against the ground on the opposite side of the island, I felt the tremors of the concrete floors under my sensitive feet. The two Luxites sat down and began belting in booming voices. As much as I tried not to, I heard bits over the rushing faucet.

"Good day Robert . . . party tonight . . . mansion next door?"

The person who I assumed to be Robert answered, "5pm start, right? . . . networking before . . . my promotion to executive." They must not have noticed me when they came in or as I repeatedly dunked the same dishes in soapy water.

". . . company shirt . . . entry ticket. Quality assurance is essential . . . this major release?"

I wondered who was speaking to Robert. But I ignored that inquiry, trying to mind my business and finish scrubbing mugs mired in green stains.

"No problem . . . garbage glow worms will work late . . . free food and unlimited emerald elixir, right?"

The derogatory moniker for my people piqued my impedance. I left the faucet running and snuck a bit closer to hear better without raising suspicions.

"Of course, Robert, it's a celebration of *your* achievements. I'm happy you whipped them glowers into shape while remaining uninfluenced by their unrefined ways and disconcerting presence. Those meds are brilliant! I know how difficult they are to tame, but we need more like the last one you brought in – albeit with less rambunctiousness. It's so productive. I'd invest in technology that performs like that one with the obedience of the others. I see big things for you. You'll have your own Opp-erator team soon enough if you deliver an autonomous acculturation advancement algorithm that performs like that."

I circled the same dry bowl with a rag, acting like I was still drying it, while ear hustling across the island.

"Most definitely, I appreciate the opportunity. The data gathering system is still learning from them. While tonight's party cracks on, I'll have them put together a roadmap for how we can scale." I bent myself over the island. I didn't want to miss any part of the juicy tea. I contorted myself deeper into their business and they continued to speak as if I wasn't there. As I leaned closer, the saucer I was rubbing obsessively almost slipped out of my hand.

My body shook in fear and I blurted out, "Oh sh–"

They stopped talking. I watched as they sipped their celery-colored drinks and looked through me. I stood a few feet in front of them, too scared to duck behind the island, but was as imperceptible from an inanimate object in the background as a painting on the wall. In my mind I silently begged to not get caught. They blinked . . . and I blinked. We stared at each other in silence for some long seconds. I held my breath the entire time. The only sound was the steady stream from the faucet. That and my heart beating out of my chest. Then they turned back towards each other and started sipping again. They couldn't notice a Kuroban cleaning right beside them, their pretentious peepers couldn't even process me.

[Cloak of Invisibility Activated]

Finally they started talking again. "Yup, I gotta head out to update our Board on the summit resettlement initiative. They'll be expecting a plan as well as a report on the GELD mole very soon, Robert."

I waved my hands and jumped up and down. They didn't notice or at least didn't let me know they noticed me. The paranoid thought that they might be faking made me duck under the island and roll into a ball to protect myself.

"Yes ma'am!" The stools screeched in pain as they were dragged across the polished concrete floor.

Panic coursed through my veins. After a few minutes I realized I was safe, for now. I still couldn't believe they hadn't seen me the entire time. Not when they walked in or through the corners of their eyes as they spoke. My Libook sat plugged in at the edge of the island and they hadn't noticed my reincarnated device. Clear Kuroban contraband. They hadn't questioned the faucet or even my exclamation.

I didn't want to celebrate because I wasn't certain I was in the clear yet. And the troubling news I overheard had me concerned. It sounded like bossman Robsie was recording our testing data to train an AI model to do our jobs. Would we all be fired? I needed to tell someone. The QA-robans were below subpar at their jobs, but they didn't deserve to be eliminated like that. They at least deserved the opportunity to grow and learn just like anyone else.

I waited for a minute or two to make sure the area was clear of Luxites. I struggled a bit to stand up, slipping while trying to grip on the island with sweaty, soapy hands. As soon as I confirmed the coast was clear, I cleaned at light speed to finish my tasks. Then I gathered my strategic study supplies and retreated back to our cramped closet, hankering to share my illicit news with the other QA-robans once they returned. How could we prove our worth, keep our jobs, and maintain this career as an option for us post-30? I especially needed this job; my options were limited without my master's. If I could convince Robert, it would be my only chance to make my game dev dreams come true. Become a game developer, develop the games of the revolution, and save Kurobans.

STAGE COMPLETE

The QA-robans Have Left Your Party!

Health Points 50%
Magic Power 5%

Mission #1: Get Work Done for the Day [Week] . . . . FOR THE MOST PART
Mission #2: Make It Through the Rest of the Day
               Without any Mishaps . . . . JUST BARELY
Side Quest #1: Enjoy Pre-Birthday Game Guide . . . . A LITTLE BIT
Side Quest #2: Hide What I Ate From the Fridge . . . . BEST I COULD

Experience Points Gained [357]
Coins [-20] . . . Payday Soon Come
Items Received [eduGames Tea about QA-robans]
Status Effect [CLOAK OF INVISIBILITY]

Chapter 4: Error Code x000017

Mission #1: Tell the QA-robans What I Heard
Mission #2: Convince QA-robans to Crash the Party to Save our Jobs

The QA-robans rushed back into our little room where I eagerly waited for their arrival. They rumbled in, bumping against each other and even squishing me against the back wall. When they finally settled down, the QA-robans let out a collective sigh.

Bodi slumped into his shaky seat. "That was rough!"

"My bank account got the brunt of the abuse. I wiped out my entire savings," the recliner QA-roban whined while avoiding an exposed spring in their recliner.

"Not only that, we only got a speck of food for all that we paid, sat far away from everyone, and they made us walk on our own as they zoomed by in p3s. Both ways!" Bodi's arms flailed in every direction as he spoke. He almost smacked me a couple times with his veiny, plate-sized hands. I heard bass in his voice that I never got from him other than toward his sister.

The lawnchair QA-roban whispered, "I mean, Mr. Rob wasn't there, but at least we were invited, right?"

I tried to hold my tongue. I saw how defeated they looked so I bottled up my words, but the tea was burning my tongue. "At least, my ass! They don't care about any of us. It was a bait and switch just like this job."

Bodi twisted around in his seat and sharpened his eyes. "What you talkin' bout? You weren't there."

I closed my fists and puffed out a little sigh so no one could see, trying to maintain my composure. "This is bigger than some little lunch. Or any other singular event. I bet y'all don't know they're having some big company event tonight that *doesn't* include us."

"I love a good party." The recliner QA-roban looked up at the ceiling licking their lips, "I bet a Luxite party is *too* lit. Way more luxurious than anything at home." The recliner QA-roban gulped down the last bits of the yellow liquid from their mangled bottle.

"It'll be flowing with *free* food."

The recliner QA-roban almost spit their liquid all over our tiny room.

The lawnchair QA-roban and Bodi both gasped, darted, and massaged at their neckline delicately.

When the QA-robans finally collected themselves, they mumbled amongst one another. They tried to reconcile the money they just wasted at lunch when their company was giving away free food tonight without them. They were falling into the wrong trap: blaming themselves, taking their frustration out on me rather than directing it at our true adversary. I added more evidence to set the foundation for what we were facing. "Even worse, they're celebrating Rob for some Quawd-forsaken reason."

"Mr. Robert?" Bodi said. "Our *never*-present boss?"

"The one and only," I piped in.

"Nah, can't be. F-for what? He's never here! Even for his

Luxite subordinates. And we do all the work to drive how eduGames products look, feel, and educate." Bodi was huffing and puffing at that point.

"Don't y'all go denigrating bossman now. That's not how we speak of someone who has given us this amazing opportunity." Lawnchair launched a dried-out pen at Bodi, which missed and bounced off the wall, almost hitting me.

The recliner QA-roban sassed, "Right, he's doing work *way* above our mental tax bracket."

"Exactly, and we're the *first* Kurobans to break this knowledge-worker barrier in tech. We are making Kuroban history here," the lawnchair QA-roban added, seeming to take the sarcasm as truth.

I debated how much to tell them. What would Baldie do to rally reluctant Kurobans toward *active* resistance? I could only imagine the groundwork the GELD laid before it was twisted by Luxite saboteurs. The revolutionary spark has since been snuffed out of almost every Kuroban soul. The QA-robans needed to know the stakes.

"Do you think they're planning to employ us in perpetuity?" I asked.

Bodi almost fell forward out of his chair again as he stuttered and coughed out a defiant response. "Y-yeah, at some point waaay down the line, maybe not, but at this point they *ne-need* us, right? We're essential to providing quality, *authentic* education to Kuroba. Without the remote educator software we test, Lux would not fulfill section 3b of the Seed Armistice. A-and Kurobans wouldn't have any pathway to lucrative Luxite employment. They could never create anything culturally relevant without *us*."

"But do they really *use* anything we do?" The recliner QA-roban said.

"Good question, *do they*? The same way they ignored our

needs in the Seed Armistice? They created a complex arrangement that benefitted Lux, deprived Kuroba of resources, and kept control to judge nuances on either end. They had the power to make Kuroba even more dependent while also becoming more detached. You think they're looking out for us? Don't make me pity you." I tried to temper my frustration by pressing my hands down on my rickety desk and taking a breath.. "I-I'm not tryin' to debate this. I'm going to the party tonight to confront Robert. We deserve respect. Starting with upgrading this shithole space they hide us in. Y'all were right, it's the least I can do to scrape back a morsel of reciprocity from him and eduGames. Someone has to say something. Y'all don't have to, but won't you at least back me up?"

They all started mumbling and groaning, making a show of ducking every which way to avoid my question.

"They're going to make us work late while they all go to the party. I swear. I heard it!"

Bodi pulled his head down into his lap with one hand and gestured vociferously with the other as if he was using a hand puppet to speak for him. "That may be true. It truly might be a possibility. I believe you, but what can we do about it? HR won't do anything; their role is to protect the company. And like you threatened before, this won't just blow back on one of us, it could impact us all . . . Or they may choose to punish Kuroba as a whole in unimaginable ways."

The recliner QA-roban muttered softly without looking up at any of us, "I'm willing to miss this party and stay cramped in here with y'all if I get to keep this job, because you know I gotta eat. I just want to make it to my 30th and get moms off my back."

The lawnchair QA-roban added while shaking his head violently, "Don't do this! This will be seen as an act of aggression. An open affront to the Armistice. I know you know they're watching us as we move about Lux. Hell, we're not even allowed to enter any Luxite property without an escort or a properly credentialed work assignment. Do you want to cause another massacre!? Because that's surely bound to happen if us four glowing soil-skinned Kurobans step foot into that party."

Bodi spoke with a tremble in his voice this time, "It's *my* name on the line if you do anything. We'll get them next time. The Elders will work on it. For Quawd's sake, please don't risk *my* job too."

I turned back around and slid down into my seat, landing in a deep slouch. "Ok, ok, I won't. Geez! But when is next time? We both know the Elders haven't been able to get shit done! They're out there sacrificing our future for their current comfort."

DING! We all received a blaring notification as a tsunami of tasks flooded our digital task lists. Each of our translucent clipboards instantly stretched into the floor.

"This is exactly what I said would happen! Luckily, I have a plan. I do your tests and in exchange y'all come crash the party that should be celebrating *us*. Deal?"

The QA-robans squirmed into every empty inch of our narrow space to evade me once again. I shut my mouth and waited for them to respond. I let the mounting work in front of them induce their decision as notifications continued to go off and tasks piled up even further.

The recliner QA-roban was the first to make a peep. "I'm fine with spending the night here in order to get this done." I didn't expect that kind of commitment to an evaporating employment environment. They'd rather guarantee failure at a career that was soon to be canceled instead of demanding a bit of humanity. After what I heard, going to that party was a no-brainer for me.

Bodi started poking holes in my plan. I felt the smirk in his voice as I sulked in the corner. "You really expect them to let *us* in. Just walk into *their* party? You might not be a genius after all."

"Yeah, we just need company T-shirts." It was simple to me. I trusted in our ability to figure it out, like our people had figured out how to survive for generations.

"We don't even have that. I don't think they'll let us in even *if* we had company T-shirts. You're tripping," the lawnchair QA-roban said.

I stood up and slammed my hands onto my feeble desk. My rapid rise pushed my chair back and it bounced off the wall, almost knocking me back onto my butt. I stumbled onto my desk causing my monitor to slide off its already tilted surface. Luckily I caught everything, saving my monitor and input devices from falling onto the Bodi's lap beside me. I shuffled around to face all the QA-robans in what little space I could muster to assuage their unnecessary worries. "I'll figure out how we get the company T-shirts and everything we need to get in. Trust me. Please!"

The lawnchair QA-roban flatly responded, "I will clearly have to decline your request. You can ruin *your* future if you want."

The recliner QA-roban pulled out another misshapen water bottle full of deeper yellow liquid and turned their head towards their monitor without saying anything. They didn't have to tell me, I knew their response.

Bodi remained silent, awkward, and still. He attempted to start working without saying anything, then put his hands back down in his lap and stared forward. The weight of his silence made the entire little room a thousand times more tense. I dared not say anything because I could taste the viscous QA-roban disdain wafting in the air and drying out on my tongue.

I sat down and shifted my equipment back into position. On my desk was a small note in Bodi's handwriting.

I'm not in support of this and neither is Quawd. I will pray that he does not punish you for your disobedience. But if you're going to do this, please be safe. And make sure everyone knows this is solely your mission of insubordination.

I flipped the paper over and picked up the dead pen the lawnchair QA-roban threw at Bodi. After a quick lick on the tip I was able to scribble out a response that was barely visible and mostly etched into the paper itself.

Don't you want better, or more in life? To thrive and get out of this quicksand we Kurobans are drowning in? This personal risk is the beg–

I didn't see Bodi watching until he grabbed my head to whisper in my ear. "No. I want to survive. That's it!"

I left it there, feeling defeated after being dismissed by each and every QA-roban. Was it me they denied or was this a larger mechanic of the tragic game we lived pulling them closer? Both prospects fueled my frustration. What denied them even I-need-the-tools-to-toil hope?

I went on with my work day, completing my new mountain of testing responsibilities with electronic efficiency, as if I was the impending program replacing us. I was done quickly, within the hour once again. Most of the work was retesting functionality the other QA-robans had done inaccurately and incompletely. It looked like more than it really was.

As much as I didn't want to, I took to heart what the QA-robans said. They were right, it was a major risk. A risk not just for me, but for all of Kuroba. Maybe the QA-robans didn't trust me or themselves. I imagined it might be uncomfortable for an anomalous antagonizer like me to stumble into success while they followed the rules expecting to be reciprocally rewarded. At the same time, I heard what Robert and his buddy had said. How they talked about us, like we're disposable. We're screwed either way.

I thought more about my dilemma as I finished reading my game guide. If we didn't have this work assignment in our pocket, I *really* needed to hurry and figure out my next career move. Regardless of whether we forgoed an alternative or continued with a career that was automated away then we were at risk of being Seed Armistice violators just the same. Lux had all the reasoning they needed to remand a violating Kuroban into their sub-city sweatshops where the Blaus would simply harvest us for everything we had. That was it. Nothing was going to change unless we did something about it. Stand up for this one or find a new work assignment, but my time and career clout was too short to find anything new. Our situation would continue to degrade unless I changed the course of its deterioration. That's what Baldie would do, I'm sure of it.

The more I ran away from the idea of crashing the celebration, the more it came back stronger over the afternoon. I couldn't hide it or confine it in some forgotten compartment of my mind. Every time I wiped it away, it coalesced in my gut and fueled the spark stirring in my stomach. Especially after completing my task list and reading my new game guide, my mind was unsettled. The final straw was when I heard our rowdy Luxite coworkers yipping and yelling as they exited for the party. It was like a rush of rabid water buffalo stampeding. They were all mobbing into a short p3 ride next door. The QA-robans sat locked onto their screens, absorbed in their work.

I stared at the recliner QA-roban's deformed water bottle that was half drunk now. That bottle had been used once, thrown away, resuscitated with great effort and lackluster cleaning, then used thousands more times, possibly handed down over generations. With no label it was hard to tell how old it was or if the yellow tint was actually the liquid inside or the plastic itself. I kept staring at that water bottle and gritting my teeth.

Then it hit me. I didn't have any work to do. I mean, my QA-robans were still busy and would be for a while. If they didn't want to buck the master's rules or to have me do their work for them, there wasn't any reason I couldn't pop by the party myself. I'd have a nice little conversation with Rob-man and return before they were even done.

~New Side Quest: Infiltrate eduGames Party ~

First, I had to exit our cramped room without pissing off the QA-robans anymore. They'd know exactly what I was up to and might try to stop me. For me to leave, they all needed to leave first since I was the room caboose. I barked out, "Anybody need any help on their tests. I'm willing and available. Final offer!"

Nothing. Not one of them responded.

As expected.

The recliner QA-roban squirmed in their seat, shifting their weight onto the opposite butt cheek. Bodi tried to hold his head still and keep testing while he let out a jaw-stretching yawn. And the lawnchair QA-roban looked unfazed. A few seconds later the lawnchair QA-roban moved their head closer to read something in the bottom corner of their computer screen. "Shit! I'm late. My weekly Psychiatry appointment starts in ten." The lawnchair QA-roban rushed to collect their badly-beaten therapy journal amongst a mess of scrap papers under their desk.

Bodi responded back in a deadened tone as he fought back another yawn, "Good luck. It'll be quick. You'll be back to work soon."

"Most definitely, just looking for a reup," the lawnchair QA-roban responded while slithering out with an empty pill bottle between their fingers.

The recliner QA-roban jumped up suddenly with their legs smashed together up to the knees. "Thank Quawd, I have to go so bad." And just like that two out of three were out the door too.

I looked at Bodi and he looked at me with a furrowed brow and a gaping yawn. He turned back towards his computer and I started to fake like I was working too. He didn't budge.

I tapped an old pen on my desk for a few seconds. He got up quickly and dribbled out a massive sigh. Bodi pouted while giving me his little puppet sign. "I get it, I get it. I'll go. I need coffee anyways. Just remember what I said."

Then, he was gone too. *Look at Quawd!*

Before they had a chance to return or Bodi rethought his decision, I slipped my therapy journal into my back pocket, hidden treasure and all. I swiped my coat from my seat and jetted out of the room.

I sprinted toward the front door, ruminating on what a company shirt looked like. Bodi was slowly stirring a tiny mug at the coffee cart where the Luxites were when we had our suppressive standoff earlier. His back was turned to me, but I knew he saw me. My mission was already in motion. Luck materialized as a special item box beaming on the pristine office kitchen island. There was no way anyone could stop me now, especially with the large soil-colored containers that hadn't been there before calling to me. T-shirts were scattered around the boxes. Jackpot! These must be the company shirts I needed. I swiped one and pulled it over my sweater. I reset my hair and clutched my coat in my hand. I walked towards the door before realizing I couldn't leave out the front like the Luxites without a p3. I doubled back and went out the back door. Bodi was gone by now. While walking out, I attempted to send Bodi a telepathic token of thanks in case he had his antennae turned on.

~New Side Quest: Confront Robert about QA-roban Office Space ~

It was dusk when I stepped outside. The cold attacked me, but I tensed my body knowing it would only be a short walk to my destination. The eduGames office was on the corner and every time we came into work we walked past the mansion next door. It was one of my most vivid visuals of Lux's ludicrous lavishness, so I knew exactly where to go.

I decided to keep my coat in my hand rather than put it on because I wanted to make *sure* whoever was at the door could see I was an eduGames employee. There should be no doubt that I was supposed to be at the *employee* party. Aside from my overall build, complexion, height, outfit, accent, gait, history, upbringing, resources, and especially my natural Kuroban glow, I was no different than the rest of them. An obnoxious, yet simple white T-shirt made from a thin material that seemed like it might disintegrate or miniaturize upon its first wash was my ticket in. The enlarged company logo and tacitly coded tagline adorned boldly on front of the tee, "eduGames: Games that Germinate the Greatest Graduates" was undeniable.

A low mechanical buzz had filled my ears as soon as I exited. The Eyes of Lux were tracking my every movement. Out too long post-30th without a career, on an unproductive trip like this, and the Blaus'd be called. No question. Luckily, this short trip was still a day before my 30th. I wasn't in violation . . . yet. As I was on my way to cause only a shred of trouble.

On my way over, I worked out my defense. "I'm attending a work event for my employer. *Well you weren't invited to said event.* I didn't know that, I was given a shirt and told to come." That wasn't tight enough, but I had time to refine it a bit more.

With every step an almost imperceptible pressure pulled harder and harder on every cell of my body. The farther I strayed from the office, the more the pressure increased. It pulled me back to work like an insanely-powered electromagnet. Aggressively urging me to retreat from my audacious errand.

The flame in my gut grew faster than whatever force dragged me back. Something was feeding the fire. The heat spread through my body, opposing the frightened pressure in my nerves. It helped me remain on course. Infiltration and confrontation, my objectives. I balled my fists to fight off the fear flowing faster. My palms sweat so much it felt like I was holding water, but the fire in my belly roared, pushing me onward. I was only going to the building next door, but the battle inside me made it feel like a cross-continent voyage.

My moist-clenched hands were beginning to freeze by the time I got a clear view of the awning announcing the celebration. The Colonbus Mansion presents: *eduGames 2.0 Employee Appreciation Soiree.* The enormous urban estate had long been closed except for school children on field trips . . . or for tourists branded attractions . . . or for Luxite nationalists indulging in skewed history lessons and other such false narrative narcissism. It was once owned by one of the original Luxite founders, Carter Colonbus, revered for its opulent grandeur and his expansive conquests across the globe.

I'd been working at eduGames for almost four months, but I'd only known of this next door estate from a popular first-person shooter. It was well-known to be a cramped, labyrinthian setting that allowed for "chaotic capture the flag games" according to the game guide I read on it. Everything about his palace in the city was built to protect Colonbus's riches from the people below him, Kuroban or Luxite alike.

Just like most buildings in Lux, the front door for us foot-walkers was actually in the back. This entrance was even more evasive as it was on the second floor and set away from the back alley by Colonbus's personal moat. There's even supposed to be a working vault in the basement where he locked away his plundered riches.

My heart started to race as I approached the narrow, serpentine ramp that led to the mansion's grand back entrance. I didn't know what to expect at a Luxite party, so I tried to psyche myself up by remembering what my mom told me about Kuroban celebrations. She would go on and on about the fabulous fetes we used to have with the abundance we produced in our hidden Maroon village. She said those were the only times she felt comfortable in large social settings growing up. It calmed her to be able to hide amidst the crowd and people-watch. The blissful energy they all created, felt, and reflected off one another allowed them to heal from the torturous situation they'd escaped. Everybody was too busy dancing to be on edge. They could let loose and breathe easy without worrying about being found, captured, and re-enslaved.

Despite the precarity of our underground independence, those *were* much better times in Kuroba. The era when we were closest to liberation. Until the Seed Slaughter. These days we had to be happy with the abbreviated jubilation that opened our Earth Goings. I knew *this event* wouldn't ride the same vibe, but I needed a positive grounding to keep going.

As I looked up the long, thin metal gangway leading to the landing and the front door, I saw two soil-skinned comrades milling about. Just the sight of them slowed down my thumping ticker, allowing me to loosen up and move with confidence.

The tension building up inside me dissipated like dust in the wind. These were my people. I could be myself with my people, even out here in Lux. Whatever misgiving they had about me or my family, they'd put that aside while we were behind enemy lines. Their glow was barely perceptible, muted as if covered by an opaque film, but they were definitely Kurobans. One massive hulk of person, the other as thin as the railing of the walkway. Maybe I'd be lucky again.

I walked up the rickety, ancient walkway with swagger. The moat below had dried up, and the parched concrete left was heavily choked out by natural vegetation emerging from underneath. When I finally saw my comrades up close, they were pacing on the landing right outside the door to the mansion. They were dressed in oversized, puffy hi-vis vests. Diagonally across their back they carried the same large, foldable electric batons the Blaus used. Their weapon of choice only slightly covered the big letters that said "Security."

I reached the top of the staircase and ignored the security-Kurobans, focused solely on my mission beyond the door. With one hand on the ornate door handle I was hit by what felt like the broadside of a tree trunk. I folded in half around it as the incredible force slammed into my midsection. As I coughed and spit up my insides, I heard someone bark at me.

"Hol' up. Where do you think you're going?" The bigger security-Kuroban, body so big and chiseled they seemed to be overstuffed with pressurized pillows under their outfit, walloped my abdomen with their unfolded, unelectrified baton.

I kept spitting over the side of the walkway because I tasted blood in my saliva. I caught my breath and heaved words out, "Bu-but, m-m-my shirt, I'm an employee, dammit! Quality assurance team. Probably the top performer, at that."

"That shit don't matter. Kurobans only work at *this event.*" The bass in the brolic security-Kuroban's voice rattled my bones. "Our people don't work at *eduGames*, that complex techie jazz is too advanced for us. You better get back before I call the Blaus on you." My heart skipped a beat when I noticed the raised brand on the back of their palm. "OP."

I thrusted myself toward the door, past the threatening barrier, and the security-Kuroban pressed the baton harder into my belly. I flailed in pain. "Come on, I'm gonna be quick. I guarantee I *am* an employee. This is an employee appreciation event, right?"

The other security-Kuroban, a tall, remarkably gaunt fella, popped out from behind the brolic one. "I-is there an issue here?" they said with a punch of what seemed like hollow confidence in their nasally voice.

"No, this stray garbage glow worm thinks they're supposed to be at this party," the brolic security-Kuroban answered calmly.

That slur hit me with as much force as the baton. I made a mistake. I shot my head in every angle searching for an escape path. My breaths got shorter and more labored. Intense anxiety returned. It flooded over my body and the electro-magnet of obedience yanked me back to the office. This time, I followed the feeling and turned to retreat with a rapid spin.

The svelte security-Kuroban barked out, "Where do you think you're going? I'm turning you in. I have enough camera evidence to request a full Blau team."

I only got a few steps before the svelte security-Kuroban jumped on the ramshackle railing and raced their nimble toe-knuckles along it like some sort of ninja gymnast. They sprinted with long, balanced strides past their security part-ner. They whirred past me as the railing shook and shuttered along the way. The railing creaked and cracked with every powerful stride, but the svelte security-Kuroban counter balanced every buckle and bend. I imagined their slim frame would take one wrong move and end up twisted at the bottom of the green and grey moat bed. Unfortunately, they landed gracefully on the other side of me. They blocked my only safe escape route and whipped out their electric baton, buzzing at full power. The tip of the baton detonated on my chest, shocking me back up the mansion's primeval catwalk.

The brolic security-Kuroban moved straight into us with their buzzing baton leading the way, making me the filling to their abuse sandwich. The security-Kurobans zapped me back and forth a few times using me as the fleshy tennis ball in their violent game to keep me from touching the feeble footbridge again. As I was batted about, I struggled with all of my might to maintain a grip on my coat while bracing my sizzling body. They were the worst flavor of Kuroban, Opps. Reasoning wasn't going to work with them. They were already gone.

I struggled to get past the batons beating my belly and my back, but the shock was too much. As much as I tried to stabi-lize myself on the shaky, slim bridge my arms swung every which way. Back and forth, the force of each power-boosted club rocked me about. The svelte security-Kuroban snickered as they continued swatting my charred midsection. "S-stay calm, this will all be over as soon as the Blaus arrive."

I was trapped.

And I was starting to smell a familiar smoky scent. Was this the smell of death?

I held my coat tight like a safety blanket as I was beaten back and forth. The strikes and shocks against my body sent ancestral flashbacks through my soul. My body recoiled into itself spontaneously. Bit by bit I surrendered to the suffering until the flame in my gut ignited.

My mind started scrolling through strategies from my Libook. Maybe something similar happened in a game. I needed some sort of a scheme, some escape hatch. The railing didn't look too high. Maybe I could jump to the concrete and roll away to salvation like the main character in the games I read about. Hopefully, I'd only break my legs if I actually landed and rolled the correct way, but I'd be able to drag myself to safety.

I took a breath to prepare to make the painful leap when the brolic security-Kuroban said, "Ooh, what is this?"

They stopped swatting and reached into my back pocket to pull out my therapy journal with its precious cargo. My bruised body clicked back into service and jumped away from my burly broken brethren trying to reveal my secret goodies. From my crouched landing position, I whipped around to protect my treasure. My reactionary rotation shot my coat, seized tight in my grasp, around with cosmic centrifugal force. I struck the brolic security-Kuroban upside their head.

Green sparks flew in all directions as my coat crashed upside their head. It was like a tractor trailer hit their muscle-bound noggin as they unscientifically flipped over four times before they started to drop off the side. I was so startled I let go of the coat as the security-Kuroban got tangled in it. I immediately thought to avoid any involvement in the accidental strike, especially with the Eyes of Lux recording. The mushroom outerwear stretched out and the hood tangled tightly around his thick ankle. The collision with my mycelial coat may have saved the falling security-Kuroban's life. The elevated walkway bent, creaked, and wobbled under the girth of the twisting tyranny grunt. The other security-Kuroban shoved me out the way to clutch my coat and their beefy partner.

~New Side Quest: Don't Get Caught ~

My heart accelerated like a maglev in a drag race. Adrenal courage exploded through my veins. I took shallow panicked breaths. A decision dialogue box popped up. Stay and help my kinfolk falling over the side of this soaring, shaky walkway or go forward as planned to sneak in the party. As the coat drew taut from the frenzied rescue mission, I heard a slight rip and made my decision. It was my only chance after all.

Tripping over my feet, I stumbled up the collapsing bridge toward the mansion's front door while my attackers were distressed and distracted. With both hands I threw my whole body to push open the heavy, flamboyant steel door. Once inside the foyer I twisted, latched, clicked, turned, and slid every lock on the other side to seal the fortress.

Right by the door was a tall aged wooden cabinet full of ostentatious knick-knacks, trinkets, and dishes. I squeezed in the small gap behind the cabinet and climbed up the wall. Shimmying my feet and back until my behind was near-parallel with the cabinet's midpoint, I strained and kicked against the wall. Eventually my leverage allowed me to tip over the enormous cabinet of affluence.

I panted as I landed with the nimbleness of a cat. Sweat burned my eyes as my vision danced between blurry and focused. Trying to focus with one eye, while the other started to twitch, I peeped two signs at the far end of the grand foyer. One pointed up a set of stairs with the words, "Private Suites and Restrooms." The other pointed downstairs, "Green Vault: Main Celebration." The door thundered with a barrage of banging fists and I ran downstairs as quickly as my feet would take me.

I tripped on the fourth step and rolled the rest of the way. My butter feet were at work again.

I crash landed into pulsating pandemonium. The room was packed with milling Luxites of all shades of sour cream. It took me a second to pick myself up. I was sore, but not scraped. My head throbbed in time with my heart jumping from my chest. I could barely discern between people in all of the smudges I saw. With a couple forceful blinks, I was able to regain some semblance of perception. A few Kurobans chauffeured trays of tweezer-tamed dishes and narrow glasses full of luminescent green liquid in the midst of rambunctious Luxites.

At first, no one said anything to me. But the looks, solely from the few Kurobans serving sustenance, stabbed at my distraught form. Their disgust and shame ripped through my weary body. It only intensified as I moved in deeper. The Luxites carried on like I wasn't even there.

I had never seen anything like this basement party before. It boasted an entire artificial garden. Racks of vegetables and other colorful greenery made the massive room a maze. This seemingly ornamental food production and agriculture at any scale or style was banned in Kuroba. Lights danced on the walls from projectors all over the room. An energetic DJ stood between speakers in the far corner under a colorful arch of balloons. The erratic music was disconcerting. It further aggravated my shortness of breath, racing heart, and overall sweat gland activity.

I had to shake off the stupefaction from all the new experiences as quickly as possible. Unseen strings yanked taut on my body, pulling and pleading for me to return to the office. My movements took more and more effort as the seconds crawled by. I stumbled and leaned on the bare shoulder of a Luxite guest in a flowing gown. Their skin looked as though it'd been thoroughly pickled and tanned ten thousand times in a row, with the rough, inflexible texture to match. The evening gown Luxite's face went from boisterous laughter to bloodcurdling terror as they turned and screamed.

[Cloak of Invisibility - Deactivated]
[Beacon of Hypervisibility - Activated]

My inner alarms screeched. It was only a matter of time before the security-Kurobans made it down here backed by the Blaus. My ancestral conditioning only gave me a few responses: fight, flight, freeze or fawn. I quickly chose the first option and furiously trudged through the crowd I didn't belong to. They squealed, shrieked, and sobbed as I hobbled through, leaning on one tartar sauce-tinted guest or another. I wasn't just another Kuroban-servant in the background, and everyone knew it.

My memory flipped back to the horror stories Mom screamed at me about why my independent spirit wouldn't make it in Lux. Both eyes twitched uncontrollably. My sweaty palms slipped on everything I touched. What kept me going at this point was the wildfire raging in my gut. But my internal conflagration was weakening.

I faded in and out of consciousness as I struggled through the tight crowd. My limbs had the constitution of slime-soaked tentacles as I reached out to anyone or anything for stability. My throat felt as dry as ancient bricks rubbing against one another. The entire time I kept muttering my request:

"Do you know where Robert is?"

"I need to speak to Robert"

"Tell Robert the QA team, especially me, deserves more."

I knocked hordes of folks over like bowling pins trying to force my way through the crowd. In my confusion I grabbed a narrow goblet of artichoke aperitif and spilled it into my gullet to satiate my parched voice box. Immediately my stomach inverted and knotted as sharp pangs of hunger peppered my midsection. Everyone I pleaded with shrugged me off or spat in my desperate face. Even the Kuroban waitstaff dodged me.

I was batted about two or three more times before I couldn't hear any longer, I couldn't catch my breath, and I couldn't coordinate a step any further. The fire flickered inside me and my end felt near. With the fire waning I got the hint of a soft drum beat rapping away at my soul, *Cha, cha, cha Chuga* . . . It gave me the drive to suck in all the air I could muster. All the incendiary power I had left in my form. With everything I gathered in my lungs, I screamed out, "Robert, Fu—"

Zap!

MISSION FAILED

```
Health Points . . . . . . . . . . . 40%
Magic Power . . . . . . . . . . . 0%
```

```
Mission #1: Tell the QA-robans What I Heard . . . . . . SUCCESS - THEY DIDN'T CARE
Mission #2: Convince QA-robans to Crash
                the Party to Save our Jobs . . . . . . . . . . TOTAL FAILURE
Side Quest #1: Infiltrate eduGames Party . . . . . . . . . SUCCESS
Side Quest #2: Confront Robert about QA-roban
                Office Space . . . . . . . . . . . . . . . . . . . . CERTAIN FAILURE
Side Quest #3: Don't Get Caught . . . . . . . . . . . . . . . . DOESN'T LOOK GOOD
```

```
Experience Points Gained [285]
Coins [-20] . . . Can't Wait for Payday
Items Received [eduGames Company Shirt]
Status Effect [BEACON OF HYPERVISIBILITY]
```

Stage 2: Elevated Risk

Chapter 5: Root Error

The words "Minigame Activated" flashed across the darkness of my mind's eye. My eyes snapped open and I scurried backward. The digital scaffolding of a forest loaded up before my eyes. Trillions of triangular shards that made up the skeletal structure of the scenery outlined the colorless setting. My body, a set of triangular arrangements in itself, was the only thing that moved in the mid-render environment.

I investigated the 3D anatomical representation of my hand and wiggled my fingers. The line segments arranged in the image of my hand waggled accordingly. A monsoon of colorful pixels rained down on the entire landscape. Every drop of damp color splashed into place and painted a detailed outdoor landscape. This went on for a few hectic, colorful seconds before an intense light flashed on everything, even beyond the horizon. Life was injected into everything at once. It was like a team of marionettes started their shift to string this scene into action. The wind whooshed through the trees, the river rushed into the distance, and the radiant, terrestrially-tinted people activated as if nothing was amiss.

I found myself kneeling in a moist dirt clearing surrounded by tall stalks rising toward the sun. The labyrinth of towering stalks stretched as far as the eye could see. My back throbbed with the tremors of intense pain, the sun seared my shiny, sopping skin, and a crushing pressure gripped my head. My mouth was stuffed with a scratchy fabric, it went down so far I felt it tickling my tonsils.

Something intense bore down behind me, the imposing presence trickled down my spine. In a series of discreet, micro-movements I cranked my neck backward to catch a peek at the intrusive energy. An enormous shadow ended right beside me and I carefully tracked its source. A beast-like breathing blasted my searing back with gamey moisture. My vertebrae vibrated and my arms tensed up. Then it growled at me. "Get back to work."

I scampered away from the demanding creature. A dusty Kuroban in a large straw hat sat perched on a monstrous steer. The Kuroban cattle hand, or more accurately chattel hand, was slight in stature and draped in sweaty rags. A large whip hung down from the chattel hand's tight grip.

They cracked the whip in the air so hard the sound wave, or the fear, pushed me back and briefly wet myself. Not only did they sport the scowl of an unsatisfied villain, but their ancestral iridescence was almost indiscernible. I could only assume they were Kuroban from their deep dirt-hued skin. Only continuous, inhumane, self-reinforced trauma could dim our natural dazzle that deeply. This was a warning if I'd ever seen one.

I backed up, so scared I slammed my eyes shut trying to end this tense nightmare. My body trembled in anticipation of abuse. The Kuroban chattel hand snarled. "You better get back to cutting this cane before I pull you in for reprogramming."

I cracked open one eye to see the chattel hand motion to something laying in the mud beside me.

I wiped my sweat-drenched face and dug my hand in the semisolid mud to recover the half-buried item. As I pulled it out, a glint of light reflected off the planetary heat lamp blazing above. I wiped the heavy cutlass on my scratchy pants and crudely slapped it against the stalk near me with a flat thud. My wrist twisted as it collided and the cutlass dropped back in the mud.

The tightly-braided leather whip whizzed through the air moving faster than the sound of its impact. When I flinched to brace for the sharp cracker at the end to dig into my back it transformed. The whip's composite triangles reappeared, reorganized, and re-rendered in the air mutating into a powerful pulsing lime green ray. The green ray stretched between my body and the Kuroban chattel hand's grasp. Along with the light came a swinish sucking that slurped all the way to my soul. My body spasmed in the ray's relentless grasp.

The chattel hand was emotionless as they watched my agony at the end of their beam whip. The other strange Kurobans amongst the stalks looked over at me through their peripherals. I tried to force faint cries through the onerous device binding my mouth. Masses of matcha energy bulbs moved from me, along the length of the ray, back to the whip's grip. Every bulb of light leaving me felt like a million blenders pureeing my insides while suctioning off the liquified residue. Then, as soon as it started, it was over.

I was spent, but adrenaline mixed with fear and confusion activated my latent hypervigilance. I felt no additional whip marks on my skin or other physical remnants of the green ray's onslaught. My back still sizzled like a skillet as sweat dribbled into old gaping impressions crisscrossing my spine. The same haunting hue of the ray blinked bright green in the distance.

The chattel hand gruffly yelled, "Strike from the bottom. Are you stupid or dumb?"

I fumbled the razor-sharp cutlass while trying to reset my grasp and almost sliced my fingers off. I frantically scanned around to observe how to properly chop the cane. My body couldn't take any more mistakes, as pain still beatboxed through my body. Other Kurobans in shabby rags, cutlass in hand or pushing wheelbarrows were busy working throughout the snarl of stalks. I honed in on one nearby giving assured, powerful strikes. I studied their technique and quickly duplicated it down to the smallest detail. Hopefully this would avoid another slice of my soul being snatched by that wrathful whip.

The chattel hand must've been satisfied with my improved technique because they rode away without a word.

Suddenly the soil-sheened colleague I mimicked popped up in front of me. I gasped and almost dropped my cutlass again. Their mouth wasn't bound like mine.

They slammed their fingers from their free hand onto my mouth gag. "Careful," they whispered so softly it took me two seconds to register what they'd said.

Their fingers sternly pointed at their eyes until I locked my gaze with theirs. They whipped their sights onto the chattel hand and then zipped towards a sprawling light blue house beyond the fields. The house seemed to be in the vicinity of where the bright post-whip blinking occurred. It was the only thing noticeable in that direction except more rows of cane.

The grandiose structure towered over the expansive farmland in all directions. It was like a baby blue castle wrapped in wide verandas on every level. A lighthearted legion of laughing Luxites populated the porch. One was gagging on a cigar. Little ones played with a tiny tea set. The final one sat stiff and stately in a gown matching the grandeur of the manor. The one in the show-stopping dress accepted a tray of perspiring drinks from a Kuroban swaddled in a chalky sheet further muting their wavering glow.

My buddy beside me squeezed my shoulder to get my attention again. They gently tapped my stomach before making a circle in the air above while their eyes followed their dancing digit. Then they whispered as gently as before, "The song." With that, they released my shoulder, turned around, and disappeared into the cane.

I almost yelled out, "What song?" before I remembered unspoken secrecy served as the appetizer to their cryptic message.

I rubbed my hand on my belly trying to figure out what they were talking about. Nothing came after waiting for a few seconds, so I looked up and got lost in the clear sky. An overwhelming, yet refreshing surge of energy sprung from my gut, seeping softly all over my body, settling serenely in my sore soul.

Shuka-shu. Kurobans walked a donkey hauling a cart overfilled with fresh cut cane. Every foot fell throughout the fields along a steady rhythm. It was like a sort of echolocation that linked me with a shared sentience of my surroundings. Our heartbeat.

Bling gling-gling bling. The cart creaked in concert with metal chiming melodically in a building at the end of the trail and the shackles around the driver's ankles. The bustling building erupted with a plume of smoke that swam through the sky. Further off was an area surrounded by trees followed by more trees. The extensive forest climbed up the mountainside rising above us all. The sound struck a chord with me and downloaded the full schema of what we were doing and how. I had distinct directions for how to collude with the planet. It was a way to provide for our oppressors and diminish each other's suffering. I tapped into the system at large and my part in it. Our stratagem.

Cha, cha, cha. Chuga cha-cha. The cadence of the cutlasses chopped in harmony. The sound energized me. Sadness shadowed every strike, but despite our dreadful situation we had each other. We were one. As we chopped in complement with one another our movements became the many threads, individual yet integrated, coordinated in a quilt of concealed Kuroban power. We shared that collective power to push us through our bonded drudgery. Our strength.

And then, barely audible, were soft words being sung with smooth, surreptitious confidence. The silky sound rode the breeze, wound through the cane stalks and zeroed in on my gut.

Waaaaaaalk on the wa-ter.

Our stories.

My bones quaked and my soul filled up with unbelievable power. I felt invulnerable. No matter what I faced I could easily overcome it. It wasn't just me anymore, I was amongst many who were simply other pieces of me. I worked with the grace and might of a dancer. I cut cane under the roasting sun like I'd been doing it for centuries. I tuned into the sonic assembly line. It gave me the awareness, insight, support, and guidance I needed. I still had to tune out the cries of torment, abuse, and exhaustion springing up here and there, but the music grounded me.

HOURS LATER, the sun faded away. As it dipped in the sky our tempo diminished at the same rate. Nobody said anything, yet we de-crescendoed in unison. A dull hum was all that was left of our song as the sun finally set.

The chattel hand stopped near me without a word and loomed over me in the moonlight. I was frozen with fear as he bent over from his horseback perch and fussed with the lock on the back of my head.

Suddenly, in a brief moment of confident clarity, I gripped the cutlass so hard splinters of wood dug into my sore hand. Liberation was on my mind. My heart seemed to slow down as every second stretched out. I visualized how I might chop down this lost comrade repackaging their own accumulated misery onto us. My body stuttered. Not just because I worried about harming one of my own, however they reasoned the righteousness of their reality. A more ominous figure farther away that stopped me.

A bright lantern moved on the porch of the big blue manor. The light from the lantern highlighted the wispy smoke of a crisp cigar, the cold steel of a long rifle and the translucent reflection of the Luxite's pasty skin. Their eyes were glued to me over the top of the red-tipped cigar. I let out an elated gasp as the cranial shackle fell from my face and air finally escaped my lungs, the insurgent pressure building up inside me released.

My grip loosened on the cutlass and the retaliation opportunity passed. The chattel hand pushed me into the sun-baked dirt. "Now clean yourself up. I hope you learned your lesson, but if not, my whip stays hungry."

I stumbled and scampered away like a three-legged mouse escaping a snake's supper. I followed after the other depleted Kurobans. They limped from the fields towards a small collection of wooden shacks at the edge of the forest. The structures were reminiscent of the shoddy cottages in my homelands. Except they were missing the dump's motley bits of modernity and hardened mud.

My joints felt like centuries-old rusted iron. Every muscle

shrieked out in pain. My feet thumped with every step like a wounded animal and my neck felt twisted in a stiff coil. My hands were so raw it was as if they were stuck in a transitory state between solid and liquid, like setting concrete. To avoid further excruciation, my back was frozen in a hunch. I staggered along despite the pain raging all over. The moon was the only light we had to drag our broken bodies to the wooden shacks. Old tattered clothes hung on the crumbling structures like patches on an old quilt. The same Kuroban-helper that showed me the secret of the song waved me into a shack as they hung out of the hatched-together window.

I walked in, and they directed me to sit on a cylindrical seat made of wood and topped with an old animal hide. In front of the uncomfortable stool was a misshapen stone water basin, well-seasoned liquid settled at the bottom. The rank sediment attacked my nose and overrode the pain. I stared deep into the sunken eyes and weathered face of my Kuroban-helper as they handed me a dirty cloth sopping with the funky liquid.

"You hurtin'?" they asked, looking at my bloody palms pulsing in time with my heart.

"This is nothing," I said, feigning resilience. "I'll get used to this, b-but my back. Ah." I winced at the pain shooting through my body.

The Kuroban-helper shuffled behind me to wipe my sore-ridden back while I recoiled with every touch. Mid-flinch they asked, "Come to my 30th?"

"I don't mean to be rude, but you're 30?"

"The song. That drum," — they pointed to the wooden cylinder I sat on — "The divination. We *need* you."

"Ok, sure, I *guess*," I responded. I didn't fully understand what I was agreeing to, but I wanted to avoid any disrespect. They'd been so helpful throughout this entire spooky situation.

They finished wiping my back and directed me to a pile of

hay and old rags in the corner. As soon as I hit the uneven pile, I knocked out.

I WOKE up to faint music playing far off in the distance. The silky rhythm, harmonies, and words felt like millions of acoustic hands gently rocking me awake. Darkness covered everything except for a luminous white cross floating on the opposite corner of the shack. The music drew me in with every note. It was coming from a certain direction, barely discernible. Amidst the shadows, the music directed me. And in one fluid movement, I stood up and walked over to grab the wooden drum I'd sat on to get washed up. I snatched it from the middle of the lightless one room shack. The raw wood of the cylinder bristling against my haggard hands told me what I was holding. I walked towards the floating white cross and pushed it. To my surprise, the floating cross opened up and I was enveloped by an empty void on the other side. I couldn't tell if this was a dream within a dream, some demented game, or I'd really been transported across time and space to an alternate reality.

Everything felt more than real, from the pain to the emptiness, my nerve-endings were on edge in the blatant absence of everything. It was still, like everything had ceased to exist around me. It seemed like someone had even turned off the moon because the space was even darker than in the shack. The only thing that accompanied me in the disorienting void was the song that woke me. It was still strumming in my soul, coming from inside me instead of through my ears. With nothing else, I was drawn in by mysterious music wirelessly tethered to my soul. I tuned inside in hopes to decipher where the music was coming from.

The distant melodies seemed to echo and amplify in my soul. As I walked around the unknown space, the volume increased or decreased like a metal detector. I shifted around in circles to search for the source, adjusting to maximize the delicate ringing. In a moment of perfect alignment, I stopped abruptly, almost falling over. A neon ball of green luminosity oozed from my gut, began spinning as it consolidated, and illuminated the forest floor to my surprise as it raced away. I chased after it. As I ran the soul-reverberating music got louder and louder.

The sliver of the forest I could see only confused me more. I couldn't hear, feel, taste, smell, or see anything except the bounding ethereal emerald light leading me and the symphony from the fields. The audio crescendoed as I got closer, becoming more complex, richer, and more energetic. More instruments, more singers, and more soul, all in perfect tune. As much as I wanted to run away, I was curious, almost drawn forward by the warmth and joy it sparked in me. I couldn't go anywhere anyways because I'd already gone too far to figure out how to track back to the shack. So I followed the odd green iridescence bobbing in front of me.

I zigzagged between the tendrils of trees, through the brush of bushes, and over the lip of each downed log. Every near miss reminded me that my surreal circumstances were based in an unseeable reality, and the only thing I could do was mimic the green orb of light as it guided my way.

The smack of sweltering heat swirled over me and spurred me from the inside out. The temperature rose as I got nearer to the song's source. Not the heat of a fire, but the joyful warmth of a loving embrace. A distinctly recognizable type of heat that put me at peace. The fire of overwhelming happiness. Flashes of this tender energy came from every angle and I felt each story as I continued running. An elemental taste of my connection with every piece of the ecosystem past, present, and what it would be in the future. It felt like home. The further I went, the more I was captivated by the whole experience so much so that it became my very being. That's when I came upon a crowd of Kurobans.

They were the same ones from the fields, all playing instruments. No sound stirred my ears. The forest was still completely silent, but it broke the knob in my soul. The soul sound flowed in and out of us and made us one. A strong seafoam glow surrounded us all. In the middle swirling light orbs gathered, skanking to the music.

I waddled my way into the throng. I knelt down amongst my kinfolk, setting down the small drum I brought with me. I didn't need to think, my soul steered my percussive performance. From my first whack onward my hands shifted into the swing of the music. Oddly, no sound emitted from my drum – like the rest of my impromptu bandmates – but I sensed the tune perfectly. My melodic beat mingled seamlessly with the arrangement of inaudible, yet internally blaring sounds. The chartreuse chunks of light intensified, multiplied, and sped up in the center as we played. I banged my drum with an innate expertise. This spiritual force supported me just as it had when I was cutting the cane. My muscles had a memory I never knew they possessed.

In the center of the crowd, beyond the chaotic choreography of the green light, was a circle of soil glowing and pulsing with the beat. The same Kuroban helper was intently drawing in the soil.

More of my enslaved compatriots arrived. Some came with pots they banged, some with banjos they twanged, and others with nothing at all. But their mouths moved as they sang songs solely audible to our souls. Our voiceless verses unified our mystical melody. Every word undulated throughout my body, *waaaaaaalk on the wa-ter.*

Without warning, the music stopped with a victorious, coordinated crash. Everyone halted and moved inward as the Kuroban helper began posing on their knees. They had their face lifted toward the sky and their eyes glowing in the same green as the soil. They were engulfed by the dancing chloro-phyll light orbs. All the light combined and grew into one massive beam. We all placed a hand into the beam and on the glowing soil adorned with an assortment of abstract sketches. An intense burst of heat ensnared us all as our hands met the soil. Our souls connected. As a collective, our bodies sucked in the incandescence and power of the soil. The symphony continued inside of us without a single person playing. We shuttered as one. We recovered as one. I felt my muscles, my bruises, my sores heal. My pain melted away and I got stronger by the second until we all suddenly whispered, "Ammirika."

A single word of our native tongue broke the trance. The fire from our shared divination blasted out from us in the form of a pea-tinted wave of light. It reverberated throughout the forest, lighting it up in a flash. We all ran like roaches following the intrinsic direction we'd shared in the soil.

The forest was filled with the spine-chilling sounds of dogs barking, guns shooting, hooves clomping, and fiendish Luxites hurling slurs and obscenities. Our tormentors had hunted us down and surrounded us at our midnight jaunt in the forest.

Strangely, I wasn't a bit scared. Instead I was happy, assured, and determined. Underneath it all I still felt the soul symphony powering my instincts from the inside out. In front of me a small green globe of illumination raced deeper into the woodlands and I followed as close as possible. The nearer I was, the better the harmony with the song blasting in my soul was. It filled me with certainty and peace. A tender feeling that helped me traverse towards unseen safety. Every mystical drum circle attendee was driven by the same Kuroban creole: *ammirika*, meaning to run.

My mind didn't know where I was going, but I trusted the music resounding inside my soul and this orb zooming ahead. Through the dark woods I dashed with an otherworldly focus. Other folks from the circle and the frantic fascists chasing us crossed in front and behind as I ran.

It was a messy chaos of people zigzagging at every angle through the arcane woods and fields and bushes. Lanterns blinked in and out from everywhere. Dogs ran into our dominators, handlers into horses, and crazed enslavers crashed into each other. Their left feet short-circuited as they scrambled in furious pursuit. They tripped, fell, and stumbled through the shadowy woods. We were no longer the prey constantly coerced into servitude. We all intuitively knew our escape path. One foot, then another in a coordinated line dance consummated through our connection with the land.

A horse appeared, charging right behind me. The sound of rushing water howled in front of me. The sphere of light I was following stopped suddenly near the roaring rapids, but the heinous horse behind me didn't. I didn't stop either. My mind wanted to panic, but my soul soothed me. The ball of light remained where it was ahead and waited for me to catch up. It bounced twice quickly like its own luminous version of a nod. Then it leapt forward and disappeared. I kept running, with the snout of the horse swiping my back. Without another thought, I leaped to where the light vanished to a resounding splash.

Chapter 6: Reset v1 - Vulnerability Assessment

Consciousness Regained
Bodi Has Joined Your Party!

"Ow!" The train's shaky suspension slammed my limp head against the frosty train window covered in half-frozen slobber. The abrupt crash summoned me out of my slumber and I thrashed my hands about to avoid drowning. The moisture was like a river swallowing me up. Electricity zipped through my cells. I was charged up, my body still reeling from what I'd experienced during my inadvertent rest. My hands were shaking. I couldn't tell if I was scared or just surprised.

"What happened?" were the first words that scratched themselves free of my grainy throat. My head spun around like an alcohol-dependent owl after a bank holiday bacchanal.

Bodi was sitting beside me with a scolding stank-face on. His perturbed disposition and the heavy bruising on his dark sienna face threw me for a loop. Blood was splattered all over his disheveled button-up and his voluminous tweed coat was gone. He looked like he'd been jumped and thrown into a dumpster, although the dump was probably where his clothes came from anyways. I squirmed backward, looking down at myself to check whether I was injured or not. I deflated with a sigh of relief when I realized I was intact, except for a few wet spots on my crusty eduGames shirt and my pants felt particularly moist and sticky. Bodi noticed my erratic movements and hissed out a huff of irritation.

I pushed myself upward in my seat. As I moved, I felt something drop from my lap. My hand swooped downward to catch the therapy journal encasing my secret strategy tablet. As I looked around everything seemed like a normal train ride home, distinct from the trip in. I leaned back and looked through the frosted window to double-check my direction. The sight of the troubling, yet recognizable factories fuming plumes of doom confirmed I was on the correct commuter train to Kuroba.

Remnants of spittle still clung to my face. I bent over to coax the cold slime onto the bottom of my shirt. While looking at the new wet spot on my shirt, I thought about the dream I woke from. I tried to hold all the pieces floating about in my head as tightly as possible.

Mission #1: Figure Out What Happened While I Was Dreaming
Mission #2: Return Home
Mission #3: Don't Let Mom Know about the Party

"You lied! You never listen," Bodi snipped at me.

"Huh? What are you talking about? What happened to you?" His immediate accusation confused me. I was mostly okay, just a dull soreness across my midsection. But he'd obviously gone through something that he was taking out on me.

He shouted back in disgust, "What happened to *me*? Bredren, Quawd brought his righteous justice upon you once again!"

His response spurred more questions. I tried to bop my hand against my forehead to jostle my memories into place. "How did I get on the train . . . Wait! Where's my coat?" I searched my surroundings to find my missing mycelial coat. I only found the shabby vinyl train seat cover with cigarette burns and scuff marks. I sighed. A complex mix of disappointment and dread came over me. Mom's gonna be pissed. Her scolding was already setting in preemptively.

Bodi barked, "I barely got you out. I wasn't worried about your damn coat. I knew you'd be out of pocket at that party. You couldn't help yourself, could you?"

He was looking out for me, as he'd done when I was growing up. I took it because I owed him. "You knew!?" I laughed to soften the tension. "You ain't know shit because I just wanted a little convo with Massa Roberto. Do you know what *did* happen though? Things got a little gray after I ran inside."

He turned his face abruptly. A tear of blood dripped down his cheek from a small gash under his nearest eye. I stared at the blood trickling toward his chin. "Elder Mama can't take care of you forever, *genius*. Tomorrow you truly transition into adulthood. And because of you, none of *my* work is done. For real, the whole team is behind because of you."

"I offered then, and the offer still stands. I'll do whatever y'all need to get the work done." I spotted an old, but lightly used piece of tissue tucked in the seat back pocket in front of me and fished it out. I reached out to wipe the bloody trail from Bodi's face.

He slapped my hand away with boisterous vigor. "Don't touch me. Worry about yourself. Scripture says we must bear the fruit of our own labor and suffer the poison for our sins. Plus, you never know who at eduGames is watching."

Over the loudspeaker the recording announced in a flat,

dry voice, "Now arriving at the Western Lux Manufacturing Park, please exit in an orderly, professional manner. Have a productive day."

I responded quickly since we had to get off soon, "Whatever! *You* can suffer solo in silence abiding by bogus bylaws. Do you know what happened at the party though?"

Bodi gripped my arm so hard I felt his short, jagged nails dig their tiny barbs in. "Let's go."

He tore me from my seat. My legs wobbled like a newborn giraffe and the soreness in my midsection throbbed. My entire torso felt like the anesthesia was wearing off and repercussions were returning. I winced while still enduring enough to gather my Libook and shove it into my back pocket before Bodi yanked me off the train.

My lungs filled with noxious particles as soon as I stepped from the train's airlock. On the packed platform, I stretched my stiff arms out and winced in pain as my abdomen howled. The crowd parted around me without any acknowledgement as they bumped my sore body. The accumulated amalgam of oil, dirt, grime, sweat, and blood from the filthy work of Lux other working Kurobans endured rubbed off on me. It reminded me that their positions were much harder to automate away, although the QA-robans and I were subjected to a totally different emotional and mental duress. No less, no more. Just different control mechanics effectively extracting power on the entire populace to satisfy the unsatisfiable at the controls.

I reached out for the last rays of masked sunlight still glinting through the dense pollution as light barely bent over the mountaintop. Bodi and I both looked up towards the daunting hike to Kuroba when an energetic voice surprised us from the other end of the platform.

Amid the soft grumbles of disgruntled comrades embarking on the long march home, a familiar sound triggered my ears. I paused and twisted my head to Bodi. "Bods, is that your sister, or am I tripping?" He was already rushing through the throng to confront her. I followed.

"What are you doing here? I thought you'd be *home* overwhelmed by homework now."

She looked down and softly swiped her foot back and forth across the ground with her hands behind her back. "Well, what had happened was . . . I got kicked out. So-so-so . . . I was sitting at the station waiting for you."

Bodi was already pissed at me, but smoke seemed to pour from his ears, "WHAT THE FU–"

She turned towards her brother with the cutest smile she could muster. She placed her hands on his bulging arms as he clenched his fists and rattled off her reasoning to calm him down. "I'm sorry. It was only for the day. I'll do better tomorrow, I promise."

"You're just delaying the inevitable, you can't hide from Father. He's the principal. What did you do?" Bodi asked.

"It was . . ." She stepped back and looked down again before slightly tilting her head towards me. Bodi jumped at me, but Soma slid between our beef. "It was *my* decision. The holographic teacher said I asked too many questions and wrote me up for *prospective insubordination.*"

"How could you tell my sister to do this? She can't become a failure like you!" Bodi yelled with his saliva in support.

"I–"

"Stop! It wasn't their fault. I said it was all *me.* Talking to them actually gave me the confidence to remain composed in the moment, unlike other students. A bunch of students were kicked out permanently, for no reason," she explained.

The tension was thick as Soma and Bodi stared at each other, gritting their teeth, without a word. It was now just the three of us standing at the desolate train station. The rest of our train mates were already past the abandoned mine.

"Bodi, you know this school's inner workings, we test the software that it runs on. Them algos've been tuned up." I saw his blank stare. It made me sigh heavily and grab his hand to make sure he understood me clearly. "You know this school is just a filter. And you, of everyone, know it's getting more strict after you and the other QA-robans were all co-valedictorians."

Bodi swatted my hand away and stomped off the platform. I could barely hear his last words before he left. "This is *your* fault. You put this in her head. Solve it before our father fi–" He was already far into the barren lands surrounding the deserted mine by the time I had a chance to respond.

~ New Side Quest: Support Soma's Curiosity
While Keeping Her Safe ~
~ New Side Quest: Keep Bodi as My Ally ~

I felt bad for Soma, but her situation wasn't good for me. I needed Bodi on my side. I grabbed Soma's hand and tried to catch up with him. A soft rhythm rang out from a corner deep in my gut. It went *Shuku-Shu* over and over. It steadied me and served as a sense of peace.

Soma squeezed my hand as I dragged her along. "I didn't just come to avoid my father. I also wanted to hear how you survived school as long as you did. I thought it might give me some hope for how to endure this for years on end."

"I don't think now is the best time. I'm already on thin ice," I said. We jogged, kicking up a whirling cloud of dry top soil before we finally caught up with Bodi.

"You know, I don't actually care what happened, Soma," Bodi said "This is *your* future that you're ruining, but you know how Father is. He tightens the screws across the board no matter who slips up. And he has a *special* penance for each of us."

Soma opened her mouth before I squeezed her hand. I attempted to channel my tranquility to her as I put my index finger over my mouth and shook my head softly from side to side. It wasn't worth it for her to get into a back and forth with him in this state. It would only lead to more trouble for us all.

"I'm actually more disappointed in your genius idol here. They wouldn't have anything without me. Do you want to be worthless like them?"

Who was this sorrowful sycophant calling worthless? Bodi followed the rules, did what his dubious dada demanded of him, and had amazing opportunities, but he couldn't do any of the work without my *worthless* ass. I let go of Soma's hand and prepared to run up on Bodi. Soma grabbed me before I was out of arm's reach.

I stayed beside her and yelled at Bodi, who was getting further ahead of us. "Hol' up. I appreciate everything that you've done for me. Truly I do, but I'm very happy with the decisions I've made. Just this morning *you* were interested in *my* experiences. Remember?"

My clapback shut him up, but only for a second. "Look, I didn't really care about that stuff. I was just making conversation. Trying to pass the time in this dump."

"Hey, stop! Don't you think your life could've gone any other way? Do you think you made it to this situation completely on your own?"

He turned and charged backwards, getting right in my face. His broad forehead pressed hard against my dainty brow. "Yes, I've put in the blood, sweat, and tears for this. I've followed all the steps to make sure I've done what I'm supposed to do to survive. It's hanging out with scum like y'all that slows me down. I would've been my own boss in a huge, gorgeous Luxite villa by now if I wasn't slumming it with you all. Hell, I don't even know if we're really related Soma. Unc just dropped you off when you were a baby and I was nice enough to care for you when Father wouldn't."

My face and Soma's both fell. He turned and walked away

like it was nothing. With unoiled robotic awkwardness, Bodi straddled and jumped over the naked land sores at the transition point between the mine and the dump. Soma grabbed my hand and pulled me forward. The metronome of peace returned. *Shuku-Shu.* We ran hand in hand into the dump to catch up with her resentful brother.

Soma had us moving quickly to catch up to Bodi. When we finally caught him, she blurted out, "Ouch bro, is that how you see your sister? Unc told Anan everything, it's not our fault he hasn't shared anything about Mom with us. And look at our noses, you can't deny the resemblance."

Bodi moved much more slowly now. Still, my ankles wobbled as soon as I entered the shifty base of decaying refuse. I fought to steady myself and make my case to Bodi. "Yeah, that's pretty harsh *bredren*. You don't have any responsibility to me, but at least don't do your sister like that. Do you think–" I looked down and found an old cell phone which I picked up with my free hand. I pulled off the battery and continued my response. "Look at this battery. I want you to think outside the box, just a little bit. I promise it'll pay off. Think about this battery's birth, its life, and now its slow descent to death."

Bodi turned. "I don't have time for your little genius games. Who cares about that battery or whatever technology you're into now?"

I took a deep breath and used my optimistic creativity to remind myself his fiery reaction was only a defense mechanism. Another sound overlapped the steady rhythm in my gut. *Bling-gling.*

A response jumped to the front of the queue in my mind. Even though it was a new situation, the words came so clearly that reciting them felt like a flashback. "Work with me for a second, we're literally in the midst of a torrential trophic cascade. Do you think this battery was destined for the life it had and, especially," I tapped the old battery a few times to cause the filth covering it to dribble downward, "this particular end?"

"Yeah, it was probably used extensively and now it doesn't work anymore," Bodi stated nonchalantly with a skeptical shrug to match. He turned away from me and kept walking through the waste.

"Ok, that's *a* perspective, but we can look a little deeper. I promise I won't get too deep without a life vest. Instead, let's focus on one of the most important elements that makes the battery work: lithium. Before it was the main ingredient in this rechargeable smartphone battery, lithium was probably sitting around chilling in rocks. Then all of a sudden there was a loud crash and it was dug out at a mine like the one we walk by every day. From there it was refined into the most useful form the extractors could come up with, forced to become this battery to power their world. Tragically, this prescribed profession all ends when:

1. A newer and better way to hold power was ushered into the minds of the extractors or . . .
2. Lithium can no longer meet the extractors' shifting standards for holding power anymore or . . .
3. The device it powered was no longer of use (whether the device was obsolete or not) to the extractors . . .

"When one of those conditions occurs, the lithium, in this fabricated form and without any recourse or possibility of reorientation, is discarded. Now it's trapped, waiting for the synthetic, hazardous elements around it to degrade. At that point it will finally seep back to the earth in an exhausted, poisonous state."

"If that's what lithium's destiny is, then so what?" Bodi asked, facing forward and plodding leisurely through the trash.

"Who knows if this was lithium's destiny because it was groomed for this particular path. Selected, shaped, and submitted into this existence solely to serve the extractors. Other destinies this lithium could've probably had were eliminated. Some destinies may've been more elongated, some more enlivened, or maybe more empowered, but it was forced into this particular one only."

Bodi stopped without turning around to respond, "But wasn't it a good life? Any other version is a what-if, nothing more than a hapless dream."

"Yeah, if that's what *lithium* truly wanted."

Bodi's head turned slightly to me. "But wasn't it fulfilled?"

"What are you really trying to ask Bodi?" I tried to hide my chuckle. I needed him to say it out loud.

Bodi turned around all the way. We had stopped right in front of him in the middle of the widespread wasteband. He replied with the most distress I've heard in his voice, "Like, how could it do any more than what it was meant to do?"

I moved to meet his eyes and comfort him telepathically. "And who determines what anyone or anything is *meant* to do? What if lithium knew no better because that's the only fate that'd been drilled into them, and every lithium, for generations? Not even lithium themselves could be trusted to imagine an alternate future for themselves at that point. They have no reference points from which to fantasize. To me, everyone, no *everything*, has infinite options, opportunities, and openings in this and every one of our many lifetimes."

"Y-you're tripping. We cannot be more than what Quawd demands of us in this *singular* lifetime." Bodi sputtered out forcefully as he took a small step backwards.

I tried to hold in my laughter. I wanted to respect his perspective when I replied to him. "Quawd isn't deciding these things, we *all* have agency, even if it's minute. Plus, actual people are creating the conditions we must fit to meet *their* needs. We're contorting to a human-made mold."

Bodi moved in closer to Soma and me. He took a deep breath and responded, "S-so this old-ass lithium was doomed by who exactly?"

I moved towards Bodi, turned him around and hooked his arm in mine. With Bodi on one side and Soma on the other I started walking to lead us home together. Turning my head to Bodi I answered his question, "Who else do you think? The Luxites you're always trying to impress. Without lithium becoming these batteries, their technological domination and exploitation has limits. Molding lithium to this singular existence deprives it of being a medicine, a lubricant, a lover, a liberator, or any other possibility. Because Luxite colonial compulsion only sees the world as a collection from which to cull."

Bodi looked down, but as he detached his gaze from mine, I saw sadness shimmering in his eyes. He stared at the trash thinning below our feet as we got closer to our community. "I want that to be true, you weird ass genius. I mean, Kurobans do reuse all the stuff out here in any number of ways beyond their original use. We're always giving a chair, a desk, a bottle, or a radio a 2nd, 3rd, or 10,000th life. But I don't think Father or Lux would want us thinking that way."

Soma

This was the Bodi I knew. The one that could think for himself; seeing the forest, the trees, and the entire ecosystem. I just helped him connect it all together. I shared the conjoining nugget that helped me detect the dissonance sitting right in front of us all. "Anything can be food or poison to the planet as a whole. In Luxite *civilization*, the 'lithium' in question is *one thing* and the instant that *one thing* is no longer necessary or feasible, it is discarded for dead. Then Lux moves on to the *next thing,* searching for whatever will fill the voracious void growing within them.

"Everything has the potential for regeneration. It's a choice whether you honor that or not. Honoring the full lifecycle is part of our ancestral practices. For example, our . . ." — I looked around and moved closer to whisper in his ear—"burial ground." I went back to my normal volume once I was sure no Luxites were in earshot. "There, we're part of an intentional, circular system that returns *us* back to the earth. We flower as special fungi that provide the healing and strength we need to survive this inhumane existence."

Bodi squirmed from the hook of my arm and replied in a meek voice, "That's not true, that's just death. When we pass on, we go to be with Quawd if we follow his will in life."

I pushed him too hard. My raw honesty stretched him far beyond his comfort zone, but I'd already created so much momentum for vulnerability between us I couldn't stop. "Sure, that's *your* thing. Those fictional guardrails steering and interpreting your life may help you, but I've found possibilities elsewhere for myself. People, society, needs, and context multiply outside of that framework. It's much, much more work, if I'm being honest, but to me, my life feels authentic. I don't know what I'm doing or where I'm going half the time, but I've hit phenomenal peaks and permutations of joy and harmony that are simply beyond explanation."

"Yeah, seems exhausting and lonely to me," Bodi strained out an awkward laugh.

I grabbed his hands and stopped him. I moved into his downward view to make sure he saw how serious I was. "It doesn't have to be, you could come too."

"Ooh, ooh. I will," Soma yelled from behind us.

Bodi and I kept staring intently at each other. Our breathing synchronized mere meters away from Kuroba.

He finally threw my hands to the side and barked at Soma, "No the hell you won't!" Then he returned his attention back to me. "S-see what you did!? We gotta go. And you can commute on your own. I can't have you poisoning Soma or *my* success. We're going to Father right now!" He turned and walked indignantly down the dusty Kuroban village path, but I noticed a dimming in his glow as a few green streaks of light wisp towards the steeple at the top of the enormous, well-lit school building.

I could hear him shouting at Soma in the distance as they marched closer to the school building looming over Kuroba. Anansi would certainly still be holed up in his office scheming what conditions he could implement in order to more effectively *civilize* students. I felt bad. So much malice was coming down on her instead of me. And Bodi was simply sacrificing his sister, giving her over to their predatory patriarch to save his ass. Anansi would take pride in punishing his disillusioned dependent, it really didn't matter who it was, it's what he's always done.

I walked the rest of the way home by myself. Whenever I had a peaceful moment, one of my indulgences was people-watching. Mom said I got it from her. The younger her, at least. The evening activity of Kuroba entranced me. By this time of day, worn down-looking Kurobans and pre-assimilation Opps – pompous, pristine, and pumped full of funds– were flooding back to the village. Kuroba was approaching its richest hour, both with relationships and Luxite funds. Folks were gathered along the street trading, purchasing, and providing services. These were the transient times when all of us were together, making life happen before exhaustion and starvation caught up with us. We all worked in concert to pass around what little promissory potential energy we could scrape together to fulfill our perpetually unmet needs.

The commotion of people allowed me to hide in the background. I didn't get the judgmental looks I typically had to parry. I blended in. The collective community cheer quotient was at its highest at this time as well. Nods of support and admiration were thrown between one other and laughter filled the air. It would be hard to tell that this community was hungry, depleted, and generally trapped. But when all of this ephemeral excitement settled down and they had nothing to distract them from their situation, distress returned. They were too tired and broken down to keep the act up once they slid back to whatever shack they rested their head in.

I walked our large dirt boulevard, soaking it all in as I went. I happened to lock eyes with an older soul surrounded by a large crowd. The frail figure quickly avoided my gaze and returned to their jovial activity. They'd assembled a table adorned with refurbished tools to repair old shoes. This cobbler's services were in high demand and they seemed to enjoy their craft. Each customer gave up all sorts of recovered and reinvigorated morsels to the clearly malnourished mortal who preserved their most precious sneakers, slippers, pumps, and boots. Even so, they seemed even more elated than the cobbler, jokes and daps were abundant as they waited for their footwear's rebirth. Whenever I saw an isolated moment of happiness being exuded and shared, I transplanted the characters to an alternate dimension.

I tried to tap into a parallel universe where Kurobans had the resources and the freedom to do as we wished. Even my deftly honed imagination didn't allow me to see my people as they *could be*, as we truly were underneath thick layers of trauma weighing us down. I tried to use my video game reading as inspiration, but it was like my mind glitched every time. I could force a different background, but nothing materially changed. It was still the same scene, with the same people, the same gangly digits, same hollowed eyes, and the exact same sadness right under their momentary disguise. They found a scrawny slice of joy in what most would see as tragedy. I wished we didn't have to generate our own bliss as it was simultaneously being siphoned away. Their symbiotic support for one another manufactured some semblance of happiness despite their deprived circumstances.

These moments encouraged me to build a better world for us, even if I couldn't conceptualize what it might look like in its fullest form. Their energy was captivating, heartwarming, and inspiring. It filled me with more hope after Bodi's Quawd-riddled resistance.

I finally made it to my front yard. I took off my shoes and walked around piles of unsorted junk toward the door. When I made it to the pile nearest our front door, I threw my slime and soot-covered shoes away before stepping inside.

It was eerily quiet, which had me on alert. Usually, Mom was already shouting at me as soon as I stepped in the yard. Something was off. Did she already know what happened at the party? If she did, I was dead.

My breathing got short and my mind cranked into high gear. I had to figure out how to avoid her before she popped up on me. I took swift and soft steps into my room. Maybe I could sneak into my bed and go straight to sleep without being noticed. That way I'd just sneak back out in the morning before she realized I was even here.

I was almost to my room before Mom materialized behind me in a terrifying bubbly voice, "Good day at work today, my child?"

Startled, my knees buckled and I fell right through the thin threshold of my room onto the floor. I clutched my head and squirmed to peek behind the see-through sheet that served as my door, "Whew! Don't sneak up on me like that. I died, I literally thought I was dead. I thought Lux had popped you for the burial ground and I was next. To tie up the loose ends."

In the same gentle, unfamiliar falsetto she responded, "Sorry, I didn't mean to frighten you, my child. I just had a good day and wanted to hear about yours."

What did she mean? Was this some twisted way to convince me to confess to what she already knew? I wasn't going to fall for it. She cared about how things looked for her and for Kurobans as a whole through the eyes of Lux. So I put on an act matching the appearances she wanted to maintain with only a hint of the truth in case she already knew what happened. I stood up and brushed myself off. "G-good. Work was good. I finished all of my assignments for the week already, even the surprises they dropped on us are done and dusted." I noticed her arms were hidden behind her back and guilt coursed through my veins. I closed my eyes and clenched my body to brace myself for whatever atonement she'd cooked up for my dishonesty and misbehavior. Her forced pleasantness had me on edge.

"That's good to hear. You're such a *good* worker. I know we've been through a lot, but I'm proud of how you've got yourself back on track." She pulled out two decorated dirt cookies from behind her, one with a three emblazoned on it in red something and the other with a zero. "I know it's tomorrow, but I wanted to be the first one to wish you a happy 30th."

Whew! She didn't know. Maybe everything that happened in Lux today would just blow over. I could only hope. She was in such a good mood, I wasn't going to burst her bubble. "Um . . . Oh, thanks!" I responded shakily as I used my finger to taste the "frosting" to find out it was a well-aged ketchup. Mom fidgeted her hand holding the partly melted plastic plate of dirt cookies. She continued to look down and had a dreamy longing in her voice. "I know I expect a lot from you. I expect even more from myself. A-and I know I keep pushing you to make a decision for your 30th, b-bu–"

It was always the same story. "Here she is. That's the mom I expect." I struck up a loud ass standing ovation clap. "Please tell me how much of a failure I am. As a matter of fact, tell me how much I'm not helping my people by bringing in enough bread or earning enough 'cred' with the Luxites. Go in on me again to tell me that I'm just like Baldie. Well, you don't know how hard it is! I just can't allow myself to enrich those milky marauders like you. That can't be part of my legacy. Baldie was always true to their values. On top of that, you don't know for certain what their plan was. They wouldn't be taken away so easily. They might be living happy and free beyond the confines of this decrepit existence. Maybe they're waiting for the right moment to free us all and *you're* stopping it," I roared back at her with nearly thirty years of accumulated exasperation. I made sure to keep my distance, enough space to avoid a reactionary strike across my mug.

She moved forward quickly and I leapt back just as quick. She tried to grab my hands while I wiggled free. Mom finally quit advancing and spoke with remorse. "Whoa, whoa, whoa. That's not what I was going to say, darling." Her apologetic tone was something I'd only heard her use around Luxites. "I wanted to apologize for how I've been. All of it. I know that I've forced you to become an adult much faster than any other child should have to. I've leaned on you for everything. For a whole decade of your youth. It took all the former elders mysteriously disappearing and Anan attempting to vault from Elder's page to supreme ruler to shock me back to reality. I'm so sorry it took me so long.

Coming up in the aftermath of the Seed Slaughter times were hard and we expected so much more for our children. That's what *Be*-Baldie and I were focused on in our own ways.

We are the legacy of those that escaped execrable enslavement to merge mycelial mansions with plentiful pocket gardens. Now we're deeply depressed in decaying dirt domes while living on Luxite leftovers. I know you're doing the best you can despite these catastrophic circumstances we're all enduring."

Her nurturing tone transformed my anger into embarrassment. "O-oh, thanks, I guess. And sorry I've been popping off, Mom."

She looked back up and smiled, showing teeth I'd never seen in her mouth. She tilted her head and said, "There *was* something I wanted to tell you about Baldie . . ."

"What! You found them? They're going to free us from Lux like they said they would, right? I knew they were just biding their time. I looked in the sewers every day because I figured that was where they'd hide even though it was a dungeon for divergents." I exclaimed, giddy like a kid on Quawdmas.

She squeezed the plate of cookies and held them up close to my face as she responded, "No. Sorry. But I think I'm ready to get rid of their stuff and move on–"

I slapped the plate out of her hand. "Fuck you mean move on? What's going on with you?" I barely held back a bundle more inflammatory words piling up at the tip of my tongue.

At first Mom just looked shocked, but soon she tensed up and squeezed her eyes closed like she was holding back a huge shit. "Anan said some things today. It was during our consensus meeting to finalize evolving our community stewardship, you know, to make it more equitable. He was making sense. I agree with him. We can all make small shifts, tiny transfigurations, to move our existence to a better space. Moving on is *my* shift. He even recommended you to the Opp-erator corps. He thinks you'd be a star Opp-erator. That could be your shift. It's a ton more money and pres—"

I threw my hands out wide, stuck out my neck, and

shook it rapidly side to side, jolted by utter disbelief and discontent. "I'm sorry, but you can't be serious. I cannot believe the words coming outta your mouth. Anan is a fucking trickster! Everyone knows that. And I don't want to be no damn Opp! You do realize that they'll be watching me 24/7 and scrutinizing everything I do. They're checking if I'll be a good little traitor. If I slip up in the slightest I'll briskly be sent to the subterranean sweatshops. Why don't you pass down your land healing skills to me instead? I'd rather do that."

"You see me laughing?" She looked dead in my eyes. Her gaze was so piercing I could feel her digging around in my brain. She was trying to change my opinion without any of the violence I saw assembling behind her titanium gaze, "Land healing ain't gonna make no money. You can't do shit with it because of the Seed Armistice. You *can* pass their scrutiny if you focus. You are an amazing worker, especially with those technology thinga-ma-jigs. And Anan says Lux needs more of that these days. This is a great opportunity."

I turned to the side and crossed my hands. While side eyeing mom I snapped back at her with a smug smile on my face, "What did Anansi do to twist your mind? You're strict about tradition and respectability, but I never thought you'd pimp your child out to Lux like this. You'd rather let traditional Kuroban land healing die with you? You know Baldie wouldn't've been down with this."

Her smile morphed into a trembling frown, every vein in her face bulged, and she clenched her fists as her breathing got heavy and hurried. "What do you know, you idealistic little fuck? You *need* this." She swung her authoritative momma hand to emphasize her point, but I reflexively dodged. "This will be good for you. You're turning 30 tomorrow and have nothing to show for it. I've tried everything to whip you into shape for this world. I've sacrificed so much. Everything I've done is for your own good. I'm a good mom!"

I started pacing at a frenzied tempo. With every point I made sure to stop and point at her with repugnance pouring from my face. "Oh, I forgot that. Except . . . for a near decade I was busy keeping *your ass* together, right? And remember, when I was six – still so fucking young. Cooking for you, cleaning for you, and taking all your aimless anger. Hell, I'm still walking on eggshells with you bawling at anything that reminds you of your loooong loooost partner. But now you're sooooo ready to let them go. I've given up so much for *you*!"

She stood in front of me and roared at the top of her lungs, wagging her finger the entire time. "You better watch how you talk to me. I'm still your mother. Have some respect. I put a roof over your head, didn't I? Sheesh! I've tried to be nice and support you. Look at how you act. And where is your coat anyways? Huh! You probably traded it for one of your little game books, didn't you? You'll never grow up. That's why I threw out all of that shit already."

I didn't even look to check if she was telling the truth. With the number of times she had threatened me with that, I knew she was ready to walk it like she talked it. I snapped, roaring right the fuck back at her maternal finger of might. "Oh, *now* you want respect. Sure, I'll just materialize some out of no-*fucking*-where. You need me to bring home food from Lux for you tomorrow too? And tithe my whole fucking paycheck to fulfill our household's obligation to the Earth Going fund? Because I know your scary ass don't have shit here! You really have no idea, do you? No matter how hard I work in Lux, there'll still be too much month at the end of the money. You're too busy crying into some old fourth-hand shirts and tending to that mushroom cemetery to see the writing on the wall."

She lowered her volume and waved me off with enough

dismissiveness that I felt the hefty slap across my face I dodged earlier. "Pssht! What the fuck ever. You don't know any better. You're just like *them*. Ungrateful! You'll have a worse fate if you don't watch out. Plus you smell like shit!"

Her dig cut me to the white meat, but I wouldn't admit it. "I'm proud of it. I'm going to bed. Some of us have work tomorrow. And don't you gotta run around making Kurobans lives worse. You might need a little rest for that too, right?"

I turned around and stomped behind the tattered sheet dividing my room from the rest of our home dome. My time changing into ratty pajamas was a brief solace, filling my soul back up with thoughts about Baldie. I wish they were here so fucking bad. Clinging to the childish faith that they would somehow reappear over twenty years later to save us all. In the meantime, I'd keep trying to perform as if I was the new and improved version of them.

Back then they told me Kuroba wasn't ready for a liberator, that's why they were "exiled." I laid in my bed wrestling with how I was doing any better. I didn't know if Kuroba was ready for anything different. Especially if the Elders, Mom included, were devolving toward devout acquiescence. Staring up at the ceiling in the dark my brain was revving up. The splotchy surface seemed to be covered with Mom's words and millions of other concerns racing through my mind, layering and complicating one another. Tonight was going to be another restless night. I had no idea how I'd sleep peacefully again.

STAGE COMPLETE

```
Health Points . . . . . . . . . . . 50%
Magic Power . . . . . . . . . . . 30%
```

Mission #1: Figure Out What Happened While
            I Was Dreaming . . . . BITS AND PIECES
Mission #2: Return Home . . . . SUCCESS
Mission #3: Don't Let Mom Know About Party . . . . SUCCESS BUT TOUGH
                                                            TO MAINTAIN
Side Quest #1: Support Soma's Curiosity
               While Keeping Her Safe . . . . FAILURE
Side Quest #2: Keep Bodi as My Ally . . . . I CAN ONLY HOPE

Experience Points Gained [190]
Coins [-20] . . . Can't Wait for Payday
Items Received [NONE]
Status Effect [NONE]

Liberation Spell Cast on Soma.
Bodi Has Left Your Party!

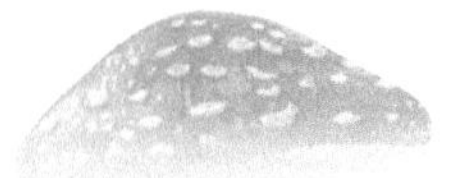

Stage 3: Software Update

Chapter 7: Firewall Removed

A muted knock slithered from the heavy front door. Before I heard it creak open and closed again, hushed farewells signified some voices left and some stayed.

The people left inside were muffled, but I could definitely tell they were arguing.

One voice was unmistakably Mom, yet in a version with much more light, life, and levity. Without the ever-present bristle years of yelling left on her esophagus. The opposing voice was unfamiliar, but its melodic cadence sparked a burning in my belly. The words, "Congratulations! Memory access granted," scrolled across my blurry point of view. The scene was pre-rendered, without the billions of triangles being constructed and colored in. My eyes were slowly focusing. With every passing second I could discern more of the detail around me. The first thing I recognized was the ceiling of my room. I was staring at the same ceiling I went to sleep scanning. My room seemed a little off though. The clearest difference I determined was the missing sheet separating me from the central living space. Then the yelling got clearer.

The unfamiliar voice whined to Mom, "We can't live like this anymore, my love. None of us should stand for this. You of all people know what we've been through since the Seed Slaughter – forced to grow up instantly amid countless atrocities – this shit ain't getting better. Even the trash we scrounge to scrape by is worthless now. Where does that leave us? There's much, much more stuff, but it's so poor quality it may only last one more reuse, if that. Then its highly processed, toxic, artificial bonds can no longer hold the form Lux has forced it into."

"Don't be so extreme. Remember what your Maame used to say, the land will provide for us. We just have to trust it," Mom snapped back.

The entire building shook as the unrecognizable person banged their hand against the wall. "Puh-lease!" the voice said. "I'm tired of fighting so hard to still starve. There's way too much month at the end of the money. We can't just eat fungi, hun. The Elders are too worried about their *own* grip on power. We could cultivate a stable food supply if we really tried."

"At least they're here with us trying to figure it out day by day," Mom retorted.

"Do you understand that I've planned, quite possibly, the most pivotal rebellious ultimatum ever devised? It has the potential to topple the whole power structure, the proxy one *here* as well as the very foundation of Lux itself. I don't have time for an Earth Going Reconciliation, I have GELD allies to free sweetie," the first voice stressed confidently.

"That may be true, but you've been gone for months," Mom replied back. "Does my partner even want to spend time with their child, much less me, before they disappear again?" Hearing those words triggered me to sit up on my tattered mattress to probe my suspicions as to who Mom was sparring with. Why today? Was this real?

Mom's nameless partner shot back, "Yes I do – I do, I really, really, really do. Believe me. B-but this action will – *essentially* – liberate us. Do you understand what that means? Babe, this will allow me to spend time with y'all *forever*. We can do the Earth Going after this if they still want it. That's their business if they want to hold a grudge after that!" They didn't deny it. But was it really Baldie? I clenched my teeth to contain my excitement. If this wasn't real, I'd be devastated.

Mom replied, "Huh-ha! And what about the next direct action o-or your next mission or the next grand campaign to pour yourself into? Lux is onto you, *you do know that*? They've been waiting for you to resurface and your dumbass pops up the day after your 30th. You haven't made a career decision and you're still moving through their nasty-ass sewers provoking Lux. That's why the Elders came. They had to name you the Person Who Harmed (PWH). This isn't just about you. The whole community is at risk. What do you think will happen to us if you don't show up in the next hour?"

I moved closer and peered into the living area to see shadows stretching from the moonlight beaming over them through the front door. A youthful Mom was standing on the far side and her partner, distorted and pixelated like a futuristic contre-jour interview, stood in front of a messy stack of papers. Even their strong glow was grainy, like it was being obscured by an opaque filter.

The blurred-out Baldie's voice seemed to inflate with optimism and curiosity. "Wait! Honeylove, you're onto something. This'll be perfect. I may not have to spread these pamphlets. This could be a better way to spread our mission through Kuroba. I can collectively spark their consciousness at the ceremony."

I was too nervous to go any closer, shocked by the mere presence of the person I'd modeled my life's mission after. But the burning feeling in my gut built up with every word they spoke.

"No, this isn't a chance for revolution!" Mom scolded.

"Listen to the Elders, 'this is your last opportunity for account-ability.' You've harmed our *delicate* relationship with Lux. This is about more than you. You might be able to get away, but who knows what Lux will add to the Seed Armistice if you embarrass them. This is serious!"

I felt their resolve and couldn't help myself. Wailing my little eyes out, I scurried over. I was my six-year-old self again. On that tearful dash over, I was so distraught and focused my dramtic reunion I slipped on an errant pamphlet on the floor. My diminutive hands flailed in every direction in an attempt to slow my momentum before slamming into the pile of pamphlets behind blurry-Baldie.

Both of my parents stopped to stare at me, eyes wide at my sudden appearance. I climbed my way out of the clutter of papers and clenched onto my darling parent's distorted leg. Gripping tight with my arms and legs wrapped around their clouded calf I exclaimed, "No, please be careful *Whurump-rump*. Don't get in trouble." I called them something. It came out and everybody else heard it. But all *I* heard was a digitized, dissolving log drum.

"Oh, my sweetness. Don't worry, I can handle this." I let go of their leg and they bent down with open arms. Jumping into their embrace, the vibration of their voice traveled through my chest. "My Maame, your grand-Maame, who you never got to meet, held many of our ancestral practices. The Earth Going is one of the few we still maintain, that's all. Nothing scary. Have faith, I'll use my ceremonial PWH statement wisely."

Mom rolled her eyes as her partner hugged and kissed me while looking at her. Up close I canoodled with a fuzzy form, their unmistakable resplendent cranium was indistinguishable even behind a blur. Their affection was infectious. Before Mom walked out on our cuddle extravaganza, she shouted out across the threshold into the kitchen area, "Fifty-five minutes

Whurump-rump! You better be ready." That distorted name again. It seemed to only be me that couldn't hear Baldie's real name, something was blocking it.

Baldie shouted back, "Don't worry about me, love-love. It's a no-brainer as long as they follow the agenda we've honed for generations. This Earth Going holds as much potential for salvation as it does for damnation. I want to spend more time with Copykid here until then." They turned to give me an exaggerated smile before asking, "Do *you* know about what goes on at our great Earth Going Reconciliations, babylove?"

I shook my head with a quick, frightened rattle from side to side.

They knelt closer and opened their arms. "It's nothing to be frightened of. It's a judiciously curated space, developed and brought over from our homelands. It's been maintained as a space for authentic community accountability and transformation. We used it to get to the roots of harm. As we all dig into that shared why, we reconstruct our relational receptacle. This is our collective craft toward creating a community devoid of abuse. Individual, collective, and societal violence are all attributed and addressed. It's our distinctive justice process. Kurobans unearthing the root of harm in order to re-steady the entire tree. Oh honeybee, you'll love it."

I crunched one of my shoulders into my ear and responded sheepishly, "Sounds like you're in big trouble though, Baldie."

"Not at all my Copykid. It's a glorious, generative experience that's become a continuous part of Kuroban advancement, babe. It kicks off with a grand celebration on our mycelial burial grounds. Music. Dancing. Mushrooms. Pure revelry, just like the old days. Everyone relinquishes control and concern to channel our ancestors and descendants. It helps us make aligned, more inclusive, long-term decisions. That, along with our agreements, boundaries, and organic processes construct a container for us to work through the most trying topics."

Their fantastical explanation seemed too good to be true. I scooted forward. "*Everyone* is involved?"

"Past, present, and future, hun. We all have some accountability and impact on harm that happens in *our* community, even if it's miniscule. So we should all assist, appropriately weighted, in its eradication, right?"

"I guess so. What about harm from outside of Kuroba? How're you gonna bring Kuroba together? What are you going to say?" I stared longingly, ready to soak up their wisdom.

They held my tiny hands to my mouth and nuzzled their hands while they answered. "Good questions my clever child. *We all* decide how to deal with harm. We debate, discuss, and deliberate on how systemic power impacts us all. In our discovery phase, after the initial statements, we collaborate to develop strategies to counteract external forces.

"I have no personal agenda for this ceremony. I trust the reciprocal process as-is. It shouldn't matter what forces we're confronting, even one as powerful, widespread, and ingrained as Lux. This is about *our* people. I know I've been away a bunch, but it's all been for us, for Kuroba. The strategies I tell you before you slumber have been honed by all of us in GELD, not just me. GELD's dwindling defenders and I are laser-focused on subverting Lux's oppressive tentacles.

"We've been protecting Kuroba. Ever since the Seed Slaughter, we've defended against the menacing culture of alienation, acculturation, and abandonment seeping into our township. But time is running out, sweetheart."

Baldie's statement made me whimper while snuggling deep into them. "Can I help?"

They patted my serpentine spine curled up in their lap. The beat of their heart lulled me into a peaceful state, the rush of their blood pumping, and the churn of their stomach. "Rest your pretty little heart Copykid. I see a great future for Kuroba. Your generation will bring about change better than I could ever imagine. We even have a new GELD recruit not much older than yourself, Wafaa'. I've already learned a lot from their youthful insight. They'll be leading the effort to build power systems for our village. We'll use the mountain to store solar power, thus bending time and capability. Soon we'll introduce water harvesting and recycling. Who knows, maybe by the time you're my age we'll figure out a food source besides furtive fungi and lavish Luxite leftovers.

"Just like Wafaa's skills are needed to drive our future, your skills will be needed as well. You'll discover your place because we need everyone. And I mean *everyone*. For now, do better than me. Be freer than me. I've been ready for this. I'll speak from my gut and the right words'll find me. But I do need an escort. Would you be available?"

Their response made me feel like nothing in the world would hurt me. I nodded my head, bubbling with glee.

My blurry, distorted parent and I got up. Little hand in obscured bigger hand, we walked to the front door. As we crossed the doorway, a bright pea-tinged light burst from my gut and flashed into the sky overhead. I released Baldie's hand, ran behind them, and wrapped myself around their legs again. Light illuminated the entire landscape before disappearing over the horizon. Baldie tried to detach me from their leg. "What are you doing? Come on, let's go."

"Y-you didn't see that in the sky? It came outta me!" I whined at my placid parent.

A befuddled Baldie shouted, "What!? I was taking a last ogle at the Drinking Gourd before–"

Quicker than we could decipher what happened, we noticed a small stream of early morning commuters shuffling down the boulevard in their shoddy suits steer clear of something obstructing their flow. As that something got closer I saw a younger, much thinner, more sinister, more frazzled Anansi, marching briskly toward us. He charged towards our dirt dome with a scowl on his face, flanked by two stoic Luxites in lock-step just behind him.

One arctic assailant wore a finely-fitted and pressed dinner suit, the other rocked a priestly vestment with the symbol of Quawd around his neck. They stood in direct contrast to the meek mess of activity from my illuminated people.

Anansi announced his arrival before he made it to our yard. "I, Anansi, the first and only Elder's page of Kuroba and liaison to Lux, have arrived on orders from the great Elders and our emissaries from Lux to escort *Whurump-rump* to the *new and improved* Earth Going Reconciliation."

Baldie let go of my hand slowly and knelt down to whisper in my ear. "Stay here, I'll handle this."

They scooted out to face the youthful Anansi at attention beyond our feeble fence. I stared on from our front yard fighting my feet from running after my indiscernible idol. The sharp-suited Luxite moved in closer and tapped a random rock with the tip of their toe. Anansi jumped down to wipe the Luxite's glistening boots faster than the rock stopped rolling across the dirt. He blasted out a glob of spit that swallowed up the microscopic speck of dirt before scrubbing it vigorously with the bottom of his baggy, misshapen polo shirt.

The Luxite scoffed. "Disgusting! That's coming out of your allowance."

Baldie approached them and pointed in the opposite direction. The three visitors glanced at me before turning their back and began to talk. I couldn't hear them so I scanned my surroundings to distract my worried mind.

The front yard trade markets were just getting up and

running at this early hour. Our neighbor specialized in books. I used to sneak a couple from time to time when I was jonesin' for learning. They switched out a makeshift sign in front of their yard to mark their opening. As they primped one of their large sorted piles of tattered textbooks and mangled magazines, our eyes connected. They gave me a toothy smile. I smiled back and the neighbor sauntered over to me. "How are ya?"

Behind me, I heard forceful peaks from Baldie's intensifying discussion with Anansi and the Luxites. By the time I turned around my parent was spitting blood. The mozzarella-skinned missionary tucked their hefty, hairy leg back under their thick gown. Baldie's midsection still had an indention where the missionary's leg had struck. The other Luxite muscled Baldie into a whirring electro-mechanical harness, binding their body in place.

I cried out, running toward them. Baldie yelled, "No, my sweetness, just get your mother and meet us at the school they've been erecting. Hurry!"

I rushed back inside and shouted for Mom. She dashed into the living area as I screamed frantically, "They're taking *Whurump-rump* to the school. Let's go!" She grabbed a ratty robe and ran out in her crêpe-thin house shoes dragging my shocked skeleton behind.

Outside, the streets were suddenly desolate. The yard shops were abandoned, not a Kuroban in sight as far as the eye could see. The silence was heavy. Nothing but a foreboding wind blowing down the boulevard.

We rushed to the unblemished Luxite-funded school at the entrance to our dilapidated community. We arrived to pandemonium. The entire populace was there, whether they were work bound or not. Everyone was clamoring to pass the impenetrable Blau barriers surrounding the steps to the school building. Confusion, anger, and fear were already at a rolling boil when we landed. It was a cacophony of shouts, banging pots, and electricity sparking in every direction. Overhead, blue and white helicopters touting the symbol of the Blaus circled, adding a background noise that heightened the tension. At the top of the school steps my blurry Baldie was on their knees, still bound by the metallic ligature. Behind them stood the three Elders in their colorful ceremonial garb, with Anansi and his Luxite enforcers looming in the rear.

Mom and I fought to the front corner of the school's incomplete stairs, as close as we could. Baldie looked even more distorted, blurred, and faded atop the landing to go into the school filled with construction scaffolding. We reached out for them as the weight of the frenzied crowd pressed forward from behind, crushing my lungs. Suddenly, a spotlight shot down from one of the helicopters and further illuminated the main show at the landing atop the stairs. Every Kuroban jumped backward and I could breathe again. The intense light overpowered the morning sunshine and made my parent, Anansi, and the Elders squint while the Luxite emissaries didn't flinch. The suited one slipped on dark glasses which triggered the preacher to step forward. A booming voice shook the ground. "Order, order, I call this trial to order. For the Lord's sake, I need silence!"

My sharp little mind snapped to the source of the ground-rattling sound hovering overhead. But beside Baldie, the Luxite reverend's bizarre behavior was noteworthy. They didn't react like the rest of us, even their pearlescent pal looked up to the helicopter. Instead, the floury friar raised their arms in the sign of Quawd with their head bowed as the commands thundered down from above. From below I spied their slight jaw movements as they spoke into their rippling robe. Somehow they must've projected their voice through the powerful helicopter speakers.

Anansi motioned forward to someone in their powerful stair top tribunal. One of the Elders wiped their brow, gave a sigh, and stepped forward to start their announcement. "Medaase family, the PWH–" the sunglassed Luxite looked at Anansi.

"I think you mean 'Welcome all' and you are referring to the suspect. The *suspect* has arrived, but please continue, Y-Your G-Grace," Anansi awkwardly interrupted.

"S-sure, of course," the Elder stammered. "Not used to that terminology, but yes, in this case we are doing things a little" — they turned and looked at the Luxites with Anansi standing right behind like a confused puppy— "different. We've found an understanding with Lux to handle this Earth Going in a more *direct* manner in order for us all to receive immediate forgiveness. We will *all* be absolved for the various atrocities committed by the P–suspect and any other Kuroban accomplice. It's a clean start for us all." The elder flashed their eyes at Anansi and he nodded in approval.

Anansi stepped in front of the Elders. "We have all the evidence on what the suspect has done. This is an open and shut case. They are the quintessential aimless Kuroban over 30 without a career conscription. A shiftless, shady scoundrel. They've been a thorn in the side of our tranquility with Lux. They must be punished. There is no need for a drawn-out ceremony nor any trust that the PWH will change in any way. This is who they are: irredeemable and unrepentant. Luckily, Lux has committed to forgive us for everything, including our gravest collective violation, harboring this hardened criminal. They've even offered us a new, *extremely* well-funded field of work assignments that have stability as well as room for advancement. The Opp-erators corps. Only the most *professional* Kurobans will be accepted into this most generous opportunity. For this gracious gift we have to commit to Quawd and remand this heinous villain into Luxite custody to atone for their crimes against harmonious advancement between Kuroban and Luxite communities."

I choked hearing Anansi's confounding assertion. Without a second for us to breathe or digest Anansi's audacious claims, the bleached bodyguard in a suit marched over and grabbed the bound Baldie.

The collective cries of the crowd struck up once again as the tag team of Luxites wrenched my struggling parent like they were an untamable Tarpan. Until Baldie wriggled their confined form free. They fell flat on their stomach facing me on the side of the steps. They looked deep into my soul, their eyes holding back tears as they wailed, "I'm sorry. Kuroba isn't ready for a liberator yet. Lead better than me, and remember . . . we're still free."

I tried to remain strong watching them not cry in their

painful situation. "I could never measure up to you. I need you. Promise me you have a plan . . ." I couldn't hold back shit as I whimpered watching them being hauled up from the floor of the school entryway.

They yelled back before they were swallowed up. "Please worry about yourself Copykid, no matter what you believe, your mother can handle herself. I'm just impatient."

I reached out, but Anansi slapped my hand back. I drew on every fiber of force in my tiny form to free myself from the raucous crowd; bawling and screaming as my heart was ripped out once again. Mom sat frozen behind us.

The crowd of Kurobans banged on the barriers in a calculated cadence that sped up as their cries were ignored. Our mad mob started to swarm the Luxites, dragging a broken Baldie to a helicopter that landed on the edge of the wasteband. A voice bellowed out from the helicopter. "Back up or you'll be next to the labor camp."

The agitated crowd stumbled backward and died down. I looked back at Mom. My eyes begged her to do something. She was my last hope to save them. But she was down in the dirt howling in agony as tears poured from her face. She swung her arms in every direction, ripped at her clothes, and clawed at her skin in anguish. And at that moment, I knew there was nothing else that could be done.

A leafy light flared out from my midsection once again and flashed across the sky. The collective illumination quickly dimmed across Kuroba. I blinked and found myself back at a messy home.

～

A FEW DAYS HAD PASSED. It was my seventh birthday and our home was flooded up to my eyes with sadness. A misery so solid and sticky it spilled from our dome home. The heartache was so heavy, it suppressed our movements. Mom hadn't stopped crying since the ceremony – no – public kidnapping. She hadn't eaten or bathed. I could barely get her to drink water to keep her tears flowing, yet she cursed at me the entire time. I did everything in my adolescent ability to maintain our household and livelihood. It was all I knew. But of course our meager abode was in shambles. This was nothing to thrust upon a six or seven-year-old under any circumstance, especially after what I'd been through. I was barely eating, not because I didn't want to, but I'd already eaten everything we had the day Baldie was taken away. For a little traumatized kid like me, it was too daunting to forage for scraps alone in the vast wasteband. So I made my first major survival decision to keep myself and the parent I had left alive. The repercussions came knocking.

It was the detestable Anansi with the deferential Elders in tow.

"How are you doing, little one? Are your parents available?" Anansi asked in a sweet, inquisitive voice with a twisted smile on his face.

I moved slightly to the side and cracked the door open so that they could hear Mom's crying. "I'm sorry, I'm all you got. What do *you* need?" I replied while looking down to avoid Anansi. Besides hearing Mom, our visitors got a whiff of the funk wafting from inside and spotted the rodents rooming with us.

"Can't you see this is the family *Whurump-rump* left behind Anansi? They're hurting," one of the Elders hissed at Anansi.

"Yeah, but someone has been pilfering the burial fruit. Would you know anything about that young wo-*meh*-person?" he sputtered out as he lost his way enroute to his accusation.

I tapped into Baldie's honest brilliance. I was too tired to craft an evasive fiction. "Yes. I was starving so I swiped a few mushrooms from the burial grounds. I needed to. So that I could have the energy to fetch our daily water and run our family trading grounds and keep this place clean an–"

"We get it!" one of the Elders said.

"Sorry, of course. I needed *something* to eat! Not enough to get noticed o-or make a dent in *all* that we have or even to get full. Just enough to calm my tummy. I didn't know what else to do."

"Aha, just as I suspected. I knew I saw you! The apple doesn't fall far, does it? We need to punish swiftly or this will blowback much worse with Lux," Anansi said.

I answered back in defeat, "Sure, take me. I'd rather be wherever Baldie is rather than here. This is the worst birthday ever!"

One of the Elders stepped forward and knelt down to pull my trembling hands close to their chest. "Don't be hasty Anansi. What does alerting Lux solve? It will only cause more problems for an already precarious community. This is a child. There is no issue with Lux. This is purely an internal issue, so it can be solved with a *community* solution. You want to learn how to lead Kuroba, do it through your actions," The Elder didn't look back when they made their mandate to Anansi. Instead, they held me closer. "You're assigned to support this family in any way they need until they can provide for themselves. Treasure this sweet child as your own. Do I make myself clear, Anansi?"

Anansi gritted his ragged teeth, but managed to force out a response. "Uh-uh, yeah, as you command, great Elder."

The Elder released their embrace and looked me in my eyes. "I'm sorry about all of this and for not being here sooner.

Happy birthday little one. It's your birthday, right? How old are you turning?"

I looked down and my response fell down like the tears that seeped from the corners of my eyes. "Se-seven."

The comforting-Elder wiped my eyes. "Wow, you're really growing up. I want to personally apologize to you for bringing any negativity on this seventh anniversary of your earthside arrival. We did what we had to do for *all* of Kuroba, but what it has done to you is not right. Sometimes I think the few birthdays we have are some of the most rare treasures that Lux can never take away from us. We were wrapped up in our own struggles. If I'm honest, we were frightened to lose our — *uh* – depressing stability. So much so that we didn't realize the ripples from our tough decisions. Mr. Anansi will take care of you. You are in good hands, I promise. We don't have much, but you will not worry about food again. And he'll make sure to get you something really yummy for your celebration today. Right Anansi?"

"Most definitely, great Elder." Anansi saluted from behind the Elders who had now all moved in to surround me in apologetic cuddles.

"Now, I'm sorry we can't stay any longer. We have to work with many more families struggling and in need, but Anansi will be your personal connection to us. If you need anything let him know and we will make it happen," the comforting-Elder said with a polite smile.

I nodded my head, forcing a deadpan face to hide my frustration with their misjudgment. The comforting-Elder rose back up gracefully and waved goodbye along with the other two Elders close behind. I noticed the stern glance they gave Anansi as they passed him and walked off to handle their duties.

Anansi and I stared at each other for a few long minutes, a

true squint and brow standoff. He broke first. "Well, what do you want, squirt?"

I furrowed my brow deeper and right on cue my stomach growled like a protective lion to answer him.

"W-well go inside and I'll be back with something for you to eat," Anansi said as he awkwardly shuttled me inside while jerking the door closed. My unforgiving gaze tracked him through the window, turning around all the way through his walk, skip, and jog out of our yard.

He never did return. I sat around the house feeling sorry for myself. Mom's melancholy finally unlocked my own sadness. I'd been hiding it since Baldie was stripped away. But having to rely on a sadistic asshole to live felt like a new kind of hell. Especially the very asshole that sacrificed Baldie for his short-sighted credibility. It left me feeling vulnerable, anxious, and conquered. I knew I needed the help, but my little mind short-circuited trying to figure out how to request another tempo-rary guardian. Anyone other than Anansi.

A liquid-like glob of lime light squirted from my stomach and flowed upward through the roof. I stared at the spot where it came from inside me, too scared to look around at what tragedy the light was responding to this time.

Another, lighter, knock came at the door. Maybe the Elders realized their mistake in subjecting me to Anansi's "care." But I was surprised to see a lanky, mini-Anansi on the other side of the door.

"Grand risings! I'm Bodi, he/him. My venerable father, Anansi the Righteous, sent me with provisions for you." He looked about the same age as me, but about twice the height and heft. On his back he had a dusty backpack. The zipper was hanging on by threads which was probably why the bag was cinched closed with a long dirty sock instead. I held my breath and braced for Anansi's trickery to unravel itself. He swung the ravaged bag around and unknotted the sock holding it closed. His hands dug in to pull out a vinyl bag whose broken handles had been retied to make usable once again. I moved cautiously closer, curious as to what rations he'd deliver, but then the smell of the scrumptious sustenance hit my nose.

It only took an instant before I ripped the bag from Bodi's grasp, tore it open and stuffed every edible bit into my mouth. I threw my hand in each greasy takeout container and crammed the contents in my mouth without concern for chewing. It was a mess of food that my little body hadn't ever experienced, especially over the last painful days. I couldn't help but smile as I crushed the meal in front of Bodi. "Thanks – *mmm* – so much. This food is so – *mmm* – good and warm. How did you get it – *mmm* – hot?"

Bodi kept a stone-face while answering me. "Father said to deliver this food and leave immediately without engaging in any frivolous conversation."

"Come on – *mmm* – I don't get to – *mmm* – talk to many – mmm – kids."

"I can't. Father is strict, and he'll know if I'm lying."

"Here, how about you not lie and instead let *someone else* 'talk with me." I grabbed the sock that he used to tie his bag and put my arm in it. I shaped my fingers and thumb into a beak inside the sock. I opened and closed the puppet's mouth to demonstrate the frivolous stand-in I had in mind. "You wouldn't be talking Bodi, it'll be me. I'm just an innocent little sock puppet trying to be honest with my new friend."

Bodi laughed as I took off the sock and gave it to him. "That might work. The sock puppet will tell you all the things I can't." He stuffed his ample arm into the sock and awkwardly operated the sock mouth as he talked to me. "Father was bequeathed a gently used solar oven directly from a Luxite household he helped a couple weeks ago. We've been using it every day since! Also, this is just a small sampling of the special leftovers we started receiving directly from Luxite restaurants, event venues, and grocery stores. Father said the request to feed you was short notice so he let me share some of our food with you." Bodi, beaming and hugging his new sock buddy, looked as if a weight had been lifted off him. He bounced from side to side as he'd finally been uncorked.

I noticed his excitement and the hot food had me feeling hospitable. "Come on in. This has officially become the best birthday. *Mmmm.* You want some?"

He walked in with shaky steps, looking around the entire time, while he spoke through his puppet proxy. "I didn't know it was your birthday. Happy Earthstrong! How old?"

I replied back with a ton of food in my mouth, "*Mmm-even.*"

He grinned as he sat down in the main living area with the sock still displayed prominently on his long arm. "Oh great, that'll be me in 2 months," he said. I squatted nearby like a voracious vulture when he asked, "Wait, is someone . . . *crying?*"

"*Mmm*-that's Mom. *Mmm* – she's been like that since your Dad had her partner *–mmm* – m-my other parent – *mmm* – locked up – *mmm*," I replied matter-of-factly between bites.

"S-sorry. B-b-but hold on," Bodi said through the sock again. He rummaged through his raggedy rucksack with his un-socked hand to pull out a thick, wilting magazine. "Here's a little gift for you, if you're open to it. It might be a little messed up since it was sitting under the food."

With my sad stomach somewhat satiated I turned towards him to check out his gift. "To-wer A-ark 2200?"

"Oh, so you *do* know how to read? Perfect! All the kids in Lux fight over the things in this book. Father says they're called video games," Bodi boasted, holding the sock puppet without moving the mouth. He came closer to give me a better look inside.

"Yeah, I've been reading since I was about 3. My kidnapped parent taught me. Reading was one of their strategies to keep my mind free, they said." I rifled through the strange book and was drawn in by the detailed contents. Story, statistics, screenshots, and strategy. There was so much bursting from this little book that I'd never seen. But it was certainly the strategy that drew me in. It reminded me of Baldie. This book seemed like something they'd create if they weren't defending Kuroba. It gave me a little comfort, like they were still around.

As I was gushing over the game guide, Bodi crept over my shoulder and talked to me without the sock as a proxy. "I'm sorry about your parents, both of them. But our parent situations are kinda similar, you know?"

I slapped the book closed and turned to look back at Bodi. "What you talkin 'bout? Your dad is literally the reason I'm at least 75% on the orphan scale."

Bodi shied away, looking embarrassed. "W-well, you see my mom is missing too."

"*Probably had to get away from your slimy-ass daddy,*" I mumbled to myself while looking away from Bodi. I turned back to him, ready to spit some sass, but his head was drooping. I couldn't take my frustrations out on him anymore. "That sucks."

"It does. I really miss her. She was a spiritual guide that specialized in the stories of our original homelands. Father says she couldn't take it when Lux introduced us to Quawd." He looked up slightly and I could see the twinkle in his eyes as he spoke about his mother.

"That's too bad, but at least you have your dad. You hear my mom in the other room, I have no one." I shot back, unsatisfied with his comparison of our situations.

"It's not the same, but Father isn't around much. He's always busy with the Elders or taking trips to Lux. He's pretty demanding too. He put me in charge of taking care of everything at home. He says, 'this will help you develop the maturity you need to succeed.' Then Father brings home fancy Luxite gifts and food from time to time and leaves out again. If I need anything my uncle, my mom's younger brother, helps out," Bodi said with conviction. His situation sounded closer to mine, especially because that kind of despicable behavior sounded like the type of parenting expected from Anansi.

"Yeah, your dad is the worst," I said with a hearty laugh. He didn't laugh at first which made me a little nervous. We stared at each other before he let out a loud cackle and I continued my satisfied guffaw.

As our shared laughter died down, Bodi's face got serious again. "You're pretty smart. Could you read the rest of this game guide to me, *bredren*?"

I replied with a grin, "Sure, bredren. I got you. And I'll always look out for you. But I expect honesty from you. Even if I might not like it, or you do it through a sock, just give me a signal that you're still with me despite our daily difficulties. Please tell me the truth. My other parent always said honesty is the foundation of true relationships. And I need people that I can trust right now."

Bodi nodded emphatically.

We spent the better part of the next hour reading and laughing at the video game book he gave me. The whole scene faded to black gracefully. When the memory was finally gone and I could no longer see nor hear myself or Bodi. I only saw a blank loading screen.

**Minigame Complete!
Loading Next Stage . . .**

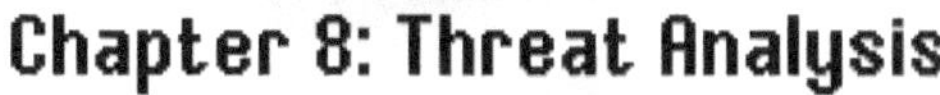

Chapter 8: Threat Analysis

Mission #1: Make Amends with Bodi
Mission #2: Make It Through the Work Day
Mission #3: Avoid Implicating Other Kurobans
Mission #4: Maintain Work Assignment

Another raucous rising. When I woke up my body was even more drained than when I went to sleep, but my soul was scintillating. The smell of the rotting dump assaulted my nostrils. Normally the cool mountain sea breeze came down from the summit to counteract the dump's funk, but this morning isolated packets of stank broke through the still, ominous air. I rolled over and gripped my Libook with determination. Curled up in my bed I could almost imagine the warmth of Baldie's lap, their heartbeat, the rhythmic treble of their voice, and even the friggin' peaceful pressure of their blood pumping. It gave life to my tired body after a particularly restless night. I had the drive to prove my doubters wrong. I *had* to make my dreams come true, for me, for Baldie, and for the future of Kuroba.

Speaking of doubters, the house was *extra* quiet. I didn't hear mom's sobs, which was odd. I tucked my Libook into my loose waistband and scurried over to her cramped alcove. She was nowhere to be seen, just an old, patched-up gray suit laid out on the assemblage of worn-out cushions she used as her mattress. I sighed from the bottom of my belly, hoping today would have less drama. I was ready to start fresh after waking up with new inspiration.

I was getting ready for work slower than a disenchanted sloth on salary. While I was splashing some water on my undercarriage to rinse off any residue leftover from the post-party evacuation, I spotted a scrap of paper. It was tucked in the bottom corner of the cracked mirror in our makeshift bathroom, in between the mirror and the crusty cup where we compiled leftover soap shards. I opened up the neatly folded, weathered shred of paper.

My child,

I couldn't bear to tell you in person, especially on this special birthday. I am extremely disappointed in you. The trouble you've caused in Lux is weighing heavily on Kuroba. We've all been put in a tough position, but I've made amends to save you. I expect to see you straight home after work. I laid out clothes for you in my room. Tonight, there will be an Earth Going Reconciliation and you will be the PWH.

*Just in case you're worried, there will be no Luxite involvement. It'll only be slightly different from our typical payday celebrations. All you have to do is make the **right** career decision and everything will go as planned. Instead of midnight, you must make your decision during your PWH statement at the ceremony. And how lucky you are, you have two excellent options to choose from. Most barely have one.*

*All in all, you **must** choose either your current work assign-*

*ment or the Opp-erators. That's all. We expect your decision
at or before the ceremony. Or else we can't protect you from
Lux any longer.*

*With Sadness and Love,
Your mother – Mama*

I was livid. She knew how much my career *conscription* was already burdening me, but to make it a spectacle at the Earth Going tonight was irresponsible. Did she know what I did yesterday at the Luxite party? What did she agree to on my behalf? And with whom? It better not be Lux. That's exactly what happened with Baldie.

I should at least find some way to enjoy this birthday without worrying about my looming dilemma. So I went to grab the original Tower Ark 2200 game guide Bodi gave me when we met on my seventh birthday. It didn't matter if I had work or a huge career conscription to decide on today, I was going to continue my birthday tradition no matter what.

I panicked when the ripped, wrinkled, and well-read game guide was nowhere to be found. Then I remembered my argument with Mom last night and realized she really hadn't been playing. She'd re-trashed it all. My entire stack of reading materials: game guides, user manuals, textbooks, and all the technology I was tinkering with was gone.

I squeezed my fists as tight as I could, hoping to crush time and space itself. I didn't want to deal with any of it. The need to yell rumbled in my throat, but my rage dissipated when I saw the threatening letter from Mom again. Crappy birthday to me! My anger morphed into embarrassment. A mortification that despite all I had done to set myself apart, my own mother still saw me as a traitor. I still might face a similar fate as my long-lost parent. And now I had to deal with whatever consequences were coming at work.

The first change was Bodi. He never came. I waited and waited, but he never arrived to walk to work with me. Bodi had actually followed through and cut ties with me like he said he would.

After watching the crowd of commuters thin out, I decided to go on my own. I didn't want to make my situation any worse than it already was. Excessive tardiness wasn't worth it.

My first solo commute ever was lonely. It gave too much time for my imagination to dredge up visions of fantastic failure.

Walking into Lux sent a shiver down my spine. It wasn't only because I no longer had my mycelial coat to weather the Luxite December, but something felt cosmically off. My gut winced with worry.

I made it to eduGames to witness major construction going down all over the cold, concrete building. My felt-but-never-seen boss Robert was there in the flesh too. I recognized him from when I eavesdropped on his conversation in the kitchen yesterday. He was lounging with the door rising skyward in his premium p3 parked in front of the back door. He must be waiting for me. My blood began pumping hard before he even opened his mouth. This could be good.

Maybe crashing the party last night made a statement so powerful old Bob showed up for the discussion I was hoping to have. Maybe this would be when I convince him that his ambitions of automation wouldn't be as profitable as he thought. I'd convince him by sacrificing myself. Sacrificing my skills to create a team of Kurobans working on culturally-relevant video games for them. He wouldn't be able to recreate my mind into some faceless testing algorithm without my consent. And knowing his plans gave me a bit of leverage.

Robbie slid out of his pod and steadied his shapely legs before stepping face to face with me. I scraped the far corners of my spirit to gather all my confidence and charisma. Now I could tell him that he needed us, the QA-robans, to achieve his aspirations. That we needed to be treated better so that we could serve *him* more effectively. I'd sell the long-term benefit of my connective capability to translate constantly-changing Kuroban culture into Luxite code. How tapping into that would mask their educational efforts better than their antiseptic approach using an algorithm from afar.

But reality wasn't the same as the theoretical conversations I practiced in my Libook.

Robbie's eyes only strayed from his foldable tablet and his flashing smartwatch when he looked through me with his smart glasses. And as Rob scolded me, out of duty rather than caring or concern, he chomped on mouthfuls of seeds. "You know you're in a heap of trouble, kid?"

I opened my mouth to make my bold requests. "I—"

"You should've stayed your ass in your pen," Robbie said, scattering spit and seed residue in all directions as he spoke.

I wiped my face of his debris while Robbie stood motionless, staring off in the distance for about 30 awkward seconds..

He started again before I could defend myself. "You're not eduGames material. You're not even mature enough to be a professional in this town. I don't know if your little pea brain can comprehend the full picture of what we're up to here at eduGames."

I dodged more syrupy saliva as he continued. "You don't even deserve the job you have. We take a chance on you bums, and this is the thanks we get? Ridiculous, I tell ya . . ." He wiggled his watch, unfurled his massive mobile, and scrolled through his shining screen, as he kept going in on me with his rambling diatribe. I could barely keep track of all of the insults and innuendos he buried me in, but the gist was clear.

He eventually got everything off his chest and stopped for a moment before adding, "You must attend an emergency appointment with Doc before the end of the day or you're fired." Without another glance in my direction, Robbie hopped back in his p3 and zoomed off into morning traffic.

I sighed. Opportunity gone. The power he had over my source of income, my career, and if I'm honest, my life, sent me on my submissive way.

~ New Side Quest: Don't Upset Doc ~

I had a few hours until my appointment, but I left as soon as Robbie zoomed off. Negative energy was eating away at the bit of optimism I'd coaxed up to enjoy my birthday. I didn't know why I expected an effortless, empowering day of celebration when it hadn't ever been that for me, but I did. Now I needed time to prepare for the momentous mess I found myself in. So leaving early to prepare made sense.

Since I've had this job, I've had a psychiatry appointment every week, but this was the first same day visit, the first time I had two in one week, and my first Friday appointment. Double the directed duress bookending my week as my visits were typically Monday mornings. Working full-time in central conquistador command required these thinly-veiled compliance checkups. At least it did for luminous, soil-skinned people like me. I knew my psychiatrist wasn't there to help me as their medicinal role in mental mediation might suggest. Compliance was their goal, precisely to mitigate the freedom-fighting maelstrom any Kuroban may find in their mind. Much more was in jeopardy with this appointment because of my stark divergence yesterday.

MY MIND RACED as I traversed Lux's piss-poor pedestrian infrastructure to Doc's office. I didn't even bother checking the gutters as I strolled past. I wasn't bothered by the buzz of the Eye of Lux following me through the streets. I ignored the mosaic of kinetic screens covering buildings and roads. I survived many close calls with p3s while trying to cross the street, navigate narrow sidewalks, or avoid dangerous passenger drop-offs.

The walls were closing in around me. On the outside I fought to keep my performance up. I didn't dare give off a whiff of the true tempest inside. But with every step, as reality crept in more and more, the façade of confidence I clung to fell apart.

I eventually landed at the bleak concrete building adorned with LEDs overselling some all-purpose fragrance the color of a watermelon rind that helped with weight loss, attracting mates, and mental health. I was early. The psychiatrist made his own schedule and worked only when he wanted to, which was usually pretty late in the day and only for a few hours. Doc's receptionist hadn't even arrived yet. Since the building was open, I presumed Doc was already inside getting a virtual briefing from the big bosses in charge of Lux's cultural compliance program. Before I went into his office, I tiptoed into the lobby bathroom to freshen up my body, then mind, and then soul.

I stood in front of the bathroom mirror, overthinking, assembling a combination attack of searing spells to defeat Doc.

I was always attempting to predict and circumvent the next obstacle blocking my dreams in order to break free from ceaseless struggle. I needed these moments alone. I stared off, scrolled through all of the nuggets from my Libook that I could recall, and reformed my character. Mom called it daydreaming, I simply called it loading. Loading the proper persona that the situation called for. But it took time and solitude to align and refine the many revolutionary potentials I'd pulled from books, online, and Baldie. Time away from the hustle, bustle, aggression, acting, defending, and dejection in all its maniacal manifestations was necessary for me to sculpt the most cohesive, nuanced depiction.

These moments for me to breathe, reset, and strategize were actually the least lonely. I had comfort in accepting company in myself. It felt like I had power. The power to actually do something once I tapped into my persuasive powers. Sometimes I tricked myself and forgot about the pervasive judgment and control outside. Only briefly, as the truth was always lurking around the corner. Consciousness amid militantly-induced submission was a heavy cross to bear.

In this particular loading event, revision #63 wasn't hitting like it needed to. It had shards of serviceable snippets, but time was ticking. I needed to dial in my statement perfectly, and fast. Doc's amorphous hot seat of deluded doom was waiting for my death-defying deposition. I reminded myself to breathe. My mind kept returning to Bodi's warning, "Don't implicate us," and Mom's scolding, "Don't cause any trouble."

It wasn't just me on trial. I was an isolated representative, but this situation was pressurized in all directions. And as hard as I tried to tap into the charisma and persuasive confidence of Baldie, I kept feeling inadequate. I had to fight back the fear that I was going to be sent to the sewers, disgrace the legacy of the former GELD leader, and incite another brutal assault on

Kuroba. All before I even got the chance to make my career conscription and toil through my 30s and beyond.

Doc would know something was up if I came into his office sweating like a Luxite outside the metropolitan barrier barefoot and baking in the summer. Staring at the uneasy energy bubbling from my gaping pores in the high-definition, LED-lined bathroom mirror, I tried to push my perspiration back inside. The pressure I was facing had me in the early stages of melting down. I tried to calm my breathing.

Looking around the irritatingly immaculate bathroom, I found it devoid of the rust and sitting water I was used to. All the paper towels and soap, as much as they resembled a roll of sandpaper and radioactive sludge, remained full. It made me uncomfortable that it was so . . . undefiled, so detached, so unalive. It wasn't that I was used to the haphazardly hand-dug communal wastewater recycling troughs, it was that this wondrous water closet reeked of Lux's signature moves.

This half my-own-shit, half socially-imposed critic made it much harder to prepare the linguistic capoeira necessary to survive my upcoming encounter. It was circuitous and self-defeating. I navigated a maze in my mind, lost in my thoughts. Still, when I stepped out of this bathroom, or anywhere in Lux, I had to be on point.

I took a second to center myself. Finding and holding onto a spore-sized bit of hope, I mockingly called out to the universe, "This will be Dr. Chattel-tamer proof. Guaranteed." It felt good to say.

I took in a belly full of the chemically fragrant air. The cool, stale air, heavy with ammonia and all its abrasive cousins, dried out my jittery nostrils. I held it in for a second, stirring my stomach closer toward regurgitation as I took control of my body again. I exhaled through my mouth while pursing my lips in an oddly satisfying kissy face. I massaged my temples with the heel of my hands.

This was the worst place and time for anxiety. I had to get a hold of myself or Doc would unleash his wrath whether I was guilty or not.

I moved to splash water on my face to wash off the nascent neuroticism still blistering on my forehead. The automated faucet couldn't identify my hands or my face when I stuck it under the sensor. In my frustration, I reached for a piece of craggy cardboard to dry off, but that wouldn't identify me either.

I was certain Doc would want to "hear" my interpretation about yesterday's events. The utmost care was necessary to overcome Doc's perilous probing. The tone of my voice, my body language, how I addressed him, what I wore, my hair, the amount of happiness I exuded, my breathing, and every word I uttered would be scrutinized. I would balance that all *and* deliver my truth.

I bet those snowy suppressors don't think this much when they go to their work-mandated psych. Oh, right, they probably didn't have this unnecessary additional medical scrutiny that Kurobans endured. Doc was probably having a good old oblivious morning himself. All while I was down the hall ripping myself apart, trying to rebuild a more suitable version. All for him.

I tried to put as much worry out of my head and looked down at my Libook. The small, shabby device was perched on the side of the sink. Within arm's reach, but far enough from the liquid residue threatening its electrical organs. I dried my hands on my shabby slacks and scrolled through the icons on the Libook's notepad app until I found a new spot to draft how I'd read Doc for filth. He wasn't about to push me or any of my people around anymore. I tapped into my extensive, yet solely theoretical, gaming experience to find the best tactic to subvert his dogmatic defenses. And then it hit me. *Honesty.* But of course, with Luxites, it would need to be more strategic honesty. Honesty straight from my gut, but tailored for the ears of a vanilla vigilante, was what I needed to survive this upcoming appointment. A shrouded attack of realness.

As I started typing a familiar tune rang in my soul. *Shuka-shu. Bling gling.*

Serving Doc v.64:

Yeah Doc, I did it.
I took food from the fridge. But who was hurt? Y'all had
many more sandwiches and salad left for your celebration
anyways.

Much like the Greeks did when they presented a gargantuan wooden horse to the Trojans, I would present my carefully-curated confession.

I unsuccessfully tried to stir my Kuroban co-workers to
action. But as you've heard, I ended up crashing the party
alone. Just me, that's it.

Another admission would add more weight to Doc's trust in me, moving me another step closer to his inner sanctum of softheartedness. A small sliver of his heart that only reserved compassion and empathy and belief for a select group of Luxites. Admitting to this thwarted transgression would only further open him up for my offensive. Also, it doesn't hurt to deflect blame away from the QA-robans.

I may or may not have slapped up your security folks at the door, but I know you don't really care about Kuroban-on-Kuroban violence.

I mean, I didn't really touch them. And everything I *did* do, was inadvertent. Still, even accidentally hitting an Opp with my coat could be dressed-up as an act of aggression against the Luxite establishment. In line with the terms of the Seed Armistice, I could be punished. Or, Doc might make a more prejudiced interpretation. One in which my whole community is at fault and thus subject to swift eradication. It all depended on the day Doc has had more than the infraction itself. And he's consistently shown he has no chill, so I centralized any errant blame solely on myself.

Nothing happened when I ran into the party.
I did have a teensy request for my absent supervisor, since my team and I have sent him messages he's just never responded to. So I decided to meet him on his turf.

Either way, Quawd zapped me before I got the chance to do anything. Much before I threatened your cultural supremacy in the slightest. There was some minor pearl-clutching in the room, but I was a grain of sand pushing back against the toxic ocean of power we all drown in.

A couple Kurobans were hurt from what I was told. But that's an expected result from your automated abuse machines. Those Blaus y'all Luxites call on as soon as a Kuroban strays from your dominion don't have much lati-tude for interpretation, do they? But that's not a concern of yours, am I right?

It might not matter what I say, and my unfiltered opinions

might be my undoing, but I needed Doc's frustrations directed at me and only me. I paused my hurried typing and took another breath to settle myself. My emotions couldn't seep too deep into my decisive declaration. I ogled at what I'd written so far, reflecting on my assertive acknowledgment of misbehavior. It was a good opening, just not great. At this point Doc's defenses should be disintegrated and his well-rooted, rapacious reaction redirected. And because of his socially super-powered hubris, he'd be vulnerable to assume default success. Now I needed to set the stage for my full onslaught. And get his mind as far away from the Blaus as possible.

*What are y'all upset about? What I did yesterday, not a bit of it, had a meaningful impact on the society y'all created. But do you understand **why** I did it?*

*My community's goal is to cultivate the planetary ecology we see as part of ourselves. We do this through authentic ways of being and intentional relations designed to nurture our connection to **all** around us.*
In contradiction, y'all set up a system to siphon and deplete all you contact. Whether it's the land, the oceans, the animals, or the people — like Kurobans — the game is the same. The horrific wrinkle y'all have added is to foist the work of this universal extraction onto your dependent flock, your trusty glowing, soil-skinned captives.

As a result, my people have long since been transformed into tools. Yet we remain peaceful and obedient. We walk around on autopilot, mere husks serving your mission at all costs. Am I wrong for attempting to scrape back a scrap of humanity for myself, my co-workers, or my people? Even as we continue our eternal exertion unchanged? We only

*wanted office space and maybe, just possibly, a little
gratitude.*

I paced away from the glossy, granite sink only to circle
back brimming with satisfaction. My Libook was full of lyrical
lacerations, but this one was piercing. I set him up, tickled his
thirst to bask in his birthright, but brought it back to my
people's herculean hardships. At least subconsciously, I hoped
to expose Doc to something that'd never crossed his hijacked
headspace.

I felt some tingling need deep inside, pulling me to fix my
oppressors for some reason. Exposure to another's experience
might engender a more positive future for us all. My sneaky
shot at revolt. Hell, they were suffering too, albeit on a totally
different plane of pain.

That was a pipe dream though. It wasn't like these hue-less
haters listen anyways. They'd rather twist our stories every
which way to serve their ends. They clung to an armada of
inhuman tropes to invalidate our existence. Evidence didn't
matter. Nobody, neither Kuroban nor Luxite, seemed to see
what I saw. They all just wanted order in the chaos they lived
through.

But I had to keep my eyes on the prize. Doc might be bored
or irritated at this point. Bored at the mere utterance of
Kuroban struggle, yet irritated that someone undeserving
wastes his time complaining about a game he supports. So, I
needed to let all of the soldiers out of the Trojan horse before
Doc realized he was under attack.

*The real issue, I'm realizing, is the unrecognized struggle
you Luxites suffer. Admittedly, you, yourself are simply a
cog. An essential, yet immaterial agent of domestication.
You aid us to become more numb yet still productive. Artifi-*

cially fertilizing us for a more productive harvest sooner rather than later. We're all victims in your systematically-segregated community's continual conquest. But it goes beyond the medicine you push or your curation of our reality. When y'all believe and treat us as sub-human, your own struggle intensifies exponentially. Just like our persecution pains us more day in and day out, your deceitful duties drain your humanity over time.

I let out all of the air building up in my bloated lungs. Breathing, even subconsciously, was the last thing my mind could comprehend while I typed those pointed lines. I sucked in air and trapped it with every keystroke. It made me feel a little better to just think about telling Doc my truth. Like some soul cleansing, standing-up-to-the-man type shit. He may not care or hear me, but the intrinsic relief of saying it helped. Especially for a solitary insurgent like me. What I've done before and my rebellious attitude were mild annoyances to the despotic, pervasive culture I was up against. But in this 64th statement, this confluence of acute accusations, might be the spark to raze Kuroba to ashes again or release us from bondage. I was certain of it. Baldie would be proud. Honesty honed from my gut just like they used to guide GELD.

I hesitated. My mom would be pissed at me for speaking like this to someone of Doc's status. Despite her lived experience with the futility of subservience, she was a judgmental traditionalist, especially when it came to her expectations for me.

After some thinking, I tracked back for a way to soften the blow in case Mom might be right. Some way to channel Doc toward his connection to our pain without letting my foot off the gas. I just wanted to serve a more digestible dish for the fickle folk I'd be talking to. He shouldn't be stuck on my boldness. Instead, he should remain engaged with the fact that this world was a bigoted fever dream. One that's brazenly constructed to hinder his own thriving.

> *As y'all heist our humanity, it dehumanizes y'all. Think of it like this: All of society is a skyscraper above a flooded, inhospitable world. My people are the foundation, literally and figuratively, holding up the entire structure from a basement that constantly floods. Y'all are sitting pretty in the penthouse. Sadly there's a crack forming in your pristine pearlescent flooring. And instead of actually doing the work to fix your rotting residence, you loot whatever you can from the foundation to further distract you with added riches. Not only does reaping from us devastate Kurobans, it does nothing to curb the rot spreading in your regal chambers while destroying the very bedrock of our entire high-rise society. We can't provide what you all truly need, so you're only feeding a voracious void. You'd rather destabilize the source of your indulgent imperviousness instead. In the end, either by losing us or the very earth holding up your precious tower, you'll perish. Broken and helpless. But at least you've squeezed every bit of life force from every earthly speck on the way, am I right?*

I chuckled thinking how well the world of Tower Ark 2200 fit as a metaphor for the world we lived in. It was the perfect setup to spark his interest and curiosity. It took the focus off of me and my naked affronts to their supremacy and opened up a path to our *mutual* need for liberation. He probably won't notice I'm describing an extremely popular Massively Multiplayer Online Role Playing Game that I'd never played but studied intensely. Just the existence of the game shows that some Luxite game designer understood what was going on, at least subconsciously.

Now I needed to bring my testimony home. To fully unveil the façade he was enabling. Hopefully, recruiting him as an agent of systemic overthrow. It was constructed by the collective efforts of an ever-changing spectrum over generations of varied trauma. But that can also be *de*-constructed, hopefully faster, with shared intention. Everyone must be involved to overcome centuries of insatiable planetary destruction. I also had to tie it back to why neither Kuroba nor I should be punished for my aberrant activity yesterday. If not, this would all be for naught. Something to show how everything I did was an effort to save *him,* if you get down to the nitty-gritty.

*Regarding my situation yesterday and any other occurrence of Kuroban divergence, this question is for you and all your conscious and unconscious co-conspirators: How do you remain human while you dehumanize other homo-sapiens? For centuries! Or pillage the world at large without regard or respect to its necessity to your life. Because everything I was doing yesterday was an attempt to stop the basement from flooding. To stem **our** foundation's expeditious erosion. Or do you want to metaphorically, then literally, drown your people . . . as well as yourself?*

Flawless victory. Doc won't know what hit him. I tested out a couple awkward-looking hooks and uppercuts with my reflection in the mirror. I looked clumsy because I'd never thrown a punch before. I just copied what I saw in one of the videos during a secret web surfing binge in class.

I took another deep breath, held it in, then let it out so slow I knew it was procrastinating not breathing. I looked up at a digital clock embedded within the bathroom mirror flashing on the hour. "Fuck, it's 10 o'clock. I'm late."

I rushed out of the bathroom to meet my fate, however it materialized. I'm not really a believer, but I made the sign of Quawd for the first time as I walked into Doc's office. For Quawd's sake. For Kuroba's existence. I hoped Doc was in a good mood today, otherwise this already crappy birthday was going to be disastrous.

~ New Side Quest: Avoid Meds ~

Doc was sipping from a mug filled to the brim with a radiant libation when I walked in. It reflected a bright neon green off his fogged up little lenses sitting near the tip of his nose. He cut his sip short and motioned for me to sit on the familiar brushed velvet beanbag. In front of him sat a smorgasbord: the biggest, sloppiest burger squirting and slipping on all sides, a blue steak the size of an ox's midsection, a grilled lobster the size of my leg – but much thicker – bathing in a pool of butter, and an assortment of crusty, fragrant, and sweet breads still steaming from the stove.

One rump cheek at a time, I gently primped myself into the amorphous, bean-filled seat. As slow as humanly possible, I squirmed in front of his desk. My hope was to stretch out the time before Doc's inevitable pre-pill scolding commenced. My body shivered slightly as I tried to bottle up my fierce reaction to gusts of wintertime air-conditioning whirring about the room. After walking the long trek from eduGames without a coat, this arctic air made it impossible to hide my intense discomfort.

I hadn't fully settled into my blob seat when Doc swatted

his entire decadent breakfast onto the floor. "You know why you're here right?" Despite his evasion of pleasantries, he maintained a soft, embracing voice. As if he *actually* cared. A preemptive strike of Luxite acting in its purest form.

My body melted into the beanbag as I watched a swarm of cleaning bots roll in to suck up the grand meal he'd just hurled onto the floor. A lone bottle of pills smirked at me from Doc's desk. I wasn't even done with last week's meds, or any week's. I didn't take dem shits. It was a slippery slope before I was just another living, breathing drone of drudgery.

Doc leaned forward and cracked out two rapid snaps to get my attention. "Are you listening to me? This is serious. I have a laundry list of charges including theft, both time and retail, corporate espionage, inciting a riot, breaking and entering, as well as numerous close combat assaults. That's before they searched your desk and found a treasure trove of contraband. You and your office mates are in some deep trouble. Any of this could be considered a clear armistice violation for you people. Lucky for you, Robert is willing to drop the charges if you answer one question."

My whole body seized up. My insides twisted and ignited with unease. All the courage and groundwork I'd done had been whipped out of me. I immediately devolved into this meek, subordinate Kuroban. Just like they expected. They had so many allegations against me, *against us*. I hadn't expected him to already know what happened, or search our office, though I shouldn't be surprised. Any opportunity to make a Kuroban cower. But why would Robert drop all the charges like that? What kind of question did he want Doc to ask?

I fell back into the timid thespian trying to outlive this moment rather than topple tyranny itself. My face appeared unfazed, but I was terrified underneath it all. My fear trickled out in the tremble of my voice. "Y-yes. S-s-sure. How can I help, s-sir?"

Doc leaned in and looked me in the eyes. "We know this was part of a Glowing Earth terrorist plot. We know you people are working on a larger offensive. But we need the traitor leading this insurrection. I thought we properly managed your rebel ruler. So who is your new leader?"

My mind went blank. His reaction and question came from a dark corner of the multiverse that I'd never imagined. I thought GELD died out when they exiled and enslaved Baldie to the sewers. I hadn't heard a word about GELD since then. Nervously, I muttered the truth, "I-I don't kn-now."

Doc leaned back in his chair and twiddled his fingers. He closed his eyes after a few seconds staring up at the ceiling. "Now, one of the founders of the illustrious Opp-erator Corps told me you are looking to become an Opp-erator. Is that true?"

I opened my mouth to answer and he started back again without letting me squeak a peep out. "That's an impressive recommendation. We can definitely make that happen. Indubitably! And we can put you in *any* position your puny heart desires." He paused so long it was as if time froze and folded in on itself. I winced before he dropped what he needed from me. "All you have to do is let us know who our double agent is. Who is betraying us to inform these terrorists?"

Was Doc serious or just teasing me to get what he wants? Any position. Really? Even . . . maybe . . . I don't know . . . a video game producer! He probably had the power to make that happen, right?

Tragically, I had no idea about double agents or how GELD could still be in operation without Baldie. I'd have to lie and give someone up to make my dreams come true. That was my price of admission to topple Luxite power.

But I couldn't.

Could I?

I responded softly, "Uh-uh–"

Doc lurched forward, seemingly gripping invisible handlebars on his desk for leverage "How about this? Take the day. I hear it's your birthday. And a big one at that. Major career decision by the stroke of midnight. When our monitoring systems update your age, you've gotta have a career assigned to you or it throws up a ton of flags in the virtual visitor's visa platform. But you shall not need to worry about that, you magnificent mahogany light stick you!

"We'll *look out* for you, b-bro. You come back anytime before midnight with the GELD information we're looking for and we'll whisk you away. To whatever future, whatever luxury, whatever power you can dream up.

"I'll even send one of my own p3s for you. Seriously, anytime. If you come late, the Metropolitan Security System knows your face and I'll be alerted. Hell, I can just send my Repligraph with the necessary contractual documentation."

I twisted up my face and reflexively blurted out, "Your whaaat?"

He sighed and gritted his teeth. "You know, those three-dimensional visualizations you all program at eduGames are holographic replications of well-off, well-known, or well-respected Luxites like myself. Just tell me who your leader is and you can be the first *gl*-Kuroban to have one. I'll be your genie. Anything that pea brain can imagine is yours. You have until the end of the day."

I tried to open my mouth again.

Doc stared as if he was trying to bore a hole through me with his eyes. "Don't tell me, and you'll endure unbearable, listless mediocrity at best. But realistically, my bosses, the ones really pulling the strings, will inflict protracted, excruciating torment for many, many of your kind. We'll still get the next great economic epoch up and running, on the backs of your kind *eventually*. And I'm sure that'll smoke the grimy, glow worm, flip flopper we're looking for out of hiding. They'll throw the book at ya. It'll be out of my hands then." He flicked up his hands like he was spewing a showy stage magician's stardust and ended it with a clownish smile.

"Oh-oh kay. Sure." I sputtered as he stared, stationary and smiling. I nervously darted my head around the room, watching for the other shoe to drop. Right on my face. From any direction. Thirty seconds of panicked breathing later, I was lifting myself out of my seat. With cautious disbelief I rose up out of the beanbag.

Doc took a breath and I dropped back down. It was too good to be true. I was ready for Doc to pull the rug from under me when he said, "Oh yeah, don't forget to take your new prescription. I whipped up a special batch for you. Packed full of the good stuff. It'll help you stay preoccupied, productive, and professional. And remember, you have until midnight. You have to make your decision then anyways, right? So nothing more than what you were already going to do. Easy-peasey. This is actually a bonus. I'd say you're getting a steal."

I took the pill bottle and shot up like a rocket. After a covert check to make sure my Libook, in its therapeutic costume, was still in my waistband, I escaped. Too scared to believe my own luck, I crushed the pill bottle tight in my grasp. The rugged cap dug into my palm as I sped out into the concrete tundra, before the Doc came back with an even more problematic deal. Once again, I braved the cold Luxite city coatless, but still, I let out a sigh of relief. Not what I expected, but I was unscathed, *for now.*

STAGE COMPLETE

```
Health Points . . . . . . . . . . . . 30%
Magic Power . . . . . . . . . . . 50%
```

```
Mission #1: Make Amends with Bodi . . . . . . . . . . . FOR THE MOST PART, NO
Mission #2: Make It Through the Work Day . . . . . . TO BE CONTINUED . . .
Mission #3: Avoid Implicating Other Kurobans . . . SUCCESS FOR NOW
Mission #4: Maintain Work Assignment . . . . . . . . SUCCESS FOR TODAY, AT LEAST
Side Quest #1: Don't Upset Doc . . . . . . . . . . . . . . . DIDN'T ADD TO IT
Side Quest #2: Avoid Meds . . . . . . . . . . . . . . . . . . COMPLETE FAILURE
```

```
Experience Points Gained [860]
Coins [+180]
Items Received [COMPLIANCE POWER PILLS]
Status Effect [NONE]
```

Chapter 9: Antivirus Updated

Mission #1: Decide Whether to Sacrifice Random
Kuroban to Achieve my Dreams
Mission #2: Mend Relationship with Bodi
Mission #3: Maintain Work Assignment

U s Kurobans aren't cold climate people. Despite our community's eye-popping elevation, the insulation of our seaside cliff and the latitude of the locale itself kept our climate fairly warm and stable year-round. Thus, we never adapted our tropical DNA to become more resilient to the cold conditions crafted by Lux for Luxites. I don't know what humans would *naturally* thrive in those tundra temps. People may adapt over time or build microclimates that mimic the warmth that keeps us energetic and enthusiastic, but in *my* experience, those are energy-intensive delusions.

Our ancestors passed down stories of our homelands and the lush, humid, equatorial environments we came from. But that was many years before the Seed Slaughter. Legends of a time before Kurobans were first captured and shipped to these foreign lands. Now, because of the Luxite lifestyle imposed upon their global dominion, temperatures have gone haywire across the planet.

In the congested urban valley of Lux, temperatures fluctuated on the frigid end of the spectrum, like the inside of a poorly maintained deep freezer. Outside of their metropolitan barrier, sandstorms, earthquakes, and sulfuric belches regularly reminded us of the demonstrative volcanic peak we only realized was active after the Seed Slaughter. At this time of year, the Kuroban air was stale with the rank of the wasteband hanging in the hot air until a sulfur-tinged sea breeze came over the cliff in the morning. At night a cheerless cold waited for the moment we left our well-insulated mud huts. Kuroban kids were told that the stabbing cold was a shapeshifting spirit, eager to suck out your life force. Through that conditioning, the frosty conditions of Lux felt like an icy, day walking soucouyant sapping me of life during my entire monitored march back to work.

Icicles crystallized on my exposed, *and unexposed*, skin. It stabbed at me like thousands of diminutive daggers. Instead of spending time looking down, I dashed between exhaust vents on the sidewalk to warm up. The subsurface heat was my focus instead of my parent potentially toiling under foot. The cold slowed my muscles and my bones, persisting despite all my attempts to avert frostbite in this polar metropole. I struggled to maintain focus. Still, I forced myself to break away momentarily to mull over my major decision, even if just as a distraction.

Would a single Kuroban sacrifice be worth the total salvation of Kurobans? My technology knowledge was essential for our revolution. Especially if we hoped to do it before they automate us away. Kurobans would be abandoned. We'd all be forgotten. Everyone was doomed to waste away like the rubbish consuming our community. But I'd be condemning an innocent person to the same fate as my parent to unlock that opportunity. Could I live with that guilt?

Liberation was my goal all along, maybe not precisely through this particular vehicle, but it was a clear step in my plan. While squatted over a toasty exhaust vent, I dug five frozen phalanges into my waistband to pull out my Libook. I scrolled through my poorly organized pitches, portrayals, and plans before I found my favorite. At the top of the list was my visionary five step plan for **Liberation Gaming**.

Not a snazzy name, but the path was all there. Once I got the game dev company started, I trusted that I had the knowhow to build the games that would unlock Kurobans. I trusted my people more. Once awakened from their submissive slumber, we'd arrest Lux's algorithmic world, drain their digital funds, shut off their streamlined security, interject our narrative into the information superhighway, salvage our seeds, and discharge our detainees.

This may be the best, clearest chance to jumpstart my ambitions. Or I'd be forty years down the road still unsuccessfully scheming. I just had to give someone up. But who? It had to be someone who would fit the bill for Doc and his superiors. Someone that'd make sense to them as the threatening clandestine leader of GELD.

As much as I wanted to, I couldn't use Anansi. They'd never believe it. Who else? Mom or some other random Kuroban just trying to make it? It was a tough decision now that I thought about it. I had to tap into all I knew about these frightened Luxites. Who would they be most afraid of, yet least harmful to my credibility with Kuroba?

Forsaking Mom like that would be unforgivable. I'd already felt terrible leaving our adobe in such animosity. Mom's relentless disappointment weighed heavy on me. The dilemma Doc presented was no match for her dissatisfaction with my divergence. All of it came down to my pivotal career conscription. Everybody wanted a piece of my decision, but I was the one who had to live with it. And I had too much honor to sacrifice a Kuroban, innocent or not. I had to find another way.

I walked up to the sidewalk surrounding eduGames and was met with a confusing sight. A strange structure was built directly into the front of the entryway, right below the p3 drop off port. I had seen these types of devices in games before, mostly in military shooters, but I never expected this at the entrance of an ed-tech company. The entire building was caged in like a fortress with high concrete walls wrapped in barbed wire. No way for me to go around back like before. The heat I needed so desperately was on the other side of this new metallic tunnel leading into the building.

I spotted a sign:

<u>Anti-Terror Scanner</u>

1. Remove all outerwear and enter one at a time.
2. Walk fully inside the frame.
3. Cover your eyes, mouth, and nose.
4. Hold your breath for 5 seconds as the scanner completes its analysis.
5. Review your results and have a great day.

My limbs trembled as I walked under the doorway's scanning frame. I was freezing and the scanner unnerved me further. Anything new from Lux only meant trouble. Five large rainwater shower heads surrounded me, attached to the metal frame of the doorway. One above, two to my left, shoulder and knee height, and two to my right in the same setup as the left.

I winced as I slipped into position like a broken-hearted badger. My lips quivered as I pleaded with the machine. "Please nothing cold, please, please no cold." Turning around to retreat was becoming more appealing by the second. Going into reverse would avoid any further frustration this system would foist upon me. I couldn't take a second more of this icy, dehumanizing climate. Maybe I'd just run away.

But I kept going, almost like a lemming marching to its doom. As soon as my body was in line with the shower heads, the scanner whirred louder and louder. Horns blared, the air shuddered, and the mechanism beeped out a topsy-turvy tune. I shivered as the scanner revved up. From every direction clouds of warmth blasted me until I was fully shrouded within the mysterious mist. The chemical scent of rusted iron and noxious sulfur slipped into my stunned nostrils. The hot vapor flash-thawed my frigid form. My reflexes zipped my arms upward to clasp my nose shut. I held in a train of coughs imploding one by one inside me.

Then it was over.

Moments after the contraption hummed into action, it powered down and a sliding door opened on the other side. I hacked up whatever manufactured fumes snuck into my strained lungs. A small screen beeped, flashed an orange check mark with the words "Passed: Monitoring Recommended" and the door to eduGames swung open.

My internal temperature stabilized in the cozy office while I reeled from the scanning experience. That's when another transformation at eduGames startled me. The whole office had been reconfigured into perfectly aligned rows of shared cubicles. I surveyed the new landscape trying to decipher what was going on. Robert must have turned me away this morning to set this all up. He was probably forced to make this happen immediately because his treasured thoroughbred stepped out of line.

Across the savannah of low-lying cubicles, I spotted specks of illuminated seasoning gleaming amidst the snow and steel background. We'd been released from our closet cage. Huzzah!

The QA-robans were spread across the office, but it was better than nothing. Free from our cramped corporate cleaning closet. I pumped my fist in stealthy satisfaction.

My confrontation at the party last night must've worked. I may not have asked Robert directly, but he received the message somehow. He saw how far I was willing to go to demand our basic respect. I don't think I scared up a soft spot in his hardened heart, but I produced results. It wasn't according to plan, but it seemed that everything had turned out for the best.

All of the cubicles were made of heavy brushed steel. Walls one might expect to separate each employee's assigned seat were nowhere to be seen. We were fully integrated amongst our cauliflower co-workers, in plain view from every angle. We might finally be appreciated for our work instead of hidden and disregarded.

I was giddy to gloat to Bodi. My conformist homie was probably having fits right now. He couldn't take it that my bold action actually resolved our demeaning work situation. He didn't believe in confronting Robbie at the party but look at these results! I mean, it was undeniable. They were finally taking us seriously. Maybe our careers would be safe here and the Robster wouldn't automate us away. The progress when I pushed forward with my infiltration would surely squash any leftover beef Bodi had yesterday.

I scanned the beaming bodies breaking up the dull scenery. Each and every QA-roban seemed elated with their new environment. Eventually I spotted Bodi in the back corner typing awkwardly near Rob's abandoned corner office.

My ears tuned into a familiar low buzz rising in force as I walked through the office. My eyes cut from side to side to locate the origin of this recognizable, yet unsettling sound. I stopped and the swarm dispersed into silence. I questioned if I was tripping or not. Hopefully it was only a temporary hypothermia-induced delusion.

I took another step and the swarm buzzed where it left off. I stopped and started again. The buzz matched my every step, perfectly aligned with my movements. Tremors of terror wriggled up my spine as I started to piece together where I recognized this sound. It reminded me of the algorithmically-biased motion-sensing AI connected to CCTV cameras blanketing the streets of Lux. With my discernment on high alert, I spotted a little computerized Eye of Lux. Each one was as tiny as a honeybee, its many eyes watching me. When I walked by, it roused from its light slumber against the wall. After seeing the first one I noticed them completely surrounding me, camouflaged in the wall decor. Watching every millimeter of the office.

We had been safe from scrutiny inside our closet catacomb before today. Now binary bloodhounds trained on our radiant, earth-toned complexions were everywhere. These partisan peepers tapped into the larger urban security apparatus like an omnipresent optical minefield. The trigger was us, and they were waiting for any slight impropriety to incriminate us. And that was just the start of the new office modifications.

In the center of the corporate plains and at the end of every regimented row, steel rods emerged from the polished concrete. Affixed to these poles were large blue buttons at eye-level, crowned with a regal blue siren. The blue color, a triggering symbol of the Blaus, signified that these might be some kind of Blau alert system.

I finally saw the back of Bodi's meaty melon a few rows ahead of me. He didn't see me as I approached from behind. I shouted out as I skipped eagerly to hide my worry. "EK are you wit me! Hey Bodi, sorry about yesterday again, but have you seen the results? I mean . . ."

Bodi didn't respond, but I scanned his computer as I came up behind him. Another email from our digital overlord Robert was up on his screen. I only saw the word "Congratulations!!!" at the beginning and his signature at the end. It must've been my well-trained trauma-vision. When I was close enough to finally see Bodi's face, I saw the joy oozing from his squishy cheeks. He was too busy kiki-ing with his new Luxite desk buddy to realize I was right beside him.

I tried to get his attention another way. "Y-you forget my birthday?" I let out a boisterous laugh until I realized I was the only guffaw in the room. "B-Bodi! Heeeeey Bodi! I'm sure your sister won't take all the nonsense I was talking about seriously. And to make it up to you, I'll take over your tests. Feel free to dip out when you want."

Bodi turned his head further away from me while responding in a quick, light voice, "Call me Bobby." He resumed his jolly chat with his chalky comrade without missing a beat.

I stepped in to bump up against him and said, "Aight, no problem. Going by your aristocratic alias then. Sure, be my guest."

The meddling mannequin of Miracle Whip sharing *Bobby's* cubicle butted in, "Erm? Hey, I'm Ally. What's your name?"

I ignored Ally and stayed locked onto Bodi. His eyes repelled every attempt I made at ocular connection, dodging and darting in every direction but mine. I got fed up and blurted at him while beating my chest. "You know, you're probably just embarrassed. My plan worked out. Look at what *I* did. I'm ready for your apology when you're ready to give me my flowe–"

Ally forced their head between Bodi and I. "My brilliant Bobby, is this *miscreant* bothering you? Need me to push the panic button?"

"No, no, it's okay, Ally. I can handle . . ." Bodi turned to me with an embarrassed redness spreading over his mahogany face. I'd never seen so many rouge undertones fighting for the limelight on Kuroban skin. His genetic glow looked more muted now than ever, even from what I remembered yesterday. He pulled me close with a tight clamp on my arm. Our foreheads pressed hard against each other and he whisper-yelled at me. "EK, enough!" Bodi's face strained and his teeth clenched hard as if to prevent his frustration with me from bursting through.

"You mad?" I snarked back.

His response seethed through his teeth, "Please . . . leave . . . me . . . alone."

"Is this how you treat me, and on my birthday at that? After I got us out of that damn closet? The other QA-robans seem happy, look at them," I retorted while scoping out the other two sporting macaroni grins.

Bodi stood up at the speed of let-me-tell-you-about-your-self before he remembered his current company. The cameras buzzed back into consciousness, whipping their computational corneas on us, activated by the possibility of Kuroban commotion. He retreated back into rigid respectability and let out a long, belabored sigh, bowed his head, and mouthed quietly, "Please forgive me, oh Quawd. Our savior of saviors, please let me honor your sacrifice and follow your footsteps. My thoughts may be impure, but my hope for this lost soul is everlasting."

Bodi smashed his hands together with faithful focus. Veins bulged in his backhands. The narrow steeple he created pointed upwards, collecting all of his energy at its peak. He mumbled in tongues and twisted up the fingers on his left hand to make the sign of Quawd across his head, heart, right shoulder, and left shoulder. Bodi raised his head and looked at me with frustration streaking down his squishy face. "Ju-just leave me alone. Puh-leeze!"

"Why? I'm trying to help," I whined.

"I don't need your help. I'm your *boss* now. If you haven't noticed, I've been promoted. We've all made our career decisions early. We were offered promotions if we committed to eduGames. We didn't want to procrastinate like you. We'd love to have you, but you need to take this career seriously. No games. This is *real* life. With *real* implications for the money, food, and livelihood our community depends on so dearly."

My stomach churned, overcome by a tsunami of sickness after hearing his braggadocious admonishment, but I tried to stiffen my face to keep my cool. "Oh really, big boss *Bobby*. Is this what you want for yourself? For our people? You fu–"

"Did you forget the Armistice? You're not some sort of fantasy freedom fighter with unlimited lives. Grow up and get real. You're thirty, decide your career and make something of yourself," he whispered through his teeth.

I moved in closer to whisper in his ear. "What if the rules we hold so tightly to, the ones that define our *entire* interpretation of reality, are wrong? What does 'commitment' mean then?"

Bodi pushed me away. "What are you talking about?" he barked. "Reality isn't wrong, you're the only one who's wrong."

The whole office, including the mechanized cameras all around, turned to look at our bridled beef. I chuckled, smiled, and gave Bodi an unwelcome hug before waving all of our nosey, desk-bound onlookers back to whatever they were doing. I backed away slowly and spoke softly, "So our submission, susceptibility, and suffering is ordained by Quawd?"

Bodi stood up straight and gave me a smug look. "You act like you're so smart. Like, like . . . your shit don't stink. *I* got you this work assignment, remember that!"

"Of course, and I thank you very much for that. As it stands, those deciding what is right and wrong might be misguided. It's at least possible, right? And that may cause centuries-long torment for some people. Or harm the planet in the teensiest of ways. That may at least be the case in some potential timeline in a far away corner of this multiverse?" I shrugged with my arms out wide as I slowly bounced away in reverse from Bodi.

Bodi leapt forward, snatched a handful of my tired clothes, and pulled me close. I thought his massive fist was cocked and ready to knock my head from my spindly neck, but he just whispered in my ear. "Let the holy spirit of Quawd guide you. Everyone's single assignment is to watch and record you, and you alone." He pushed me in the opposite direction.

A sinister laugh rose in the distance which coincided with someone hacking up a lung. The cameras buzzed across the room like an alarming wave of mechanized mayhem. The clamorous sound made me tense up and move more intentionally. Had we been caught? Two subjugated peoples caught coordinating in plain sight. I didn't know if Bodi was being real, so I turned around more cautiously than a traumatized feline, hoping not to trigger the cameras.

Luckily, the cameras went after the commotion surrounding another QA-roban being bullied into eating laxative chocolates by their new pasty cubicle-mate. I looked back at Bodi to see his hand low and slightly hidden behind his leg in the shape of his sock puppet's beak. This was real. As real as could be. Bodi's furtive warning had flown under the radar because one of ours broke from their well-rehearsed decorum.

"You're right," I said with a nervous laugh, moving my eyes around to swiftly scrutinize my surroundings. "I still got you Bodi. But this is neither the place nor the time for pleasantries," I said to myself and walked away.

I pranced with my head on a swivel across the office space, moving past coworkers while avoiding eye contact. Maintaining a volume lower than the buzz of the cameras allowed me to keep my senses tuned for whatever surveillance I couldn't detect yet. I had to assume my every move was being tracked, as Bodi had warned. It was probably more intense than even he knew. After a few minutes of searching, I stumbled upon an empty desk in the direct center of the office with my Lux name on it. My new assigned seat came with my very own intercultural colleague too.

The blonde ghoul of a kid kept their blue-eyes locked on me as I walked up. Their gaze was both oblivious and piercing without any regard to how uncomfortable it made me feel. It incited a strong, startling shiver that almost shook me out of my chair. Strewn across their side of the desk and spilling over onto mine was a cornucopia of snacks. I'd never seen so much food just laying around since . . . probably the office fridge yesterday.

As I settled into my chair, my seatmate hurried to swipe their massive haul of snacks into their desk drawer. A few open wrappers fell on the floor, prompting the entrance of a small battalion of carpet cleaning bots. Some snacks dropped in their lap as they navigated around cords and accessories to hide their snack spoils. They ducked into their own lap to scarf up every one of the cakes and cookies and crackers that amassed on their pants. Like I hadn't already seen what they were stowing away literally three feet in front of me. They locked their desk of noms and feigned innocence with a twisted smile before they resumed staring at me.

This overanxious observer was pretty strange, their movements shifty as they guzzled from a massive opaque canteen that gleamed every time it opened to their energetic silence. But something more felt amiss. More problematic than the typical unsociable, yet controlling child of dominant culture. I remained vigilant while still trying to ignore them and settle into my new space.

A key was lodged in the top drawer of my new desk. I'd never had a real desk, much less one with a lock. I was moving on up. With a twist of the key, I opened up the empty drawer, releasing a strong metallic scent. I pulled my Libook wrapped in its therapy journal outerwear from my back pocket and dropped it in the drawer. Warm satisfaction filled my heart as I closed the drawer. I couldn't believe I had something of my own, something . . . private.

While trying to lock it, I flubbed the key. Missing the minuscule hole when trying to turn simultaneously, the small key squirted out of my grasp. It fell and bounced on the rigid floor. I started toward the key, but before I moved forward an albino aardvark attacked first.

From the ground under our desk, my new deskmate's mouth moved, but shock diverted all sound away from my ears. My first reflex was to close my legs and retreat backward from their under desk approach. I had no idea what that oddball was on, but I did see them go past my key and fumble with something on the back of my PC tower. While this strange little Luxite was under our desk fussing with my equipment, something on the back of their chair caught my attention. It was a mycelial coat. My mind spun theories and excuses for how a tofu-tinged taskmaster might have mushroom clothing. Mycelial manufacturing was still the one cultural practice my people had retained in secret. It'd probably be profitable to have a place in the Luxite marketplace but they just didn't have the fungal knowhow. Unless . . . had they co-opted that too?

My ground-bound desk mate popped back up on their side and handed me my keys without any further funny business. They said nothing and I didn't either. I was still processing all

I'd seen. It wasn't like a Luxite to sully themselves in any way, much less to aid a Kuroban. Once back in their seat, those oceanic eyes bore through me once again as I locked up my desk without issue.

I logged onto my computer and saw my desk mate's mouth open without a sound. Then it closed. Opened, closed. It was getting far beyond unnerving. Still, I kept minding my business. Their bizarre behavior set off my internal alarms one by one. My desk mate glared at me and adjusted their oversized frames clumsily as if I was a nude mime they lusted over. They continued to take gaping gulps from their luminous jug. After every sip they'd quickly snatch a snack from their desk and cram a cookie or two in their mouth while still holding eye contact. Confused, I checked myself to find what drew such impassioned interest, but saw nothing out of the ordinary. They still stared at me as they tried to chew. Saliva-soaked crumbs dribbled out of their sloppy mouth. Disgusting.

After about twenty minutes of this game of social chicken, I got frustrated and pushed my head towards them, stretching my neck out with my eyes wide. They stumbled backward in their chair. For a brief moment, they dodged my eyes and pretended to be busy rifling through papers and aimlessly scrolling on their computer.

Taking a second to analyze my desk mate beyond their unbecoming behavior, I sensed a little familiar flavor. More sauce than most bleached boneheads who all rocked the same standard issue pale blue to white button-up shirts tucked into billowy khakis. Beyond their large, likely fake, glasses, this fair-skinned fascism facilitator felt oddly umm . . . dare I say, welcoming?

It was like I'd seen them before. Maybe even I'd grown up with them. It really confused me because I didn't know Luxites like that. Hell, I barely even recognized my boss and not just because of his poor attendance. To me, most Luxites looked like duplicates of one another, small permutations of the same mutation.

Maybe it was my callowness or their conformity that made me think Lux was made up of a simple set of societal suppressors, either way it always seemed as if they were all replicating within a narrow range from the same codebase. But not this one. Their colorful guayabera with an obnoxiously large top button and with errant splashes of glowing green sludge, camo pants covered in crumbs, and neon sneakers distressed just enough to appear worn, looked out of place draped over their pale skin. I also noticed the way they sat in their chair with a laissez-faire lean instead of the board-stiff posture the other melanin-less misers maintained.

Optimism bubbled up in me. Maybe my desk mate had actually taken the time to understand my people's plight and was just clumsy with their interpretation. Maybe they couldn't figure out how to engage in conversation with someone suffering under the societal game design they feasted on. A sympathetic subjugator feeling the weight of their intentional — and potentially incidental — repression. A low bar but I was hopeful.

My adapted assumption allowed me to give a little grace to their unwavering gaze. Still, something in my gut was singing for me to remain on guard, more than my classic cautiousness. I leaned into my gut and kept working, defenses on full force. They'd have to make the first move.

Despite my constant evasion, I still caught all their punctuated gawks and glimpses only slightly interrupted by shimmering swallows and surreptitious snack attacks. An hour in, they seemed to have amassed enough spunk to speak. "H-hey, I'm B-Brad. He/h-him. I-isn't that how you-all-introduce-yourselves?" Before I had a chance to respond, they vomited a barrage of words. "Saw . . . your-name . . . on-chart . . . excited . . . meet." He let out a belabored gasp for air. "I heard you're really an ace with technology. T-t-t-true?"

His staccato words and frantic breathing sounded like his tongue tripped over his thin lips as he spewed out his statement. The unease he emitted only increased with his words. It was not the natural social ineptitude I'd expect someone to grow from, but more like amateur delivery of something prepared. Even in that little bit he said, his accent favored a Kuroban. A Kuroban that'd spent most of their life in Lux, but a Kuroban nonetheless. I could hear the fluidity and bounce he attempted. He might've genuinely been trying to be nice. At the same time, how did he know anything about me? It's not like we were truly part of this company before today. All my relational and physical defenses remained up. I responded with a crooked challenge. Straight from his people's reductive playbook. "What do you do here, *Brad*?"

"Well, I'm a junior software engineer. Where were you this morning, bro?" he responded with a more intrusive energy. The reckless relatability device he ended with turned me off even more.

"Busy," I replied sternly. I was doing "nunya" Brad, I thought to myself.

"Today's my first day, bro. I was so excited to start at such a cool, impactful company. We're doing the work that *really* matters, don't you think? I was sent here after struggling at one of my father's game design studios."

I had to check if I was hearing him clearly. It might've been a type of slang with Luxites. I didn't know better, so I asked, "What types of 'games.'"

His answer seemed effortless. "A wide variety team, they all specialize in different styles and genres, but mobile and computer. There are a few teams that specialize in old-school console or the growing environmental gaming worlds. But he is trying to solidify his dominance in the corporate gaming field, eduGames is a portfolio company, didn't you know?"

My defensiveness evaporated instantly. I jumped up out of my seat without fully digesting all of what he dropped on me. "Really? Studio*s*? With an 's'? Like multiple? Which ones? Refer me to any one, please! I can pull together a portfolio if you need one."

He shrugged and said, "I don't think so, bro. Things didn't end on the best of terms."

"With your *father*? Oh, okay," I replied flatly and sat back down to re-embody the very essence of unwavering ambivalence. I was a little ashamed that I broke from my stoic character in front of hostile company. The mammoth distance between my dreams and my reduced reality slipped my mind in that brief moment of desperation. I locked back into reality. Hiding my embarrassment, I excused myself from the nosy small talk by turning my head toward my computer screen. Back to solitary work.

He got the hint, zipped his lips, and only stared when chugging from his jug. He couldn't help himself from taking a peek here and there. The relative peace didn't last very long. Groans and grumbles from his side of the desk interrupted my concentration.

I fought as hard as I could before I finally snapped. "What's going on with you?" I hoped he hadn't heard me as soon as I said it. I just wanted his petulant noise pollution to cease.

"I'm having some issues, bro – *gulp* – this algorithm. I've been trying to compile it since this morning. It's kicking my tail, ya know?" he replied in a defeated tone.

I kissed my teeth and tried to get back to what I was doing. I saw him squirm in his chair trying to catch my eyes as he groaned again. It was only a few minutes before I relented. I had to empty my lungs, pout, and close my eyes before responding. "Let me see." I stood up and slinked, heavy with regret, over to Brad's screen.

I hadn't ever done software programming for real. My knowledge in this, and most technology topics, was totally theoretical. I'd soaked up writings with a pinch of online info on a number of topics. From technology and psychology to design and economics. Basically whatever knowledge was the next level down the rabbit hole to assemble my masterpiece of strategic freedom. My grand plan for liberation through gaming necessitated me having a broad technical foundation. I excelled at connecting dots and identifying patterns. With that particular battle skill, I could jump between interrelated topics with ease while still understanding the whole picture. I knew *of* software development because of its centrality to the games I loved, but I was by no means a programmer. It was just something I read about in old books Bodi found or in the illicit research that led to my expulsion.

All I could recall of programming was from a ratty Ethics of Software book that ended up being way too convoluted for me:

> *. . . architecting processable logic and procedure to a software system. When clear logic is provided to a system that follows the pre-designated procedure the system can interpret, operating as designed.*

I didn't think I could actually help Brad. He was supposedly an actual developer. This might've been his version of a sick joke. Something to reinforce my plebeian position. Or possibly it was an under-the-table test.

I took a look at Brad's screen. Right above the badly-chewed mouthpiece of the jug of glowing slime-green sludge crowding his desk, I immediately saw his error. I didn't have to decipher the logic or sequencing or any of that bullshit. I tried to tell him with respectful curiosity so I didn't bruise his ego too badly. "Is there supposed to be a semicolon on line 62?" I dropped my wiry finger on the line of code in question and out of the corner of my eye I caught Brad trying to stretch the outlandishly big top button of his shirt closer to me.

Brad responded with an unconvinced, yet surprised "Huh," but still added the semicolon and compiled the code. "It works," he said with greedy delight. "How did you know, bro?"

I walked back to my seat feeling myself, but trying to keep my glee under wraps. "I read a lot. You said I was smart, right?"

Brad's voice jumped up a couple octaves, gained a nasally filter, and his pseudo-Kuroban twang disappeared. He lost the nonchalant slouch in his chair that made his whole performance work. His back straightened up. His aquamarine eyes twinkled and his big teeth glinted in the fluorescent light. He screamed at me from across the desk. "Genius level, chap! That was exquisite. I hope your Elders aren't too harsh tonight." He proceeded to gargle a mouthful of his jug sludge as every brake in my mind screeched to a halt.

"What?" I cut my eyes and twisted my head at an angle almost parallel with the floor. Anxiety ambled its way into my heart. How did he know that? He's a Luxite! I had to tread lightly with Brad. He may be friendly on the face of things, but I was still talking to a Luxite. Cold, calculated, and cutthroat, even if they didn't know it. I tensed to keep my recognition to myself. I wasn't about to freak out like at the party last night, not if I could help it. This all felt like a trap.

The unnerving undercurrent undulating in my underbelly was certainly warranted. Something fiendish was afoot. Only Kurobans should know about anything going on with the Elders. Unless Lux was actually involved in the Earth Going somehow. A Kuroban would never speak of such a sanctified ceremony. That's why it was moved deeper into Kuroba. We all had too much to lose with an outright breach of the Seed Armistice. It was one of the only things we could do to maintain our culture and keep a stockpile of healthy calories when foraging wasn't fruitful. If any fair-skinned fascists were involved, and knew that much, then something much bigger was going on. Shit wasn't as sweet as Mom or Doc made it out to be.

My antenna went on high alert as I awaited Brad's response.

"I mean, I mean . . . I hope I g-g-get-the-chance-to-repay you." He fell back into the same hurried, breathless stammering from before, "A-all-this-surveillance . . . for-you . . . it's-nothing, right?" He wheezed and tried to stuff his words back into his mouth. I side-eyed so hard my eyes closed.

With my eyes shut, I shook my head in disgust trying to wade through his bullshit. "No. No. No. That's not it. You said Elders. And what surveillance were you stammering about? Take a breath Brad, it's okay, speak slow. My b-b-bro?"

He took another hefty drink from his jug before huffing up a whole chestful of air and promptly deflating back down into his seat. He responded in a careful tone, "I-I wasn't supposed to say. The e-e-exchange student living with my family was talking about it. You know Bradley, right?"

I furrowed my brow in complete confusion. I didn't know no Kuroban named Bradley, and if I did, I damn sure didn't know that sad-ass Luxite name.

Brad used his hands as he spoke. "You know, he's pretty tall and slim. Pretty agile fellow too. He's been living on our compound for a couple years since he earned his Master's and started with the Opp-erators."

I stared back at him with a dead face. I had no idea who he was talking about. A woozy feeling of wretchedness flared up inside me. My mouth wanted to ask Brad more and gather intel, but safety was my main concern. My soul warned me to retreat into my shell like a threatened turtle. This was a trap. I didn't respond to Brad. With my eyes affixed to my computer screen, my fingers went to work on my keyboard. In my peripherals I saw him scurry in every direction, waving his hands, while blabbering on to get my attention. But for me, it was definitely time to say less. A trustworthy timbre rang out once again. *Shuka-shu, shuka-shu.*

[Beacon of Hypervisibility - Activated]

I wasn't about to be the next sucker. Kuroban history taught me to be careful with folks like Luxite-Brad whether he was just a bumbling buffoon or an intentional interloper. The reason we had the Seed Armistice in the first place was because his people massacred my Maroon ancestors. Hell, both of my parents barely survived the slaughter, so the pain was relatively fresh. I heard it all started when a Luxite spy manipulated a susceptible Maroon by twisting their trust to locate our hidden community.

Brad may have really thought he was my buddy. He may have honestly believed he was down for the cause. But he had no idea what it would take to completely commit to Kuroban liberation. I'd been lulled asleep by the veneer of victory. Now I saw the plot. Neither his relatable swag nor his "charitable" foster brotherhood convinced me he wasn't just an asset to further advance Luxite supremacy. He was their very own Kuroban cosplayer.

His plump rosy cheeks perked up as he tried to over-smile his mistakes away. It only served to make me more upset. This stooge probably had no idea the insidious impact he was facili-tating. This blundering mole sharing my desk was simply a honeypot waiting to lure me in. Connecting this revelation to his seemingly innocuous imitation and extrapolating out to Lux's headless, self-replicating cultural algorithm made me rethink my game plan.

This simpleton wasn't simply here to watch me; he was bait to tempt me toward bondage. To catch me slipping. To make me think I truly had a chance against this automorphic social algorithm reigning over us both.

There I was, overthinking again. It was all I could do. I was on a deserted island in the middle of a radioactive ocean. Unmoored. Uncomfortable. Unwelcome. These unforgiving environments forced me to make a trillion novel life decisions in succession. My drive to survive a world trying to swallow me up was unmatched.

I drew on a sad specter of Baldie being ushered away. It gave me the strength I needed to do what was required next. That memory stimulated purposeful paranoia propelling me to persist. I dissected every detail around me. What was going on here and how were they watching me? Were Kuroba and Lux working together or against one another? What should I do to preserve and progress towards my dream? How should I protect the QA-robans and all Kurobans – because I surely didn't want to cause any more drama than I'd already aroused?

Constantly curating the minimal information brought up more questions than actions. I froze like I was under a dastardly denial-of-service attack. I couldn't see a way to squeeze even a bit of hope from the rock or the hard place I was in. It was all too confusing and complex. The only certainty was the tiny ember sizzling in my gut. It was the only earnest support I had in these tense, solitary times.

My new work situation only made the weight of my 30th

birthday bear down on me even harder with Mom, Doc, and Bodi all turning the colossal clamp around me tighter to force my compliance. Always fighting back was exhausting. The simplest, yet most unpleasant path was what I kept falling towards as my mind scrambled to figure out how to deal with Brad and the almighty surveillance trained on me. Succumb. Obey. Serve. I fear I was the sacrificial lamb to appease the Luxite overlords, just like Baldie.

I needed a way to withstand work. I'd decide my career on the way home. I could fake it, but that was a tall task to maintain under an unknown level of added acquiescence auditing. Without knowing the surveillance triggers, I had nothing to determine what kind of performance I needed to pull out to appease the powers judging me. To be safe amidst that level of ambiguity I had to maintain — nay, *become* — the obedient oaf to make it through the day. To commit completely. That meant full subservience to Brad, to eduStream, and to the entire Luxite power structure. And the only way I knew that might happen was by taking Doc's meds. I'd avoided them up to this point, but now there was nowhere to hide.

Maybe it wouldn't be so bad. At least for today, I'd be the "good little 'roban." No acting this time. I'll survive to fight another day. Doc's passivity pills supposedly only lasted a couple hours according to the label. I just needed to make a career choice where I wouldn't rely on them. Dependence is what kept Kuroba in its current vulnerable position. If I leaned into these pills, I'd certainly lose myself along with my dreams of gaming liberation.

My gut told me to resist. There was another way. There had to be. But I had to survive long enough to figure it out. I didn't see a timer ticking down, but I knew myself. I couldn't *not* be myself for too long. I was running out of time and options.

Before I could question myself again or make up another

excuse, I hid behind my monitor and did it. Bottom's up. I placed a pair of two-tone capsules on my tongue and jostled them around a little. I took a deep breath with just my nose before I used my trembling tongue to force the pills down my throat. It was a fight to squeeze the sizable pellets down my gullet with no water in sight, but soon enough I didn't feel them squirming down my throat.

[Curse of Lux - Activated]

Bit by bit every cell in my body contracted, then quivered, and then tightened up once again. The pressure was intense; it felt like my eyes were bursting out of my skull. A surge of energy coursed through my body. My heart felt like it was going to tear itself apart. I was wound so tight I might spontaneously combust or blast off like a rocket. I looked at my hands and saw my glow flicker, then ratchet down to a low dull. My senses retreated, and I zoomed in on the computer in front of me. It was my only focus.

My body started moving on its own along a haphazard rhythm I'd never felt before. My heart pounded like a jackhammer. My entire body was as stiff as a board. Every move I made was relentlessly robotic. My cheeks hurt as I assumed my mouth was overwhelmed with a face-stretching smile. I couldn't recognize myself anymore.

Still, I felt every lie my body told. The inauthenticity was piling up in my soul. This must've been it, the chemically-induced version of Lux's cultural command.

I regretted my decision. I was now another melanated miser aiding in my own bondage. I wasn't using my magnificent mind for generative means like liberating my people or even slowing down our erosion. Instead I steadfastly ensured eduGames's indoctrination products converted targets more efficiently. I tested a brand-new early education module and suggested a lesson that introduced Luxite values to transposed-upon traditional Kuroban decorum. I slipped in references to Luxites being a gift from Quawd to bring Kurobans to a better future. And I commented on how eduGames could use Kurobans' affinity for the world around them to help Lux "discover" suitable places yet to be conquered. I was the agent training my glowing earth community to police and mule themselves. Turning their learning, through which they hoped to escape their dire circumstances, into a tyrannical tool for untold Luxite exploitation.

To try to make myself feel better, I qualified my actions. I told the disappointment pouring into my soul that I was being subversive. But as I typed away, following the forceful tugs of what Kurobans called the spirit of Quawd, the pain I was designing into Kuroban lives struck across my body.

Even so, I had to endure. At least for the day. This was bigger than me. Bigger than a couple improbable design notes that I'd surely undo once I took control of this vendor contract. This was a sacrifice for my community's future too. This time under the Curse of Lux allowed me to clear my mind. I had big decisions ahead of me, and this was only the preamble. But it all boiled down whether I'd continue sacrificing myself or just one other Kuroban. Lux was watching me closely, and it seemed like anything would set them off. So, I kept on typing.

STAGE COMPLETE

Health Points 30%
Magic Power 50%

Mission #1: Decide Whether to Sacrifice Random
              Kuroban to Achieve my Dreams . . . . COULD I?
Mission #2: Mend Relationship with Bodi . . . . NOT LOOKING GOOD
Mission #3: Maintain Work Assignment . . . . ON SHAKEY GROUND

Experience Points Gained [150]
Coins [+180]
Items Received [NONE]
Status Effect [BEACON OF HYPERVISIBILITY, CURSE OF LUX]

Chapter 10: Reset v2 - Node Isolation

Mission #1: Get Home Safely
Mission #2: Make Career Conscription Decision

"Bye, bro. Have a good weekend. See you on Monday. We can't wait to have you onboard producing like this everyday," my new work bestie Luxite-Brad hollered as he rose up to put on *his* mycelial coat.

I didn't say anything. He grabbed his alligator briefcase and walked towards the door. I still didn't utter a word and remained locked into my work.

He threw the hood up to reveal a gaping tear in the back flapping in the gust of cold air that rushed in through the open p3 bay door.

When I finally registered what he'd said to me, and what I'd seen, he was already outside. The biochemical hold the spirit of Quawd had over me was beginning to loosen.

A few hours later, as the day ended and the office was almost empty. The power of those new pills from Doc had completely subsided. My heart had stopped beating out of my chest. My eyes had receded back into my skull. Over the course of the day I was subjected to a dramatic dis-harmony of chemical explosions driving me to work harder, faster, and to just do more. It was all disorientating. The experience left me feeling disembodied.

The pills had engaged every one of my muscles whether necessary for sitting and typing or not. A day of that whole body arousal left me feeling diminished, like a phone on 2% and dropping. The power of Quawd was ceding the wheel, steering my life back to me, with the tank nearly depleted. I was on the verge of collapsing and not waking up until Monday morning.

I let out a melodramatic yawn. My jaw stretched out like an overworked viper while my arms twisted and stretched in all directions around me. It was a warning shot for the coming crash. If I didn't get home, or at least on the train, I'd be in for an unpleasant weekend strewn about these concrete streets.

The life force leeches that lived in this valley molted at this hour. These were the in-between hours: After work, but before the well-documented weekend debauchery was in full effect. Everyone was at home charging up, pre-pregaming for a consumption-concentrated turn up. When the sun slumbers, another raucous horde of revelers flood the presently dead streets. They'll lose every bit of the sophistication, respectability, and professionalism they exude and enforce during the workweek. Their animalistic attitudes bear their true fangs. Every Kuroban knows not to be caught in Lux during these times. Even Quawd couldn't save us. Never during the unruly hours.

I needed to get out before it all popped off. A Luxite activated by the moonlight was a hate crime waiting to happen.

The timing might've been perfect though. I still had twenty minutes until the last train home left. Enough time to make it to the station and knock out on the ride home. That'll allow me to regenerate enough juice for the long slog home. I'd be closer to my normal self by then.

I cleaned up my desk, shut down my desktop, and reflected on my experience being under the chemical command of Lux. Could I do this every day and still maintain my main mission? Could I maintain my identity under the influence?

On top of my exhaustion, when I tapped back into my body I felt my ancestors and descendants crying out from inside me. We all lost hit points. Being a pill-powered puppet was more than being simply out of alignment. It was a systematic deconstruction of my personal and cultural identity, experience by experience. The internal harm wouldn't end if I kept this up. I'd be unfulfilled with the void inside me growing more voluminous every day. It didn't matter whether I performed my duties exquisitely as a good worker or popped pills to get by. Every day I'd fight to maintain my sense of self, depleting what minute capacity I could regenerate at home until I'm totally tapped out and I'm just a bitter, self-serving adversary to Kuroba instead of the savior I'm supposed to be. There was no escape from this onerous game except through the destruction of its very mechanics and critical infrastructure.

At the same time, today wasn't as bad as I anticipated. It was easy to be led, to be fully unconscious. Taking a break from parsing and performing once in a while, in order to temporarily ward off the encircling, engrossing cultural command might be beneficial . . . in doses. It might sustain my resistance for longer, offering just a little intellectual intermission so that in critical moments I could endure and tip the momentum of societal fate toward justice. Hell, maybe other Kurobans would have the capacity to join in if they knew someone modeling another narrative.

A little Luxite lie to myself and my lineage shouldn't matter in the grand scheme of liberation. Especially if it keeps me and my community kicking. I mean . . . I did get a lot of work done while under the influence. Probably more than I had since I started here. I finished my tests and even wrote recommendations for them all. I gave the developers and designers step-by-step directions for how to best educate (read: indoctrinate) my people on the other end of this tech. With a little more craftiness, possibly through messages only Kurobans understand, I'd nurture more nonconformists like myself. Eventually, I'd be able to inoculate the populace from their helpless acceptance of Luxite persecution. Maybe this would actually be a subversive path for me to move up. To be the video game creator I wanted to be. Damn, I might be able to work *with* the system to get the position and power I needed to make material change for Kurobans. All while we build a new world free from Luxite domination.

The only other option was being an Opp. I couldn't bring myself to commit to that type of long-term, active treachery. Just the notion of the entry fee it required gave me nausea. Direct disloyalty was simply something no narrative could spin to sit right with my soul.

Mom and Bodi wanted me to quit fighting and enjoy what little I'd lucked into while it was still being offered. They'd be ecstatic for either choice I made, even if they each wanted different versions of me. I was at least imagining the concessions I'd make for both and not dismissing them outright. They should be happy to get as much from me. It was *my* life, and I had to live with the decisions.

Today's pill-powered psychosis was a taste of what taking the career at eduGames would be, however short-lived. I needed more time to reflect on it all. I was exhausted and had a train home to catch. So I pushed my ergonomic rolling chair away from the bolted down desk.

Standing up from my desk made my legs liquify like overcooked linguini. I struggled for stability, but my body was weaker than wet tissue paper. Gravity alone was almost enough to pull me to the ground. My eyelids were heavy, like they were attached to the invisible anchors dangling far below. A smidgen of excitement to return home kept me active and alert. It was concerning how much these meds wiped me out. I had to lock in and pull from my reserves if I was going to make it back home without passing out on the way. I daydreamed about the nap waiting for me on the train as I shuffled outside.

The chilly air whipped my exposed body and woke me up. Walking was an effort in itself. My noodle legs wobbled no matter what I did to keep them on mission. I hurled one in front of the other with my body bobbing behind. I slinked my way up and out, constantly on the verge of stumbling. It didn't matter if this was the 80th time I'd traveled these silent, somber roads from deep in the urban valley up to the central train station above. A constant buzz followed me and reminded me that it wasn't my curtain call just yet.

I was happy to arrive at the packed platform. It was a relief to see other Kurobans. It didn't matter if they were covered in grime, barely glowing, or if they ignored me. I smiled at them in secret anyways. They were all scrambling about, encroaching on what was going to be my mobile bed for the forty-five-minute ride back to the manufacturing district. A general scent of hurry gripped the air as everyone rushed onto the whistling train. The pent-up anxiety in anticipation of imminent departure was heavy in the air. My feet continued to tug me up the steps onto the train despite the havoc around. I dropped into an open seat, let out a sigh, and blinked.

"Wake up! Wake up! Come on, get up," a voice cried out.

My eyes ripped open and I found myself laid out on the platform with one leg dangling over the tracks. Luckily, it was the Western Lux Manufacturing stop. The train was gone, and Soma's little body stood over me. She had her hand cocked. Pain pulsated across my face. I covered my cheek and blurted out, "Wh-what happened?"

Soma stepped from over me and helped me up. "You were sleepwalking off the train and just collapsed here. Everyone scattered and left when they saw you fall."

"Wow! Those pills from Doc were a doozie. Wait! What are you doing here?" She should've been neck deep in homework by now.

She replied with a mischievous smile, her small hands clasped behind her back.

"Don't tell me. Again? Day one *and* two? Soma, you got me beat," I said with a smirk. After rubbing dirt off the back of my head I started walking towards the deserted mine. Soma's little hand snatched mine before I got away.

It only took a few steps before she whimpered, "Yeah, I got kicked out again. I didn't want to go home. Father got chewed out by the powder people and now he's on one. If I go home while he's in that kind of mood, he'd ship me to some far off Luxite military camp for sure. Sometimes I don't even think we're related the way he treats me."

"And you came to me?" I was both in disbelief and flattered. I turned my face so it didn't give off a confusing message.

"Of course. You're the only one that'd understand. That school is the absolute worst." Soma served a small snicker and a light wretch.

"What's the *real* problem you're having?" I inquired with a warm smile.

She rubbed her tiny temple with her free hand and closed her eyes. When she finally responded, her normally cheery voice overflowed with shame. "Well, it's not hard work, most definitely. It's actually *super* easy. I-it's just not interesting or helpful. Being there makes me itch. My body feels icky and I get overwhelmed. It's like we're all being forced to be the same listless Kuroban. That feeling gets worse and worse until I j-j-just gotta say something.

"For example: They're teaching us 'history,' but really they're just lying. Like, like they said Kurobans had *tails* until Luxites found and domesticated our ancestors. Or that we're naturally *violent* and can't be tamed unless we have the most back-breaking labor to tire our idle, barbaric hands. I was even called lazy just because I was doodling on the back of my *completed* assignment. I wasn't bothering anyone! I didn't want to distract the other kids suffering through a simple math assignment. And the holo teacher started going off on me.

"I tried your advice yesterday and they kicked me out immediately. Today I kept quiet, even though I was itching to speak up and challenge them. But because I completed my quiz using the Ethnomathematics I learned from my mama's stories, they kicked me out for 'insubordination.'"

"Yeeeah, they playing the same game, they just updated the battle system. If you know what I mean. But how do you think *I* can help?" I was truly curious as to what ideas her little mind had in store. This felt like a setup to bring more trouble my way. Without a doubt, Bodi and Anansi already blamed me for her misbehavior. Still, her words made me recollect my own educational distress and connect it to the predicament my semi-grown ass faced as an employee in Lux. Her descriptions were slightly different from my own interpretation, but I *over*stood her somatic discomfort.

She moved closer and nuzzled against my side, flashing her innocent little eyes up at me as only a child on a mission could. "I know this is *my* problem to deal with. B-b-but just tell me how you dealt with it. You got expelled and all, but you almost made it to the end. And, and, and you're about to be set up with a cushy career anyways. Plus, you're soooo smart and I really value your opinion. It's lonely, you know. Everyone seems to just go along with whatever the school says. No matter how messed up it is, they dig in deeper, like there is no other option. You're the only one that said no."

I looked forward and stared for a little bit, frozen by her ingratiating words. I was shocked by her authentic appreciation and her analogous alienation. I scanned beyond the mine we circumnavigated trying to find inspiration for the right response.

"Well, thanks for that. I don't know if I'll be helpful though. The school and the entire educational ecosystem with all the extra tutors, incessant testing, and pervasive rigor was intense. And I know they've ratcheted it up a lot since I was there. Mostly because of *me*." I shrugged with my free hand and giggled at my humility. In this golden opportunity to talk to someone honestly and completely about my experiences and perspectives I felt the urge, or really, the obligation, to hold back a bit.

"Then you're probably the most important person to talk to," Soma said. I need to figure out how to get through school so I can make *my* dreams come true. Like you! I know you've probably got some big announcement for the Earth Going. I just wanted to hear your story. And, and t-they said if I mess up on Monday I'm expelled. From kindergarten. I mean, where they do that at?" Soma chuckled nervously while looking down in defeat.

She needed as much help as she could get, but I read between her little lines. She was holding back too. And I knew she wouldn't get an empathetic, sympathetic, or even a listening ear back home.

Just hearing the threat they saddled this innocent child to

carry made my skin itch all over. They were prepared to kick such a young child out of the only education institution available to our mountaintop Maroon village. A "genius" kid, enthusiastic to learn. Truly inhumane. They weren't taking chances, cutting bycatch immediately. Maybe she was right. My story might help find her own compromising character to endure that oppressive institution. "Sure, I guess I can tell you what I went through. It couldn't hurt."

Soma pumped her fist in the air as she hopped alongside me. "Yes, thank you so much."

I couldn't bring my cheerful cheeks down as I shared my truth with Soma. "Ok, so you already know about my gaming — uh, let me be honest — *infatuation*, right?"

"Yeah, that's so cool. You're like the only one in the community doing something *original* like that." I saw the sparkle of imagination still burning in her innocent eyes. Most thought I flirted with an impossible dream. They said I was delving into the business of our bosses. But it was something I authentically enjoyed. It was where I found the joy to keep going every day.

My energy was rising. The words were queuing and jostling to spill out. "Check this, it all started with a strategy guide your brother gave me." I nodded with a flat look, so she knew it was real. "But that's just where it started. My studies expanded to all kinds of books until I'd amassed enough knowledge to tinker with technology from the dump. Everything was so I could figure out how to create my own games."

"Really, *Bodi* Bodi? My brother Bodi. Goodie old shoes Bodi . . . gave you something cool?" She was flabbergasted, but her excitement seemed to match my own.

We were at the land sores that divided the mine from the dump at this point. I dodged a cesspool of rancid runoff bubbling nearby, but in that moment it didn't even bother me.

I laughed heartily and continued. "Yeah, he's trying to figure out his way to survive this inhumane world we live in. He's got a good heart underneath all the pain he stomachs.

"But for me there was only so much I could learn through books and tinkering. I needed more. Without the wizardry behind the devices I rehabilitated, I was only dabbling with inert instruments. Life was injected into them through the internet. And the only place I knew that had internet access was school. But that gateway to the world wide web was only a heavily monitored slice of the pie, if I could access it at all. When I finally saw the full breadth of their virtual library — from technical ebooks and academic audio to vibrant videos along with the few informational webpages sprinkled in, I was able to clearly decipher the core gameplay behind the world we navigate:

1. External — Categorize and weaken your 'cash cow.'
   Internal — Increase the threat of violence to 'cash cow.'
2. External — Milk the 'cash cow' dry.
   Internal — Indulge in the finest dairy-derived products.
3. External — Automate the milking.
   Internal — When the 'cash cow' starts to become depleted 'discover' the next 'cash cow' and start back at Step 1."

Soma squeezed my hand in between hers then swung our hand sandwich back and forth as she said, "Wow! So that's why you got expelled? How'd you do it? What did you see besides all of that technical stuff? Probably some amazing things."

I wobbled over the clutter of unconstrained consumption at my own delicate pace while dumping all that spun around my head since the day I was expelled. "Just a second, I'll get to it.

"At that point I devised a path to access the full web. I needed to become the maestro of the school's game mechanics by identifying its vulnerabilities." Soma squinted briefly and I realized she might not understand all of my technical terms. "Ways to outsmart the school. In essence, shortcuts. L-look at it like this: the school is a simulated stable and we're a herd of hungry bovines. They designed the whole limited, highly curated meadow to cater to *their* needs. They see us as rabid beasts that need to be broken down and retrained. Part of their domestication efforts were the many little lies they had us all grazing on. I needed to find a way to see through the virtual cage they trapped us in. I'd need to divert just a single dot of the projecting propaganda in order to peek at reality. I may not be able to fully escape yet, but I could chip away at the inconsistencies calcifying in my soul from time to time. I just needed to cover my tracks before they noticed what I was doing."

"Yeah, but they're always watching, especially on their internet?"

Kurobans were always good at seeing why something *wasn't* possible — an adaptation from long-term trauma. I was always determined to *make* it possible. "They didn't notice my tiny hacks, stretched out over time. After each one I'd start again, refine my approach to lessen the difficulties I faced, research for the next hack, and try again. But I couldn't do that outside the building. No device ever connected. No matter how I twisted, turned, angled, or even spoofed. But I had a plan for all Kurobans to see what I saw. And I needed a device from the inside."

"You didn't get discouraged by failing over and over? That's why you're the best!" She shrieked out with excitement. "Dad is the only person in the community that gets new stuff, he never even has to forage. Lux provides him a regular stipend on top of large gifts after big projects."

"It was tough, but my voracious need to learn more about video games drove me. Sluggish progress encouraged me to continue instead of shy away. Let me build the background so you can see what I noticed about our pretend pasture that led to my breakthrough. What might be a valuable detail about the teachers at school?"

Soma responded instantly. "Holographic teachers, of course! But I'd rather not have Luxites in person. There might be a Spore Slaughter if they were here in the flesh."

"That part! You see it. They don't even give us the respect of presence to brainwash us. They project Luxite teachers instead. I saw that as an opportunity to claw back a bit of power. Even very young I always had a certain vision. A focused way of noticing that allowed me analyze the world, zooming in and out, cataloging and mapping the mechanics of the many intersecting games that make up our world. I'd use all of this information to develop strategies, connect dots, and find cheat codes inherent in our computerized conditioning camp. Gray areas that weren't necessarily violations, but I knew they'd make our shiftless shepherds mad. I think my unique abilities are what prevent Lux from eliminating me on the spot, but unluckily, their ego spotlights me as, one may say, "extra exploitable." Thus, to protect myself or fight back against being taken advantage of, identifying the hologram opportunity had to be part of my much larger plan. Close your eyes and notice for yourself. What else in the classroom might stand out as an opportunity to pull back a bit more autonomy? I know there may be a ton now that I've flipped your lens."

She took a little longer to noodle my question while I led her through the waste with her eyes clenched shut. "School supplies! That process is weird. A-am I right? We ask for things and then they have to be returned to our desk by the end of the day. The next day the desk is empty until we make another request."

That's exactly what I thought. "But that's how it works *currently*.

"You're exactly right though, we ask *holographic* teachers for *real* school supplies. As long as we explain the 'educational necessity' it appears inside our desk.

"Before you get too excited, do not try any of this . . . yet. Take your time. Keep looking, listening, and learning for now, please." I made sure to add the disclaimer before things went too far. It was my plausible deniability if this ever got back to

Bodi or Anansi. "The next cheat I found were the substitutes. Through my reading on holographic technology, I figured out that our regular teachers were simply well-trained AI apparitions. But when they had to be retrained, updated, or patched, our substitutes were remotely operated by *real people* in Lux."

"Yeah, yeah, yeah. That is strange. Substitutes, even though the teachers were holograms, almost every week," Soma responded eagerly.

"Strange as hell that they would have faulty eduGames technology running these classrooms in the first place, but that's beside the point. The final cheat revealed itself when you layer all of these oddities together. Ordering 'educational necessities' from substitute holograms. When a class ordered all at once, we'd overwhelm the remote substitute. Resulting in a blanket 'yes' every time.

"They didn't flag this as harmful as long as we tested well and we didn't take anything out of class. So I initiated a batch request one day. It took *a lot*, but I got the entire class on board. Even your big bro." *A lot* was glossing over the elaborate and messy organizing I did. It doesn't even approximate the weeks of dealmaking, planning, hushing, and sucking up to a bunch of mindless 20-somethings dead-set on making massa' proud. None of them wanted to rock the boat or do anything to jeopardize their graduation or work assignment prospects. I eventually concocted enough compromises to spur each of my classmates to become an accomplice. I learned a lot about them and the effect the school was having on us all. My former classmates still hold a grudge against me for getting them involved in my risky scheme. To them, that was worse than the shame the community had for me as the child of the captured GELD leader. And that ostracization made me super cynical. I lost much of the hope that drove me along the slow, laborious, inclusive path to my dreams. Instead I figured they needed to see it to believe it.

"Really? What did Bodi ask for?" Soma asked with a sly smile.

I hid my mouth trying to be coy, but I eventually moved my hand to whisper, "Diamond prayer beads. He said it reminded him of y'all's mother."

She flung her free hand around and her whole demeanor changed to displeasure. "Boring, but it definitely sounds like him."

"Some folks asked for colored pencils and others for backpacks. One twerp asked for an entire encyclopedia set on the 50 Laws of Luxite Power that couldn't even fit in his poor desk. Such limited creativity. But *I* asked for a brand-new tablet, and surprisingly, it worked." I said it casually even though I knew how big of a deal it was for a Kuroban. I'd used the system in some small way to serve my own needs. Instead of the other way around.

"I bet that was an exciting day. You actually got to surf the Luxite internet," Soma said as the central Kuroban community was coming closer. The waste diminished and divided at our feet to give way to hearty, heated soil. The gentle glint off the ground was just the welcome I needed.

"One more detail first. I wasn't allowed to take it out of class, and I had to ensure this was more than a one day thing for me. The only place where I had access to the internet was in class anyway. I loaded a script I adapted from an old cybersecurity book to cloak my digital presence. I spent most of class for the next few months watching videos or reading info online. I was supposed to be learning about whatever nonsense they were teaching, but instead I was leading my own learning journey. I used context clues to scrape by with my schoolwork.

"Regretfully, access to all of that information online lured my hungry little mind deep into a complex quagmire of more questions. There were new devices and shows and memes and stories and trends and jokes and Luxite culture rapidly devolving online. The problem was I got greedy."

We finally made it back to Kuroba. We walked down the barren dirt boulevard. The air was bulging with silence, every building was shut with the lights off, and even the yards, usually full of piles of plucked goodies, were empty. Large dead spots of pale soil scarred the dirt yard of each humble hut. Instead of the abundant connection and commerce I loved, the community was dead. It was as if all life in Kuroba had been extinguished at once, without a struggle or residential damage.

The anxious voice in my head worried that everybody had packed up and teleported to our homelands, many oceans beyond our clifftop community, without Soma and I. A bone-chilling wind creeped up the mountain bringing with it the stench of the dump and the exhaust from the factories. An old plastic jug tumbled across the main boulevard, hurled by the strong summit-seeking gust. I tried to put worries out of my mind and continue my conversation with Soma, but her shifty eyes and rapid breathing revealed her concern.

"G-g-greedy? How did you get the – uh, uh – tablet to stay in your desk?" Soma asked.

As we kept walking nothing stirred. It made me even more uneasy with each step. "They created the rule that supplies only lasted a single day *because of* me. It's not at all as cool as it seems. Definitely don't do this, for real Soma. Promise me, please!"

She gave me a stern face and stopped our progress. "I promise." That moment of sincerity was disturbed as emerald lights streaked across the sky. This time not only did I look up and see it, it seemed like Soma did as well because her head shot up in time with mine.

We both looked at each other for a second and only acknowledged the strange green light telepathically before I edited my promise for her. "Do better than me."

I fought to hold in a satisfied laugh before I continued my story. "I wanted to share what I'd learned with the rest of the community. They would only trust me if they saw it themselves, so I found a dead tablet in the dump. I fixed it to work offline. I snuck the dummy tablet into class. But I forgot these classrooms were also surveillance centers. As soon as I brought in the refurbished tablet to smuggle out my illicit information, the digital indoctrinator running the class knew. They expelled me for illegitimate use of school supplies right before I got my master's degree."

"Really? You were so close. Then what happened?" Soma asked while racing ahead of me.

The Elders, including my mom, had to beg our metropolitan managers for forgiveness. But I didn't want her to focus on that. "I didn't get to keep either tablet. That didn't matter so much though. I fixed a new tablet and tried to record anything I had straight from memory. Th-that's . . ." I grabbed my therapy journal with my Libook resting inside, but hesitated before showing it to her. I knew she'd spotted it yesterday morning, but showing it to her felt like I was involving her in an ongoing crime.

"Nice! You gotta teach me to do that with tablets and stuff. You can really take tablets and stuff from the dump and revive them? Who knows what riches are waiting to be reborn from the dump." Soma was so energetic, but I could see her crib up ahead. I needed to wrap it up in case an irate Bodi or Anansi were inside waiting to teleport with the rest of the town.

"Sorry I *can't*." I gave her an exaggerated wink to not be too obvious on the empty road. "You'll have to find your own way. In the end I didn't get a work assignment and I only have a bachelor's. That's nothing for Kurobans to get hired in Lux. But thanks to Bigtime Bodi, I eventually got an amazing work assignment. Interestingly enough, I'm working on the same education system that tried to abort me."

"That's wild. I'll definitely do my best to take my time to figure out my way." We made it to her yard. It was empty, not even a dead spot surrounded her well-modeled hut.

It felt good to have a moment of connection. She was at least open to another way of thinking even though she was too young to do anything about it. Soma was a glimmer of hope for the next generation. She was the next evolution of the work Baldie picked up and left for me. And I'd hand it off to Soma. "You really have to pay attention, Soma. I'm talking about high-level noticing. You're literally walking in two worlds. Building your dreams covertly while staying in character for the forces in charge, Luxite or otherwise." The silence broke when I stepped on a stick in her yard. I jumped backwards and almost ran away thinking her family had come out to give me a piece of their mind.

After a few seconds of panicked breathing, I realized no one but Soma was around. Before I left Soma to her silent house, I composed myself enough to begin succession planning. I didn't know what was going to happen after I made my career conscription decision and the time was ticking. I whipped out my Libook and gave her the rundown. "This tablet is my Libook, liberation + notebook. Liblet didn't have the same revolutionary energy. I'm putting together all the pieces I've found to overcome this oppressive game Lux holds us in. I also write my plans and testimonies for pivotal situations like the ceremony tonight. In fact, here is my Five Step Plan for Liberation:

1. *Build video games*
2. *Get my "educational" games in the Kuroban school.*
   a. *Use my connection to Kuroba to receive the Kuroban/Luxite coalition government contract to replace eduGames.*
3. *Nudge narratives, catalyze countervailing ideas, seed seditious science, and raise rebels en masse.*
4. *Kuroba stops Lux using my game as our organizing platform.*
   a. *Let the people decide how they overcome their oppressors once they have the tools and the consciousness to act.*
5. *Freedom!*

The notes in here are where I reflect on what went wrong, right, and how to improve. It's my love letter to Kuroba. To our emancipation."

Soma let out a frenzied howl. "Ooooh, and this works? Can I see?"

I was going to deny her request and share more of what I had written when a strong voice yelled from the door. "Soma, if you don't bring your narrow ass in this house. What are you doing hanging out with that hoodlum again?

"Only half an hour before your ceremony starts, you bum! And you better get ready because this one'll be a doozy," Anansi roared in his raspy, reptilian voice from deep inside their luxury hut.

I didn't stay around to have a conversation. I yelled bye and ran away. So Anansi hadn't been teleported. Then what was going on in Kuroba?

He was right though. I was running short on time. I needed to get back home ASAP because this wasn't the time to make a bad impression.

STAGE COMPLETE

Health Points 25%
Magic Power 15%

Mission #1: Get Home Safely . . . . MADE IT, BUT SOMETHING
FEELS STRANGE
Mission #2: Make Career
Conscription Decision . . . . FAILURE, MORE IMPORTANT
BUSINESS CAME UP

Experience Points Gained [150]
Coins [+80] Auto Pay Kuroban Food Fund
Items Received [NONE]
Status Effect [NONE]

Chapter 11: Overclocking

Mission #1: Get Cleaned Up
Mission #2: Write Statement for Ceremony
Mission #3: Arrive on Time to Ceremony

Impending duress pressed upon me. It was a whopping weed planted deep within us all, fed by conscious and unconscious agents of cultural curation. Its weight multiplied as time ticked by. Each moment increased the tremendous tension building up inside. I didn't feel this anxiety-inducing duty at work like Bodi and the rest of the compliant Kuroban commuters, but it was a different story when it came to Mom. My punctuality would be the first statement I made at the Earth Going, much before a word was uttered.

My second impression was my appearance. I didn't have time to *hope* I found a full tuxedo somewhere in the vast wasteband. It was a crapshoot to find one in good enough shape to wear off the "rack." So I figured I'd go for the first outfit with no visible holes and focus on cleanliness instead. Kurobans knew maintaining the "professional" standard demanded by floury folks down the mountain wasn't the simplest task, but it was expected just the same.

Mom always drilled into me, "A shower and a change of clothes are the antidote to nasal disrespect." The combined funk from a day under the pill's influence and the commute through the dump would only add insult to indiscretion. So when I made it home, I hurried to take a grueling shower. Grueling because shower supplies needed to be procured and *hot* showers needed time and effort for the water to percolate properly.

In addition, I needed a plan to quickly dry off afterwards. Too much to do and not enough time. Then I had to pick out the perfect outfit, make my career decision, and cede a couple minutes to script my testimony.

After a shower that took longer to prepare than take, I was shivering in front of our simple solar stove trying to speed up the drying process. Anansi's foreboding time check echoed in my head. I searched around on the kitchen shelf beside me until I found an expired lotion container Mom sometimes used as a cooking fat in her leftover remixes. I had to squeeze out crusted globs of ancient lotion that replaced the missing pump before I got to anything usable deep inside. What lotion I coaxed out liquified into a creamy paste as I applied it to my moist skin. As fast as I squeezed and banged out the dregs of the discarded lotion, its watery form baked onto my body. I didn't mind the opaque coating covering my skin because my mind was already preparing my ceremonial statement. I had to multitask to battle the clock.

My teeth chattered as I kicked my prep process into over-drive. Before all the water-logged lotion completely crusted over, I dashed to a pile of clothes. I reached in to seize some drawers to throw on while I got everything else squared away. My room looked empty without all of my books and game guides piled everywhere. I wanted to share them with Soma, but without my comfort items I realized I had to prepare for a big change.

The Libook was still sitting in the clump of clothes I ripped off on the way to shower. I rushed to wipe my hands off on anything around to safely type my game-changing statement. I grabbed my Libook and laid across my concave mattress. My midsection collapsed inside the mattress's sinkhole.

I batted away water dripping from my hair into my face as I racked my brain. Going by the traditional agenda, as the PWH I'd be asked to account for the harm I caused. I'd need to be honest with myself and my community. In the end I'd also need to reconcile with all sides of the truth. Truthfully, my focused hope to aid my kinfolk may've actually caused more hurt than I'd expected. If that was true, then I'd need to formulate a path forward for a better Kuroba. Just like Baldie planned to do. My hope was that if I did this right, it was an early crack at liberation. My statement itself and my actions yesterday needed a perfect balance between saving myself and taking accountability. That had to be superimposed upon the need for systemic accountability. In particular, it required subtle elements to release the self-reinforcing rage roaring inside Mom. Because whatever happened tonight, I'd have to come back to her house. I'd also need to impress the Opps, the youth, the elders, the religious, on top of inspiring my latent revolutionaries.

This was my apology and rallying cry. All the proper words, inflections, meanings, mannerisms, and illustrations needed to be assembled precisely. A spell to conjure a fusion of social magic with the power to reanimate and galvanize my community. That was the careful balance I attempted to compose.

Suddenly, the call to begin the Earth Going rang out. The ground trembled under the reverberations of the powerful tone. From the burial site hidden in the center of Kuroba, the ceremony's initiation stretched through the entire settlement like a mass text. "KU-KU-KUUUUUUU!"

"Shit, I'm late," I screamed, snapping out of my thought spiral with nothing typed on my pad.

My rush to get ready had failed. Near my bed were some recently rescued slacks Mom left for me the day before. I shot my legs through them. As swiftly and as safely as possible I smashed my Libook in its journalistic jacket under my arm and rushed toward the door. I realized I didn't have a top on, and I spun back around to my room.

I tripped trying to scramble for a top and stumbled upon a new pile Mom had moved to the main room. I paused briefly because I knew whose clothes those were. Mom was serious about dismantling her memorial and moving on from her unresolved loss. But what about me? The leftover clothes that made up her shrine to her partner were the best I could get.

I didn't have time to tussle with the long-term repercussions or potential disrespect. I ripped into the pile to uncover an aged, but charming mycelial turtleneck. I ducked my head in and slid my arms out. Throwing my tattered belt in one loop, I completed my outfit while running out the door. I clutched a heft of belt and slack with my left hand while I squished the therapy journal under my right arm. This sloppy system kept a hand free to string up my belt while on the run. I smashed the door shut and was off to the ceremony.

I was technically late, but if I ran hard enough, I might reduce *how* late I was.

As I ran, a welcoming, serene power rose ever so gently from my feet and pushed me faster along the soft glow of the dirt road. The streets were illuminated with a hint of arugula, as if covered in reflective paint. I hobbled as I ran, trying to put myself together while maintaining a grip on the therapy journal. I came down the main boulevard of our clifftop barrio flanked by a succession of shanty structures built from trash and dingy dirt. Every step induced a mysterious micro pulse of purpose to wash over my body. Although I was rushed and unprepared for the intense incoming social crucible, my body remained at peace.

The ground palpitated under my feet. The ceremonial music was rocking at my hallowed destination. The sensual, driving shakers rattled down to the sandy sod of the ocean below. Their sound rooted the whole ceremony with a steady *"shuka-shu shuka-shu shuka-shu shuka-shu shuka-shu,"* on and on, lazily accelerating its invite to all within earshot.

Then, as the stars began to dominate the early night sky, the twinkle of the bells and glass rang out, *"bling gling-gling bling gling-gling."* These sounds connected us to an ecological intelligence irrespective of time, space, and dimension. The rich ringing resounded inside me, drawing me in soul-first. My legs automagically caught the cadence of the chords vibrating throughout my body. My feet slapped the ground with the certainty and intention to rip open some spacetime distortion allowing me to arrive early.

An enormous crowd milled around the burial ground as I approached. I arrived at the same time the beat dropped. The bass whizzed through my body, echoing down my pores. *"Cha, cha, cha. Chuga cha-cha. Cha, cha, cha. Cha-cha."*

The swagger and personality of this unfolding orchestra ballooned as more community members had their cells serenaded. Intricacies and nuances arose as the sound gained fortitude. More drums and pots and sticks and cups and strings and stomps pounded out the celestial conjuring.

Whatever the dump offered, my people used. Everyone added their bit of energy into the beautiful arrangement of sonic summoning. Here, at this pious plot, sat our most sumptuous soil. Hallowed humus cultivated for generations. Now it fed our hidden field of fungi, the same place where we returned our ancestors to the land they served throughout their lives. It was our last little secret from Lux. Every Kuroban samba-ed amidst the bounty of mycelial fruit in a synchronized stupor. Our skin melded and mixed into a vibrant mess of earth-tones sliding through one another.

The mushrooms grew before my eyes, feeding off the music ricocheting over and through each teetering toadstool. Vocal healers let out their song of syncopated storytelling to complete the ceremonial charm, guiding our souls to commune with those of our ancestors and our descendants. *"Connected to earth, we live among trees. Skin smilin' like the sun, in all shades of sand . . ."*

Every one of us were drawn in as if by magnetic strings attracting, repelling, and twirling amongst the cavorting caps. We all tapped into the ecological groove engulfing the mycelial burial grounds. Not a single shroom was threatened in the process. The entrancing music gave us the innate direction to dance *with* the fungi instead of on them. It was the perfect cover for me to sneak in unnoticed. I used my two-step as camouflage. Mixing into the miraculous musical menagerie.

I scouted the setup of the ceremony as I danced my way through the mosh of melanin. A large, ornate chair was set up right in front of me. If I remembered right, that was the witness(es) seat. The section for the youth was on my right, and the Elders would be to the left. I knew my seat as the PWH was on the other side of the scene. Directly through the dancing. I couldn't see beyond the mass of bodies blocking my view, but I knew the empty chair was waiting for my tardy ass.

I did a couple body rolls and cabbage patches, letting my feet do their fanciful flit through the jazzy crowd. I made my way over to the youth first. They all sat on a gnarled, old bleacher section that had long been dragged here from the dump. Soma was pouting in the corner of the front row. The other juveniles sat up straight with smiles so big their back teeth bumped against their ears.

"Hey Soma, why so sad? Are *you* actually the one on trial?" I burped up a laugh through the awkwardness of being the butt of the joke.

She snapped back to me, "Why does he treat us like this? Forcing us to sit quietly with fake-old grins. All while y'all have fun and dance."

I smiled hard to reflect the gigantic grin from the rest of the youth to bring some levity to the situation. "Sorry. Sucks for y'all. But who told y'all to, you know, be little statues of false joy?"

She dropped deeper into her pout as she answered, "You know who."

I didn't even need her covert nod across the burial grounds and the crowds. I knew exactly who she was insinuating. My face twisted up in disgust. "Your pops is definitely tripping."

Soma let out an exasperated sigh and slowly rocked her head side to side. "Mmm-mmm-mmm. You're telling me! He's been beefing with the other Elders too."

"What's he been doing to my momma?" I clutched my hand to my heart with a quizzical look on my face.

She shot up from her rusting seat. The entire bleachers wobbled. Soma quickly sat back down to steady the shared seat for the other youth. Their faces remained the same despite the near collapse. Soma had the noticeable strain of stress to her voice as she exclaimed, "He's changing everything. He's trying to force us to spend more time studying at the education center. You know how he already thinks Wafaa' is illegitimate because she ain't old and anti-Kuroban like him. An-and there've been rumors he's gonna snitch to Lux to get Elder Mama removed."

"You know, that's no way to be. I'm rubbing off on you too much. Don't talk about yo daddy like that. And yes, school sucks, but that tracks. Although. . . Mom's additional anger and superior strangeness the last few days makes sense now."

I stroked my chin putting the pieces together. Despite Mom's own experience with the futility of subservience, she was a judgmental traditionalist. Especially when it came to me. That belief would surely make her more vulnerable to Anansi's trickery. She was stuck in the Maroon days before the Seed Slaughter. Those were the richest times for Kurobans after being stolen from our homelands. The possibility to restore that livelihood was the only thing that pulled her from despondency after her partner was incarcerated.

She was the head Elder not only because she possessed the most traditional Kuroban wisdom, but she also poured her whole self into this community, this land, and what remained of our culture. With complex trauma accumulation from our original kidnapping, the twisted torture centuries afterward, the Maroon village massacre she witnessed, and her partner being ripped away, she was holding unimaginable pain. Pain that drove her toward a spineless safe space. It didn't matter how strong she acted in front of everyone else. It was all a mask she put on. She reminded us all, especially me, that draconian respectability and societal rules defined by the vampires of the valley, were safety incarnate. It was the survival of Kuroba over everything with her. This philosophical failing, in my opinion, remained as the ruling rift in our relationship. That and the adolescent grudge I just couldn't kick.

I couldn't even look in Mom's direction. I stared off in the distance and let the music cool me back down until Soma disrupted my daydreaming. "Elder Mama's no different from the rest of us though. Pop is pulling the strings in his own favor. I've heard him talking about moving, *assimi*-something, and *bored* schools . . . I think. That's confusing because school is already so boring, but the way he's been talking, something is already in motion."

She caught my attention and brought my smile back. "You're so right. You're very wise for your age. You know that? As soon as I get this ceremony and my career squared away, Mom and I need to have a heart to heart. Oh! And here's a little something for you to hold until after the ceremony. I know it'll be safe with you. It's no use to me since I didn't have the time to write anything." I whipped my therapy journal holding its clandestine cargo from under my arm and quickly slipped it into Soma's grasp.

She let out a tiny little jig as I handed the guide to her. "Oooh, thanks so much. Hol' up, why aren't you wearing any shoes?" She pointed to my bare, dusty feet. I was sorely out of place amongst all the fourthhand shoes jigging at the ceremony. Unfortunately, I was too distracted to notice she was pointing out my impression's indisputable impropriety.

"Yeah, yeah, I got you," I responded. "Hold onto it tightly. Don't lose it." Something in my soul blared like the alarm of looming harm. My eyes diverted elsewhere, zipping around the circle until I zoned in on the Elders' section.

Hopefully Mommy-dearest hadn't spotted me yet. Mom was deep in conversation with Wafaa', the Elder she brought in last year. Wafaa', the third and final Elder, was like the community's young, fun, forward-thinking auncle. They were only a handful of years ahead of me and well-known as the Extinguisher. They possessed the unique healing power to diffuse, diminish, or douse any escalating situation. And they'd honed their planning and execution abilities for developing dump-derived solutions to community needs during their brief time in GELD. Those skills made them invaluable and was why Mom campaigned to add more "youths" to lead Kuroba forward. That and their connection to Baldie. Mom may have been the head, but Wafaa' was already both the brains and the soul.

Both Mama and Wafaa' were draped in traditional regalia. Their colorful tunic shirts draped over their flowing asymmetrical wrap skirts. Bright beads crowned their heads and complemented their colorful outfit. Emerging from her elegant skirt, Mama's regal legs stretched into the ground like shapely twin tree trunks whose bark had been smoothed, glazed, and waxed to shine. The long end of Wafaa''s skirt hit their ankles, so only one leg peeked out, but Mama's barely grazed her knee. Mama looked as though she'd sprouted from the pristine earth she stood on.

Off to the side, looking way out of place amidst an unsettling cloud of controversy, was the final Elder, Anansi. I tried to hide behind the gyrating crowd to get a better view through the gaps without being noticed. I was still missing whatever was triggering my internal alarms. They echoed louder when I finally had him in view. Anansi was dressed in a fine Luxite suit and tie. His shoes shined so bright I saw my reflection in them from across the circle.

This bootlicker was busy talking to the slim security-Kuroban from the party. The same Opp who pushed me around when I tried to get into the eduGames party. The tall, slender Opp bounced around with a toothy grin and passionately spoke with Anansi throwing their partially gloved hands in every direction. An uneasy feeling bounced around in my body, making my nerves erupt from an avalanche of anxiety. They were obviously here for some nefarious reason. Anything involving Anansi was bad news.

The music waned away gracefully until it was completely replaced by Mama's gravitas. She stood up centimeter by centimeter, letting all of her elegance and poise cascade upon us. The dancers retreated from the mushrooms in reverence of her powerful presence. The entirety of Kuroba encircled the burial ground, titillating with anticipation. The whole community was under her spell. Except me. I knew the real her. Behind those powerful, bright eyes was the pain she wrestled with and the arguments we had.

Mama was tall. Me, not so much. She told me Baldie passed down their short, solid frame to me. I couldn't corroborate her words with the spotty memories I struggled to decipher. My mental mementos were too disjointed and opaque to distill the connection I thirsted for. Still, I never dared to ask Mom for a name, stories, or pictures — like we would have any. I didn't want to bring her back to the painful place she was in after Baldie was stolen away. I might've walked past or over my long-lost parent a million times without a word. I just couldn't remember enough to tell.

Mom's newfound self-assuredness, as surface-level as it was, held our people together through these tenuous times when our systemic starvation sharpened in severity. The superficial satisfaction she fashioned out of refuse and resourcefulness mitigated the communal calamity brought on after the armistice. These days we danced from crisis to crisis, literally every payday and figuratively through gradual famine. Always a moment or two away from the next daily disaster that had to be managed or mitigated. Her instrumental influence, even just bringing on Wafaa' to represent the spirit of the youth, amplified not only her height but also her power over Kuroba's path forward. These moments were exactly why she put on a good face for the public. Knowing she did not share that grace and love with me, much less herself, made me more disappointed than proud.

Oh no! Everyone was staring at me. I was front and center, but not in the way I wanted. I had been lost in thought and left alone standing in the hallowed burial ground. *There went my good impression.* Mom shelled me with an optical strike of shame shurikens. Her disapproving glance alone was enough to unfreeze me in that mortifying moment.

I scurried to my seat like a roach on speed and plopped my butt into the gaudy throne taken from the trash. The alarms blaring in my gut evaporated like spit in the desert as soon as I sat down. My soul went silent all of a sudden.

I watched my feet dangle from the chair, and Soma's words finally registered. I was totally barefoot. Soil residue clung haphazardly to the bottom of my feet. Add sacrosanct site desecration to my list of fatal faux pas. I shook off my feet and slapped them together before crossing them in my seat in an attempt to hide my blunder. Maybe less soil on my feet would lessen my cultural disrespect. Either way, I would've been even later if I'd taken the time to dig through the dump for ceremony-appropriate shoes. Or that's how I reasoned away my latest lapse.

Mama held the sacred vial of seed-humus. It twinkled like an iced-out bracelet. This ancient, robust soil was one of our most treasured community heirlooms. It was one of the few that weren't razed or pilfered or legislated away during the Seed Slaughter. Succulent soil imbued with the essence of our ancestors all the way back to our original homelands. It was the most potent, perfected bit of earth we possessed. Passed down and utilized at every settlement my people had ever maintained. It had been cared for and cultivated to record our history over centuries. As our ancestors pass on, they become the fertile stardust feeding the mycelium fields here. And like the sky twinkling above seasoned with billions of stars, this soil sparkled as well. It was well-seasoned with the souls of our genetic source code. The soil shone so brightly we saw each other clearly from anywhere around the ceremonial circle in the darkness of the new night. Just my luck!

Mama beamed bright, matching the land she so tenderly cared for. She was the healer and voice for the land. Her and her healing medium had such a deep connection she resembled it more than any of us. Her deep mahogany tint gave off a soft, creamy glint in the moonlight. Her healing specialty was the most revered in our society. It was what sustained us for generations before, during, and after our enslavement.

Mama didn't say anything. She suspended us all in shared silence. We were all on the edge of our seats ,eager for what would emerge from her mouth. She looked around at everyone assembled and seemed to lock eyes with every single one of us.

Anansi stopped talking to his gangly guest. He turned around with careful curiosity and immediately fell backwards, grabbing the back of his head as if someone had popped him. His partner-in-arms ducked their head and struck up a careful, clandestine jog toward the witness area.

Mama gave me a stinging side eye without breaking her crowd-scanning flow. No one else probably saw it, but I sure did. Her telepathic tongue-lashing hit me like a chi blast straight to my chest. She was already upset and wanted to make sure *I* knew that *she* knew. A second micro-movement in her side eye said it all. I saw the anger building up in her strong shoulders, tensing more by the second. When she took her eyes off of me, I instantly wished I'd spent more time preparing. My miscues were mounting by the minute. A well-crafted response might be my only way out of this deepening pit I was in.

STAGE COMPLETE

Health Points 25%
Magic Power 15%

Mission #1: Get Cleaned Up . . . . SUCCESS BUT NO SHOES
Mission #2: Write Statement for Ceremony . . . . THOUGHT ABOUT IT AT LEAST
Mission #3: Arrive on Time for Ceremony . . . . FAILURE, HOPEFULLY NOBODY
                                                        NOTICED

Experience Points Gained [340]
Coins [+80]
Items Received [NONE]
Status Effect [NONE]

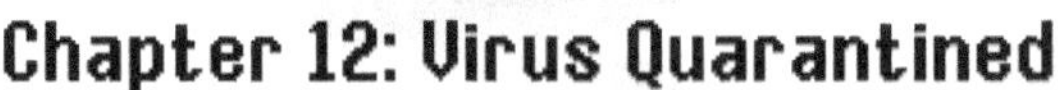

Chapter 12: Virus Quarantined

Mission #1: Don't Upset Mom Anymore
Mission #2: Survive the Ceremony
Mission #3: Make Career Conscription Decision

Mom's powerful words initiated the Earth Going. "With all the grace and power of Quawd, akwaaba Kuroba!"

As one cheery chorus we responded together, "Medaase Elder Mama! Praise Quawd on high."

"Family of Kuroba, remember, we are no longer Elders. We're mere *stewards* of this great community. And, of course, I love you all."

The crowd responded in chorus, "And we love you too!"

She stood up even straighter as she introduced the ceremony, but her voice shifted from caring and chipper to stern and solemn. "Every other week, on paydays, we hold this Earth Going ceremony to reconstruct us as Kurobans. First we celebrated, now we will commune, and I know most of y'all hungry-asses are eager to consume as we typically do after our celebration, but this ceremony will be a little different. We will explain these differences, but I wanted to address the lack of nourishment being provided at its normal phase in our ceremony right off the bat. This time we must wait — for good reason. Normally we provide a feeble feast, procured with meager tithes from our employed community members.

"I know the scant rations we provide are worth its weight in soil, but this time Lux is blessing us. They've provided a complementary feast so fine, so fancy, and so multifaceted it'll surely fill our bellies not only physically, but also mentally, emotionally, and spiritually. Altogether this ceremony is not just a community response to harm, it is our convalescence. And Lux's generous culinary contribution will do a great deal of healing. We simply must wait patiently and follow an altered schedule before we enjoy our communion.

"This ceremony will also be special as we only have a single issue, concerning a single individual this time. That fact should tame your bellies as you all should not have to wait too long. The single individual who is the source of the presumed harm in question, simply known to us as the Person Who Harmed, will henceforth be referred to as P-W-H. The PWH is seated to my left as usual." As she motioned toward me, boos and taunts piped up from pockets of the surrounding Kuroban mass. "We stand by this formality to ensure we rectify the harm's deepest taproot. In the end, we will all be evolved individually and collectively.

"And before I'm bombarded with questions and concerns, I have an additional note on the peculiar procedure we will employ to effectively conduct this unique solo session. As you all may be able to tell, this ceremony is especially difficult for me. Because, of course, the PWH is my own — *ahem* — beautiful, but burdensome baby."

I couldn't stop myself from yelling, "Mom! Really!? I'm lit-er-al-ly 30."

She shook me off and continued, "Don't be worried. I will remain as objective as a mother can be. But to ensure objectivity, our newest *Steward* Wafaa', they/them, will facilitate. Wafaa', please."

Mom sat down on her towering throne of trash and released us from her hold. Wafaa', much shorter, but captivating in their own right, stood up. Their effortless, authentic, familial charisma was what always defused any tense moment she faced. They were smooth like a soft breeze sailing over the surface of the sea, convincing the combative to cooperate and the stubborn to sacrifice. Normally, every word, step, movement, and thought was perfectly balanced with the energy and elegance befitting the room. But as Mama handed Wafaa' the seed-humus, it slipped through their fingers. Luckily, Mama saved it from smashing on a heavy, rusty lead pipe that served as the armrest for her throne.

Wafaa' carefully held the precious seed-humus in one hand and shook off their near cultural massacre. From behind their back, they whipped out a sizable bundle of papers with their free hand. Wafaa' began to read from an uninspired script in a monotonous drone. "The initial request for this session was made by fellow Steward Anan, who handles and heals the vaunted relationship between Lux and Kuroba. He remarked about the immense harm the PWH provoked on Kuroba's relationship with Lux. Anan's significant expertise in this realm — with regard to maintaining and improving the quality of life for us — makes this a very serious concern to us all."

A raucous chorus of cheers rang out in appreciation of Anansi's introduction. Noteworthy because he rarely had many fans here. His primped and powdered fans lived charmed lives under the protected valley below. But tonight, he was the big man in the shanty settlement. Yet another bad sign.

Wafaa' continued after the cheers subsided, but with the script down by their side. They spoke with their standard seductive cadence and inflection this time. "All of us community Stewards have adopted our new title as you may have heard. It emphasizes a renewed requirement and direction for our guidance of Kuroba. This is simply the first shift to ensure our stewardship better mirrors our critical, creative, yet youthful population. In exchange, Anan has insisted on a much altered and accelerated version of this ceremony.

"After the sudden disappearance of all three former Elders, we've taken over the *stewardship* of this great community. In that transition, compromise and cooperation have been key to our continued march towards a greater standard of living for all Kurobans. These changes may be uncomfortable, but are necessary for our survival. Therefore, it has been brought to our attention that as long as we also introduce more 'professionalism,' as Anan puts it, Lux will be more amenable in adversities such as the one we're discussing today. And backing that promise up with unctuous goodies on the house! So that is why I am reading from the agreed upon instructions."

"Psssht," I grumbled to myself, irritated at the foreseen fraudulence that rang empty to realistic reconstruction. Somehow my mom caught wind of my exasperation and whipped her eyes at me. Her gaze was so powerful, even at a distance, it welded my mouth shut. I sat up straight and tightened up. She cranked out an eerie exaggerated smile with her head cocked to cover up her obvious contempt.

Wafaa' went back to their mechanical monologue. "To begin the ceremony, we dance with one another alongside our ancestors to appease Quawd. We hope to welcome him to guide our reconstruction. This ancestral asymptote serves as our portal to his kingdom. We will then hear statements from the most impacted by the PWH's harm. Through the grace of Quawd we will hold space for our victims."

Everyone in the crowd stammered out with their own prayer, proclamation, or proverb to Quawd. I tried as hard as I could to hide my disgust with this cult-like behavior. Every pious Kuroban made the sign of Quawd and begged for blessings in concert with one another.

"We have two direct eyewitnesses. Their testimony will determine how yesterday's events can be reconciled. The first victim is Agymah, he/him. He is currently on his initial work assignment as a security official—"

Agymah, the rail-thin security-Kuroban who was talking to Anan, raised a finger-gloved hand to interrupt from their plush witness seat. "Ma'am, my name is Bradley." He was now stuffed in a neck brace, with an eye patched and a bandaged body. His left arm was hanging in a well-constructed sling and his right leg was confined in a conspicuously clean walking boot. Across the burial grounds, the moonlight glimmered from a massive bruise on his arm to an angled cut on his cheek. I had seen him only a few moments ago. He didn't have all of that medical equipment when he was talking to Anansi, did he? My heart dropped and I cranked up my antenna to track any other tricks teeing up.

"Yes, thank you," Wafaa' said, breaking from their rigid reading. "That wasn't noted here but please don't ma'am me, bruh." They let their request settle in a smidge before their text-to-talk voice returned. "*Bradley* was working security yesterday evening at the event where the PWH committed their — ahem — *mass terror assau*— come on, really!?"

Anansi coughed out, "again." His fingerprints were all over this ruse.

Wafaa' gritted their teeth and turned the robotic recitation back on. "I apologize, I meant to say the PWH committed their mass terror assault on a private gathering of innocent Luxites.

"After Bradley's testimony we will hear from our star

community member, Bodi, he/him. He was coerced by the PWH to arrive afterwards in order to extricate the PWH back home, to this very hard-working community. We'll then allow the PWH to make their procedural apology — which *will* include their 30th year career decision — before they are dismissed. Finally, we will take these statements into consideration to advise fair consequences and hold the PWH accountable. Accountability that will address the confluence *of depravity* that the PWH represents.

"If we allow Quawd to use us as his vessel, then we will conclude this in a rapid and effective manner and get to nosh immediately afterwards. As a bonus, flavor-bursting dishes from a selection of three-star restaurants from the Luxite Mining Conglomerate's Dining Guide have been donated for this meeting. Praise Quawd!"

The restless crowd chanted and stomped with the furor of a battle-bound army. "Praise Quawd, Praise Quawd!" The ground and a bright green bolt of lightning struck slightly down the mountain near the dump's edge. The erosive energy was palpable. It weighed us down, made it hard to breathe, and ate away at the joy that normally came with this blessed celebration. Anansi struggled to hide the glee growing on his face.

Wafaa' looked unsettled by the sheer force of the crowd. They rifled through their papers, frantically flipping sheets as their hand trembled. The congregation kept chanting and stomping until my mom, still seated comfortably in her throne, made a stiff upward motion with her hand. Her strong palm flew up and swiped downward, instantly silencing the crowd.

Wafaa' took a deep breath and nodded to Mama with a look of relief. Then they dropped the crumple of papers to their side and spoke with their back straight up and conviction behind their voice. "As usual, we use the sacred seed-humus.

Now, this little thing holds our lineage to the land, back to our earliest ancestors and our original home lands. The one holding the vial of our communal soul force will be the only one speaking. Period, point-blank. Ya heard? Its connection to Kurobans past, present, and future will bestow clarity, control, and candor on the holder . . . or so the legend goes. The decisions we make now impact our people irrespective of time and context. Now let's welcome our first witness, *Bradley*."

Out of the corner of my eye, I spotted Anansi. He must have slipped out of sight during all the chanting and raving. Now he was way back in the distance, at my four o'clock. To his pre-tapped testifiers he was an easy ten thirty-five. Cool, calm Anansi was back there jumping and waving his hands back and forth trying to get Bradley's attention. Nobody noticed as they were all captivated, waiting for Bradley's response.

Wafaa' made a smooth slide towards Bradley to hand him the seed-humus. He stood up out of his chair and outstretched his hand to stop Wafaa' in their tracks. With a slick wink and a quick smirk Bradley launched into his testimony with the dramatic flair of a victimized wrestler. "*Elder* Wafaa' thank you, but I will not need the vial to make my statement. The horrid occurrence still haunts me vividly. It replays constantly in my head like a waking nightmare."

The crowd mumbled about the ostentatious departure from cultural customs. This whole ceremony was out of the norm. These were typically centered on how we, as a community, stamp out internal harm. And even deeper, root out any egregious or emergent violence on our list of complaints borne from Kuroban-Luxite relations.

I wasn't surprised at the change. I'd hoped for a fair chance to avoid the most restrictive retribution. At this point the odds of that seemed to be poor at best. Two versus one with a whole lot of help, Bodi and I versus Bradley . . . with an antagonistic arachnid weighing down the scales of justice with a well-crafted narrative of negativity. Hopefully, my advantage would be enough to get me out of this only slightly scathed.

Bradley spoke with a bellowing voice, "Thank you all for having me. And I'd like to extend special appreciation to Elder Mama for the professionalism you've brought into these ceremonies since I've moved to Lux. Even though I no longer reside here regularly, I've longed for more moral and upstanding leadership in my former homelands. And your openness to adopting aspects of Luxite judicial procedure will get us just that much closer to civilization." He held his pointer and thumb so close together I could barely see his beady eyes staring through the teensy gap.

Bradely continued with even more passion, "As the glamorous Wafaa' stated, I am Bradley. I have been on work assignment for just over two years now since I earned my master's degree at our glorious Kuroban learning center — *sponsored by Lux and powered by eduGames.* I now work in strategic security management.

"Now for the situation we are all gathered here today to discuss: Yesterday evening, I was on assignment to lead the security efforts for an exclusive Luxite event when I was brutally attacked. The attacking individual acted in gross disregard to what should be our well-known respectability standards. And it clearly disregarded the guidance of Quawd.

"It started when they stormed me with an armory of unapproved deadly weapons, pummeling me into the state you see before you now. They then terrorized a party full of Luxite workers and donors. The same saviors who run the glorious company behind our state-of-the-art learning center and facilitate the path to employment for hard-working, honest, humble Kurobans. This barbarism was carried out by the traitor to Kuroba straight across from me!" Bradley flung both arms towards me, including the arm wrapped tightly in a sling, in a dramatic display of disgust. The entire crowd gulped simultaneously.

Mother clutched her imaginary pearls and gasped audibly. I saw her temple throbbing. Her face did some twisting and turning before it dropped in disappointment. Her daily denunciations popped into my head: "Just follow the rules, have faith, that's all I ask of you. How you spend your time will be your downfall, trust me."

She didn't need to say a thing. This was exactly what she was trying to prevent.

I was pissed. Bradley was bold-faced lying. Pure, unadulterated falsehoods without flinching. Shame bubbled up inside me, latching onto my insecurities, and ready to pounce on the first external victim. I didn't even touch him, or anyone, at the party. If we're being really real, I didn't even touch his other security-Kuroban buddy. My *coat* hit him, not my hands. I jumped in my defense when the excitement died down. "Why you lying? You're lying your frickin' ass off. I didn't touch anyone. You ain't even injured. I saw you—"

"Child!" Mom jumped in. "I mean PWH. That was uncalled for on so many levels. I know this is uncomfortable, but maybe you need to hear the truth from someone besides me. You don't have the seed-humus — er, no one has it, b-but you know what I mean.

"Just follow the guidelines, please . . . please. Don't embarrass me any further. Your erratic, abhorrent thuggery has threatened our stability enough. You've put us all at risk. You're too old to be acting like this. Bradley darling, please continue."

Bradley tried to feign pain flaring up with an exaggerated grimace. He rubbed the shoulder of his arm *without* a sling in slow circles. A sly smile snuck through his flimsy performance.

"Ooh, ow, ow. Thank you, Elder Mama. As I was saying, the PWH came to the event in question harboring malice. The PWH intended to destroy the tenuous peace between our collaborative communities. Possibly to mass murder our Luxite benefactors, we just don't know.

"The gracious allies investing heavily in Kuroban education and employment opportunities were at grave risk. We can't even determine the inhuman depravity this psychopathic deviant intended to dole out. Why would they have such ill will for good people? The PWH came to the event disheveled and probably hopped up on some potent upper. They weren't even wearing a coat. And if you know about the Luxite winters, you know how reckless that is. The PWH stole alcohol, food, and was on their way to rob every Luxite and Kuroban . . ."

It was impossible for me to focus on the fabrication he spouted. I was flabbergasted, bewildered, disgusted. Everyone was nodding along, buying his tall tale of terror with their snorts and salutes.

Throughout the rest of Bradley's delusional description, my mind fluctuated between listening and semi-autonomously trying to assemble a plan for how to get out of my public character assassination. I bounced between Bradley's structured fallacy and my own psychic safe space. Bradley went on snitching and embellishing like I was more damning to Kuroba than the living, breathing Luxite slave masters he served.

I stood up to Lux yesterday. Or, at least, that's how I viewed it. Each and every person in this crowd was too scared to do anything in the universe of what I did. How else were we to find a way from under Lux's boot heel? My imagination might've been limited as far as strategy and execution, I can admit that, but whatever Kurobans had done before wasn't working. I was open to other options if anyone had any, but they seemed to want to extinguish me without even listening.

I clenched my teeth tight and grumbled under my breath. The community cooed like eager infants, sopping up all the shade without questioning its validity. They had no idea what was looming over them, creating that shadow in the first place.

Bradley blabbed on and on. "Five good, trustworthy, hard-working Kurobans employed at the event. Two, including myself at the door, and three inside serving the food and drinks. The PWH was so out of control I had to call the Blaus. It put us Kurobans working the event in danger. Tasing the PWH and calling in reinforcements was the only solution I saw. It would've been worse if this brave, yet confused former class-mate of ours hadn't arrived. He so graciously saved the PWH's life!"

Bradley moved to the side of the witness seat and Bodi walked up with a disheartened look dragging down his face. Bradley put an arm around Bodi's neck and shoulders. "All in all, this is a recurring issue with the PWH. They have already been expelled from the education center for sedition. Plus my Luxite foster brother shared a laundry list of run-ins the PWH has had with the Blaus while working in Lux. They've only been employed a couple months, who knows what cruelty they'll commit if allowed to roam free. Even how they showed up to work today, according to my foster brother, brash and unrepentant. We need to stop the PWH now. They must be taught a significant lesson or this will never end. Right Bobby?" Bradley said, his mention of Bobby — Bodi — the finishing touch to his veil of villainy.

Bradley's fingertips pranced along Bodi's shoulders before stopping to give a quick squeeze or two while snaking his neck around to whisper in his ear. Bradley's backbiting may have had the crowd in the palm of hands, but his icky aura creeped me to my core. And Bodi surely wouldn't let it stand.

Bodi hung his now bruise-less head in disgrace. He faced directly in front of me from the other side of the burial grounds. He avoided my eyes no matter how much I tried to catch his gaze. I'd assumed he'd be on my side, but his avoidance gave me pause. Maybe he knew this whole charade was coming. Still, he was silent.

A small section near Anansi led cheers and jeers throughout the ceremony. His local fan club sparked a mutual mantra of "Trai-tor, trai-tor" that quickly consumed the crowd. I watched Bradley hobble away, with a little pep in his phony limp, looking completely satisfied. My standing with the home team was in tatters. I stared at him, hoping my telepathic disgust would unearth some subterranean shame hidden inside of him. Then it hit me.

I knew this fool. "Bradley" was so familiar because *Agymah*, the name his parents gave him, went to school with Bodi and me. Same year and everything. His words and proclamation about being "our classmate" when talking about Bodi finally made sense.

He had always been the teacher's snitch, and then he ran off as soon as our class graduated. Word was he was silently selected for a special job that gave him the big break. The official backing to betray his brethren just like he'd always begged for. It took the most arguing and sweet talking to get him to go along with my class-wide supply request. And this joker requested the 50 Laws of Luxite Power encyclopedia set. As a matter of fact, he was probably the tattler who tipped off the system administrators that I was doing something "non-compliant." There had to be a reason they were monitoring me so thoroughly that day when I'd been hiding under their nose for years.

Bradley truly believed his people should be ruled and exploited. He justified it as the fate of the frail. The curse of the uncouth. If we all followed the dominant society's game play we'd be the exploiters ourselves soon enough. A mirage of immaculate meritocracy . . . or at least order.

Now he'd demonized me from top to bottom in front of my community. Fitting, isn't it? A traitor deflected blame and convinced the people he'd forsaken that *I* was a traitor. A traitor to the very people *I* served. I constantly fought for our freedom, or at least a down payment on it. But an Opp's gonna Opp. They're at least consistent in their opposition to liberation.

Another bolt of bright green lightning struck the same spot on the dump's edge as it did before the ceremony started.

I bit my lip until I tasted a bit of iron. It was the only way to stop myself from interrupting this spurious open-air scolding anymore. It was hard to endure this blatant rejection by the community I loved so hard. I held back the tears sloshing behind my clenched eyelids and tensed my body up.

Wafaa' started again, "Thank you Bradley for your – *uh* – candor and such a-*umm* graphic explanation. I know you have to get back to your foster home in Lux before Kuroban curfew. You are excused, and we will continue to our next witness. Bodi, will you please remain at the witness's seat and begin your testimony? Would *you* like the seed-humus?"

"No thank you, Steward Wafaa'. I don't need it. This is hard as it is," he said as he plodded in a stiff, anxious manner with his head hanging low. He was even more rigid than normal. Like he was clenching his butt cheeks so he didn't let his emotions leak out back. He lifted his head a vertebra at a time before he finally spoke. "A-ahem. I've thought long and hard about what I would say. I've known the PWH for most of our lives. They are my dear friend, but they've always, *always* been adversarial to Kuroba's stability."

The crowd whispered and whooped at the courageous callout from my close friend. I scooted to the edge of my seat and zoned into every word, overtone, and undertone he delivered. I had to know what Bodi really thought of me. Ignoring an Opp was easy, but not good old Bodi. My dog, my brethren, my ace grace glowa. The only one that stood up for me before and even after my expulsion. He was the only Kuroban left that hadn't discarded me as a lost cause.

Bodi took a deep breath before continuing. "I don't want to take too much of your time, so I'll get straight to the point. It's obvious the PWH has always been fighting Quawd's will from day one. Consistently diverging from how a Kuroban should dress, speak, work, behave, and overall represent our community. They have always been the true essence of a boundary-breaker, even during school. They're very smart, but it was this rebelliousness that got them expelled. Eventually, after continuing to interact with the expelled PWH while I was on work assignment and they were not, I pitied them.

"Their destitution made me feel guilty about my own success. They performed an assortment of odd jobs on top of begging and stealing to survive. Never able to scrape up enough to eat more than once a week, they disgraced this very burial ground by munching on the hallowed mushrooms before us. They'd been doing it in secret ever since they were young. They never stopped, even out of respect for our sacred crop. Now I know hunger is a normal occurrence here, but I don't know any one of us who would stoop to that level of brazen desecration. They had so, so, so much potential. And-and what they went through early in their life . . ." He closed his eyes and shook his head while still talking to the ancestors below. "That would break the strongest among us."

Damn, was he gonna tell *all* my business? The privacy breach urged me to stretch my hand in protest, but Mom's ocular admonishment blast sent a similar sentiment to Bodi. He was close enough to our family to feel the full force of her powerful peepers. Her body was as tense as a petrified rock. She wasn't on trial, but it was hard to tell by the way she acted. Mom obviously wasn't ready to face the decade of disarray I struggled through while she cried in the background. She wanted to keep our family business under wraps.

"But that's beside the point," Bodi continued. "I frankly got tired of hearing about their *many* failed patchwork plans to escape indigence. From dreams of making Kuroban "video" games to *free* us. Really? Without the requisite experience or education, and coming from this shithole! And freeing us from what? Dealing with reality? It's like they'd forgotten they're just a broke, hopeless, dirty Kuroban. And probably the laziest one of us at that. They need to put in the work and swallow their pride in order to approach their potential. There's no way around it. My pity drove me to recommend the PWH for a work assignment with me at eduGames, despite the PWH's repeated resistance to appropriate behavior. Maybe that's me being too nice or giving too much credit—"

The crowd came in with comforting groans.

"It's not your fault baby."

"Such a good heart."

"Had a similar situation last week."

"You know better now, son."

"They didn't deserve you."

Unbelievable. My friend, my day one, my — well, *to me*, we were close. I never expected him to be in on my communal cancellation. And it hurt worse because his opposition came at such a critical moment for me. He knew exactly how the work assignment referral came about. I was grateful, but I wasn't begging him for anything. The tension holding me up in my seat released and felt like I was adrift, floating on a vessel away from everyone.

He was feeling alienated at eduGames before I came. And *he* came to me for help with *his* work every night when *he* came home bawling about how *he* was being treated. He really benefited the most from referring me. I helped him without expecting anything in return.

Lying must be spreading around this burial site. But what healing item could I provide to dispense the maligned status effect being concocted of me, much less the malignity molding the masses?

I squeezed my knuckles in frustration as he dragged me while avoiding eye contact. "I-I hope I keep my job. I love it. I treasure it. I *need* it. I told the PWH many times to not get involved in Luxite business. Earlier *that* day, I pleaded with them not to go. But you see what happened. I wasn't convincing enough."

The crowd groaned as one. Bodi's voice began to tremble. "A-a-after they left the office in a hurry I kept working until I heard the Blau sirens blaring around the office. Luckily. Luckily. I mean, pure luck. The other two Kurobans we work with had already left. One had a post-Quawd pill collapse and the other was evacuating from both ends in the bathroom after overindulging in tainted water. That left me scared and alone. First, I scrambled to hide under my desk amid vacuums, wires, and detergent in terror. Eventually I realized the Blaus weren't coming for me, they were at the party next door. I knew immediately it had to do with the PWH.

"And pity swept me up once again. I blamed myself. I knew the PWH wasn't ready for this opportunity and I had to save them as usual.

"Luxites had gathered in the streets. Some put up chairs,

others set up picnic blankets. Vendors sold their wares. Kids danced and played at the jovial event. Screens on all nearby buildings streamed the violence going on inside the party along with energetic color commentary. Closer in, Blau vehicles and barricades blocked in the party venue. I ran through the laughing crowd, hopped over barricades, and dashed into the building. Someone screamed when they saw me, 'there's another one!' I was bombarded by Blaus before I took my next breath." Bodi spoke faster as tears fell from his eyes. But he continued his retelling.

"I-I tried with every bit of me to tell them why I was there. But they still beat me without remorse. Between every vicious strike against my body I saw other Kuroban bodies being tenderized while the large crowd watched as if it was a family-friendly outdoor concert. The PWH was nowhere to be seen, but it was hard to see anything while being pounded into the ground. The Blaus attacked Kurobans without regard to our life, except Bradley. He walked around supervising the whole bacchanal of beatings while I begged for death. Rods and shields and cattle prods and boots blitzed my body. The chords of bones breaking outplayed our screams. I prayed to Quawd, but the beating didn't stop until Bradley called off the Blaus."

My body felt hot. Everything was extremely uncomfortable and itchy. I didn't know my actions drove Bodi to go through such intense, public agony. I didn't ask him for help, but he did it anyways – like a real friend. Who knows, I might've been locked up, tortured, or publicly lynched had it not been for him. I'd be a gift to our harassers. A shining example of the fatal result of insurgency. I was ready to suffer the consequences of my actions, but not for my people to suffer too.

Still, the blame wasn't all on me. Bodi said himself that the Blaus were under Bradley's command. It was *very* much his fault too. The community had to see that, right?

Bodi, still looking down, sniffled. "Bradley then dragged what was left of my body like a blood-soaked bag of broken parts and pinned me against the wall. He poured some strange liquid down my tattered throat. Every molecule of the fluid tasted rancid and smelled of melting plastic. He released his arm and pointed to the PWH before walking away.

"The PWH was sleeping like a baby owl face down in a pool of sweat. The same result I'd seen multiple times when the PWH tested Quawd's will. He'd been shocked into submission by a judicious strike from our savior above. I always told the PWH to heed the great power of Quawd to protect us in Lux. Sadly, the PWH never listened.

"Bradley walked out *with* the Blaus. He hauled the other broken Kurobans in a handheld flatbed. He smiled and nodded judiciously on the way out. My body started reassembling itself as I slithered down the wall. Soon enough I had the power to pull myself together and carry the PWH to the train home.

And that's the end. Can I go now please?"

Anansi jumped up from his seat in the back of the crowd. "M-My dear Kurobans. Please focus on the most important details on my dear boy's brave testimony. Young Bradley only did what he had to do to save Kuroba. He was fulfilling his duty as a security Opp-erator. The PWH is the problem here. Their family has always been a burden on us."

Wafaa' turned quickly to Anansi. "Really? That is how you diffuse the situation? Does that 'protect' us? Sub-bashing another Steward? You're sick in the head—"

Anansi balled his fists as he snapped back at Wafaa'. "Don't derail this. Remember our agreement. You both promised. Are you not ready for this? You said you'd follow my rules if I brought Lux to the table for a large aid package. I will keep my word—"

"Now," Mom said in a voice that danced between control and chaos. "I only agreed to this because you said it'd be quick and easy. Just a little scare for my baby to get back on path. *Without* delving into 'personal' business. You know our history. I'm not here for an indictment on my leadership *or* my motherhood."

Silent green lightning struck again at the same dump's edge without anyone noticing except me. It was like something was channeling the green bolts. The crowd was too busy cheering like a raucous pub entranced in a pivotal championship match. The discord had elevated as the ceremony went on. Everyone seemed to be settling into this odious fever dream. Animalistic animosity salivated for Mom and me.

A confusing, multifaceted rage overcame me. I was embarrassed that Mom was getting hit too. Even if I was upset at myself, my logical brain was more disturbed by my community. It was as if they'd all lost any capability to engage in critical analysis. Anansi was an agent of abuse, plain and simple. And they were clearly shunning a — maybe ill-prepared and improperly popularized — revolutionary . . . as well as my family.

I had to defend myself before I didn't have the chance to. My hand shot up again and I belted out, "Um, excuse me exalted S-Steward Wafaa', is it my turn yet?"

~ New Side Quest: Deliver Statement to Save Kuroba AND Myself ~

Wafaa' paused for a second before looking back at my mom. Now back near his fellow leaders, Anansi opened his mouth. Luckily, Wafaa' answered before Anansi had a chance to block. "Sure, I guess since Bodi has ceded his time, it is now yours, PWH. Let me get the directions you must follow for your procedural statement." They shuffled around the sheets of paper in their grasp until they found what they were looking for.

Bradley leapt out of the crowd. He motioned at me with both hands un-slinged and creaked out a callous cackle. "Can we take the PWH seriously? They didn't even wear shoes to this sanctified ceremony. They have no respect for that which is consecrated. They have no common decency. Anything from their mouth is hollow."

He had spotted my nude feet sitting crossed into my lap. The crowd lost it. They broke out in a torrent of laughter, berating, and degrading. I felt even smaller as I looked down at my undressed, dirt-tinged feet curled up against my pre-owned pants.

"That's beside the point. Shoes don't make the person. How they show up does." Wafaa''s words managed to quiet the crowd. "Ok, ok, but here are the *explicit* instructions for the PWH's statement:

"'Please provide a full apology, centering your state of mind and the impetus that drove you to this harm. This should be accompanied by your plan to rectify the situation with regular accountability checkpoints. It is paramount we under-stand how you will reconcile the relationship between Kuroba, Lux, and Quawd before we make our community decision on your consequences. And the final, but most important piece, we need your career decision as today is your 30th birth anniversary.'

"Now would *you* like the seed-humus?"

I started sweating. Raw, uncut worry streamed down my arms and both sides of my midsection as my pits squirted out sweat. I was alone. It seemed like everyone had fallen head over heels for the masterfully localized exploitation being instituted during the ceremony. We'd been invaded once again. Lux didn't need weapons or to risk even one snowy soldier to get what they wanted. And now it was time for me, an unpunctual, uncouth, divergent dreamer, to save us all with my words. I had to counteract a more delightful disguise on our same-old servitude. The only counter I knew to take on such a well-bonded belief was an even more enticing reality.

"Yes, I would like the seed-humus Steward Wafaa'." I stood up and walked my bare feet over the sacred soil with pride. A familiar flood of peace and clarity swept through me, replenishing and emboldening my soul with each step. My nerves settled down and my pit sprinklers dried up as I made my way. I tried with all my might to evade Mom's piercing glance even though it didn't seem to have the same oomph it normally packed.

Wafaa' handed me the cherished vial of seed-humus, and the tranquility ruminating in my gut detonated into every fiber of my body. Everything I'd ever said, heard, thought, experienced, or felt seemed like fiction. I'd been disconnected from the simulation feeding me signals all my life. Now I could feel every life force all the way back through to my ancestral history. All the programming and protective paranoia was peeled away until my deepest yearnings sang out.

A bright light consumed everything in my view, and modals popped up over every Kuroban in the crowd rolling clips and revealing the precise fluctuations in luminosity from the brightness of said motion picture. Every snippet was the moment the world, as it was, had diminished each Kuroban. I looked up and saw a browser window above me pulsing and creeping higher. The short film above me was flickering and burning brighter, but I saw a reflective bald head hanging down in defeat.

My mind ingested all of the traumatic experiences scrolling

above and weaved them into a healing story I needed to share. The veil had been lifted. The truth was clear, but would my words be absorbed by my ailing allies? An innate knowledge and instinctual rhythm connected my situation to what was at stake for my people. I don't know if anyone else heard it, but the music was back. The same song that saved me from the cane fields, guiding me through the forest, and that started this ceremony. That deeply Kuroban tune was bouncing in my body and swinging in my soul.

I couldn't wait to return to my seat to start my statement. I was too amped. I turned towards the center and went in. Right in front of the Stewards. Mom was surely staring holes through the back of my head as I snatched the crowd's attention. My bare toes brushed up against fruiting mushrooms. My mind, body, and soul were firing a symphony of resonant rhythm. The sound reverberated with the promise of our ancestors and the will of our descendants. What they all wanted coalesced at the tip of my tongue.

"Thank you . . .very . . . much. All of you bright, beautiful, brilliant, brave Kurobans. Thank you for caring so much about me and Kuroba. Your presence shows your concern. I want to share my deepest apologies. I am truly sorry. First, I'm sorry for the physical harm any of you have suffered. I have certainly provided the Blaus with additional reasons, that they may or may not have needed, to subject Kurobans to added violence."

I glanced over at Bodi and bowed my head in reverence. My pace was calm and measured. "I promise to do better. To *be* better. I can become more subversive to Quawd's power and imposed Luxite norms.

"In addition, I'm sorry for the collective trauma I've triggered in all Kurobans."

I took a second, enough time to let my apology sink in. Time for the crowd to fully embrace my remorse. In that mighty moment of silence, I turned and surprised Mom with a tender embrace. With just a reciprocated glance for consent, I held her tight. Long enough for her body to soften and relax as I whispered my apology to her.

I released her and turned back to the crowd. "The emotional pain I've caused Kuroba doubly damages me because I feel the agony of the people I love. As you all hurt, I hurt. And I love Kuroba with everything I am. To me, liberation is pure love actualized and embodied. And from time to time this exuberant, efflorescent love for Kuroba leads me to—"

Anansi blurted out, "Love? *Love* you say child? You've set our community back generations with your actions. You are nothing more than a wily hoodlum. Am I right?"

The crowd roared in a muddled mess of praise. He hammed it up for a second before he went on. "You heard Bradley. And even my son, who has foolishly spent his life desperately trying to drag this hopeless soul to salvation, admits it. The PWH is hopeless. They're a traitor. A hopeless traitor. Stop protecting this hopeless traitor or we'll suffer . . . greatly."

A large contingent agreed with Anansi. Passing around "uh huhs" and "yups'" and "that's rights."

Wafaa' jumped up. "Anan, you hateful hermit, you're not holding the seed-humus. So just listen and latch your yap. Follow *your* procedure."

Anansi sat down, crossed his arms, and sulked in silence.

Mom sat frozen, staring off into the distance.

"Thank you, great Steward Wafaa'," I said as I began to address the audience once again. "I want us, collectively as Kurobans, including myself, to regain our stolen self-respect. To *re-claim* our hijacked humanity.

"The problem is I, no, *we* can't reconstitute ourselves individually. Not when parts of us are beholden to others. Right Mom?" Somehow, I saved enough of my spirit to snipe a stray at my mom. I saw her shake in shock and then sink into her seat. Her mouth struggled to mutter a defense, but I continued before she could react. "Our current experience was enacted through cruel coordination. It must be sunk through shared, summative, strategy forged by our deepest desires. But we've been deceived into division; divorced from ourselves and each other to instead see our enemy in our reflection. For what?

"We can never expect anything better from a Luxite or their unjust society if we can't do it ourselves, to each other. Our inner Blau or, or the specter of Quawd shackle us. Trapping us while Luxites thoroughly trample our souls. This perpetual deterioration thus relegates us to fight each other for Lux's chewed-up crumbs. Completing a cycle towards complete collapse." From my slightly elevated position in front of the Stewards I waved my arms to direct the crowd to look below at the fields of trash stretching far and wide around our settlement.

Mom sat forward on her grand throne looking intrigued yet weighed down by confusion and fear. "But, but what do you mean my child, I mean, PWH?"

I stood up straighter, dug my feet in the soil, and smiled as I took center stage. "Take this 'traditional' Earth Going ceremony for example. It's being purposefully perverted. This process *was* Kuroba's way to collectively heal from external *as well as* internal harm. It was supposed to align our values with our actuality. To maintain our society's peace and prosperity through evolution. This is our system of justice outside Lux's murderous exploitation, enforcement, and eradication complex.

"I can't stand by and let this consistent erosion of our collective reality slide. A colonial illusion has spread like wildfire in our communal psychology. This started before our last Elders mysteriously disappeared. Even before the Seed Slaughter. This poison pill has been systematically dripped into our souls since we were ripped from our homelands. And it only takes a few that fully submit to the . . . sometimes uncompromising obedience our societal torturers instill in us. The numbers of those caught in that hallucination have risen steadily with every raid on our resilience, whether it be verbal, physical, mental, emotional, metaphysical, or spiritual. Evangelists of enslavement enforce their insecure abdication of self onto their country folk. All while knowingly kneecapping Kuroba's freedom at every step. Because we're more than individuals, we're one. We're Kuroba.

"Again, I'm here to take responsibility for the harm I caused. And I take it all. For sure. I am at full fault.

"At the exact same time we must *all* take accountability for the ways we compromise with the system designed to harvest our humanity. If not, this situation will keep popping up in different spaces and places, with different people, and in different manifestations. We must heal the core of this vital vulnerability. And some of us are much more culpable than others. I'm talking directly to you, Bradley, *and* your intermediary puppet master, Anansi!"

Once again, the cloudless, thunderless night sky dotted with the stars shook silently as a bolt of green lightning flashed. It landed around the same spot once again. A crescendo of confusion washed over the crowd.

Anansi shot up so fast I thought he was jet propelled. I swore I saw flames flicking from the surface of his skin. His veins bulged, visibly fighting to be free from his face. "Wafaa', young lady, this is blasphemy and treason! This is no Kuroban love. The PWH is sowing *division* among us. And as an Elder of this community, it should be disgraceful to allow this delinquent to disrespect me. This is exactly what Lux wants. And-and the PWH has contraband on them right now. Check them!

This inflammatory affront to Quawd on top of baseless accusations against community leaders are an act of treason—"

"Chill, Anan. Stop being so suspicious and combative to a young Kuroban adult speaking their truth. Allow the PWH to speak. We've accepted your truths, then heard Bradley's and your son's. So we must accept the PWH's," my mom said as she snapped back into reality. She caught my gaze and sighed. It wasn't disapproving like most of her glances to me. I felt her authenticity, like she had an intense weight lifted from her shoulders. She finally saw *me* instead of what she wanted *from* me.

Too bad, because her words didn't reach the uproarious Anansi and his cultish fans. They were looking for action, not answers. The potential energy of the event was heavy and tense.

Wafaa' spoke up. "Thank you very much for your very impassioned plea, but there was one key request that I do not think I heard in all of this. Your career decision. I heard you're lucky enough to have two options available to you, your current position at eduGames or an alternative position within the Opp-erator corps. Have you made a selection?"

The tense crowd teetered on the edge waiting for my response. Seconds felt like hours. My body felt like it was floating, like there was no distinction between me and the soil I stood upon. My decision came to me so easily to my lips when I spoke out confidently, "Neither, I choose myself and K—"

Pandemonium broke out.

Shouting came from every direction.

Then all the objects the community used to play music in the beginning of the ceremony went flying. People were throwing instruments in every direction at no one in particular. The crowd pushed, crushed, and clawed to get over one another.

Wafaa' and Mama tugged on Anansi's taut suit, seemingly begging for him to take control of the situation, but he brushed them off and kept on his warpath. "Take the PWH and their contraband device," Anansi commanded. "Leave them on the streets of Lux. They'll have at 'em without a career decision." A group of Anansi-sympathizers pushed into the burial ground to fulfill the directives of their idol.

Wafaa' hopelessly screamed out, "Order! Order! Bring order to these proceedings. Come on y'all. Chill out! And I'm nonbinary, Anan, I've told you this a million times. Y'all don't get it . . ."

I looked at Bodi and Bradley. One was destroyed, the other ecstatic. I wondered how Anansi knew about my Libook. Bradley waved like a beauty queen basking in my downfall. I stared, hoping Bodi would slide me a quick little puppet hand or even a pinky wiggle to assure me of our bond, but I saw nothing. When Bodi finally looked up he only gave me a deadened, apologetic shrug.

The intuitive power within circulated energy and information from the soil surrounding my feet to the vial in my hand. I felt like I was about to explode as the energy increased to the point where I almost lost my footing. Then it stopped and only a single melodic word was left. I connected eyes with Mom and saw softness in her stone gaze. That gentle person was only present when she cried for her partner. In that moment of connection, she mouthed to me, "Ammirika." The libretto booming in my body was already singing the same word. And I was off.

~ New Side Quest: Save Myself ~

I slipped the seed-humus into my pocket and pirouetted in the other direction. With every step, the ground's explosive energy conducted through me, pushing my feet faster than they've ever moved in my life.

Mom screamed to the chaotic crowd, "The PWH has been dismissed." She stood above the stampeding swarm and raised her hands in an attempt to quell the commotion. "We will come to a decision *as a community*. Our decision and accountability measures will be relayed back to the PWH before the clock strikes midnights. Control yourselves. For the sake of Quawd!"

I ran as fast I could without looking back to see if her words worked. I didn't know if home or anywhere was safe with Anansi and his earth-toned mafia on high alert. My feet naturally slowed as I got closer to my mom's house. I smelled smoke.

When I was finally near enough to put eyes on the mud abode I'd called home my entire life, it was engulfed in flames.

Dammit! Was that where the lighting was striking or had I forgotten to turn off the stove again? She'd never want to see me again after this. All her partner's paraphernalia was up in smoke as well as the home they built together. If that didn't break her, I knew Anansi would use this to crack apart what little confidence she had left. I gasped and kept pushing dirt behind me as I sprinted out of the settlement.

I felt a drop of liquid run down my face and splash onto my swinging arm.

It wasn't raining. Was it sweat? I mean, I was out of shape, but this much sweat? Then another drop. Again and again.

It was pouring now. I wiped my forehead mid-stride, and it was dry as a bone. I stopped at a dirty broken mirror attached to an antique vanity lying at the edge of the dump. My faint outline told the whole story. I was crying. Bawling.

The synthesis of all the hurt and despair I was hiding from came rushing in at once. Everything I tried to strategize past and hold in was streaming down my face. In the background of my weeping image, I spotted the mammoth school building. At the top, an electric green light raced around in a halo above the apex, over and over. It ballooned and circled faster and faster as a boisterous bolt of lightning blasted into the building's pinnacle once again. It wasn't safe to break down here. Who knows how far behind the Anansi-mob would be. They wouldn't have any sympathy for me in their current psychosis.

I kept running to find a hiding place for the night. Some-where I could rest and come up with a plan. I ran through the snarl of the dump with bare feet as the random refuse ravaged my tender feet. Sadness blocked out any damage I was incur-ring. Emotional injuries outweighed the physical.

Eventually I scoped out the shell of an old car. I contorted my way into the cold rind of metal. The chilly air found every nook and cranny to cuddle up against me. The distance between me and the warmth of home provided the opening for the cold climate to colonize my body. All I had was the seed-humus. I held onto it tightly. The ancestral heat pumping through the vial kept me warm.

I couldn't stop crying. Heartache poured from me until I had no more. I was swimming in it after running from it, planning through it, dreaming beyond it, and fighting against it every day. I was lost. I had no idea what to do with myself. I might as well have been the only person on Pluto. And I didn't have a ship to escape my solitude. I was alone in an insurmountable battle inside and around me. Those who I thought were my allies had dropped by the second. They were just bandwagon backers looking out for themselves rather than Kuroba's shared success. Or had I tagged onto them when they didn't see themselves tethered to me? Maybe it was just best for me to leave all this with only the clothes on my back.

I took stock of my bleak situation and my worry drained what little energy I still had. Fear, agony, and estrangement gushed from my eyes and thundered from my heart. I wasn't only crying for myself and my situation. I was crying for Kuroba. We were in such a bad state. I needed to find a way out of this shit. But tonight, I needed to feel this pain. I passed out with tears still pouring from my eyes.

STAGE COMPLETE

Health Points 20%
Magic Power 80%

Mission #1: Don't Upset Mom Anymore . . . . FLAMING FAILURE
Mission #2: Survive the Ceremony . . . . BARELY
Mission #3: Make Career
          Conscription Decision . . . . NO DECISION IS A DECISION
Side Quest #1: Deliver Statement to Save
          Kuroba AND Myself. . . . . NOT LIKELY
Side Quest #2: Save Myself. . . . . TEMPORARY SUCCESS

Experience Points Gained [840]
Coins [+80]
Items Received [SEED HUMMUS VIAL]
Status Effect [NONE]

Stage 4: Resilient Vulnerability

Chapter 13: Previous OS Upgrade

Mission #1: Survive

I was drowning. I heard the muffled sounds of underwater currents and thunderous splashes as I flailed for safety. The water was freezing and sapped any strength I had to keep afloat. Like most Kurobans, I never learned to swim and was screwed from the jump. A wet, icy grave was calling me. When I succumbed to the ice water grave I sunk into a gelatinous film. I started flailing again and stretched through the sticky membrane until it popped. And I landed gently on my butt.

I was bone-dry, sitting on a fallen tree trunk. An assortment of adolescent Kurobans sat with me. We all wore light mycelial clothing and sandals. We were in a quiet wooded area with more of our people walking peacefully in small groups in the background. Across the middle of my view, the words "Congrats! Maroon Portal found." scrolled by. My eyes jumped around to see if anyone else saw those words, but they all seemed unbothered.

My nose latched onto a familiar funk. A soft scent similar to loamy essence undergirding the diversity of decaying stenches I was used to in Kuroba.

On the fallen log, we were all facing towards a middle-aged, what I assumed to be pregnant, Kuroban. Their mesmerizing mocha hand rested on the shoulder of a stoic child. I could only guess, but the child seemed somewhere in the pre-teen phase. The young one's face was twisted up with twelve different kinds of annoyance as they clutched a well-worn metal wagon filled with a stack of empty mason jars. Beside them both was a large pile of what looked like plastic bags, from grocery to zip-lock, strapped down with stakes in the ground.

The land was lush. Vegetation grew in every direction, but these two stood in a patch of deep black soil. The dirt under them was so vivid I had to squint to see it clearly. It looked like someone had painted black on black and finished it with a luminescent green gloss. It reflected so much light that it looked as if it hovered just above the ground.

The soil twinkled brighter than any speck of dirt I'd ever seen at home aside from our hallowed seed-humus. It demonstrated an unmatched level of ecological harmony. We didn't have the resources, much less the skill, to match this level of care. My mom was the only one with the skill to heal the land, but the luster of this soil had to have been achieved by multiple healers over lifetimes.

The midday sun poked out between the dispersed gaps in the thick canopy above. Succulent gardens overflowed with enormous edible goodies. Plots of inconceivable combinations of fruits, vegetables, and grains were scattered everywhere in this wooded wonderland. In the darker areas under the canopy were cornucopian fields of fungi.

Bountiful mushroom varieties I'd never seen before took up most of the ground that wasn't saved for a thin network of walking paths. The lavish bounty of this wooded oasis must've curated the most exquisite soil ever raised by humankind. The little patch in front of us was so active it propagated its own climate, its soul-tickling heat wafted over us in waves. My whole body seemed drawn into this ethereal example of abundant co-creation.

A cool breeze dove in from the west. This strong seaborne mountain air smelled of salt and freedom. In spite of the gust, the soil's radiant heat instinctively intensified to balance the breeze's intrusion.

The older, expectant Kuroban's words snapped me out of my awestruck survey. "Akwaaba future healers. I am Afreyea, and this little prodigy is my first progeny and partner-in-learning Bekoe. Both of our pronouns are they/them." Afreyea patted Bekoe on the back. "Say hi, Baby."

"They or them, that's it! Got it? Oh, and hey new learners," Bekoe roared while shaking a raised fist.

Afreyea continued, "This learning journey is both personal and shared. This is the beginning of your *individual* healing journey. We are not the source for your learning, we are custodians curating this journey alongside you, learning along the way ourselves. You are your own leader. We are all mere co-conspirators. This is the start of salvation.

"First, we must awaken your souls through a soil sacrament. It's something like an — um — introduction, if you will. An opening line to begin a conversation with both our ancestors and our descendants. We harness this time-independent connection to overcome struggles alongside generations before and upcoming. It will guide your healing odyssey."

The rest of the students on the stump hooped and hollered, excited and energized by Afreyea's magical proclamation. My "classmates" all shrieked with excited musings of emancipated life with each other.

I slouched, uncomfortable with the situation. I was ready for someone to scold them for speaking so freely and optimistically, half-expecting treacherous eyes and full-blown spies to give them up to Lux. The twin emotions of panic and pleasure confused me. This was exactly what I've always wanted, yet I grew up in an environment where everyone tiptoed around their dreams.

"Ahem!" Afreyea said, halting the chatter. "Stay vigilant. We are still under imminent threat. To them, we're still wayward Maroons they've yet to re-enslave. We've created our own bountiful utopia veiled behind the waste Lux indiscriminately dumps around us. This pile of plastic is a meager example of what we've liberated from those massive mounds of refuse. So it goes without saying that we'd like to remain hidden. At least until negotiations between the Luxites and our Elders conclude. Then we'll go from Maroons toward the Open Green era. We will indulge in a world bursting with open collaboration, free movement, constant learning, and abundant healing. A world our progeny whisper about in their dreams."

The class broke out into another hushed cacophony of fervent chatter. When someone beside me asked about what my "Open Green" entailed, only an indecipherable dribble of mumbles fell from my lips. My chipper comrade twisted their face and moved on to ask the person over their other shoulder.

To my knowledge, I was the only one in my day-to-day life testing the boundaries of our bondage. If not in action, at least in my private Libook lyrics. But not these folks, no, they were 'bout it, 'bout it. I mean, as much as I struggled to keep up, I felt at home. These were *my* people. The ones I was descended from. They talked that salvation talk. They spoke of thriving, not simply surviving hidden away. They verbalized and acted on the liberation dreams that interrupted our living nightmare. These people. Their intentions. Their hopes. It soothed the yearning in my soul. My original, radical people.

~ New Side Quest: Learn from My Ancestors ~

Afreyea clasped their hands together, closed their eyes, smiled, and took a deep breath as if they safely released a bit of exhilaration building up inside. They said to the class, "Ready to learn?"

Everyone nodded in boisterous coordination. The unbridled enthusiasm I was amongst made my neck hot and my breathing shallow. No one was being strategic or guarded, yet they were still under threat. That's what had me tripping. This level of inner peace was something I could only dream about in my daily life. I never felt safe enough to let my heart pour out in public. I pushed myself in the moment to overcome my cautious conditioning and nodded. It was like constipation: all my cheeriness was backed up inside me and I involuntarily grunted as I moved my head. Ashamed, I only hoped I had what was needed for the upcoming revolution my new comrades were planning.

Afreyea smiled back and welcomed little Bekoe to the front of our group.

They jumped in with a ferrous frown. "Rookies! By the sun's last light, I'll show you how to nurture this plot of soil we stand on. We'll provide you each with a small colony of *curated* mycelium, and with it you'll be ready to conduct your own land healing research. This particular mycelial breed consumes plastic and excretes nutrients." Bekoe dropped a load on us without so much as a single extraneous facial movement while Afreyea raised their hand to underscore something around us.

It was undetectable at first, but amidst the trees were homes and buildings camouflaged into the flora and bedrock. Built into the environment, mycelial structures served as homes and shops and gathering places for the community. No wonder they hid for so long from their former enslavers. The township was fully integrated into the bountiful mountaintop forest.

These Maroons didn't live in refurbished trash and mud domes on poisoned, sterilized land like my people did. They lived in perfect harmony with the rich environment around them. It was a stark difference from the dead charcoal husks poking up from rampant refuse asphyxiating any area outside of the Luxite bubble.

Bekoe maintained their mean-mug as they started digging into their long locks tied up in a messy bun teetering on top of their head. They pulled out a couple tiny unrecognizable objects. They held them tight in one hand and dug a small hole in the soft, gleaming soil with the other. Then Bekoe placed the tiny objects in the dirt before covering them up.

Afreyea started again. "Bekoe has planted a few pepper seeds to provide a more visceral example of healing art in action. Before we show you how to use this soil to spawn your mycelium, we must all connect with the soil ourselves. This binds us with our ancestors. They are the ones whose sweat, as forced captives, communed these lands ever since caustic colonizers kidnapped them. Now everyone—"

A whirling dervish came crashing in to interrupt our lesson. At a full sprint someone small yet hefty slammed into the log we sat on. It was so much force we tumbled into the tall, gentle grassy area surrounding us like a line of meticulously placed dominoes. I looked up to see the kid who crashed into us. They seemed to be about Bekoe's age.

The tardy preteen heaved like they'd been drowning in the dense vegetation. Their gasps were so loud it drowned out our groans and giggles from the ground. The situation was even more comical because the new kid tried to feign like they hadn't just rushed in and knocked everyone patiently listening off the log. They sat on the log alone, dripping sweat, still heaving.

Most of the class, including me, just laughed the clearly accidental incident off. Except one judgmental teen who kissed their teeth in disgust. I was starting to feel more comfortable as the seconds passed, like I truly belonged here. The students and I slowly picked ourselves up while Afreyea barked out, "Nice of you to join us, Mama. It's she/her right hun?"

"Yes Elder Afreyea. I'm Mama, she/her. I'm so sorry. I—"

"No need for excuses or apologies. It's your choice when you arrive at *your* rebirth. Now, take a second to catch your breath, sweets?"

Out of the corner of my eye I spotted Bekoe's stone face morph into a euphoric grin. Their hands rocketed up to their mouth to cover a coy giggle. Before we were all back on the log paying attention, Bekoe snuck a glance of amorous glee towards the new kid.

Mama responded with a fidgety bow of her head. "Yes, of course. Sor – I mean, I'm ready."

Afreyea's voice remained in its natural buttery tone as she spoke. "Everyone come up here and put a hand on the soil. Bekoe will conduct the ritual while I explain what is going on."

We let out a chorus of affirmatives and stampeded into the radiant patch of soil. We all assembled with our knees in the duller dirt encircling the special class plot. Each of us held a hand on the edges of the shining soil and slid forward in unison.

When my hand touched the soil, an orchestral arrangement slid into my soul. It massaged my whole body. It was the same music from the forest near the cane fields. Again, the music didn't catch my ears. The instruments strummed my soul.

The class encircled Bekoe as they pranced their small, but assured form in the middle. They took a deep breath, and looked up at the sun. Bekoe bent down with the stoic face of intention. They began drawing familiar, yet unintelligible lines and curves in the soil. The arc of their inscriptions circumscribed the small mound where they initially planted the seeds.

Afreyea paced pensively behind our circle. "Everyone close your eyes and tune inside."

The music crawled upward, traveling via a conscientious crescendo. More and more I was wrapped up in the rhythm as it grew. I peeled everything else from my concentration except the soul-soothing music. A fiery feeling of the soil worked its way up my arm until it filled my entire body. It was like I'd been empty my entire life and now I was finally being filled. *Shuka-shu, bling gling, cha cha, waaaaaalk.*

Afreyea continued, "This is your inheritance. The offering from the ones enslaved on and saved by these foreign lands. This is their love. Listen to the stories, learn from the knowledge, and feel yourself being healed as you heal the land. Load your inheritance into this little plot of land, because throughout your life you'll have much more to share. It will save your spirit to the ancestral repository. An innate repository that connects our people."

Afreyea's words walked my mind through the complex experience my body was going through. Every one of my neurons fired at once. Pulses traveled from me to the soil and other ones came back. I was an information superhighway sending signals back and forth. The spent energy of this explosive spiritual exchange built up an intense heat, which increased as more data was transferred through the sound waves echoing inside me. I felt it saturate me with more power, insight, and love. Then it whispered in the most delicate way possible, through a strange synthesis of a thousand voices, "Ammirika."

Something hit me in the head. It broke my concentration. My link with the land evaporated, and I opened my eyes to see a gigantic, juicy scotch bonnet pepper laying on my noggin. A stupendous bush full of prodigious peppers had sprung up out of the sumptuous three-dimension black soil.

Bekoe and Afreyea jumped into each other's arms, cheesing with pride at the magic they'd catalyzed. Childlike awe was how I'd characterize the moment for all others involved. Our jaws dropped to the dirt and we rubbed our eyes red to make sure they still worked. Everyone except for that teeth-kissing-ass student. They seemed less than unimpressed with an exaggerated pout and their arms crossed. They seemed actually disappointed.

The disbeliever raised their hand so fast they almost jumped out of their loose mycelial shirt. They didn't wait to be called on and instead shouted their inquiry, "What type of fertilizer did you use to get the soil so rich, Ma'ams?"

Bekoe stammered, "I may present . . . no! I'm not a ma'am, buddy."

"Anan, use our names if you do not wish to use our preferred pronouns, please," Afreyea said, backing up their little one. "And we don't use fertilizers here in Kuroba. Not only because of the harm it causes the ecosystem, but also because we don't have the resources for it. What inspired that idea, child?"

"My mistake," Anan responded with sheepish confidence. "I'm a man in case y'all need to know." He paused and waited for some unrequited validation. He finally took the hint and continued his statement. "Well, I've been spending time helping the foragers near the old mine. And that's where I met this pure, porcelain glowless goddess with an aura of confidence that was undeniable." His voice was indignant as he looked around with annoying arrogance beaming from his face. "I've been hanging with her in the dump outside these woods. She's super nice and banging to boot. Skin as fresh as an overnight snowfall. A-and she's taught me so much. Like how to create arable land at scale almost immediately. She even shared food I'd never seen before. It was super good, and made indoors. In huge mechanized factories . . . she says. And the most important element they used to grow more and quicker was fertilizer."

Afreyea gave a curious look. "I see. Let's talk after class. I'd like to meet this 'friend' as well." Anan looked around, satisfied that he'd sufficiently demonstrated his "advanced" insight. Everyone looked away until Afreyea jumped back in, "Ok class, let's continue. The sacrament you all experienced took immense preparation. And all ten of you had a hand in stewarding the simple seeds through rapid growth. Wasn't it amazing?"

The whole class, including me, was brimming with joy. Except Anan. He was stewing somewhere away from us. His beady eyes scampered from side to side. To me it looked like he was plotting imaginary insults to package with any infinitesimal imperfection in our incredible feat that he could find.

Afreyea spoke with a soft tone, drawing us closer. "It all starts with seed-humus. It's been passed down for centuries. It catalyzes special mycelium which purifies the soil. And that's where we'll start today. Using a mycelial strain that feeds on plastic, transforming it into a supplement for the topsoil. Bekoe will set you up for our initial learning experiment together."

"Everyone, please come up to get a jar," Bekoe said in a tone chocked full of cheer. "Fill it approximately one-third full with the newly sowed seed-humus below the pepper plant. After that, grab a few pieces of plastic from the pile and return to your seats. Then I'll walk you through the next steps."

I stood up for my supplies and the entire background glitched. The scenery flashed quickly and the outlines of the polygons that composed the scene shined the bright color of avocado guts. Their fill flickered between all sorts of colors. I paused and stared at the alarming error on my way to Bekoe. An ectoplasmic light flickered across the forest and then disappeared. The rest of the class didn't flinch, but I watched it until our scenery returned to normal. They didn't see what I saw. I walked warily once it was over, each move tentative and tense at the same time. A colossal boom rumbled out in the distance.

The ground trembled. A few frantic countryfolk covered in branches, bushes, and bark streaked through the forest. One screamed, "They found us!" Footsteps and heavy breathing began to attack my ears from all angles. The sounds of terror, from eerily familiar screams to scattered explosions, ripped through the air. Another shockwave, close behind, blew us meters away from the learning log. The heat from the explosion fried our clothes like a broiler on high. Small bits of shrapnel sliced through our flesh from every direction.

I scrambled on the forest floor like a cat. Shock and anticipatory pain were the first things on my mind. I faltered briefly before finally darting away. It was hard to concentrate and strategize under a mayhem of bullets, detonations, cries, and people scrambling.

We all scattered in a mess of directions. Sirens similar to the Blau's sinister serenade of slaughter clanged out chords of catastrophe. Kuroba's hope for harmony was being disemboweled. The staggered sounds of violence erupted around me and ravaged my ears. Smoke billowed in the eastern sky. I choked on my choice. I was too terrified to move. Filling up my airways was the scent of a quickly moving blaze mixed with the scent of flesh frying, blood boiling, and shrooms searing. It was becoming more pronounced by the second.

All of a sudden the clearest thing I felt — not heard — was a hollow echoing *shuka-shu, shuka-shu, shuka-shu.* The soil had already warned me to run when we were experiencing the sacrament. The symphony building up inside guided me like it had done in the cane fields. The tune got louder and louder. A sizzle in my stomach intensified into a roaring blaze. It got so harsh I had to stop scampering for my life to check under my shirt. Pixelated polygons were seeping from my midsection and coalescing into a familiar spinach-shaded orb. The fully formed orb popped out and bounced in front of me briefly before zooming off through the bountiful, yet balding forest. I knew damn well to chase before it was out of sight. So off I scurried.

The ancestral symphony navigated me from inside. It grounded me like the metronome of the waves crashing on a placid beach. Without any doubt, I heard a voice sing out, "*Waaaaaalk on the wa-ter. They put us in chains, but we're born free. Connected to earth, we live among trees . . .*" My conscious mind connected that I needed to find water. Except I had no idea where. Only the boiling lake that capped the massive volcanic summit. I had to trust the sage sphere guiding me toward aquatic salvation.

Deeper into the woods we went. The illuminated GPS took me higher and higher, further west, through the mad scramble of screams. Until the trees rapidly got thinner and more sparse. The orb kept zipping upward through the rocky terrain scattered with shrubs and serpentine greenery. As I ran behind the kiwi-green ball of light, I was struck by the feeling that I was watching myself in action rather than being in it. It was like my camera view had been switched to second person. I was running and dodging through the rocky plains nearing the water-filled caldera while watching my body running and dodging behind.

I sprinted past, around, and over the booms, cracks, and smoke razing this peaceful, wooded mountain settlement. Ahead and around me Kurobans began gathering as the scent of boiling sulfur and vinegar swallowed our sweaty residue. Out of the corner of my eye I peeped Bekoe and Mama's little bodies hauling a cart with the pregnant Afreya in tow. Every Kuroban was going the same direction, with all hands on deck to shepherd every body to safety. The power of our ancestors moved us together like a murmuration of iridescent starlings.

AMIDST THE SCRAMBLE TO escape our hidden homelands, we all instinctively rushed higher up the peak. No matter what path we took, eventually we all amassed at a bubbling body of water within the cavernous caldera at the summit. Watching the chaotic, roaring liquid we saw the volcano we lived on was as activated as we were. The air was thick and hot, oversaturated with moisture that reeked of rotting eggs. The steamy, effervescent natural jacuzzi wasn't a safe site for us to stay; not one of us could swim those scorching waters and our invaders encroached steadily from below.

The Luxites intentionally scorched their path upward, setting the scenery on fire with torches, flamethrowers, and incendiary devices. We were trapped at altitude, between the vicious onslaught and the rocky ocean on the other side of the boiling lake. I quickly took hold of my anger before it took me over and used that energy to help the early Kurobans set up a rough camp for the distressed and injured. More refugees streamed in over the next daunting days.

As our numbers ticked up, little Bekoe held it all together. They provided leadership to turn the turmoil we witnessed into positive action. They assembled us, Elders and community members of all ages and abilities alike, to develop a detailed plan of resistance. Our caldera rally point became our home base. It was where we mixed our capabilities as a community into a coordinated counter strike. It was a place for us to rest, plan, and orchestrate our guerrilla survival operation.

I was huddled around a tiny fire, a blaze barely big enough for one, soothing a trembling, groaning mass. We were over a hundred Kurobans up late passionately discussing resistance tactics when my entire visual frame zoomed out. I wasn't just watching myself involved in this rebellious action, I saw the whole volcano face at once. Like a drone camera flying high above the sulfur spring, the entire battlefield came into view.

Below our lakeside camp, ferocious Luxites haphazardly used fire to clear their way through the fuming forest. Titanic tanks tumbled over the grasslands near the base of the peak spewing gallons of garbage over wide swaths, all the way to the energetic excavation site where legions of loathsome Luxites boarded armored vehicles parked en masse.

Luxites continued to stream off an extra-large locomotive snaking all the way back into Luxite valley. We were surrounded on all sides with only more mayhem on the way. As my view zoomed back to camp, I watched my Maroons comforting one another. The contours and colors became solid and artificial, like a digitally developed film instead of the shambolic, saturated, seamless scene I'd been a part of. My former character, now some faceless Kuroban teenager, moved autonomously while my disembodied spirit floated above. As my camera reached its maximum distance overhead, the words "Minigame Completed Successfully," faded in and overlaid on top of the scene. The words faded out as a list of stats and updates scrolled up from the bottom to calculate current "HP" and accumulated "Experience Points." After the last piece of information scrolled by my view, the camera zoomed back in to watch the ensuing action.

The entire Maroon community cooperated as one under the confident guidance of young, assured Bekoe. They led reconnaissance teams that tracked Luxite movements while also rescuing supplies from the ruins of old Kuroba. To enhance our security, Bekoe designed defensive fortifications to protect our cluttered camp and organized strategic attack units to minimize Luxite momentum. As iff that wasn't enough, the juvenile Bekoe also built and maintained the temporary food, water, and housing stock for our summit survival site. Everybody, young, old, strong, frail, incompetent, and smart were enlisted in some way, including my faceless character. I watched as Bekoe led the front line offensive to take back our mycelial municipality.

For over three weeks, the Maroons took turns in small, specialized teams to expand Bekoe's vision to survive, save trapped comrades, and push back the infamous invasion. The Maroons knew the land better, but the impact of their grass-roots methods were limited. They hid in trees and tactically cornered their assaulters until they had them on the ropes. Using creative controlled burn techniques, the Kurobans turned the forest-clearing fires against the pillagers, disconnecting them from their pristine metropolis far below. The attacking Luxites could no longer receive supplies and reinforcements to sustain their massacre. The Maroons' limited supplies waned as well, but they maintained the mirage of an immortal menace. Both were trapped in different spots of the wooded wasteland, but the cunning of Bekoe and the Maroons threatened the Luxites enough to force a peace deal after twenty-two bloody days of battle. That agreement was eventually called the Seed Armistice.

A montage skimmed through those last days of battle and faded to black. The terms of the Seed Armistice came up as the system rebooted. I'd been told these stories of our past, but it was much sadder to experience in real time. It made me want to cry as the credits rolled because I knew it was the birth of the insidious world I grew up in.

The Seed Armistice*

1. *Termination of hostilities between Kuroba and Lux provided:*
   a. *Slavery or involuntary servitude is abolished, except as a punishment for a crime.*

2. *Kuroba must relinquish all seeds and halt all local farming as payment for using stolen Luxite lands provided:*
   a. *Lux provides universal access for the sale of food and goods to Kuroba.*
   b. *Lux offers Kuroba a 99-year limited equity lease to the current Kuroban lands.*
3. *Every Kuroban must fulfill their required work assignment in Lux and choose a career by their 30th birthday provided:*
   a. *They successfully complete their compulsory education at least to the master's degree level.*
   b. *Lux offers free, culturally-relevant education to every Kuroban at all levels.*

**Any violations of these terms will be determined by the offended party and punishments sentenced therein.*

STAGE COMPLETE

```
Health Points . . . . . . . . . . . . 60%
Magic Power . . . . . . . . . . . 40%
```

```
Mission #1: Survive . . . . . . . . . . . . . . . . . . . . . . . . . . . . . SUCCESS
Side Quest #1: Learn from My Ancestors . . . . . . . . . . SUCCESS, A LOT TO LEARN
```

```
Experience Points Gained (680)
Coins (-) Non-Existent
Items Received (SEED HUMMUS VIAL)
Status Effect (NONE)
```

```
Level Up (30)
New Ability Obtained (Ancestral Instinct)
```

System Reboot Initiated . . .

290

Chapter 14: CTRL - Sing

Mission #1: Make Career Conscription Choice in a Hurry!

Shuka-shu.

The same warm, welcoming feeling tiptoed into my consciousness. It felt good, but it came with an urgent alert. Something was awry. A sudden influx of adrenaline stiffened my lethargic body like a slap bracelet, snapping me out of my sorrowful, sleepy malaise. I was still caressing the exothermic seed-humus. The moon was high above and I was cramped into a cold, crumbling car carcass.

I quickly connected with reality. I yelled out, "What have I done? Is there still time?" I regretted everything from the Earth Going. My brash behavior left me alone with no options and I already begged for some sense of stability. I felt bare. An untethered free radical detached from any and everything. I needed to make my career decision as fast as possible, but was it after midnight or not?

A flood of shameful urges sent me scrambling to Lux. My community wouldn't accept me unless I fulfilled my commitment and Lux would simply send me to the sewers unless I made my decision. I hoped I wasn't too late. I was orphaned and disgraced once again, and this time Bodi couldn't save me.

In a frantic mess, I rummaged through the trash surrounding me to find a pair of shoes to cover my dirty, ravaged feet. I was fortunate enough to quickly scrounge together a mismatched pair: one shoe too big, the other too small. I tied both as tight as I could and sprinted toward the train station with the seed-humus stuffed in my pocket.

My shame metastasized as I ran, slipped, and searched for the stars to tell time like Baldie had taught me. I was ashamed at the chaos I'd caused my community and my family. The dishonor made me panic. I scanned to find the Drinking Gourd and lined it up with the North Star. The trick from Baldie to read the night sky's clock worked. The stars whispered to me that there was about an hour left before midnight. I wanted to gasp, but the timing was still tight. Unless I arrived precisely when a train going to Lux rolled into the station I was screwed. So I let shame hurry me along the toxic terrain, struggling to keep my feet churning over the unstable wasteband.

What came over me to make such a rash decision? Was I in some sort of fugue state? Because I couldn't actually *not* make a decision. There was no way I could ever stitch together a living out in this pitiful purgatory on my own. My liberation dream was nowhere among this rotting refuse. So as I ran, I tried to sort through my decision on the off chance I made it in time.

First, I thought it'd be best to keep work consistent and stay at eduGames. It was the game I knew. And I knew it very well. But that wouldn't work at all. Not with the new setup and the ephemeral nature to the role itself. If I stayed at eduGames I'd be in the sewers slaving away in a few short months tops. Once they gathered enough data on me, I'd be automated away and left worse off. Besides, how would I find Rob to let him know at this hour? Before I had time to discuss my only other option, I saw the incoming headlights of the train. I hustled even harder to make sure I didn't miss it.

Huffing and puffing, I arrived just as the train announced, "Now arriving at the Western Lux Manufacturing Park, please exit in an orderly, professional manner. Have a nice day." I dragged my heaving frame onto the platform to wait for the doors to open when I was startled by an outlandish sight.

A gaggle of Luxite tourists in sharp, albeit soaked suits were surrounded by scores of suitcases bursting at the seams. The floor of the train car was jam packed with snacks. Food was piled almost two feet high, from crispy chips and luscious muffins to seasoned nuts and what looked like scrapple stuffing. On top of it all, these well-dressed folks were wrestling each other over an enormous glowing glass bottle.

The fluorescent contents of the double Nebuchadnezzar-sized bottle spilled in every direction. They clawed and kicked each other to reach the narrow opening at the top. As they reached the overflowing aperture of the bulbous bottle they chugged down as much spillage as possible before they were overtaken by one of their coconut meat combatants. They were all sopping wet and scratched from head to toe. And while some rested and crammed down snacks, others joined the fight to get another glowing sip. Not waiting for them to notice me, I ran further up the train to a car free of Luxite shenanigans.

I didn't get much further. The doors began closing as soon as they'd opened. I had to leap into the next open doorway. Luckily, the next car was completely empty, but I was still reminded of the strange situation going on next to me. Here and there slams echoed from the bottle battle next door. I tried to ignore it and focus inward on the ride into Lux. I had to pray to Quawd to get me there in time, so I closed my eyes.

There was no way I could find Rob and grovel for my career at this hour. I would have to find Doc. After the ruined Earth Going, he was my only chance. The only option I saw left were the Opp-erator Corps. It hurt to even think I had to submit to the Opps. Despite what I thought about them or how they were connected to Baldie's exile, I *had* to be one of them. But maybe it could work. It was an unfamiliar game, but maybe I could take advantage of the ambiguity. Enough to reimagine what being an Opp meant. And what I did know was that they'd make my gaming dreams come true. They'd finally provide me with consistent income, opportunity, and food I'd literally starved for. I had to find a way to make it work, no matter how disgusting it was. I just had to figure out my sacrifice.

My senses heightened. The shameful panic that woke me up intensified as the train got closer to Lux. Louder than the clattering of the train itself, my anxious foot tapped out of control. I was so out of it that I didn't even notice when we crossed into Lux. Shame and anxiety were building up in me, clogging up every bodily process I had. Listening to the rhythm of the ballasts as we traveled, it sounded as if the cadence slowed. I moved next to the train door, nervously bouncing as we approached every stop. I was ready to sprint to plead for Doc's offer.

The doors opened, as usual, at one of the first stops right inside the Luxite bubble. It was before we entered the urban core where Doc's office was located. An announcement came over the intercom. "The train will be stopping momentarily, please keep seated and wait patiently. We will be on our way shortly."

A fire sparked inside my gut, shocking me out of my shame spiral. I walked off the train, following that feeling and scanned the area. A massive, mingling late night crowd began dispersing from the platform. Sirens whined in all directions. And a group of elite FEEs hauled semiconscious Luxites, exploding from both ends, from the car behind me into ambulance drones. I could see them getting hooked up so that they would get their stomach pumped and do it all again. But still that wasn't what was triggering my instinctual alarm.

Then I heard it. "*You people* need to be more respectful."

I choked. My body tensed up and my breathing shortened. I could only catch murmurs of intermittent verbal abuse interspersed with debasing denominations like "criminal" and "animal" and "worthless."

I jumped off the train steps to track down the source of the audible abuse shocking my soul. I looked over the throng hastily thinning from the platform as the train prepared to depart for downtown and the entertainment district. *Shuka-shu shuka-shu.*

~ New Side Quest: Investigate Commotion on Platform ~

More semi-audible insults about "ruining the city" and "being a drain on resources" punched my eardrums. I intimately knew Luxite verbal aggression, an early step in the decomposition of Kuroban identity. Unrequited fury flared from inside me. I rushed like a river over a cliff toward the south end of the platform.

Wrong way. My soul sirens silenced going south. I turned around and caught the smell of the victim's panic on the other end of the platform. *Shuka-shu, shuka-shu, shuka-shu.* My gut led me like the annoying beep of a metal detector.

The horn of the train blared out. It was about to leave. I hesitated and jumped forward then back then onward to the source of my soul's signals.

"I gave you the coffee you ordered, sir. I just made a mistake. You said if I got you coffee you'd forgive me. What's so bad about purchasing an adult ticket instead of the youth ticket. It costs more anyways. Please let me call my foster family. I just wanna go home."

"No! My order wasn't right, you idiotic scum. I asked for almond, not cashew milk. You don't belong here. After we teach you a lesson, we'll make sure the rest of your dirty people remember their place."

I locked eyes with my young comrade boxed in by the gang of ruthless ivory interlopers. The horror-struck victim vibrated with fear. Their saucer-sized eyes hemorrhaged tears. I had to do something. *Bling gling-gling bling . . .*

"Let's get rid of—"

I jumped in between my frightened kinfolk and the alabaster wall of aggressive, societally-aggrandized assailants. "What do you think you're doing?"

I turned my head slightly towards the kid and said, "Ammirika, go home." My intrusion gave them a path to another train door to board. The terrified teen turned, fell, and scampered onto the train as it started chugging. The train blared for me once again.

"All aboard," the intercom rumbled across the almost empty platform. The engine churned. It increased momentum steadily until it left me alone with a Luxite horde hopped up on hate.

Now I'd done it. I got myself involved in someone else's issues and now I was stuck in the capital of cultural corruption not knowing if I was in conscription violation or not — more trouble I'd caused for myself and my people.

I was supposed to be on my way to make my dreams come true and salvage the shit show I'd caused with my rebellious-ness. I probably would've been in relative safety if it was before midnight. Instead I was face to face with an even worse situa-tion than anything I'd faced in the last few days. I'd typically code switch into my Quawd-driven character to get out of sticky situations like this. But even the best performance wouldn't cut it now. I'd walked into this conflagration myself. And no one was coming to save me on a late Friday night in the heart of harm central.

I turned ever so slightly to catch a peep of the young Kuroban. They smiled from ear to ear with their face plastered on the train window. I saw the innocence brimming from their face. The same vibe I saw in Soma, qualities I'd lost a long time ago. I hoped they took advantage of the possibilities I'd forsaken for them, because I was a goner.

But I had to meet whatever was coming next head-on. No blending into the background or creatively retelling what had happened. I was unquestionably in it. Optimism was the only perspective that provided some relief in such a dire situation. Every muscle in my body expanded as adrenaline coursed through my weary frame. I had prepared my entire life to resist, and here was my chance to put it all into action. All the scenarios, expectations, plans, and tactics I'd imagined and penned were preparation for a moment like this. It was the reason for my Libook.

The corners of my mouth turned up into a wry smile, and my eye twitched on its own. I was preparing to parry the assault from these enraged cultural enforcers.

After a few seconds of staring each other down, I ever so carefully traced my hand across my body toward my backside. I didn't want to make any sudden movements that might spook the Luxite predators before me. I was in search of my escape hatch. One of my previously prepared plans, tactics, or spells to save myself from the bosses on this stage of my survival. These despots of societal deprivation were rearing to fortify their fragile power. But I had something for that ass. Once I . . . pulled . . . my, my — uh huh. *It was gone.*

My Libook was not in my pants. I frantically slapped

around and checked every pocket and crevice. The only thing I had on me was the vial from the Earth Going. Kwasia! I didn't like to talk bad about myself, but what a dumb thing for me to put myself in this situation. I slowly moved backward to put more distance between me and the Luxites approaching with villainous vigilance.

But who was I kidding? I wouldn't have had enough time even if I *did* have my Libook. They weren't going to just let me pull it out, scroll to the perfect plea, and cast it before I was bombarded by their bloodlust. It was then that I remembered giving it to Soma at the ceremony. As I backed up to the edge of the platform, I kept one hand gripped on the vial in my pocket. I wouldn't lose a sacred community heirloom on top of my Libook. *Bling gling-gling bling.*

~ New Side Quest: Evade Luxite Aggressors ~

The music in my gut took over. The stirring in my stomach sharply accelerated. Every move I made from then on zipped with instinctual intention.

We tangoed tenuously around one another until mere inches separated me, them, and the train tracks behind me. I used my back foot to check my proximity to the platform's precipice. Another step backward I'd be barbecued by the third rail. Right before they pounced, I flashed my hands out of my pockets.

They jumped backwards as I gradually raised my fists in a circular motion. It stalled my attackers, and I took the opportunity to scan my enemies for any vulnerability. I needed something quick before they swooped in to beat me into submission.

First of all, each of them were costumed in their own unique character. They didn't attack on instinct like typical tyrants off the street. These elite FEEs seemed to have more refined victimization methods to sustain their stolen social superiority. These ravenous reprimanders were more prudent, purposeful, and pernicious.

One of the jokers looked like a bloated, bleached lemon wrapped in a dark, precisely tailored three-piece pinstripe suit. Their Oxford shirt seemed to blend into their almost sheer skin until I caught the contrast of red blistering across their face. Their golden hair was gelled backwards in the shape of a low-profile helmet, and they held onto a briefcase matching the leather shielding their feet. *The Red-Faced Reaper.*

The next one was a bulging beanstalk. A burly bloke with an urchin of hair-looking spines or spine-shaped hair extended from their head — I couldn't tell which. They wore a dusty pair of coveralls and battered boots. The reflection of the train tracks flashed in the metal emerging from the toes of their well-worn footwear. They cracked their knuckles, stretched their limbs, and popped their neck as they followed close behind their suited compadre. *The Dusty Degrader.*

The final person was a strong yet petite individual in a flowing white blouse accented by a dark pearl necklace. Their aura oozed of immense power yet composure. Despite their skin tight crimson skirt split at the side flowing down to their feet and sky-high platform boots they moved effortlessly. A literal firecracker ready to combust at any moment, their stance seemed set to snag me at any second. It was as if they floated over the ground rather than the rest of us drudging about. Over their torso they wore a brown leather shoulder holster filled with the familiar electric batons of the Blaus, the same ones the security-Kurobans used to bat me around. Their deep, dark brown hair was tied back in a coarse bun as tight as their calves, but I peeped flyaway strands curling asunder by the second. *The Bloused Batoner.*

The last one. Something felt familiar about them despite their ominous presence, something I couldn't put my finger on. No time to dissect that feeling . . . they moved in.

The Red-Faced Reaper rolled towards me. I made a quick step to the side as if I was evading a closeout defender. It was the only way to dodge them without going over the cavernous drop onto the tracks. I was uncomfortable operating in peril. I preferred planning to instinctual action. Fortunately, my body knew exactly what to do.

I shot my empty hands forward and back with explosive speed as if I pushed a wall of wind at my aggressors. They backed up ever so slightly. One hand focused towards the Red-Faced Reaper and the other towards their partners poised to pounce as a pair. I spread my fingers out and in and out and in using a patient pulse to grab their attention. Then I twirled each finger independently while simultaneously cranking my knuckles in a wild mess of directions.

Their faces were frozen, agape with awe. I started to dance my hands like they each had a mind of their own and wriggled my body to accentuate my fervent fluidity. My eyes rolled in the back of my head. My head jolted skyward. I froze. My head dropped. My fingers elongated directly towards the shivering deputies of dominant culture in front of me when I belted out my incantation, "Ammirika."

The sky cracked out thunder and green streaks of light flashed across the sky. The morally bereft bullies seized like someone had paused their game. The Red-Faced Reaper and the Dusty Degrader became bulbous balls of fear. Those beefy beings curled into such compact masses on the ground their cowering was actually remarkable. In that moment the tempest roiling in my gut accelerated to the point of detonation. A green orb ripped from my midsection. It bounced a few times between me and the goons before whizzing off the platform to a quaint neighborhood nearby.

The Bloused Batoner stood, a confused look carved on their face before blurting out, "R-run? Wait, the stinkin' 'robans's running."

I was gone before they coordinated with one another. I made it off the platform, off in chase of the green light zooming deeper into a gated township. The bloused one yelled at their associates, "What are y'all doing? The glowa's gone, come on." *Cha, cha, cha. Chuga cha-cha.*

A faction of footsteps rumbled behind me as I whipped through the tangled streets surrounding the outer rim of the valley. I didn't know these suburban outskirts very well because they were typically off limits to migrant workers like me. We only passed by this picturesque area on the train.

I jumped through the gates of the model community chasing after the green glow. It looked as though someone was stuck copying and pasting a singular concept of home. The repetition of the same impotent buildings and blank yards stretched far in the distance. I slipped into a grassy alley between two indistinguishable boxy, cream-ribbed houses on pristine grass plots. From there I watched an unassuming rice-skinned resident unclip their tie and stuff it into the back pocket of his spacious slacks.

They walked around to the back of a monumental, nondescript vehicle with tires almost their height. Once they reappeared, their arms were weighed down by a bundle of dangling bags on each arm. They took a couple steps forward and put down the two plastic clusters. They bumbled a set of keys before slipping one sharply into a door to one of the carbon copy houses. The green globe waltzed inside as the resident turned around to gather their bags again. I moved in closer as I watched them stumble to transfer their haul into the wide-open house.

With the stillness of a mouse and the fleet feet of a gazelle, I glided across the pavement and slipped into the open house. I hid behind the first thing I found inside. The green ball of light bounced beside me. We were huddled behind a dusty plastic fern near the door. The bag wrangler hadn't noticed us in our poor hiding place. I searched for an exit while the wrangling resident was distracted, scanning for a backdoor or a large window somewhere deeper inside.

I couldn't hold back the overwhelming onslaught of dust on my nostrils any longer. "Achoo."

I gave away my position. I stood up, put my hands behind my back like a butler, and smiled so hard my eyes hurt.

"Eek! Milton honey, you didn't tell me the contractor was going to be *this* late?" a person dressed similarly to the Bloused Batoner exclaimed in alarmed confusion. The poor excuse for a body double didn't have the same aura as the powerful batoner. Not only did they not exude the same self-assured strength, they were as pale as a newborn golf ball and wore a novelty apron instead of a baton holster. The apron was embossed with the quip "It's not a Home without a Homemaker."

I piped up instinctively, "Yes, I am the contractor. Sorry v-very l-late." I tapped into a dorky yet confident character to finesse my way out of the situation. As I walked further into the house, I scoped out how clean, put together, and chock full of tacky stuff it was. I made a smooth move forward, wiping my hand on my thigh before offering a formal handshake to the bloused homemaker. I brushed up against the warm vial in my pocket while wiping my hand. It passed on a pulse of poise to aid in my evasive bluff. *Bling gling-gling bling.*

After the homemaker recoiled, I walked with determination to the schmuck in billowy slacks. "Milton, I presume." I shook his hand energetically while patting him on the back. He stood slack-jawed.

Milton eventually managed to mutter, "How . . . did . . . you—"

"I'll get to work then," I said with a slight nod to cut him off before I had to answer. I took advantage of their stunned state and kept moving. My legs pranced across the room toward what I prayed was a rear exit. I was determined to make my departure before they sounded the alarms on the recalcitrant Kuroban in their midst.

Before I made my escape, the bloused-homemaker cornered me in the kitchen. "I-I'm Sharon. I'm glad you finally made it, but your service window was 8-12 *this morning*?"

"Th-this morning, lots of calls. This was the first time I could make it. You know, *traffic*. Where's the problem again?" I replied without turning around. I was trying to get a grip on my nerves and search for their back door.

Sharon answered with enthusiasm that filled the room. "Oh goodie! I told you on the phone, it's the sink in our guest bathroom on your left. It's spouting sewage. Yuck! But-but where are your tools?" When I turned around Sharon was smiling so hard the corners of her mouth cracked and flashed a dark red. Her bright eyes locked onto the guest bathroom right beside me.

I looked at the door and the hair-raising stench of raw sewage snuck into my nose. Maintaining my composure I responded with confidence, "Ma'am. My tools are out in my truck. Assessment first, then I'll know what tools are necessary for the job."

The beep-beep of a mobile phone broke through the tense silence of the moment.

"Wait." The word shot like a cannon out of Milton's mouth.

He'd remarkably been resuscitated back into operation by the text he'd received.

"What do you need, sir?" I asked with the oblivious mediocrity of an obedient Opp despite my nerves wailing. Quawd was back, pulling me full force back into my submissive place. Nerve ending by nerve ending, the new tension jumpstarted my sweat glands, reminding me of the combustible stress from the party I crashed the other night.

Milton stepped towards me with a cheesy smile across his face. "Let me shake your hand again. I really appreciate you coming so late. Did you come all the way from rough old Kuroba or are you a lucky local?"

I raised my now sweat-soaked hand towards Milton trying to keep my tremble at bay. "Oh, of course, sir. I t-t-typically—"

"Aha! That's what I thought." Milton grabbed my hand, which liquefied in his grip, only to twist it abruptly to reveal the bare back of my hand. "You're not a contractor. You don't have a brand. Kuroban fugitive!"

~ New Side Quest: Escape Suburban Luxite Home ~

I hit Milty with a quick swim move, chopping his arm with my free hand before diving into the bathroom beside us. I slid onto my knees to lock the door as banging echoed from the other side. The impeccable bathroom reeked of raw sewage. Despite making my eyes water, the smell oddly had a momentary calming effect. It had a hint of the familiar putrid aromas my homelands were exposed to on a daily basis.

Chaotic slamming shook the hinges, but the door didn't budge. The reverberations traveled far enough for me to feel Milton's rage through the room's quivering. The frantic beat, both desperate and diabolical, made me scuttle around to figure out how to vanish.

"Come out. Come out now!" Milton yelled at me over the sound of their bombardment on the door.

"Please, please, please, I'm stranded," I pleaded. "I got no beef with y'all. I just want to get back home to see my mom. Puh-leeze let me go."

The banging stopped. I moved closer to the door to figure out what might be going on. I faintly picked up Milton and Sharon arguing in another room.

"Stop it Milton, let's just use the BlauShare app. The Blaus will handle this," Sharon whimpered.

Milton spoke, fiendishly giddy, "No, no, no, this could be good."

Sharon drew snot back up into her nose and spoke between distressed sniffles. "What do you mean, Milton? It's dangerous . . . You let it . . . into our *home*. I'm scared!"

"Quit your belly-achin' Sharon. The neighborhood association sent a message about a Kuroban terrorist on the loose. This is it! The one they're looking for. They're offering a big, fat reward." I heard someone knocking further away from them before Milton said, "I'll handle it, Sharon. Don't. Call. Anyone."

Sharon's heaving and bawling were the only sounds left. I took a moment to catch my breath and hush my pounding heart. I scoured my surroundings for a way out of the putrid powder room. *Bling gling-gling bling.*

When I pulled back the shower curtain the green glob of light bounced in the bathtub waiting for me. It bounded up the decoratively tiled shower wall to the ledge of a tiny, frosted window. It squirted through the small window, streaked over the placid pool, and sped across the fenced yard to the other side.

I lunged at the window.

"Sharon, pull yourself together. These two gentlemen were the ones who sent the message to our neighborhood association. They're FEE's from the Opp-erator's Security Network. One of their bloodhounds is sniffing around to find the stray Kuroban. Look, there it is on the side of the house."

Sharon hurled thinly veiled shade through each hyperventilated phrase. "Ok . . . it's dressed . . . particularly civilized. I still . . . want my phone . . . just in-in . . . case."

"Sure, but trust us, Ma'am, Becky's the best at these things and wants to rid Lux of this glowing scum more than we do. Calling the Blaus will only harm *our* performance rating. We can handle this in no time," a new, velvety voice said.

Milton jumped in like an eager gamer before release day. "Gentlemen, when do we get our $250K? And is it a lump sum or an annuity? Wire or check?"

"As soon as we capture the Kuroban in question, all financing details will be arranged. Now, where is it?" the new voice responded.

"It's locked in the bathroom right there. I'm in favor of the lump sum wire myself, please and thank you," Milton remarked with childlike holiday glee.

"Bruno, handle it," the new voice commanded.

Heavier booms, certain and powerful thuds, rebounded through the bathroom and knocked me on my bum in the tidy tub. The door began to creak and I scrambled to the window like a lizard hiding under a rock. I picked up a bulky bottle of 4 in 1 bath soap and broke the glass. The door frame to the bathroom cracked and splintered with every strike from my opponents outside.

I wedged my slender upper body through the minuscule frame and scraped my protruding ribs against the shards left from my haphazard barrier removal. Surprisingly, half of me was outside quickly. I saw the luxurious lawn of escape below and managed to wriggle my right leg and the vial out, but on the left, my slacks snagged on a jagged piece of glass. I writhed and twisted to get free while hanging out the window. A loud crack rang out followed by the rumble of the whole house shivering under the brute force. Someone was inside the bathroom.

That someone seized my left foot like a super powered vice grip as the rest of me dangled outside. My left pant leg ripped in the struggle. My foot was the only thing trapped inside. I felt the bones in my foot crushing as the violent vice constricted. I kicked and contorted as their grasp got tighter.

Inside, I heard the bloused-homemaker scream, "I just got that bathroom remodeled! I'm calling." My body hung like a limp rope from the window as I battled my way free. I was caught in an awkward backbend with my hands in the grass and my left foot inside fighting feverishly for freedom. *Cha, cha, cha.*

I coaxed my foot until the ill-fitting reclaimed sneaker slid off my foot. Thankfully they got the too big shoe, not the too small one. I fell from the window onto the sharp synthetic surface below. I shot up like a rocket on grass so supple it had to be contrived of the finest plastic product. After balancing my weight on my only remaining usable foot. I took a glance back at the window and saw the Dusty Degrader trying to pinch their bulging body through what seemed like a fairy's window. One shoulder and the spiky head spilled out while they strained to snap their other shoulder outside. The corners of the window ruptured the entire wall of the building.

"Found it! Get outside, it's running again," the Bloused Batoner yelled from the right side of the yard on the outside of the fence. I staggered across the yard like my life depended on it, hauling my bare, mangled foot behind.

A daunting inground pool stood between me and the fence to get to the ridge where the green orb waited patiently for me.

It was like the orb didn't know I couldn't swim. Still, there were two bloodthirsty FEEs closing off any other escape route. So I staggered for the pool, pulling on the power of my ancestors for aquatic abilities from the Kurobans who escaped enslavement by traversing rivers and oceans. I could either wait to get captured, bleed to death, drown in this pool, or miraculously swim to the other side and escape.

Waaaaaalk on the water.

I took my first step on the water and made no splash. The surface tension of the chlorinated personal natatorium held my weight with each step like in the stories of our savior, Quawd. Step after step, I hobbled to the fence on the other side.

Clink. I threw myself over the chain-link fence with just momentum and one scratched up leg to propel myself. My pursuers hustled to keep up. Bone dry and outside of the untouched yard, I hastily picked myself up and limped toward the edge of the ridge as the green globe of light went over. A strong gust blew in and almost took me over with it into the bustling city far below. I watched the green light disappear into the concrete cacophony and knew I had to follow to escape these hunters.

Soon after, I heard a splash and the scream of the Bloused Batoner. "Argh! Tony, help me!" I tried to leap over the ridge, throwing my haggard foot first, but I couldn't. I had no adrenaline, no fumes, and I was terrified.

Before I knew it, a soaking concrete wall hit me. My head dove directly into the dirt of the steep slope towards the city. My broken foot flew up into the air, flapping like a roving plastic bag in the wind. I caught a blurred glimpse of the Bloused Batoner on top of me as we cascaded down the towering crest behind Sharon and Milton's house.

My body banged and buckled against the rocky earth

broken up by forgotten plots of concrete separating the suburbs from the urban landscape below. The increasing momentum of gravity rolled us faster and harder until we scraped across a slimy concrete patio straight into the broad side of a dumpster. One of the attackers was with me, but still, I made it to the shores of the urban valley. Closer to Doc's office.

I couldn't recall how long it was before I came to, but everything hurt when I did. My body fluttered a syncopated concerto of pain. Upon uncovering myself from a thick coating of trash, I spotted the foggy outline at the top of the hill above. And the Bloused Batoner was lurking in the same garbage pile I sat in.

I rushed to pull my battered body up. The leg that I thought was in working condition sprayed blood. Two shots rang out from the ledge above. Tending my wounds would have to wait. I crawled with every exhausted fiber of strength my body could muster. The green ball bounced joyously in front of me once again. It advanced into the city and I strained to lug my frail frame after it.

My limp, bloodied leg and wrecked foot scraped against the ground behind me as I crawled forward. It was all I had to survive. I held onto every structure I came across to gain any bit of leverage to move faster. Faster toward what, I didn't know, but I wasn't safe with these hunters in hot pursuit.

Motion cameras buzzed awake, training their digital eyes on me as I slinked between a confluence of construction and vice. I had no idea where I was. Luxites popped in and out of establishments singing and hanging onto one another. Many gripped glasses of green glowing gunk with its luminous residue dripping from their mouth and clothes. So many p3s were in line to drop off boisterous Luxites at the second level ports of surrounding buildings.

Amid their blundering joy Luxites ultimately started to notice my mutilated earth-toned body radiating against the cold roadway. Some pulled out cameras and filmed my prone form scraping across the pavement. I had no idea what to do with myself. Running or resisting was out of the question. I only had hiding and hoping. A green ball seemed to spin slowly in a loading dock in front of me. It was set in an alley behind a towering building. A hiding spot.

Every breath required my entire body. Only one of my eyes remained in operation after my crash, but it twitched like it had at the party. My leg gushed blood, and my heart pounded out of my chest. Still, I crawled my way to the loading dock and laid against the cold metal bay door.

I tracked the source of the bloody eruption in my leg to find a curved shard of glass jutting out. The blood formed a small stream trickling into a nearby sewer vent. I cried out in pain; the sight of my physical state multiplied my misery. The sheer agony and desperate reality of my situation set in. Hopefully Soma or some young Kuroban uses my Libook to continue my work.

All of a sudden someone socked me across my face. It felt like an electrified brick was thrown straight at my helpless, already bruised face. "Chile, you really thought you'd get away from me, you deplorable speck of defecation? I may be old, but I'm not dead. This is what I do." When I opened my eyes, I saw the Bloused Batoner. They'd chased me from the train station to the house, down a hill, and now to a loading dock in the city. These browbeating bounty hunters were relentless.

"Argh," I screamed, stretching my finely-grated arm out to grab the glass piercing my leg. With another scream I cleaved it out. Tears poured from my spasming eyes. The Bloused Batoner let out a hearty chuckle as I aimlessly swung the bloody shard shouting, "Back up, I swear I'll slice you up. Ow!" I dropped the glass and pulled my hand back. It was now leaking blood too.

"You held it too hard, Hun. You're pathetic. Can you stand?"

I struggled down an arid gulp to settle my frightened, fractured body before I asked, "Why do you hate us so much? We've done nothing but serve you all faithfully."

The Bloused Batoner didn't answer me and patted me down with vigor. "I can check you on the ground. Do you have anything dangerous on you that might cut or poke me?"

They slowed down near the pocket where blood spouted from my leg. They went into my bloody pocket and pulled out loose seed-humus intermingled with glass shards. "What's this in your pocket, baby? Glass and dirt? What are y'all doing these days?"

I swiped at the Bloused Batoner's handful of seed-humus and felt an intense heat erupt from our hands and swallow every other feeling fuming inside me. A bright light flashed, and we were blinded in an instant. The entire background, including the spectators and city, melted away pixel by pixel. The only thing left was . . . *cha, cha, cha. Chuga cha-cha.*

STAGE COMPLETE

Health Points 3%
Magic Power 100%

Mission #1: Make Career Conscription
          Choice in a Hurry! . . . . FAILURE
Side Quest #1: Investigate Commotion
          on Platform . . . . GOT MYSELF IN A MESS
Side Quest #2: Evade Luxite Aggressors
Side Quest #3: Escape Suburban Luxite Home . . . . SUCCESS, MINUS A FOOT

Experience Points Gained [364]
Coins [-]
Items Received [NONE]
Status Effect [NONE]

WARNING: FUNDS FREEZE AT MIDNIGHT WITHOUT CONSCRIPTION DECISION

Chapter 15: Esc

Mission #1: Free Myself
Mission #2: Free Koruba

Everything was indecipherable, like a game with no sound, no screen, and no controller. Light swallowed everything and choked on the contents. It was so blinding that I kept my eyes closed so it wouldn't trigger spontaneous migraines, yet I could sense the brightness of each individual dot reducing bit by bit. But it was far too slow to open up my eyes even after waiting what seemed like a year. Instead, I pushed my other senses to gather some semblance of circumstance. I went inward and dug up any sensation to sniff my surroundings out. There was nothing.

No fire.

No nerves.

Nothing.

I squeezed my hands and wiggled my toes. Still nothing. My mind began to fill with made-up musings of what had happened to me as I separated from my physical self. I was lost for seconds, which became minutes, which could've been hours or even days. Totally isolated. It was only me, my muddled mind, and the light all around vaporizing away at the speed of a slug sipping salt in the Saharan summer. Was this death?

My internal inquisition ended abruptly when my body was sequentially squeezed segment by segment. It was like I was being pressed through a pipe with a narrow point in the middle. Near the point of maximum contraction, I turned slightly headfirst and gushed out the other side. A delayed spasm of suffering shot through me like an 18-wheeler had run me over, backing up a couple times for good measure.

Every scrape, scratch, and dripping puncture in my body flooded my pain receptors with a surge of tooth-chattering stimulation. I lost quite a bit of hit points and was hanging on by a thread. The agony was so intense I could feel my soul clawing to cut off its dilapidated chassis. I felt faint. On top of a collection of incapacitating injuries, my eye twitched out of control and sweat pooled in every crevice. My heart raced like it was on the verge of detonation. My breathing was spastic and rushed. And now I didn't have the vial of seed-humus anymore to help subdue the storm of debilitating forces over-powering my conscious capabilities. I broiled in that pain for what seemed like days as the light surrounding me continued to retreat.

The intense light dissipated a pixel at a time as I begged for something, anything, to take away the quagmire of pain consuming me. My Libook wouldn't have helped, but it might've comforted me amidst the growing umbrage of unknowns. What I did know was that I wasn't bleeding in a loading dock anymore. And the Bloused Batoner was nowhere to be seen. Instead, I was leaking capillary fluids in some sort of infinite, indeterminable void. I might be falling without realizing it, I might've slipped into that wormhole I always wished for when late to work, or maybe I'd entered hell itself. I had no idea. All options were possible at this point.

After what felt like weeks of light dissolving and pain throttling, I was finally able to open my eyes. A heavy haze the color of basil took over where the floodlights left off. My senses were still dulled and my body shrieked in pain, but something seemed different about this haze. For some reason I wasn't worried about my extensive excruciation or my puzzling predicament anymore. It wasn't just that the absurdity of my circumstances had been normalized over time, something in the haze comforted me. The haze had a pleasant tenderness swaddling me with security. Its fluff felt like the epitome of serene softness within each infinitesimal volume of haze. Its aroma was calming. It smelled like – *sniff, sniff* – soil. A rich, dank soil that gave a hot oil massage to the insides of my nostrils. Every part of me the haze caressed was left infected with a measured reassurance. I was lost in the haze's embrace when a vicious sound vibrated in the vicinity.

Something was growling. The sound was coming from somewhere in front of me. My busted body tensed up. It was unclear where to flee, if that was at all possible. The forested haze held me throughout this panic as it diffused and unfolded to reveal its secrets. My body began to feel warmth burrow from the outside inward. I tasted my caustic saliva transform as the haze titillated all of my tastebuds. I smelled a sequential series of natural scents telling a story as they continued tickling my nose holes. From the fresh salty scent of the ocean to a warm prairie's bouquet of fragrances, I was mesmerized. Until a loud animalistic snort struck a sour note once again.

"Ah!" I screamed while scuttling away from the sound. An ominous outline materialized from the haze. The source of guttural grunts was bearing down a few feet in front of me. After a second I recognized the ferocious fiend was the Bloused Batoner. They were howling and wrestling like a starved tiger that'd been left caged for months. But as much as they struggled and roared with foam spilling from their inconsolable mouth, not a muscle moved more than an inch. Eventually I realized their body was being restricted. Their voice rang out and their eyes darted in every direction while their body remained motionless. The Bloused Batoner, locked with their heels together and arms stitched to their side, was being held in place by secure, solid nothingness. Indestructible, yet invisible shackles.

Time was warped and bloated. What felt like days were shoved into every second as the batoner distracted me from my constant pain. It felt like I watched them rampage for months on end, yet we were immune to time itself. Still, no human had the endurance to remain frenzied forever without a break or food or water.

After some time, my fright flipped into curiosity. I figured I might've been safe from the batoner, at least for now. But how were they being held in place? Maybe the answers to that singular mystery could lead me closer to understanding the sorcery encapsulating us both. I scooted my beaten body, blood and all, towards the bloused one to investigate further. Nothing was attached to them. Well, nothing I could perceive. I poked at where the restraints should've been and recoiled, expecting that I might've accidentally unlocked my attacker. Nothing happened.

I poked around and stayed to observe the results. Nothing again, except the batoner's eyes locked onto me with laser-like intensity. The ground below was translucent. The batoner's tightly bound feet stood level with the same surface that held me above a hazy abyss that stretched on and on ad infinitum. I was able to sit and crawl and bang on this invisible surface, but we seemed to just float in a never-ending haze. We were both stuck, except I wasn't restrained.

A soft, entrancing grassy glow blinked before fully illuminating the hazy cloud molecules like a large backlight. Startled, I backed up from the bloused one to assess the situation. Like an engine warming up, the pace of the haze diffusion and the emergence of lime luminosity ramped into warp speed. It was like a vacuum sucked up smog while spewing green light exhaust. Apparitional forms, the color of the superb, sunny soil of my homelands seeped into view all around us. The luminance encircling us touched my soul. They were my people.

The light pulsed in cadence once all of the haze had dissipated. It was slow at first, but sped up faster and faster until the scene twisted in on itself. We were all sucked into an infinite point until we emerged on the other side a little more pixelated, an effect which quickly subsided. Between me and the still struggling batoner I saw the words, "All Players Logged In," fly into view before it morphed into a large, rudimentary sundial. The simple shadow clock slowly ticked away between us.

A powerful, yet patient voice echoed throughout my body. The words vibrated the mossy glow's enchanted particles. "Players, ready to begin healing?"

"Arrgh, let me go," the Bloused Batoner barked as I reflexively retreated from their proximity.

"Wh-what do you mean?" I queried the disembodied voice in the aether.

The almighty voice spoke through us as it continued, "Healing is borne of real relationship, extreme empathy, reciprocal responsibility, and emergent evolution. It is a collaborative process that demands the utmost patience and trust. Heal your timelines, heal your communities to heal yourselves. Begin."

Tick Tock. The sundial between us moved faster.

"Huh?" This was confusion stacked on top of uncertainty smothered in befuddlement. Whoever was making these enigmatic proclamations in this indeterminable environment where time was becoming more arbitrary by the second deserved to, at least, answer a simple lifesaving question. How would empathy stop me from bleeding out? I was already dizzy. All the riddle-troll shit was too much. I was still actively hemorrhaging hemoglobin. I desperately yelled out to the glow around us, "I need something for the bleeding and the pain. Please, you gotta help!"

No answer. The bloused one kept grunting and moaning, unconcerned about anything happening around us.

"This Luxite won't empathize with me. Vulture-puppets like this one only want to tear me limb from limb. They get their rocks off by sucking the ripped edges like a butter-drenched crab leg."

A gale of time flew by, swirling haze and light along with it. The sundial's shadow turned like a top. Years zipped by in a mighty gust that rolled through the entire void. The batoner and I stayed in our same battered states, unimpacted by the massive passage of time, other than being a little windswept. In front of the sundial, a calendar projected itself as well, marking off days, weeks, and months before disappearing into the glow of the hazy horizon along with the gust it came in on. *Tick Tock.*

"Grr! Don't blame this on me young'n. Let . . . me . . . go. Nooow!" the batoner snapped back at me as soon as time steadied back down.

Tears snuck out of my lids as I yelled at the battle-hardened batoner, "This is your fault. You were chasing me, remember?"

I got even more frightened when the batoner calmly. "Sweetheart, you're gonna be sorry. Either I'll surely get free of these restraints soon or my backup will arrive much sooner.

The lady at the house you broke into called the Blaus. You'll learn."

I watched the batoner struggle, squirm, and stress themselves out while stationary. Finally accepting the futility of their situation, the pitch of their grunts transitioned to distressed whines. They ripped and rocked in every direction. We could've both passed on, doomed to suffer in hell, and still they served the violent urges of societal supremacy. It didn't matter what was going on around us, where we were; even how they were being held down was immaterial. The compulsion driving them seemed deep-seated. An addiction to demean and dominate.

But they didn't move at all. My mind kicked into high gear as I watched them struggle. If I was dead or going to die from my injuries, I'd at least pass on with the satisfaction of knowing I tried. It'd be a small consolation to understand this ruthless relationship the Luxites had with the world around them. A relationship where they wring the world of its substance to receive a meager claim against future exploitation. Only for said Luxite to be further hooked into repeating the same sinking spiral to justify the capital they'd just oppressively occupied. So I decided to investigate.

I shouted with composed confidence at the whining batoner. "Why are you doing this anyway? Like, really, why do y'all spend so much time squeezing out the lives of others to fuel your own deadened existence? Y'all would have less trouble and be less miserable if you spent more time on yourselves instead of using us to compensate for y'all's self-imposed insecurities."

Tick Tock. The winds of time zoomed by in a gnarly gust once again while we remained suspended in place with not a word between us. The sundial spun faster and the calendar ripped off years.

I waited intently for my nemesis to respond.

The batoner stopped their frantic yelping and dropped down like a wet napkin. "You're one of those head-in-the-clouds types aren't ya hun," they responded with smug stoicism. You prolly think the world is supposed to be nice and gentle to you, right? The youth, I tell ya, so entitled."

"Do you think Kurobans should be relegated to a reduced existence? We're forever striving and our modest momentum is nothing compared to institutional inertia. Fighting to simply recover the humanity that's been violently ripped from us is a herculean effort. Every detail, from what we learn, believe, do, think, say, eat, survive, and more is directed by and provides for others. Not for ourselves. Not for our livelihood or survival. No, everything is extracted out. Then it's used up to y'all's heart's delight and that's when y'all dump the depleted husks back onto us. Everyday we're scraping the sediment of our soul to survive."

"Hunh!" The batoner's face twisted up. They sputtered out a maniacal laugh that continued for an awkward amount of time.

Set on proving my point, I said, "I'm talking about living a life that isn't my own from birth. Hell, it's pirated to serve the dominant powers before our first breath. Y'all have created a corrupt cult guided by domination and exploitation. There's no reciprocity. No balance. We're forever-enslaved to y'all. We've lost our freedom. It's different from the chain and whip bondage you shipped us here with, but the same power and violence manifest in more indirect methods to manacle us to y'all's will. The game plan's been updated with more systemic expropriation through low-touch cultural terrorism, dele-gating disempowerment to anyone with the least bit of ambi-tion just by selling *y'all's* story."

The batoner made a lackluster squirm for freedom from

their invisible restraints. They were probably eager to get a free lick at my smart mouth, but they eventually stopped and snarled, "Grr! Who's doing that, child?"

"You! Don't you get it? You and every other indignant Luxite there ever was and will be. And-and some Kurobans too — they're not absolved of complicity, either! It's some fucked up love-your-torturers-type-shit. My people don't see their eradication happening in real time. Instead they see themselves as temporarily embarrassed Luxites. They're lying low until the loot and authority arrive via supernatural faith. They live thinking that if they work hard and pray enough, they'll alleviate their endless struggles. Struggles put in place through the same imperialistic values guiding the people and institutions who don't see much difference between a Kuroban and a smartphone. The only difference in this nightmare world is between Lux and everything that serves Lux. The complex, layered narrative running on repeat makes this whole horror a million times more insufferable."

I took some deep breaths. I didn't know what to do after finally screaming what had been ruminating in my mind all these years. Watching, analyzing, and dissecting our oppression from every angle alone with my Libook, it all finally connected. Our plight never had a place to be heard or validated or agreed with. Saying it was much more powerful than typing it out. It was a release for a starving tiger locked in a cramped steel cage. A cage where I was only allowed to see the world through videos methodically training tigers to serve Luxites and not their own natural needs. And now I'd been let out into a wide-open yard. I was still getting used to the possibility in front of me and what was truly going on in the world, but my first brush with reality was exhilarating.

The glow encircling us grabbed tight and stole my breath away like the first huge roller coaster drop.

The geyser of blood coming from my leg stopped. My eyes refocused and my heart settled down. The piney haze opened up to reveal more definition to the silhouettes observing us. *Shuka-shu, shuka-shu, shuka-shu.*

A brief breeze of time swept over and through us. The shadow clock rotated and the calendar tore months away in a matter of moments. *Tick Tock.*

The bloused one wasn't fighting anymore. Their head and limbs dangled from their invisible restraints. The same rush of serenity that clotted my leg must've also impacted them. They drooped without moving, only their chest rose and fell with every breath. The wildfire in their soul reduced to a light sizzle.

"'You Luxites, right?" the batoner said with a snarky, jovial energy. "You really think you're gonna change the Kuroban existence by yourself? The hubris."

Unsure if this was a trap, I kept the pressure up with my own sarcastic spice blend. "If I *have* to.

"I'll make it happen at any cost. I'm sure that when I do, I'll free all Kurobans. It'll be the most efficient way to help my people. My community doesn't believe our struggle is a problem. They think it builds character. They're too busy trying to 'make it' or too scared to rock the boat. Or-or they're simply greedy traitors . . . Oops, I mispronounced Opps again. Isn't that what you call the loyal puppies working with sadists like you?"

Their face softened and they lifted their head to give me a bright smile with both their mouth and their eyes. Even shackled a few feet in front of me without the possibility of ever being released, they seemed unbothered. It was like they'd accepted their circumstance and the blame I heaped on them. "Ouch! I used to think like you when I was younger, you know that? Then life hit." Their voice held a sense of calm, less bass, and a hint of relatable attitude. The batoner took a deep breath and shook their head. "And when it hits, you learn a lot. Including how to elevate beyond this transitional period of solitary, the righteous enlightenment you're deep in now. For instance, do you even understand this Quawd business baby?"

The bloused one's arms unlocked from their invisible restraints. They took a couple seconds to shake out their arms. I sat dumbfounded, my brow furrowed like it was weighed down in the middle by my dangling jaw. I move back slowly. What was the batoner going to do? Would they attack me? Who released them? And why would a Luxite ask me about Quawd? I was terrified and curious at the same time. My guard was up. They couldn't flip that fast, could they? It might at least be interesting to hear a Luxite tell me about a *Kuroban* god.

To mask my true mood, I tapped into a persona centered on confident cerebral chicanery cross stitched with candor. "It's a complicated arrangement. Part religious reassurance, part personal protection. We found Quawd during our enslavement, but it's morphed into something else since then." I connected what I had said before with what they said. "Wait! Are you gonna tell me to *follow Quawd* in order to overcome *societal* subjugation?" My words bled into nervous laughter.

Their hands punctuated every word they uttered despite their torso, legs, and feet still being tightly affixed together in the haze. "Chile, you worry too much about old folktales. Quawd isn't real. Not physically *or spiritually.*"

"What you talkin' bout? You don't know how it feels for us. I feel it fighting for control of me as soon as I cross into Lux." I scanned every memory, moment, or meaning I associated with the spirit of Quawd. Was this Luxite trying to play me?

The pea glow in the fog tightened around us even more. My heart slowed and the pain resounding with every heartbeat subsided. I found strength to quell my nerves and sat crisscross applesauce like it was story time. Simmering below my tempered anxiety, I was brimming with anticipation.

I would listen, but I wasn't about to let the batoner know that I'd give an inkling of trust to their incoming truth bomb. So I forced a defensive grimace.

Tick Tock. The sundial gyrated out of control as a whirlwind of years rolled through our conversation observed by the glowing silhouettes surrounding us. Instead of a calendar, a projection of the year appeared, ratcheting up the numbers like a chrono-slot machine.

The batoner smiled and chuckled deep, from their belly to the wrinkles in their forehead. "Chile, they twisted our homeland tales into their own propaganda. It was foisted upon Kurobans as an unwritten term in the Seed Armistice. Cosigned by gullible Elders and co-created with a compromised Kuroban narcissist. Tyrants want to keep us working while they increase the difficulty, reduce our rest, and maintain a submissive model for how they want us to live.

"Clashing with the passed-down pain only causes your trauma symptoms to flare up. Those meek-as-a-mouse urges are a survival adaptation for a world constantly beating you down. I see how it affects you. It was probably worse for myself. But if all else fails, Luxites will medicate you into shape, like me."

Impossible. I replayed their words trying to find the loose string to pull apart their quilt of lies. Their story was incongruent with how I saw the world, but most of the logic tracked. I stumbled over my words trying to make it make sense, "A-a Luxite affected by Q-Quawd? It can't be true. It's only a Kuroban affliction!"

"Are you listening, baby? It starts with excessive sweating, then eye twitching, and a jittery anxious feeling. At its peak, your chest tightens up, breathing takes everything for the smallest bit of air, your heart pounds out your chest, and then you zap-out into some other reality, am I right? Baby, that's centuries of trauma, stress, and anxiety compounded upon in your spirit." My eyes, lost in the swaying samba of the baton-er's hands, finally saw the outline of an extremely faded "OP" tattoo. They weren't lying. They really were one of my people that'd long since flipped.

As they finished their statement the tension wiped away from their torso. Their legs touched down delicately on the transparent base serving as our imperceptible floor.

"Wait! Are you-you *Kuroban*?" I squinted to see the slight glimmer and warmth in their bright sand frosted skin better. Another peaceful embrace from the cabbage haze gripped us. It reminded me of how I felt when I was speaking in the burial grounds during the Earth Going. The silhouettes around us clarified more to reveal their decorative Kuroban drip adorning their faceless forms. Our ancestors were guiding us on a journey. *Bling gling-gling bling . . .*

"Ampa ara! Now you're picking up what I'm putting down. Pretty slow, aren't ya. I never said I was Luxite. I'm Bekoe, they/them. And still Kuroban, as far as I know. I even used to help my Maame train Kuroban yute in my early days." Bekoe twisted their torso, stretched from side to side, and touched their toes. I sat before them, staring, choking on my insults.

It was too unbelievable. My jaw fell through the never-ending floor. "No way . . ."

The shadow clock between us rattled out countless rapid revolutions. The projection of the year appeared and jumped forward in chunks. Decades moved past us in a tornado of time. We were still unaffected despite the dramatic time skip. *Tick Tock.*

Bekoe

Bekoe moved in closer and crossed their legs to mirror my position. The ravenous raider who'd been itching to pummel me was well within striking distance. I was too stunned to care. Too wrapped up in their ridiculous revelations to care about the risk.

"I was kicked out of my community. The same one I sacrificed for, and saved from extermination time and time again. During and after the Seed Slaughter. But all that dedication got me sent to the sewers. I was sentenced based on the word of a Luxite in a Kuroban's glow. But while I toiled in the suburban work camps, I came up with a plan to save our people utilizing the same skills that got me swallowed by the beast, honey."

"May I ask what happened with your plan?" I asked with eyes wide.

Bekoe looked sad and distraught. "Sweetie, I didn't save anyone. Not even myself. Organizing the enslaved of the sewers provided only enough leverage for *my* emancipation. But the ensuing deal sacrificed the genuine electricity that powered my escape. I fell deeper into the system, always thinking I'd find my way back. I sucked up pain day after day until it became the only thing coursing through my veins. What kind of life is that? I became the lies I told myself. I'm a prime example of agitator attrition." When they finished, they looked up at me with whimpering eyes and a smile. I jumped, half-expecting a beating, but tears rolled down their face instead.

"Sorry about that. That all makes sense, fakin' it is draining," I responded. "I know. I've been fakin' since my school days. It's work, but work that soothes my soul. I got expelled before my first little scheme got started. But once I got a chance to get back in the good graces of Lux, I did my damndest to double-dutch between worlds until I could dream my way out.

"You see, to me, everything we experience is just a societal video game we're compelled to live in. A user-generated simulation designed to funnel the world's life force to Lux, including our own. All while continuing to 'live' without any resources. Framing oppression as a game made opposition more digestible for me. And it kept my heart at a distance. That frame has allowed me to identify and test strategies, tools, and technologies to beat this 'game.' But I haven't *fully* heard or coordinated with other players. No matter how they're playing."

"Vi–DEE-oh GUH-ay-mmz. That's a techno ting, right? You tech-heads are funny. Technology's not gonna save us no matter how powerful, advanced, or ground-breaking it is. What's gonna free us is even more difficult, multidimensional, and dynamic. It's a revolution within us all and the force truly driving society. It is the medium through which the public is manipulated and your technology is trained. *Culture.* No matter the social system, culture is the fundamental energy that runs the whole societal machine deep at the core. And tapping into that stream is tough for a solo savior. You can easily get lost, lambasted, or lynched on the way. Look at me, sweetie." Bekoe's resplendence grew as they spoke until their warmth dried remnants of sweat settled on my skin.

"That makes sense, Bekoe. Culture is the kernel that manages the mechanics of the world's dominant operating system, right?"

"What? Sure, if you say so kid. Culture is so powerful it will morph and pervert your liberator ends. I got distracted by my *own* survival and all the shiny objects along the way. I was disconnected and veered far away from anything that was real, or-or lasting, or even the mission that gives me the strength to go on, you know darling?"

"I know. I know. I know. It's not all on you. I mean, this is hard for anyone, much less for someone attempting to change the game alone. While plugged into the mainframe at that. But . . . maybe . . . if you'll have me . . . I'm here . . . only if you're open. M-maybe I could help. I'm at least passionate. I mean, we both want Kuroban freedom, right? But, but I just want to know. . . why did you do it? Y-you know, helping Lux like you did? As, as a sort of meta-oppressor. I-is that really the world you want to facilitate?"

"Heck nah! Sweetheart, I was ripped from my partner and my dear child. About thirty years ago I carried a dream for over forty-one weeks. I wanted to be with them more than anything. But I also wanted to build an interchangeable, improving, inclusive Kuroban resistance force. Not all Kurobans were open to that. And I didn't tend the soil cultivating the fruits of freedom.

"I was worried about protecting the wrong things. I should've built in public, in coordination rather than hoarding control. Allowing others the time and space to find their free selves, but instead I built a resistance rooted in myself. I reflected the same modalities as the system oppressing us. It only lived in me, and not in an unkillable, countervailing culture hosted by a committed community. That is what will sustain against the dynamic dominance we're up against.

"But when you're in it alone, who's there to tell you when you've strayed? Lux has twisted reality so much it seems like the dystopian binary they peddle, rather than simply the world *they* need. The longer I was away, the less energy, reason, and resilience I had to resist. I simply got tired of fighting, hun."

I was on the same trajectory myself, albeit to a much lesser degree. All of the violence we face is so that we're more harvestable. The very air of this society is poisoning us. This programming is cemented in place, taking over anywhere, anytime even without conscious compulsion. Unless it's forced out, it's the default.

What could I expect from someone like Bekoe? Or my mom. Or Bodi. I could even understand Kuroban-Bradley and maybe Anansi, a little. It's what we're up against. That's why Bekoe and I were at each other's throats, when at the core we're on the same page. Real revolution necessitates chaotic compromise with all involved, much like what the original Earth Going Ceremony was created to catalyze.

I watched the sundial's shadow slowly ticking as I put all the pieces together and thought to myself, "Maybe. Only after extensive healing though. I definitely could build towards something like that."

My wounds stopped throbbing and healed over as if nothing had ever happened. I patted myself to confirm the rapid regeneration. New energy surged through every vein. I was no longer ailing — no blood leaking or broken bones anymore — as a matter of fact, my body felt unusually strong and my belly was full.

Bekoe looked at me with a sunny smile which unlocked levels of comfort in my soul that I'd never known. My eyes began spilling joyful tears. It was more than newly-mended appendages exciting my emotions, my unexpected teacher soothed my soul too.

The sundial stopped suddenly and an alarm rang out all over the glowing haze. The sound danced all over the place as centuries of time burst forward and backward, then forward once again. Bekoe and I floated, staring at one another bathing in our reciprocal restoration. Then the sundial disappeared with a slight poof.

I eventually gathered myself enough to respond to Bekoe. "I appreciate you sharing. I get it. We *all* know something is wrong. We feel it, but don't have the words to express it, much less topple it. Surviving requires us to give up the culture, creativity, and cooperation which makes us who we are as a people. It keeps us in mental, physical, emotional, and spiritual bondage, right Bekoe?"

Bekoe started clapping without breaking eye contact with me. Their face looked like they were holding back tears again as they responded excitedly. "You see hun, I've been thinking 'bout this for a minute. You're the first to take me seriously in a long time. The real hurdle is exactly what you said. Much is necessary in order to reintroduce someone to themselves once they've been subsumed. Holistic captivity is some shit.

"I've wondered to myself many times if there was another life path for Kurobans. A direct path for us all to find freedom and peace. What would I give up for that? And even if I was ready to give up everything, how would I even figure out the first step toward it? Why would a Kuroban consider pausing their march to 'make it' in order to spend time for some abstract, *uncompensated* healing?"

Bekoe's inquiry hits me hard. Beyond the personal transformation much more work is left. How were we to expect to overcome our daily dreadful circumstances forever? How would we reorient ourselves within the largest systems at play? All we had was each other and potential collective power. Difficult, cross-cultural, identity-redefining healing work was all I came up with, something I've always dismissed as too astronomical, sloppy, and arduous, but I zipped my lips and listened.

Even though we had different ways of understanding, speaking about, and battling, we were on the same side. Maybe it wasn't at the top of their mind. But when we all went home at night, alone with our thoughts, there was no denying the truth. Bradley and Anansi knew the truth just as Bekoe did. They may try to mimic their master by ignoring their needs. But humanity always shines through. Whether they know it or not, the futile decline inherent in dominant culture consumes all souls.

I closed my eyes and took a deep breath. My heart was a serene metronome for each assured, full breath I took. *Cha, cha, cha. Chuga cha-cha. Cha, cha, cha. Cha-cha.* My insides relaxed. Tension swam away from my body. Then the same symphony of the fields, the Maroon village, and the Earth Going belted with impunity in my soul. "I'm sorry Bekoe. I've been selfish. I blamed and cursed you in my head and sometimes out loud. Not solely you, all Kurobans, especially Opp-erators. We are all struggling and must work together to get free."

They nodded gently toward me. "No, I should be apologizing to you, Chile. You're a victim of *my* pain. Because I was prevented from imagining my potential, I tried to end yours. For each and every one of us our promise is within reach, yet so very far. I'm sorry to you, to my family, to my people, and even to Lux itself. Because I was yet another conduit for Lux's devastation across the world."

I stood up a bone at a time with my head slinked into my chest and arms wide open. I kept my eyes closed. When I made it up on both feet, back straight, I eked out a childish request for Bekoe. "Do you mind . . . if I give you a . . . a h-hug? Puh-please?"

"Come here, baby," they said with a smile that made me feel at home. My cheeks hurt, so I must've reflected the same glee. We moved toward each other, and I noticed the glow from each of us stretch far beyond our bodies. Our personal phosphorescence blended and intertwined with the light holding us in the cloud. The fusion of radiation amplified as we embraced. Time swirled in, out, and around us in every direction. Everything became warmer and warmer until the entire ancestral orchestra enveloped us. The circumference of ancestors played and sang with every bit of their ethereal life-force. They sang out together, *"Waaaaaalk on the wa-ter."* A mighty, yet tranquil energy expelled from us both at light speed.

The voice encircling us sounded again, "Level Complete."

IN A FLASH we were back in the loading dock, standing in each other's arms. I felt like I'd had my first full night's rest. My legs were stronger than redwoods and a deeper level of the harmony swirled within me. A powerful connection tethered me to everything in the vicinity. Instead of the enormous weight holding me back, every Kuroban there ever was or would be pulled me forward. A holistic, assured, and empowering kind of support. My manic mind eased into a swift sea breeze. Everything was softer, warmer, lighter, and more joyful. We'd both begun healing.

I spotted my old blood still soaking the concrete. We released our grasp of one another. A blast of warm air blew up from a vent below. Our reorientation was rushed into high gear when sirens whined their way towards us.

"Blaus," we wailed in unison.

The sirens came from every direction. Bekoe grabbed my arms and pulled me down. "Don't turn around. They're arriving soon. Help me with this."

We both hunched over the sewer grate and wrenched it open. The rank of the wastewater rushed into my nose. It was a totally different stank from home. The upstream stench was much more subdued. The sirens approached close enough to feel the high pitch travel up my huddled back. "Please, please, please Bekoe, let's run. They're here!"

The vent swung open.

Bekoe held the grate open and directed me into the flowing sewers with a harsh neck whip downward.

From inside the urban cesspool, I motioned for Bekoe to come down as well, but they slammed the grate shut behind me. Blau vehicles screeched to a stop above, right where I was crouched. I heard the doors open and the erratic electronic buzzing of the robotic Blaus activating above. A loud slam of a thick metallic underbelly reverberated across the pavement above.

The computerized tone of calculated Kuroban criminalization blared its commands over its integrated speaker system,

"Violent Kuroban traitor . . . Put your hands up . . . You have been judged an enemy of Lux . . . You must be taken in for reprogramming."

Bekoe, still squatting above the grate, reached through the metal to hold my outstretched hand. "Baby, I know you're scared, but you're free. Choose joy, even though you don't know what it fully looks like. Ammirika and free our people. A sweet song told me to save you. The chariot has finally come to carry me home. Follow the songs of our ancestors . . . And tell your mother I will always love her."

In their final grasp, I not only felt reassured, I was stronger. I was lighter than air. All of Bekoe's items, skills, abilities, and experience flowed to me, and my glow exploded in intensity. Lighting up the entire dank catacombs under the city.

Before I could respond, Bekoe was mechanically ripped away.

I jumped down into the stream of sewage to avoid being the next Blau victim, suspended in shock as I realized who Bekoe really was. Until I remembered what Bekoe said. *Run.*

My legs churned harder than they had ever before. I kicked my legs up high to trudge through an ankle-deep current of water-logged waste flowing in from all sides, but my feet never broke the surface. I ran on top of the water past spouts draining from the walls into the main channel of urban discharge. Lining the walls on both sides was an array of iron-caged windows, each with a metal tag with a number engraved on it. Cords dripped green liquid of all hues into large vats hanging from the small lip of each caged cavity. The sirens almost completely drowned out Bekoe's miserable cries fading with every step I made.

Ahead of me I noticed the remnants of chains affixed to alcoves underground. Sporadic clinking, banging, and grunting echoed throughout the narrow waterways. Bits of water-logged clothing clogged up the foul channel. Not knowing where I was going I was nervous, but at least I was free to choose.

I'd started a path to recovery. For me, for my people. My soul was finally at peace, right down to my DNA. My ancestors and my descendants had my back. I couldn't help but crack a smile. This might actually be the best birthday ever. I kept running and running and running as the sirens faded and the new, guttural cries began louder. Still, the song in my soul sang softly to me as I sprinted:

Waaaaaalk on the water,
They put us in chains, but we're still free . . .
Born of earth's true soul, livin' wit' trees . . .
Sunny skin smilin', all shades of sand . . .
Souls healin' soil, cause we are the land.

LEVEL COMPLETE

Health Points 100%
Magic Power . . . . 101% (AND GROWING)

Mission #1: Free Myself. . . . . SUCCESS
Mission #2 Free Kuroba . . . . FAILURE

Experience Points Gained (289)
Coins (-) ACCESS UNKNOWN
Items Received (NONE)
Status Effect (NONE)

PROFILE ADDED (BEKOE'S GIFT)

Acknowledgments

R + B I love you two so much! I truly want to appreciate you two for all that you missed out on from me as I was wrapped up in writing. You both offered me so much insight and perspective whether you know it or not. You are the ones I really write this for. I write this in order to understand myself, the world I brought you into, and to heal said world. I appreciate you for dealing with me being tired, aloof at times, and sticking with me as I learn more everyday. But this is for you. I wanted to leave a written record of my interiority and mission now, for later.

I want to deeply thank my beautiful, brilliant, strong partner Steph. Without you I'd still be literature-less luddite. I wouldn't believe in myself, step boldly into my future self, or have anyone to challenge my raw reactions to the world as I decipher it. You are the one that has truly shaped every single word in this book. These are our conversations over the decades wrapped in a cute narrative so others can learn from what we've built together.

I have deep appreciation and reverence for all of the Black, Indian, and Caribbean writers that came before me and sketched out a path for how I might tame the tempest toiling betwixt my temples. All of your work inspired and enlightened me, especially those of you that wrote fiction, and most notably the works of speculative fiction. These got my gears going and my mind racing on what could be, realizing that stories were flowing from inside of me.

I want to thank Kota and the Inked in Gray team for giving me a chance with my wild idea for a book and helping me shape it into more than I believed it could be.

I have to show love to my initial editors and illustrators in my writing journey. You have all helped me build confidence, find my voice, and sharpen my style.

Interestingly enough, I also want to thank Jordan and my first pre-reader group in 2018 for *eCONomy*. That book was the beginning and precursor to this one and the entire *A Window to Liberation (AW2L)* series.

I want to thank all of the music and artists that fueled and soothed my mind as I compiled, processed, and scribed all of my visionary vignettes. Music, and the whole spectrum of deeply spiritual, melodic, percussive, wordfull and wordless was truly the auditory stories that grounded me throughout this entire process. I dabble with them in this story, but I have more ways in which to show my appreciation and admiration for your impact.

And finally, thank you to all the friends and associates I've met, learned from, laughed with, and helped along my journeys. It was your reflection that slightly subsided my pain and transformed it into treasure. Every shred of community healing helped me hone myself, this book, and the rest of this series into what it needed to be.

About Maxime Paul

Maxime wasn't always an avid reader, but he always loved experimental, emotional, and energetic storytelling. He grew up watching, discussing, deciphering, reimagining, and reenacting shows (lots of Discovery Channel and Anime), movies (Thrillers, Comedies, and Sci-Fi), video games (RPGs and every Sport), and a plethora of music. Those stories and the ones my family and I spun with each other around the house built fanciful worlds in his mind, critiques of *this* world, and further shaped his storytelling. This was much before he found the arena of literature that unlocked deeper chambers of his soul. That unlocking only began after he graduated college.

Now, as an engineer, serial social impact startup founder, and consistent boundary pusher passionate about building prefigurative platforms he has the words to understand himself and is ever closer to clarifying his full impact. In his writing he taps into his Black and Indian, US-Caribbean background. He has moved to all corners of the US and lived with all types of communities, listening and breaking bread along the way. He enjoys spending time with his partner and two young children, discovering and channeling music, all things soccer, riding his bike around town, and living out liberation more everyday.

You can find them at the socials below or on their Substack: https://maxpoetic.substack.com/

 instagram.com/maxap23

threads.net/@maxap23

linkedin.com/in/maximepaul

bsky.app/profile/maxap23.bsky.social

Also by Inked in Gray

If you enjoyed *Harvesting Game*, please consider also reading *Children with Gifts*, or any of the other Inked in Gray novels and anthologies. Support our small business by buying direct at InkedinGray.com

We also appreciate any and all reviews! You may leave a review on Goodreads, Amazon, IndieStoryGeek or on our site at Inkedingray.com

9 781952 969348